CREATURE OF THE BLACK STAR

⚜

Ailia roused to find the fire had died down to a red-eyed smolder. At the edge of its sullen light there crouched a creature: a thing that had the batlike wings of a dragon, opening and closing as if in spasms of agony, and a dragon's scales and twitching tail. But its form was like that of a man, and it was draped in some dark material. Then, as the horned and shaggy head lifted, she saw it had a man's face crusted with scales and two blazing eyes weeping tears, which, in the reflected fire-glow, seemed to leave trails of flame. The monster moaned and thrashed about as if in pain, but its burning eyes did not seem to see her. And in the next moment she recognized him.

Mandrake, she thought, sickened. Neither man nor dragon, but a horrifying blend of the two, a thing utterly unnatural . . .

[p. 218]

PRAISE FOR *THE STONE OF THE STARS*

"Legendary gods and lost temples emerge from dragon-mists. This is writing that calls enchantment forth from the shadows of Time."
—Andre Norton, author of *Beastmaster's Ark*

"Solidly entertaining . . . Baird's narrative is crisp and lucid."
—*Starlog*

"A strong contribution to the epic fantasy genre."
—*Library Journal*

Also by Alison Baird

The Stone of the Stars
The Empire of the Stars

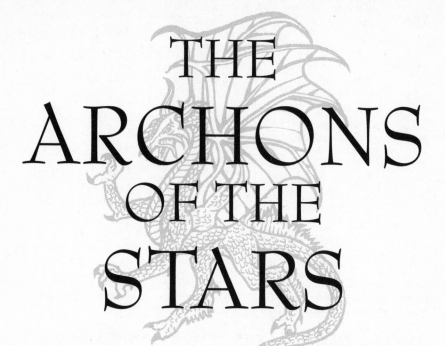

THE
ARCHONS
OF THE
STARS

THE DRAGON THRONE • BOOK III

ALISON BAIRD

ASPECT®

NEW YORK   BOSTON

This book is a work of fiction. Names, characters, places, and incidents are the product of the author's imagination or are used fictitiously. Any resemblance to actual events, locales, or persons, living or dead, is coincidental.

Aspect
Warner Books

Time Warner Book Group
1271 Avenue of the Americas, New York, NY 10020
Visit our Web site at www.twbookmark.com.

The Aspect name and logo are registered trademarks of Warner Books.

Printed in the United States of America

First Edition: August 2005
10 9 8 7 6 5 4 3 2 1

Library of Congress Cataloging-in-Publication Data
Baird, Alison, 1963–
   The archons of the stars / Alison Baird.— 1st ed.
      p. cm. — (The dragon throne : bk. 3)
   Summary: "In the third entry of the Dragon Throne series, Ailia must fulfill the age-old prophecy and become the Tryna Lia, champion of the Empire"—Provided by publisher.
   ISBN 0-446-69097-X
   I. Title.
PR9199.4.B34A89 2005
813'.6—dc22   2005004969

For my fellow "Ink Blots": Jan, Terri, Marian, and Louise

Vartara
the Black Star

Utara
(Sun of
Ombar)

Lotara

The
Worm

Iantha

Meraur
and Merilia
(Suns of Nemorah)

Miria

Arainia

Talandria

The
Dragon

Anatarva
(Sun of Alfaran)

The Planets of Auria

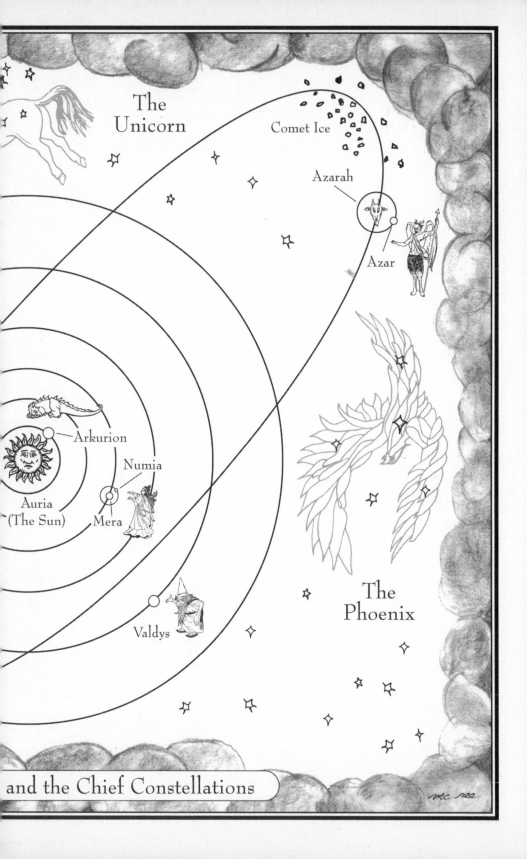

The Unicorn

Comet Ice

Azarah

Azar

Arkurion

Numia

Auria
(The Sun)

Mera

Valdys

The
Phoenix

and the Chief Constellations

PROLOGUE

(Excerpted from Maurian's *Historia Arainia*)

I T IS DIFFICULT FOR US, studying these annals, to envision the events and personages in them, so fantastic do these accounts seem; so remote and even godlike the figures that move in their midst. We must not lose sight, however, of the fact that these beings were as human as we, in their outward forms at least: that Ailia, Damion, Morlyn, and the rest lived and breathed and knew our mortal weaknesses, doubts, and fears. For any chronicler of this strange and wondrous era the principal task must be to clothe those names in flesh.

As to their story, it is elsewhere recounted in full, and a brief retelling of its main points will serve here. When the Queen Elarainia, revered throughout the world of Arainia as the incarnation of its goddess, gave birth to a daughter, the people rejoiced to see prophecy fulfilled: the *Tryna Lia*, Princess of the Stars, had been born in mortal form to deliver them from the designs of the dark god, Modrian-Valdur. When the little Princess Elmiria was still scarcely more than an infant, her mother took her from her home world and conveyed her by sorcery to the neighboring world of Mera for her protection. For Morlyn, the Avatar of Valdur, knew that she would one day challenge his rule. Also, it was in Mera that the Star Stone lay. This enchanted gem alone could give the Tryna Lia the power to defeat her foreordained foe. But upon reaching Mera, Queen Elarainia disappeared, and the little princess was left, not in the care of the holy monks on the Isle of Jana as both friend and foe would later come to believe, but on the shores of Great Island much farther to the north, where she was discovered by a lowly shipbuilder and his wife. They took the foundling into their home and raised her as their own. And when she grew older she did not seek out her true origins, for her guardians allowed her to believe that they were her true mother and father.

When she was in her seventeenth year, Ailia (as the young maiden came to be called) made a journey along with many other islanders to escape the invading armies of Khalazar, the Zimbouran tyrant king. She and her family found sanctuary in the land of Maurainia, and at the Royal Academy of Raimar she first encountered Damion Athariel, priest of the Faith of Orendyl. She secretly fell in love with him, though such a love was forbidden, but she did not guess that their lives were interwoven by destiny.

Many others were also bound by fate to Ailia. One was the aged woman known only as old Ana, a reputed witch dwelling in the coastal mountains. The "coven" that Ana led was in truth a secret company of *Nemerei*, seers and sorcerers who practiced the magical arts of elder days, and she told Father Damion of their ways and of the predestined ruler who would one day descend from the stars. At that time the girl Lorelyn, who had fled with Damion from the Isle of Jana when King Khalazar's forces menaced it, was believed to be the Tryna Lia. Damion later came to her aid again when the sorcerer-prince Morlyn, then using the name of Mandrake, abducted her and confined her deep within the ruins of Maurainia's oldest fortress. The Zimbouran king, who believed himself destined to seize and wield the Star Stone and conquer the Tryna Lia, then captured Lorelyn and with her Damion, Ana, and Ailia. He set off with his prisoners by galleon to the long-lost Isle of Trynisia: for there the holy jewel lay waiting for either the Tryna Lia or the dark god Valdur's champion to claim it. But with her sorcerous power Ana freed the prisoners after landfall was made, and they escaped together into the wilderness of Trynisia. They were joined by Jomar, a half-breed slave who hated his Zimbouran masters and rejoiced at the chance to thwart them of their prize. The Stone lay in the ruin of the holy city of Liamar, high upon the sacred mountain of Elendor, and Lorelyn and her party resolved to find it before the Zimbourans could.

But many perils lay in their path: not only the vengeful king and his soldiers, but also the misshapen and evil beast-men that dwelt on the isle, and the dragons that made their lairs on the summit of

Elendor. Morlyn, using his sorcery to take the shape of a great dragon, led the latter in an assault upon Ana's company. For it was his wish that no one should ever come near the Stone, nor awaken its wondrous powers.

Yet though he caused Ana to be separated from her charges, and though he fought Jomar and Damion in the cavern wherein he kept the Stone, and took young Lorelyn back into his power, in the end he was thwarted by Ailia. The maiden, whom he thought a harmless shipwright's daughter, ventured all alone into the treasure-cave, and took from thence the sacred Stone. She was assisted in her escape from Elendor by a great golden dragon, a servant of the celestial realm, whom she freed from the chain with which Morlyn had bound him fast. The semidivine Guardians, whose sacred duty it was to protect the Stone until the Tryna Lia came to claim it, saved her remaining companions. All were borne away through the heavens and reunited in far-distant Arainia—a world that, to them, had become merely a myth.

Morlyn met them there and once more attempted to challenge them, denying them entry to the royal palace of Halmirion. But before the others' wondering eyes Ailia took up the Star Stone and drew upon its power to put the dragon-mage to flight. In so doing she revealed at last her true identity. And before the people of Arainia she was returned to her throne.

But countless dangers still awaited. For Ailia had not destroyed her predestined adversary; and there were on other worlds many cruel and powerful beings whose aid he could summon in his fight against her. The Zimbouran God-king, Khalazar had turned to necromancy to aid his cause, and in the midst of one of his incantations Morlyn appeared before him. The Dragon Prince revealed that he was the son of the ancient king Andarion, and feigned to be an undead spirit. The seeming "spirit" then bestowed upon Khalazar a vision of Arainia, and vowed to assist Khalazar in conquering the Tryna Lia and her world—if the Zimbouran king would but accept the title of Valdur's Avatar. Khalazar did so eagerly, little suspecting that he had been deceived, and would serve but as the bait to draw Ailia out of her world and induce her to try and deliver Mera before her powers were adequate to the task.

Ailia, unaware of the threat to her life and people, was celebrating a national feast day when an ethereal image of Khalazar mate-

rialized before her court, and declared he intended to seize Arainia.
In the meantime, Mandrake continued to gather many allies against
Ailia's reign. He sought out the dragon-folk—sorcerers descended,
like him, from Loänan—and slew their ruler in a duel, taking his
place. Then Mandrake brought Khalazar and the king of the goblin race together, in a pact to conquer Arainia.

Arainia's governors then held a council of war. Jomar warned
them that all the young sorcerers and knights of that world must
train for the conflict to come. That same night, before an audience
of hundreds, Ailia entered into an oracular fit, prophesying disaster
while a storm raged with unnatural intensity over the city. At the
urging of the court sorcerer Wu, Ailia was sent to the Nemerei
academy of Melnemeron to be instructed in the lore of wizardry,
preparing her for the battle to come. Syndra, an Arainian Nemerei
turned traitor, spied upon the Tryna Lia and gave report of her
progress to Morlyn. At her command, a firedrake made an attempt
on Ailia's life, but it was foiled by Master Wu, who was revealed to
be a celestial dragon disguised in human form. His true name was
Auron, and he was the very same Loänan who had saved her life in
Mera. He explained that he believed she was the prophesied leader
who would one day unite all the worlds of the Celestial Empire.
From that point on, Ailia would be watched over by two celestial
guardians, Auron and a firebird named Taleera, who was also sworn
to protect the princess from harm.

Their new draconic allies declared that they would assist the
Arainian army, now planning to open a "dragon-gate" on the Ethereal
Plane and enter Khalazar's world. Ana also went to Mera, but to Maurainia not Zimboura, where she rejoined her Nemerei coven.
Damion, to Ailia's dismay, elected to join the army in the desert of
Zimboura. She made a last desperate effort to stop the war by ap-
pealing to Khalazar in a magical message, but he spurned her offer of
peace. The army departed; only later was it discovered that Lorelyn
had disguised herself as a knight and passed through the gate as well.

Her guardian dragon flew with Ailia through the Ether to a world
of the celestial dragons where she would be safe, and she was filled
with wonder at their fabulous city—built by the long-vanished race
of the Archons whom the Arainians believed were gods—and its extraordinary inhabitants: dragons, cherubim, sphinxes, dryads, and
many other beings long held to be mythical. On Mera, Khalazar's

forces and the Arainians clashed in a desert battle. Jomar, Damion, and Lorelyn were separated from the others, and fled to a distant oasis to join with a small band of rebel Mohara warriors. Their shaman declared that Jomar was fated to lead them to victory, and together they made daring forays against the enemy. But they had not the numbers to overthrow the tyrant Khalazar and his armies.

In the world of the dragons Ailia sought an audience with Orbion, the Celestial Emperor, to ask for his help in the war against Khalazar. The aging dragon told Ailia that he could not oblige her, since he was the servant of the Empire's many peoples, not their master. It was important that she understand this, for she must rule Talmirennia in his place when he died. In any case Mandrake had already divided the Loänan, so that they were themselves on the verge of civil war. Ailia, distressed at the prospect of a cosmic conflict that made the Meran war seem insignificant by comparison, then secretly resolved to go to Mandrake and parley with him. She took a flying ship and traveled alone through the Ether to Mandrake's homeworld of Nemorah. But on arriving there she was assailed by his firedrakes, and her winged vessel was damaged and fell from the sky. She wandered through alien jungles, hopelessly lost, until she met and saved the life of a native creature called an amphisbaena. In gratitude it offered to show her where other humans like herself lived. Following the amphisbaena, Ailia came to a city made up of human beings whose ancestors had been slaves of the old Loänei empire. A local seeress gave shelter to Ailia, and explained that Mandrake in this world was believed to be a god. Though he had been gone for centuries and a new human ruler had disbanded his cult, still he was feared and revered by many.

In Mera, Khalazar set a trap for the Tryna Lia's friends by announcing that he would sacrifice a captive princess. He knew well they could not ignore the plight of this innocent victim. The shaman Wakunga warned that Damion was the one most sought by the enemy. Lorelyn advised Damion to remain behind while the others attempted a rescue. Reluctantly he agreed, and stayed in the Mohara camp while Jomar and Lorelyn rode forth, and were captured.

Ailia confronted Mandrake in his castle on Nemorah, but he claimed that he did not wish to fight her, and merely desired to convince her that he was in the right. Ailia found herself treated not as an enemy but as an honored guest, and agreed to remain with Mandrake for a brief period of time and hear his arguments. Mandrake advised her to put her concerns for her people aside—humans, he declared, will always harm and enslave one another—and think only of herself. Soon Ailia began to believe that a union between herself and the Dragon Prince might well bring a lasting peace. She gave up her old dream of winning Damion's affections, and decided to accept Mandrake's proposal. But unknown to her, he slipped into her wine a potion, a love philter that bound her to him as a helpless thrall.

Khalazar chafed with resentment at being ordered to spare the lives of Jomar and Lorelyn, whom Mandrake planned to use for hostages. Realizing at last that he was under Mandrake's control, and not the opposite, Khalazar determined to show his independence by harming Ailia's friends. He announced that Lorelyn and Jomar would be executed if Damion did not give in. When the priest heard of his friends' impending executions he went to Khalazar and surrendered himself. The tyrant decided to disobey Mandrake's command and kill Damion in Valdur's temple. At the news of the impending sacrifice the unease of the Zimbouran people turned into open revolt against Khalazar. The king was slain, the rebels freed Jomar and Lorelyn, and the two joined in the storming of the temple. But they were too late to save Damion.

Ailia, unable to free herself from her attachment to Mandrake, was rescued against her will by her guardians, who had learned of the philter. On Arainia she was cured of its effects, but then learned the terrible news of Damion's death on Mera. Mandrake now realized that Ailia, once cured of the philter and at the peak of her power, could be a deadly adversary and that Damion's loss would only make her more vengeful. In his extremity he agreed to a pact with the goblin-folk of Ombar: he would become their ruler and Avatar of Valdur in return for their protection.

In the meantime a grieving Ailia pondered the accounts of Damion's passing. It was said that he had vanished bodily from the earth, and been transformed into an angel. On seeing him in a dream, she too became convinced that he was not dead after all, but had somehow been transported to the Ether. Disregarding the protestations of her councilors, she embarked on a search for Damion, asking her friends to follow her to Mera.

Part One

THE SIEGE

1

The Island

THE STORM RAGED THROUGH SEA and sky, a winter gale surpassing in fury any that had ever troubled these turbulent latitudes. Its massed thunderheads towered up for leagues upon leagues, black against the stars, and beneath the shadow of their opaque canopy there reared titanic waves, rising almost to mountain height. The spray blown from their rearing crests mingled with the lashing rain. It was as though the very elements of water and air were dissolving and melding one into the other, returning to a primeval unity. Cloud and sea churned together, whipped into fury by the wind that held both in sway.

The lone albatross caught in the midst of this turmoil was no longer attempting to fly, but merely allowing itself to be blown about at the storm's whim. Indeed, had it not been for the winds that buoyed up its great white wings, it would long since have fallen exhausted into the heaving surf. Once it did falter and drop, but at the last moment recovered itself with a frantic flap of its pinions and skimmed over the frothing summit of an oncoming wave. Beyond this the bird's weary eyes saw only slope after slope of slate-dark water, capped with white: the cold pale glimmer of foam was all that could be glimpsed between the lightning flickers. For a time it despaired, fearing that it had been blown altogether off its course. But as it rode the gale higher into the air, a dazzling flash revealed a shoreline only a league distant: steep, rocky, a coast of cliffs sheer and threatening as the walls of a fortress, but land nonetheless. Hope renewed the bird's vigor and it beat its wings in a last des-

perate effort. The cliffs gave way on the northern side to a long ruinous slope of boulders and jutting columns that broke the force of
the surging seas, and sent them tumbling back in confusion. There
the albatross spied a low granite shelf, and with the very last of its
strength fluttered down upon it. The surf burst around the tall
standing rocks, masking them from view, then falling back made
fleeting cascades down their jagged sides before crashing up again.
One wave, greater than all the rest, dashed over the shelf of stone
and covered it and the still white form that lay upon it. When at last
the seething foam retreated from the rock, there was no longer a
bird lying there, but a woman.

She wore a white cloak, its wide deep hood drawn up over her
head, and she lay facedown and motionless. For a moment it
seemed that the grasping surf would suck her out to sea, claiming
her at last. But then she stirred feebly, and began half to stumble,
half to crawl farther up the shelf, out of reach of the waves. By the
time she reached the top of the rocky slope beyond, the wind's
power was already abating somewhat, and she was able to stand upright, though still bowed with fatigue. Her pale face, its grayish
purple eyes deeply shadowed, looked out from the shelter of the
white hood on the bleak scene before her.

To this inhospitable shore she had come once before, as a small
child. Her sorceress mother had crafted and captained a flying ship
to take them both to a place of safety, far from their palace home.
But the ship had fallen and foundered here, off the coast of Great
Island; her mother had suffered an unknown fate, while the little
girl had been taken in by a shipwright and his childless wife to live
for the next eighteen years as their own daughter.

This was my home once, thought Ailia.

It seemed impossible to her now. The dark fields stretching before her were barren save for the harsh grasses that grew there, tall
wiry stems fused together with frost. Sleet from the diminishing
storm pattered down on the frozen dirt road that wound ahead of
her. A fresh gust whipped her wet cloak around her slight, shivering form. But the air stung even without a wind. She had forgotten,
after her long sojourn in warmer climes, how bitterly cold it was
here in winter. How had she ever borne it? And how did the Islanders bear it still? Why did they choose to remain in such a place?
It was as if harsh clime and unyielding island worked together as

hammer and anvil, hardening the bodies and spirits of those who lived here but also imparting to them a stern resilience, the power to endure adversity.

The Island had not changed; would never change, not though thousands of years should pass. The ceaseless assault of wind and wave made but little difference to its stubborn granite coast, and its people, each generation gaining strength from the stone they trod, would carry on for the centuries to come just as they had in the far distant past. It was Ailia who had been altered, completely and irrevocably. When she had departed Great Island at last, watching from her ship's stern rail as the gray cliffs dwindled and appeared to sink into the sea, she had wondered if she would ever return. It had seemed to her then that the island really had submerged beneath the waves, like an enchanted isle in a faerie tale, never more to be seen by mortal eyes. The passing years further relegated it to the past, until even the desire to see it again faded from her mind.

Yet here she was, standing once more upon its stony soil.

She had been forced to take a bird-form to come here, loath as she was to use her newly emergent gift of shape-shifting. This came from her Loänan side, the legacy of dragon-magi who could transform themselves at will and had taken human shape in order to mate with her ancestors. But she had never called upon it until her greatest adversary, taking advantage of her innocence, awakened the buried talent—all so that he might teach her the love of power. For this reason she feared and mistrusted it, but with no ship available to cross the sea, she had had no recourse but to use it. She was an unskilled flier, however, and she had not reckoned on the storm—if indeed it was a natural storm, and not a sorcerous assault by her enemies. Many of them still lingered in this world, and weather conjuring was well within their power. Clutching the cold, wet cloak tightly about her, she made her way slowly along the road. It was empty of any other passerby. The sensible Island folk would not be out on a night like this. Only the small, shaggy island ponies and a few sheep were to be seen, grazing the frostbitten grass in the meager fields. Not far off a temple stood, humble and towerless, its walls pieced together from fieldstone, the only building here not made out of wood. She knew the temple well, though her family's visits there had been somewhat infrequent. It served all the fishing villages hereabouts, her own included. Bayport was not far away now. She would reach it before midnight.

After she had walked for what felt like an hour, she spied at last the low stony hill that had marked the westernmost boundary of her childhood's territory. She had approached it always from the eastern side, climbing it on mild evenings to watch the sun sink into the sea—for so she then believed it did. The world in those days was not a ball hurtling with dizzying speed through an unfathomable void, but a wide, flat disc of earth and water: stable and stationary, immovable, circled by sun and moon and by the stars and planets that were mere lights in the heavens, not suns and worlds in their own right. How she longed for that smaller and safer cosmos of her childhood! Its very center had been this island—her village—her home. She approached the hill now from the west, and even this simple change of direction seemed to underline the permanent shift in her perception of things, and her estrangement from all that she had once known.

Why did I come back? she wondered, pausing. *Was it really to seek out my foster family? Or was it to try and reverse time—to go back to that safe and innocent past? Could I have been so foolish?*

She forced herself to still the inner voice and keep walking. As the road wound on, it grew hauntingly familiar in every twist and turn. Here a glacial boulder, and there an ancient crab apple tree with spindly, spidery limbs—the old wayside signposts she had once known as a child. Before her a light burned in the black night, yellow and steady as a star. Her heart gave a slight lift at the sight of these things—almost it seemed she *might* return to that old life, secure in its ordinariness. There had been another existence for her before her return to Arainia and the awakening of her powers. Even before Damion . . .

A tear slipped down her cheek, and was swept away by the rain.

She came presently to the barren point where a short, round tower built of granite boulders stood stalwart, the overreaching spume breaking against its westward face. Through the thick-paned windows at its top the yellow light burned: the old sea beacon, kept lit night and day for the safety of sailors. She pitied any vessel that might be riding those tempestuous waves. As she drew closer to the beacon tower she glimpsed in its western wall the carved figure in a stone niche, one hand raised in a warding gesture. The statue of

Elarainia, protector of ships and those who sailed in them: Star of the Sea, Queen of Heaven, goddess of the planet that some called the Morning Star.

And mother of the Tryna Lia, prophesied savior of the world.

She averted her eyes from the statue and toiled on, until through the gloom she could make out more lights: the houses and harbor of Bayport village, only a short walk away now. Her footsteps quickened, as did her heartbeats. She was, for an instant, that innocent small girl once more, hastening toward home and hearth, toward the warm welcoming comforts she knew . . .

And then she stopped dead in her tracks, unsure whether to trust the witness of her weary eyes. The gray granite hillock on the edge of the village was there, standing as it had for time immemorial, rising solid and firm from the midst of the meadow. But there was no longer any house upon its summit. Her home was gone.

Ailia walked slowly, in a daze of exhaustion and disbelief, toward the place where the house had stood. A mass of burnt timbers lay there, rain-wet, black and flaking at the edges. Here and there a shard of glass gleamed faintly up through earth and cinders.

Ailia dropped to her knees. *Mandrake said I could never go back to my former life*, she thought, feeling numb. *He did this—on purpose, to show me I cannot go back.*

She realized now that, while her ostensible object had been to find her foster parents and be sure they were safe, she had really been yearning for the sound of Dannor's sensible voice and the security of Nella's capable presence. Where were they now, the two people who had risked their lives, perhaps deliberately, to save hers? She *must* find them. If indeed they were not dead.

They were not here, at least. If they had perished in the fire the neighbors would have buried them in the little windswept cemetery farther inland. She stood again, scanning the village. Her uncle Nedman's wooden frame house still stood, as did her cousin Jemma's cottage down by the shore, but they were dark where the other houses showed lights in their windows. And it was not yet time to sleep.

She approached her uncle's house and knocked on the door. The sound echoed through the rooms beyond and died without any answering footsteps or voices. She pushed it open—Islanders' doors were never locked—and peered in. She expected broken furnishings and disorder, but the house was merely abandoned. The kitchen table was bare; the hearth had neither wood nor ashes in it. Ailia lit a candle and made a quick search of the home. Each room was the same, from the parents' bedroom to her cousin Jemma's former room, vacated by her on her marriage to Arran and turned into a sewing room, to her cousin Jaimon's room (still kept for him, since as a sea-roving sailor he had no home of his own). Everything was neatly put away—clothes (not many of these), tools, crockery. There was no food of any sort in the kitchen, not even a biscuit or piece of salt fish.

She left the silent house and went down to Jemma and Arran's cottage by the shore. Here it was the same again: vacant yet orderly rooms. The old wooden cradle Jemma had inherited from her mother stood forlorn and empty in the nursery, along with some of her sons' toys. Arran's fishing nets and other tackle lay in the storeroom at the back, and his green-hulled boat was anchored in the bay. But of the owners of all these things there was no sign.

Ailia returned to the main bedroom, took off her sodden cloak, and laid down her candle on the night table. Then she sat on the bed, put her head in her hands, and shook for a moment with silent sobs. Where were they? What had become of them all?

There were soft footsteps in the passage outside, and she looked up, then sprang to her feet. "Jemma? Is that you?" called a woman's voice.

Ailia went to the doorway. "Who is it? Who's there?"

A figure with a lantern stood there. "It's I—Elen. I saw the light, and I thought that Jemma was back. Who are you?"

"Elen—Elen Seaman? It's Ailia. Don't you remember me? Where is my family, Elen?"

"Ailia?" The young woman went up to her and took her by the arm. Ailia recognized the freckled face and the tow-colored hair pulled into a knot at the back. "It's Elen Fisher now, I'm married. But how did you come here—and on such a night?"

Yes—Elen must be nearly seventeen, the age Ailia had been when she left the Island. People here married young. There was a confidence in the girl's voice and manner, a forced early maturity. "Ellie, please! Where are they?" Ailia implored.

"Why, I thought you'd know! When the womenfolk went over to the Continent because of the Zimbourans, my father wouldn't let us go, you recall. And then the Zimbourans didn't come after all, and most of the women returned, but not your mamma and aunt and Jemma. They sent their menfolk a letter, saying how there'd been a misunderstanding and you'd been taken by the authorities or some such, Ailia; and would the men come at once? Dannor and Nedman went first, and then Arran followed. And then none of them returned. It's just as well for Dannor and Nella, for they've little to come back to. Your house burned down—did you see it? A great storm blew up one night out of nowhere, and a lightning bolt struck the roof and set it afire. No other house in the village was hit: I suppose yours was most at risk, sitting up on top of that hillock. We did try to put the fire out, but it was too late. A mercy no one was at home! Anyway, I hope your folks are better off where they are now, though it's a pity about their things."

"If they are on the Continent still then I must go there too." Fatigue throbbed in her limbs at the thought.

"You can't. The Armada's loose they say, and no ship will risk the crossing. The Zimbourans have gotten themselves a brand-new tyrant now, and a civil war at home. Ailia, however did you get here?"

"I found a way. Please, Ellie, I can't say any more just now. I'm fearfully tired."

"You come with me, then. I've my own place now."

Ailia thought of a warm fireside, food and other comforts, the soothing presence of people. But also there would be questions, a steady barrage of questions she could not answer truthfully, and she lacked the strength to field them. How to explain her lack of any luggage—her crossing of the sea—where she had been all these long years? "Thank you," she replied, "but I really am so exhausted at the moment I couldn't stir a step. I think I will just stay here tonight. There's fuel for a fire, I see, and plenty of candles."

Elen rose reluctantly. "Well, if you're sure. It'd be no bother to put you up. But I'll come by in the morning anyway, with some bread and milk and maybe an egg or two. Sleep well."

After Elen had gone Ailia lay down on her cousin's bed, staring up at the one small window. The sky was clearing, and in the dark starry patches between the parting clouds there were comets, at least half a dozen even in this restricted view, their long white tails streaming behind them. They had begun to appear shortly after her arrival in Zimboura. Portents of evil, many people said, but she knew them for something far worse: weapons, wielded with a deliberate malevolence by a ruthless enemy. Eons ago they had been cast out of their normal orbits by a rogue star, and they pursued still the ancient trajectories on which they had been set: the age-old enemy had intended that they strike this world of Mera and its peaceful neighboring planet.

Unable to rest, she got up and went to the window. The Evening Star was also shining tonight, and she gazed long at it: Arainia, the planet assigned in the old writings to the goddess Elarainia. These tales said that she dwelt in an enchanted garden of delights, far beyond the end of the world. Some said this land of Eldimia lay to the west, where her star sometimes shone at eventide, while another tradition insisted it could be found only in some mystical realm, "east of the sun and west of the moon." Most accounts agreed it could never be reached by mortals: a ship traveling to the world's end would only fall off the edge of its disc into bottomless deeps of sky. But the Queen of the Western Heaven must have granted to a favored few leave to journey to Eldimia and return, for in the old tales were many descriptions of that fair land: its beauty and wonders, its tame beasts and plenteous gems, its cities of crystal and gold. As a little girl Ailia had watched as the Evening Star sank slowly toward the sea, and hungered to journey with it to Eldimia. As she grew older she was forced to acknowledge that the Otherworld was only a myth, and though she still gazed westward at eventide she yearned instead to visit the mortal lands that lay there: Maurainia, and Rialain and Marakor.

And yet all along it had been true. Meran travelers had, indeed, been in that loveliest of countries, and given faithful report of what they found there. For the people of this time had long since forgotten that Eldimia lay, not in some fanciful country visited by the journeying star of Morning and Evening, but within the planet itself. The tales were not idle fancies, but faint lingering memories of an earlier age when Mera and Arainia were linked by an enchanted portal. Only the Fairfolk had remembered it all: those few still left on this side of the portal after it was closed had yearned for their true home. She recalled now the words of their hymn to Elarainia, which was also a lament:

As exiles from their native shore
Are parted by a pathless sea
So must we yearn forevermore
In halls divine to dwell with thee.

Night-blooming lily! Lady fair
Of lands unmarred by war or woe!
O Queen of Heaven, hear the prayer
Of thy lost children, here below!

What must it have been like for these exiles, unable to return to their beloved Arainia, watching that world shine remote and unattainable in the sky even as their kind dwindled and died out in this one? She herself felt an intense yearning as she gazed on the far-off planet. It shone like a beacon, or like the window of a warm and well-lit house seen by a traveler on a stormy night. She thought of its warm and teeming seas, its exotic flowering trees and plants, its greater proximity to the life-giving sun. Even its small attendant moon was filled with growing things, a celestial garden. She thought of her private apartments in the palace of Halmirion, and of her true father and family, all wondering where she was and worrying; and her soul strained toward that distant point of light even as it had years ago on this same island, when she did not yet understand the reason for that inchoate desire. How had she *known*? She leaned her forehead against the cold pane and watched the planet until a drifting cloud blotted it from sight, then she sighed and returned to the bed.

She fell at last into a light, troubled sleep, filled with restless dreams. In them she saw shadowy figures come and go, passing like ghosts before her eyes. A face appeared—a young man, blond, with gentle sky-blue eyes who vanished as Ailia reached out in longing. In his place, then, was the face of another man, his pallid face contrasting strangely with his long hair and eyes, both as bright as flame. . . . He filled her with fear, and yet her arms were still reaching out. She withdrew them and moaned, tossing in her sleep. A woman with golden hair and violet-blue eyes appeared, gazing tenderly at her, driving away the other face. Then a sequence of vivid images crowded in upon her—scenes of battle and turmoil, armies of yelling men. Dragons swooped through a black sky filled with stars. And then another face appeared, shining through all the strife and chaos—the face of an old woman with white hair pulled into a knot. Her eyes were a blank gray-white in color, and yet they were filled with compassion and an ageless wisdom.

"Ana," Ailia whimpered, tossing from side to side. "Ana . . ."

But this face vanished also, and then in its place she saw a vast burning blue-white light: a star, distorted into the shape of a tear. From its end there bled a long streamer of blue flame that curled around upon itself, making a circle with a black hole at its center. That darkness gaped at her like a mouth, pulling her toward itself. She could not resist: she would be drawn in along with the dying spiral of star-fire and devoured . . .

A voice that was not a voice spoke from the midst of the black maw. *Behold the Mouth of the Worm, the darkness no light of Heaven can pierce. There is no escaping from the void within. Who enters here comes not forth again.*

With a violent start she woke and sat up, shaking with terror, fearing for an instant that the darkness surrounding her was that of the fathomless pit. Always she had feared the dark, from her very earliest childhood, but there was in this enveloping blackness a different quality—a lurking malevolence. With unsteady hands she lit a candle, banishing the darkness back into the far corners of the room. Then she lay down once more, but did not sleep again until the light of dawn came into the sky.

AURON FLEW OUT OF THE soft dim radiance of the Ether and into the midst of battle.

All about him were the gleaming stars and the limitless black deeps of the heavens. Behind and to his left the unveiled sun blazed fiercely bright, and before him the world of Mera returned its radiance like a vast blue jewel. But directly ahead of him a great light shone, round and white and surrounded by a hazy aureole, and about it many smaller shapes swarmed like moths drawn to a lamp. As he sped onward with wings furled, propelled through the airless night by enchantment alone, proximity and changing perspective revealed the pale halo to be a cone of luminous vapors, streaming back from the bright globe as long tresses of hair are blown back in a wind. It looked to extend for many millions of leagues. The shining object was a comet, hurtling straight toward him, and shedding its outer mantle as it drew ever nearer to the fires of the sun. Dark-winged shapes were defending it, while Loänan and eagle-winged cherubim assailed it on all sides.

One of the black shapes, all but invisible against the void, lunged toward him and he swerved, avoiding its attack. Thwarted, the fire-drake snapped its jaws and glared with its cold red eye—savage as a wild beast's, yet filled also with a malign cunning. But its flaming breath could not reach him in the void, for the envelope of air that sustained the creature ended very close to its own body. As it turned to dive on him again he faced it, then at the last moment rolled to bring himself underneath his assailant's body. The plate armor on the monster's belly was not so thick and strong as the scales on its back, and a swift and deadly thrust from all four of his claws to-gether scored it deeply.

Another time he would have fought it to the finish, but Auron had been sent here by the Celestial Emperor Orbion merely to ob-serve the progress of the battle, and report back to him. He left the wounded drake to be slain by two of his fellow Loänan, and flew in closer to the comet's head. It burned only with the sun's reflected glow: the surface of its nucleus was not hot, but formed of gray-white ice, deeply seamed and fissured like the face of a glacier. It was, in truth, a gigantic hailstone, formed far out in the perpetual cold of the regions between the stars. As he passed over a dark cave in its sunward side there flew up from its depths the dark shapes of still more firedrakes. At once the other Loänan and cherubim de-scended to challenge them. Their cries were soundless, as they could not carry through the void beyond the individual cocoons of air, but Auron mentally sensed the bursts of pain and rage from the combatants. They battled all around him as he dropped toward the comet's surface. And then it was not a surface but a landscape, a gray-white plain gaping with black crevasses and walled with frozen cliffs. In the sky above, the comet's flowing tail glimmered like a pale aurora. He alighted on one of the icy crags and stood for a moment contemplating the scene before him. In days of old the Nemerei mages had ridden on comets for pleasure, and even he felt the wonderment of traveling upon this swift-moving celestial body.

An eagle-headed cherub glided down out of the sky and alighted on the ice beside him. *Well met, Loänan!* it called out silently, mind to mind.

How goes it, Falaar? he replied.

We have succeeded in changing this one's course. The firedrakes sought to prevent us and failed! We will send it flying harmlessly into the sun, Falaar answered.

But can we turn them all in time? Auron asked, eyes sweeping the blackness above him. Dozens more comets, their gauzy tails fanning behind them, shone overhead. They were aimed at Mera, like a flight of flaming arrows loosed at a target. Long ago the Loänan and cherubim had attempted to turn another bombardment of comets like this, and had succeeded with all but one, resulting in the Great Disaster on Mera.

My people shall not fail the worlds again. The firedrakes have learned to fear us: they now flee before us. Falaar shifted his strong, clawed lion's feet, eager to be off fighting again.

I am glad to hear it! You cherubim are well named the Hounds of the Gods, Auron replied with a draconic salute.

How is it with the Celestial Emperor? the cherub asked. *I have heard that Orbion's strength fails.*

The Son of Heaven is very old and very weary, Auron answered. *His end is near, I think.* Sorrow filled him as he spoke. The dragon spread his wings, and soared up again through the void and among the other comets, with the cherub following after. *He does not leave the palace now. Indeed, he does not stir from the Dragon Throne. He has coiled himself about it, as if he would protect it with what life remains to him, and there he lies day after day. Often he sleeps, but when he does not his eyes stare at nothing, and are filled with fear and sadness. He does not dread the approach of death: no Loänan does. We trust in the Power that made us to receive us into itself again. But Orbion is filled with anguish to see the Empire torn with conflict, and our people divided. He would not see Talmirennia leaderless. Yet though he asks that Ailia come to him and take the throne, ensuring the succession, she does not answer his summons. She has never desired to rule, and now her mind is filled with other cares.*

There thou touchest on another matter of urgency, the cherub told him as they passed through a comet's tail, into the bright blizzard of swirling, sunlit ice motes that to terrestrial observers looked like glowing flame: it was here that many of the firedrakes hid, lunging out at the dragons and cherubim when they flew past. *When didst thou last have words with the Tryna Lia?*

Not since we parted in Mera. I left her in the land of Zimboura. Why do you ask? he inquired, uneasy.

She departed that place while thou wast in Temendri Alfaran attending the Em-

peror, we know not whither. She did not take the Star Stone with her. Some say that she desired to see Queen Eliana again and hear her counsel, and others that she sought her Meran family, to see if they are safe. However that may be, she is gone from Zimboura.

Auron turned to him, distraught, as they burst out of the comet's tail again with their hides all diamonded with frost. *Then I must go to Mera and seek for her! Whether she will take the throne or no, the time draws near for her ordained battle.*

Even so, Falaar said. *Prince Morlyn is the chief danger. The Darklings have many powerful champions, but they mean to make greatest use of the Dragon Prince. He is heir to both Loänan and Archonic powers, and the heart of the Valei's schemes. Remove him, and the chief threat is gone. But for that we need the Tryna Lia.*

I will go, Auron said. *Another can bear my tidings back to Orbion. Fight on, hound of Athariel! I journey to Mera.*

Leaving the celestial field of battle to his fellow warriors, Auron hastened toward the blue sphere of the embattled world, and the woman he had sworn to protect since before her birth.

2

The Councils of Kings

IN THE TREASURE-CHAMBER OF the Forbidden Palace in Nemorah, four people of very different appearance sat together, speaking in low voices. One was Roglug, king of the goblin-people: bald and grotesque of feature like all of his kind, more apelike indeed than human, save for the gleam of cunning in his small dark eyes. Beside him sat the black-robed Regent of Ombar, Lord Naugra, whose wizened face bore the marks of a mixed human and goblin ancestry. With them sat another man whose youth and haughty beauty were like a living reproach to the hideousness of the other two: Erron Komora of the Loänei, tall and proud in his embroidered robes, with his straight black hair falling loose and luxuriant down his back. The enchantress Syndra sat apart from the other three, gowned in scarlet, her dark hair bound up in a crown of interwoven braids. All about the chamber were arrayed the fabulous treasures of the Dragon Prince, Morlyn, which he had gathered throughout his centuries-long life: jeweled chalices, a great scrying-globe of crystal, a brazen head upon a plinth. A suit of armor was mounted in a corner of the room, one of many that the prince had worn in battle five hundred years before, when he was a knight in the service of his father, King Andarion of Mera. This suit had been Prince Morlyn's favorite: it was of Kaanish make, a gift to him from the ruler of the Archipelagoes in Mera, and made in the island race's distinctive style. The visor was a steel mask patterned on the prince's own features, to make him proudly recognizable on the field of battle, while the helmet was topped with fierce hornlike projections. The breastplate was composed of many overlapping pieces, somewhat resembling the ventral plates of a serpent. The armor was black as onyx, and gleamed as if newly made, with only a few minor dents and scratches to show its long years of use. Next to it was mounted a sword with a dragon-patterned hilt and notched blade.

It was clear that the armor was but a curiosity now, a relic of the prince's early life before his mastery of magic. Morlyn (or Mandrake, as he preferred to be called) could, by taking on a dragon's form, sport scale-armor twenty times as strong as this: armor that need never be removed, even for sleep. Indeed, he spent as much time as possible in draconic form these days for that very reason. The suit of human armor, with its dark and vacant eyeholes, its now useless gauntlets and greaves and breastplate, had a forlorn and abandoned air. It bore mute testimony to the weaker creature who had once required these protections: the empty and discarded shell of his humanity.

"It is as I told you," Naugra said. "The plans laid by our master thousands of years ago are unfolding exactly as he foresaw. The Empire founded by Valdur's foes has been weakened and divided, and our own strength grows. Morlyn has at last accepted his role as Avatar—"

"Whatever will you do now, Naugra?" asked Roglug with a mocking look.

"What do you mean?" Naugra turned on him, cold and contemptuous.

"Well, you can't go calling yourself Regent anymore. Not now that we have our new ruler."

"You understand nothing, as is your wont. Morlyn has not yet become Avatar in full. He must journey to Ombar to take Valdur's throne and be filled with the Master's spirit there. Until then he remains as vulnerable as any mortal. We must protect this chosen vessel of our Master's as best we may."

"He is safer in draconic form at least," said Erron, "and we Loänei guard him night and day, as do the dragons that serve him. But we cannot repel the forces of the Tryna Lia unaided. Ombar must send more guardians: firedrakes, and Morugei soldiery."

"If we do as you ask, Morlyn will have no need to go to Ombar at all," returned the Regent. "He will feel secure here in Nemorah. It is our wish that he *should* be afraid, and seek for safety in our world. Once there, he will be forced to yield himself up to his master. And the Tryna Lia will be powerless against Valdur."

Syndra listened to the others speak, but said nothing. She had reasons of her own to preserve Mandrake unharmed. If he were to defeat the Tryna Lia, and become Talmirennia's ruler, then he should have a consort. One to rule by his side and give him heirs—and why should that not be Syndra herself? It had troubled her to see him drawn toward Ailia, and though there was now little chance of any reconciliation between them, she still felt pangs of resentment and jealousy. To win Mandrake for herself, she reasoned, she must become more powerful: Ailia's appeal for him had no doubt lain in her superior sorcery, which made her a consort worthy of him. The Dragon Prince was, after all, a being to whom power was the supreme goal—or so she believed, for it was what she herself had always desired, and what she most admired in him. She perceived her contest with the Tryna Lia as one of strength pitted against strength. When two animals battled over mates or food in the jungle, she had observed, it was always the stronger one that emerged victorious. And the supernatural realm was but an extension of the natural, an enlargement and expansion of its themes: within it the same rules would certainly obtain. Syndra gazed at the discarded armor in the corner, and pondered how to win her desire. There were many books of grammarye in Mandrake's library: he never made use of them now, for his mastery of magic was complete, and they had nothing more to teach him. But there might yet be something in one of those volumes, some piece of arcane lore or spellcraft that could help her to augment her own sorcery.

"It is time that the Avatar showed himself again to the Valei," Naugra went on. "They grow restless, and need reminding that their ruler has come. Roglug, go and tell him this."

"I? Why must *I* go? He's grown so suspicious, so dangerous—"

"You are safe enough. No one fears a fool."

The goblin-king rose with a grimace of reluctance, and left the room.

On the lower level of the palace a door led to a long downward-sloping tunnel, and this in turn brought Roglug to a large cavern half-filled by a hot spring. He entered the cave and approached the steaming pool's edge. "Highness," he said, bowing low.

The wisps of steam stirred, and the pool's dark surface rippled. A red scaly back appeared, glistening in the dull light, and then a horned head rose dripping from the water. The lids of the dragon's golden eyes parted, and it looked down on the goblin from the towering height of its great neck.

"We await your command, Lord Prince," Roglug said. "The enemy is massing in strength, and the Valei yearn to behold their leader!"

The dragon's reply rumbled through the cave as if the volcanic forces deep in the earth below had awakened. "They have nothing to fear. I shall be victorious. Already I wield such power as I have never known before. And it is growing."

The goblin bowed again. "Your Highness's victory is indeed assured. But—"

The dragon's golden gaze dwelled upon him. "I was as you are, once. Small, feeble, helpless. But no more. To be human is to be weak, and I must be strong to face what will come. Go now, and leave me to my rest."

Two shimmering ethereal forms suddenly appeared in the air at Roglug's side, startling the goblin considerably, though the dragon paid little attention. It was Elazar and Elombar—or so the originators of these projected images named themselves, declaring that they were the ancient Archons of Azar and Ombar. Both Mandrake and Roglug suspected that they were in fact goblin-sorcerers aligned with Naugra, for in all things they agreed with the Regent. The demonic-visaged Elombar spoke in a rasping voice: "You were right to set aside your human frailty, Prince. Your body may have been human, but your soul was always Loänan—full of power. You will defeat Ailia."

The dragon began to circle his pool restlessly, head above the water like a swimming serpent. "When I was human I pitied her, for like calls to like. But I feel no bond with her now."

The tall saturnine image of Elazar spoke next. "That is well, but you are not yet safe. You must destroy her, or lose all. It is the will of Valdur."

"I am Valdur."

"No, not yet." Elombar countered. "It is not enough to make the claim. You know that you must go to Ombar and receive the crown, and with it the power of Valdur. Until then you are the Avatar only in name."

"But I am your ruler—yes, even yours, even if you are an Archon. And Valdur himself boasted no more power than I do now." With that pronouncement the dragon closed his eyes again, and sank back into the pool. The royal audience was at an end.

Once he was submerged and his unwelcome visitors were banned from sight, the dragon curled around himself and waited, his head resting on his foreclaws. He could hold his breath for an hour and was prepared to do so, giving Roglug and the others time to leave his sanctuary. Few were suffered to enter it these days, for he trusted no one. His human form was, indeed, a thing of the past. He needed the security of this well-protected body, the natural armor and weaponry of scales and claws, and wings to fly to safety. He shuddered to recall the fragility of his human body, its vulnerability to attack, and felt little regret at the loss of his man-self. True, it had brought pleasures along with its weaknesses. But he was a creature of the elements, of elemental needs and passions, now. This new nature protected him from the human susceptibility to temptation, even as the scaly body protected him from all but a few weapons—the adamantine blades of the Paladins, and swords of cold iron. These he still feared. But he was a living fortress in this

form, and deadly as an army. With the addition of his magical powers no foe could hope to match him, save only the Tryna Lia.

Ailia! Where was she now? He dared not risk putting out a feeler
of thought into the Ether to search for her. They said that she had
grown great in power. Had the long-vanished Archons who had assigned to him this role made him adequate to the challenge? However that might be, he was caught now in their trap. Fear followed
him even in sleep. He dreamed often of seeing a dragon swoop
down upon him—a dragon with Ailia's eyes.

In the cruelest of ironies, it was he who had taught her to take
that form.

She was now adept at shape-shifting, a difficult skill. Her Loänan
powers were emerging. Before long she would command the
weather and move from world to world at will. And these were but
the first, eager graspings at a power that would, if unchecked, one
day seek to hold all the Celestial Empire in its sway. But the
Morugei, goblins especially, would never accept Ailia's rule. The
memory of Valdur's commandments was too strong in them still.
What was needed was another ruler, who could control the
Morugei and yet also prevent the Loänan and other races from warring with them—a ruler who would inspire fear on both sides. Only
he could do so—and only then would there be true peace in
Talmirennia. So he told himself, as he reposed in the depths of the
warm dark pool within his inner sanctum, and while he mused on
the future he gave no more thought to what might be happening in
the worlds beyond.

JOMAR STOOD ON THE BATTLEMENT of the fortress of Yanuvan, looking out on the great plaza beneath. It was crowded as always, but
the crowds were more orderly than they had been in earlier days.
And the Mohara and other peoples of the world of Mera now mingled with the native Zimbourans, a thing that would have been un-
heard of during Khalazar's reign. All slaves had been freed after the
tyrant's fall; even the lions and tigers and other beasts in the royal
arena had been released into the wild. The drought was ended; the
rains had been steady and constant and the crops flourished. All the
old prophecies of this land seemed to have come true in the wake
of Ailia's arrival.

The Princess had come to Zimboura months before, and had

spent many days sitting alone in the ruins of Valdur's temple. It was a grim place. The sacrificial shaft beneath its inner sanctum was no man-made delving, but a natural chasm in the earth, deep beyond reckoning: if one dropped a stone into its dark depths, no sound of it striking bottom could be heard. The Moharas in ancient days had feared and shunned this abyss, saying it was the entrance to a shadowy netherworld from which evil spirits might emerge. The Zimbourans, arriving centuries later, had made it the center of their worship and cast slain sacrifices into its gaping mouth; in later centuries they had built their temple over it. But it had claimed its final victim. The crowd in their fury had slain Farola, the priest who murdered Damion Athariel, and thrown the old man's body into the temple shaft. They would have done the same with the captive high priest Berengazi and all the clerics of Valdur, down to the half-wit acolyte who had served at Farola's side, had Ailia not intervened. They believed Farola's testimony, however, that Damion's body had not been cast into that dark hole: that the young priest had instead been transformed in the moment of sacrifice, and become a being of light who ascended to the heavens. Many claimed to have had visions of him at the site, now sacred to him rather than to Valdur.

Ailia had waited patiently in that terrible sanctuary for a vision of her own. Then she had lost faith that Damion lived still, and her intense grief in combination with her sorcerous powers had affected the very atmosphere, causing rain to fall. The water had seeped into the sands, finding there the husks of dormant seeds awaiting the end of the drought, and the desert had bloomed as it had in days of old, with greenery and flowers of many hues: so the old Mohara story of the sky-goddess and her consort had been fulfilled. As Nayah had wept for the fallen earth-god Akkar, taken from her down into the nether realm, so Ailia had mourned for Damion, and with the same result. Power had descended from the sky and breathed life back into the land.

Ailia had afterward met and talked with Wakunga the Mohara shaman, before departing from Zimboura in secret, by night. Wakunga could not say where she had gone. "I said only that she could not simply wait for Damion to appear, but must seek for him as the goddess sought her consort. She would know the place," he explained.

Jomar's response to this had been a colorful profanity, but there was no help for it: in the Princess's absence he had been forced to take the reins of power in Zimboura, as a temporary measure. He had yet to sit upon the throne itself: the jeweled and gilded Sun Throne, that Valdur's worshippers had set up centuries ago as a rival to the Tryna Lia's Moon Throne in Arainia. Khalazar and his predecessors had imagined themselves conquering the Princess even as the sun outshines the moon in the sky. Jomar regarded the great golden chair as the symbol of everything he detested: tyranny, privilege, and overweening pride. But he had accepted the onerous mantle of responsibility for his native realm.

He was hailed as a hero of the Great Revolt, and accepted by both races since he was of mixed Moharan and Zimbouran blood. And so far all had gone smoothly. Zimboura was recovering from her wounds, and Queen Marjana reported that all was well in her realm of Shurkana also, now that she was free to reclaim its Lotus Throne. But in the north Khalazar's remaining supporters had changed their allegiance to the new Avatar, Mandrake. They had an army of their own and command of the Zimbouran Armada, which still roamed the seas beyond Jomar's reach. And there were the comets too, the latest of the bombardments caused by Azarah's disruption of the ice-cloud far out in the void. Comets were viewed by all the peoples of Mera as sinister portents, a belief no doubt stemming from old memories of the first Disaster. Nothing Jomar could say would assuage the people's growing dread of these "signs" in the heavens. He knew that their apprehension, though fueled by superstition, was founded in fact.

Jomar felt very alone. Damion was lost; Taleera, Ailia's T'kiri guardian, had returned to her own distant world, Kirah-kyah, to consult with the elders of her race; and the dragon Auron, along with the other Loänan, fought another battle far beyond the sky. Lorelyn, growing restless at her lack of any useful role here, had finally chosen to join the Loänan. "You're needed here, Jo," she had told him, her blue eyes looking earnestly into his. "And so is Ailia. But I'm not."

I need you, he had wanted to say. But as always he had not managed to get the words out; and she had departed, soaring away through the heavens on a dragon's back.

He left the battlement and went back down the stone staircase to his private receiving room. Kiran Jariss was there with Yehosi the chief eunuch. The latter bowed low, but Kiran greeted Jomar with a lazy wave of the hand. "Hail, son of Jemosa, King of Zimboura!"

"I'm not your king," growled Jomar, throwing himself down on a divan. "How many times must I say that? The people can go choose themselves a ruler."

"The people choose you. They want you to take the throne, Jomar."

"I don't want it. Help yourself to some wine." He spoke the last words dryly: Kiran was already finishing the flagon on the table. But Jomar was grateful for the young Zimbouran's irreverence. It made a welcome change from the awe and obsequious veneration he received from everyone else in the castle. And Kiran had played an important role of his own in the overthrow of Khalazar, at considerable danger to himself. It was he who had sought out Jomar and Lorelyn and their fellow rebels in the desert, had spied for them, and in the last days of Khalazar's reign had helped to stir the restive populace into open revolt against him. He had led the angry mobs to the arena where Jomar battled for his life, freeing him, and then accompanied him to the storming of Yanuvan.

"Since we're on the topic of royalty, how is Jari doing?" Jomar went on, seeking to shift the subject away from the kingship.

Kiran had taken in the son of the tyrant when the boy's mother fled back to her family in the country, leaving behind the child she feared as much as her royal husband. Since he had contrived Khalazar's downfall, Kiran felt that he owed Jari a new home by way of compensation. "He is adjusting, shall we say," the young Zimbouran replied, sipping his wine. "The truth is he saw very little of his father, and does not mourn him overmuch. Jari knows he must not mention to anyone that he is Khalazar's child, and he has stopped putting on airs about it at home. My own children sit on him— quite literally—if he does."

Yehosi, who had been patiently waiting his turn to speak, now stepped forward and said, "If it please you, Zayim, an emissary from Maurainia has arrived in the city and requests a meeting with you."

"It doesn't please me. But tell him I'll see him shortly," Jomar answered.

Yehosi bowed again and turned as if to go, then paused. "The people are asking when Nayah will return to them, Zayim."

"Her name is Ailia, not Nayah. She isn't a goddess, and she never claimed she was. As to when she's returning, tell them I don't know."

Yehosi shifted his weight, looking uneasy. "They will not believe me. They will say I have not truly spoken with you, that I am lying to them. You are her trusted prophet, they will say: you must know when she will come back." Again he hesitated. "I am not young, my lord, and I have seen three kings fall from grace and power in this land. Khalazar was but the latest. The people here may worship a ruler one day, and hate him the next. I do not make threats, lord, I only wish to warn you. I would see you reign for many more years."

"But I must play to the mobs, and humor them? That is exactly why I *won't* be your king." Jomar cast a pointed glance at Kiran Jariss.

"Yehosi, you trouble yourself unnecessarily," said Kiran, patting the eunuch on the shoulder. "I know what it is that you would say. But our Zayim is no tyrant, and will never do anything to turn the people against him. It is your own welfare that you fear for. You know Jomar is better than any ruler we have ever had, and that you will continue to enjoy peace and comfort within these walls so long as he stays in power. And he will, you'll see! You shall live to a ripe old age under his reign."

Yehosi bowed again. "You are most kind. Had I known more of this Zayim and his Tryna Lia, I would never have feared them. But I did not understand . . . You have heard how Ailia once appeared before our court in a phantom form, and spoke to Khalazar?"

"Yes, though I doubted the veracity of the report, since I was not there to see and hear for myself," Kiran replied.

"I was not there either, master, but I was in an adjacent chamber. I could not see her, nor hear her properly: the screaming of the courtiers drowned out much of what she said, and I fled and hid myself under a table that was near at hand, and dared not stir until the commotion ceased. But I did hear her mention death and destruction—"

Jomar rubbed his temple and groaned. "She only meant that *Khalazar* would bring those things on his people and hers, if he started a war."

"So I understand now. And so do most other Zimbourans. But some still labor under the false impression that she means us harm, and these have gone over to Prince Morlyn. I would not see more of them do so. Her speedy return would help to ensure that they do not." One last time he bowed, lower than ever, the top of his bald head nearly touching the floor; and then he departed.

A great cry went up from the crowd outside, and Jomar rose and went back out onto the battlement. He glanced up, shielding his eyes against the sun, half-expecting to see one of the comets plunging down to the earth. Instead he saw a dragon, its scales gleaming golden as it descended toward the fortress. He relaxed. It was an Imperial dragon: these creatures were on the side of Ailia and the Emperor. This was no marauder, but a benevolent emissary. As Jomar stared, squinting against the sun, he saw it had a rider on its back, clad in armor that glinted silver. A Paladin.

With a rush of wind the great beast alighted atop the battlements. Jomar strode forward, his short cloak whipping in the wind, to greet the rider. The armored figure sprang lightly down, doffing its plumed helmet to reveal a mop of blond hair. His heart lifted. He ran forward and gave the Paladin a bear hug, armor and all.

"Lorelyn! It's you! I wondered when you'd be back."

She smiled back at him. "Oh, Jomar, it is good to see you too. We've been hearing such a lot of things about you. But what is all this about Ailia leaving Zimboura?"

"Come inside," said Jomar, his smile vanishing again. "I'll tell you all about it. Is *he* coming too?"—gesturing toward the shining bulk of the dragon.

"She," Lorelyn corrected. "No, she says she must go back to the fighting. Thank you, Gallada."

The golden dragon dipped its head, and then spread its shimmering wings again as Jomar led Lorelyn inside. The fierce-looking Mohara guards with spears in their hands snapped to attention as the pair passed along the corridors. Their dark faces blazed with pride: once they had been the slaves of Zimboura, and now the black-skinned people freely walked the halls of Yanuvan.

Jomar ushered Lorelyn into the receiving room. Seeing them, Kiran rose, grinning. "Hullo, Kiran!" said Lorelyn.

"It is good to see you again, Lady Lorelyn. I will leave the two of you alone now," the Zimbouran added, in a knowing tone that made Jomar long to hit him.

"I think I will go take my armor off first, and have a bath," Lorelyn said.

"I will show you to a guest room, then," offered Kiran.

Sitting in a mahogany chair, his sandaled feet resting on the skin of a lion, Jomar waited for Lorelyn to return. At long last she reappeared, clad in a loose-flowing green gown, her short blond hair newly washed and soft. She was beautiful, he thought, though not in any dainty, traditional way, and she looked fresh as a flower, a tall green-stemmed lily with a golden head. It was odd that he, who feared nothing in the way of mortal danger or violence, could not quite bring himself to broach his growing love for this woman. She showed no sign of feeling the same for him, and Lorelyn would not hold with any conventional nonsense about "letting the man speak first": she was open and honest with her emotions, always. To her they were fellow warriors, comrades in arms who had faced countless perils together, and she appeared content with their friendship. No doubt she would view a declaration of love—even supposing he could ever manage to find the right words—as an unwanted complication. If he wanted more from her, he would have to bide his time and hope she would learn to see him in a new light.

But it was good at least to have a friend with him again. He pushed a pitcher of citronade and a bowl of fruit toward her. "Here—you must be hungry."

"I'm ravenous," she replied cheerfully. "I've been watching the dragons turn the comets, and helping them when I could. There are beings from the other worlds joining us: I never saw so many strange-looking creatures in all my life! It's like one of Ailia's stories. Jomar, *where* is she? Is it some secret mission?"

"Ailia has run off," said Jomar in a flat voice. "She's been in a mood ever since we came here. I never saw her smile, not once. It's because she couldn't find . . ."

"Damion," said Lorelyn softly. "Yes, she told me she had begun to wonder if she dreamed it all. About him being alive still."

Jomar nodded, looking glum. "I wish he were—I'd give anything if Damion really had gotten away somehow . . ." A roughness entered his voice and he stared at the table's inlaid top. "I miss him."

Lorelyn too looked down, her pageboy hair falling about her face. Something in the mournful picture she made caused Jomar's throat to constrict even further. He cleared it with an effort, and continued. "The people just fell all over her when she came. She came in style, after all: riding on a dragon. Kiran told me all about it. He says the people were too scared to go right up to her, because of Auron, but they filled the plaza and the noise was enough to deafen a man. To them, you know, she's a sort of goddess."

"I don't think she liked that," said Lorelyn. "She had enough of that sort of treatment in Arainia."

"No, she didn't like it—but there was nothing she could do about it. According to Wakunga, Damion gave his life to grant her that title, and she couldn't let his sacrifice be for nothing. She told me so. But it ate away at her the whole time she was here. Finally she just ran off. Didn't take the Star Stone with her, didn't even tell me she was going—just left a message with Yehosi." He drew a piece of parchment from his pocket and handed it to her.

Lorelyn's blue eyes widened as she read the note scribbled on it.

Dear Jomar,

Please don't be angry. I feel a great danger is coming and I must be ready for it. I have decided to go to Maurainia and look for Ana. I feel sure that she is still alive, though we have not heard from her, and there is much I wish to consult her about.

I promise I will return, and hope I will be stronger when I do.

Ailia

"How long has she been gone?" asked Lorelyn.

"Going on a couple of weeks now. The people are growing restless, wanting to know where their goddess is, especially now that the rebels in the north are getting noisy. They're losing faith. We need Ailia, Lori."

"It's worse than you think," she said. "I know how you feel, Jomar, but this country—this whole world—is only a little speck of dust in all of Talmirennia. There are worlds going to war up there in the sky, for all it looks so peaceful of nights. Their ambassadors have been telling us about it. The Loänan empire is divided and in the middle of its own war. Goblins and firedrakes have been raiding other planets. It's all so enormous I can hardly hold it all inside my head. But there are as many stars out there as grains of sand in the desert, and they might *all* end up at war."

"I can guess who's at the bottom of it," said Jomar, looking grim.

"Yes, it's Mandrake. Or Prince Morlyn, or whatever you want to call him—he seems to have a different name for every world he's been to. He's been stirring up trouble all over the Empire, trying to carve out an empire of his own. He's taking over world after world, they say, killing any Valei who try to resist him, and now he's sending firedrakes to burn and kill on the Imperial worlds. Jomar, he must be stopped."

"I'll be glad to oblige," he replied, fingering a jeweled dagger at his hip. "How would you like a necklace made of dragon-teeth?"

"Don't be absurd!" Lorelyn burst out, rising to her feet. "You can't kill him! None of us can—except for Ailia. We've got to find her! I don't like this—her running off, I mean. It's as though—as though she were running away—from *him*. Something happened to her when he held her in his castle. I've tried to get her to tell me, but she won't talk about it. She has to defeat the Dragon Prince, or everything will keep on going wrong."

"We can take care of Mandrake. Remember our vow?"

"Our vow was nonsense," she said. "And we knew it at the time, we were just too upset to admit it. Neither of us can harm Mandrake. Only Ailia can face him."

"Well, let's go to Maurainia," said Jomar. It was a relief to act at last, after all these weeks of sitting and waiting. "Maybe Ana really is alive. We have been assuming the old woman died because no one has heard from her. But maybe she's just being cautious. Ethereal messages can be overheard by the enemy, can't they? If she and Ailia are over there we should try and get them both back. But there's no chance of crossing by ship, not with the Armada still on the loose. Ailia used some magic or other to get herself across the ocean."

"I will call for a dragon, as soon as you are ready," said Lorelyn.

Yehosi entered the room and gave his most obsequious bow. "My lord, the ambassador of Maurainia craves an audience," the chief eunuch announced.

"Oh, hang it, I forgot all about him," said Jomar. "We had better see him now. Send him in, Yehosi."

A heavyset man with a graying beard entered the room, resplendent in the gold and purple livery of Maurainia's royal house. He too bowed, but not so low, and he looked them over with an imperious eye as he straightened. Then he began to speak to them in

Elensi. Though a dead language in Mera, and used with any kind of regularity only in the liturgies of the Western Faith, the tongue of the Elei was still occasionally spoken by ambassadors and by certain tribes of the Mohara, in situations where a *lingua franca* was required. The peoples of this world had once been united under a Commonwealth dominated by the Elei, and traces of the Fairfolk's culture and influence remained. "Ambassador Jevon, servant of King Lian I and Queen Paisia of Maurainia," the diplomat announced himself in formal tones.

Jomar waved a hand. "You can speak in Maurish," he said, using that tongue. "I learned it long ago."

The man Jevon blinked in surprise, then recovered himself. "I take it I am addressing the new potentate of Zimboura?"

"There is no potentate," Jomar answered. "I'm just looking after things until the Zimbourans decide on their real leader."

Ambassador Jevon's brows rose. "Indeed? I was given to understand that you had seized the throne for yourself. You say that is not in fact the case? I find it difficult to understand—ah—how is it I am to address you, sir?"

"I'm Jomar. And this is Lorelyn." He jerked his thumb at her.

The sharp gray eyes shifted to the tall young girl. "Your—consort?"

Jomar bristled. "My friend, and my advisor. Anything you have to say can be said in front of her."

"Very well, then—Jomar. We in Maurainia are, as I said, disturbed to learn that the situation here is so unstable. It is best that a monarch be crowned immediately after the previous one perishes or is deposed. The people feel more secure. Also, we in Maurainia are wondering about your intentions." His eyes went back to Lorelyn. "I see that you are not of any Antipodean race, my lady," noted the ambassador. "You are a westerner yourself, are you not?" It was clear that he saw in her presence a possible advantage to his side.

"I was raised by monks in the Archipelagoes," Lorelyn explained. "And, well, it's rather a long story. But to return to the matter in hand, Ambassador—"

"Yes—we keep hearing of this Antipodean conflict. I understand that with the former king's demise, a struggle has arisen between two rival cults. Your own goddess religion, and another based on the worship of Valdur."

"It's the prophecy, Ambassador," Lorelyn explained. "The Tryna Lia, Princess of the Stars, against the Dragon Prince. We follow the Princess, and they worship the Prince. He's their god, you see: Valdur in an earthly form."

"So that's it—all the old heresies and superstitions have come together in this place! And the Antipodeans really believe this is the Apocalypse?" asked the ambassador.

"It's true," Lorelyn insisted. "The Dragon Prince is a real man. And the Princess is a real person too: I know her well, and she is what she claims to be. Truly!"

"With respect, we shall reserve our judgment on that. Regarding such things as prophecies, my liege lord will take some convincing," the ambassador said.

"Then let him be convinced of this," returned Jomar. "We're going to war on the Princess's side, with or without his help."

"Well, then, can I at least meet with this Princess of yours?"

Lorelyn and Jomar exchanged glances. "She—she's not here at the moment," Lorelyn said.

"I see." He made no effort to conceal his skepticism.

"Look here, Ambassador," Lorelyn said. "You simply must make up your mind whose side you're on. The fate of this whole world is at stake. We are going to do all we can at our end. But you can do your part too: send your navy against the Armada, for instance, and free the Archipelagoes. That would free *us* to do other things."

"What things? Do you think you can conquer the remaining fanatics here in Zimboura?"

"No, not them," Jomar replied. "They're just blind, deluded fools, and some are acting out of fear. We won't make any moves against them. No," he repeated, rising up to his full height. "We are going to kill their god."

3

The Book of Doom

IN MAURAINIA'S CAPITAL THE GROWING fears of its ruler were reflected on the streets. Though no war had been fought here within living memory, there were still many in Raimar who recalled the tales of Zimbouran assaults on their city long ages ago: of the vessels of their fearsome navy, armed with catapults and burning pitch, and the savage warriors who had streamed ashore to pillage and slaughter. The passage of centuries had taken little from the power and dread of these old narratives, and the city's defenses had been maintained. The old seawalls still reared their grim masonry along Raimar's seaward side, and watchtowers looked out toward the eastern horizon like the raised heads of wary beasts. The enemy was still out there, beyond the ocean's curve, and now possessed the intervening islands of the Archipelagoes: all knew there was nothing to stop the horrors of the past from happening again. Rumors had come to Maurainia of war in the east, brought by sailors who knew of what they spoke. Some citizens had fled by cart and wagon through the range of mountains to the west, to shelter in the lands that lay behind their natural rampart. For those who remained in Raimar the passing hours were filled with dread. Every day brought some dark foreboding of imminent doom: word came from the wharves, from the coastal road that ran up from the south, and from the marketplace where foodstuffs were beginning to grow scarce— and not only because it was the tag end of winter.

And now there were new tales, scarcely to be believed, of an unknown terror that came not by sea but by air.

Every face was somber, every voice edged with stress, as another day dawned bleak and chill. As the sun climbed, however, the normal rhythms of the city returned. War might come tomorrow, or even this very afternoon or evening: but for the moment there was work to be done, food to be found, necessities to be bought or bartered for. And so it was that no one noticed the old woman who came into the city from the direction of the shore. She was unremarkable, clad in a dirty white cloak and plain dress, with disheveled steel-gray hair and a pale, hollow-eyed face that was deeply lined. There were many poor women just like her, lone widows and spinsters who lived by toiling in the warehouses or on the wharves. She mingled with the crowds, walking slowly and bowed as if with weariness. When she reached the broad main streets of the city's center a voice yelled above the heads of the crowd, making her pause in apparent bewilderment.

"Out of the way, you riffraff! Make way for Their Majesties!"

She was slow to move, and the press of jostling bodies nearly swept her off her feet. As a result she was left standing in front of the crowd when the open carriage rumbled by, drawn by its matched white horses and driven by a purple-liveried coachman. The occupants were a young man with dark hair and beard and olive skin, and a fair-haired young woman at his side, gowned in white and silver. Their garments were of fine velvet and brocade, and they wore circlets of gold on their heads. It was the king of Maurainia and his queen, Paisia, daughter of the late King Stefon.

"Back, you!" shouted an armed guard, shoving the old woman roughly into the ranks of onlookers. "Make way for your betters."

As she staggered backward she heard a man's voice grumble behind her: "He's got a nerve, talking to us like that."

"It's their way, don't you know. Those Marakites! This is what comes of marrying our princess off to a foreigner," said a woman.

"Oh, hush! Would you have the Princess marry a commoner, then?" remonstrated another woman. "She'd no choice but to take Prince Lian."

The surly man spoke again. "It's just our ill luck Stefon had no male heir. A foreign queen would do little harm, for her husband would keep her in order. But Paisia must obey this Marakite husband of hers, and go along with whatever he decides. It was he signed the truce with Khalazar—"

"It's not his fault. The Holy Father talked him into it," said a second man. "I don't think any great shakes of Norvyn Winter as Supreme Patriarch, as I've said before—him and his Zimbouran converts! Spies for Khalazar, that's what they really are—everyone sees it but he—"

"Well, now Khalazar's gone, and good riddance!" said the first woman.

"Ah, but now there's this civil war brewing over there. We'll have trouble no matter which side wins, mark my words. Both are heathen, and see us as the enemy. And they do say the Armada's on the move."

"Never mind the Armada!" interjected a new voice. "What of these other ships—the ones that can fly through the air? The seawalls are useless against *them*."

"Flying ships?" repeated the gray-haired woman, her tone sharp.

The speaker turned to look at her. "Haven't you heard?" he said. "It's some new witchery the Zimbourans have come up with: they've made vessels with flapping wings in place of masts and sails. They've been seen all over the countryside, sailing in the sky. The wise ones up at the Academy say it's naught but machinery and they could do the same—but they haven't, have they?" The man shook his head.

Ailia made no reply. He was right: the builders of the old stone fortifications down by the harbor had never dreamed of an attack by air. But much as she would have liked to ask more questions, she knew that she should leave. She was filled with unease, and her weariness and hunger and lack of sleep made shape-shifting impossible, and even a glaumerie illusion hard to maintain: keeping the false image of the grizzle-haired woman before all these bystanders' eyes took all of her concentration and much of her remaining strength. She did not dare show her true face here, for fear of enemy spies. As she continued to walk up the steep sloping streets, she began to feel as if she truly were as old as her illusory guise. She felt strangely dizzy, and hot despite the chill damp air. Her lungs labored and her calves ached, but her eyes remained fixed on her destination: the escarpment that jutted over the western end of the city, and the many-towered stone building atop it. It was the Royal Academy, where once she had been a student. Longing filled her to walk its familiar halls again and rest in its quiet chapel.

When at last she reached it she had to sit on the stone steps of its threshold and catch her breath. The building's facade lowered above her, its gargoyles and other fabulous stone beasts capering about the roofs. There was a unicorn among the animals in the carvings, she now noticed, the ignorant Meran artist portraying it as a horned horse. Of course no one here had seen the exquisite grace and delicacy of the *Tarnawyn* for many centuries, and did not know they were as different from horses as swans from geese. There were also figures of cherubim—gryphons, the sculptor would have called them—and scaly firedrakes. The people here had long dismissed these otherworldly beings as fancies. Little did they know that the old dreams—and nightmares—would soon come to Mera again. And she could do nothing to warn them, for no one would ever believe her.

When she felt somewhat rested she walked up the steps and into the front hall—and there she stopped, as suddenly as if an arrow had transfixed her. On the stone wall before her hung a dark and aged painting in oils—a portrait of a former benefactor, a lord of olden times with stern narrow features and piercing eyes. She had passed it many a time as a student, but only now did she recognize its subject. The elegant beard, trimmed to a point like a spear's, masked the lower half of the face, and the eyes were gray-blue instead of golden. But all the same, the portraitist had captured more of Mandrake than the latter had no doubt intended. A glaumerie had altered his eye color and possibly other details in the painter's mind, yet something of him still showed through in the confidence of his pose, the proud tilt of his head and determined set of the shoulders under the black velvet doublet. With some difficulty, Ailia tore her eyes from the painting and walked on.

Once the Royal Academy had been a home to her, where she lived and slept and took her meals, and browsed to her heart's content in the vast library. Now no one gave her a glance as she entered it, and all the faces were strange. She moved among these people like a ghost among the living. Once she glimpsed a fair-haired young man standing with his back to her, and without thinking she cried out, "Damion, Damion," and when the man turned, startled, she retreated in confusion at his unfamiliar face. As she made herself walk on, the memory of another face, dark of skin, wrinkled with great age, rose within her mind. Wakunga. And his words came back to her as well.

"You seek Damion in the wrong place," the shaman had said to her. "The sky-goddess Nayah knew that she must find her consort in the Netherworld, and summon him forth to live again. And your tale in many ways follows hers."

Superstition: it was mere superstition. Wakunga was wise, but he had not the training of the Arainian Nemerei. Damion Athariel would not return, ever. He lingered in this place, as he had in Zimboura, only as a memory in the minds of those who had known him.

She wondered drearily if there was anyone in Maurainia she should inform of Damion's fate. He had been an orphan with no known relations, raised here at the Academy by the monks of St. Athariel. Perhaps the abbot and prior should be told. And there had been a boyhood friend of his, now an ordained priest down in the city—what was his name? She couldn't recall. Her thoughts felt thick and slow, dulled no doubt by fatigue and depression. Several people she passed in the hallway gave her ragged figure a disapproving look, and she expected at any moment to be told to leave the premises. At least she could not be thrown out of the chapel, which was open to all the Faithful: she quickened her pace, heading toward its safe haven. When she reached it, she knelt down in a pew in a prayerful attitude, and fixed her eyes on the sanctuary. Once again the familiarity of her surroundings set her heart to aching. The high vaulted ceiling with its carvings of stone, the ranks of flickering candles, the altar of the sacred flame, all were imbued with traces of a safer and happier past. Behind the altar rose the stone screen of the inner sanctum, adorned with winged figures of bronze. Angels, they were called here. But like the stone gargoyles, these statues were inspired by true accounts of beings from ancient times: the sorcerous shape-shifting Archons, onetime rulers of the Celestial Empire.

And it was here in this chapel, in that flame-lit sanctuary, that she had first seen—

No. She was *not* going to think of Damion again.

Ailia turned her attention back to the carved angels and demons on the altar screen. They made her think of the old accounts in the Meran scriptures of the war of Heaven and Hell. She picked up the illustrated Kantikant in her pew and opened it at the first part, the Book of Beginnings. There, in the accompanying woodcuts, robed and winged angels warred with fearsome fiends that sported horns, tails, and other bestial attributes. Modrian-Valdur appeared first as a crowned archangel, then as a demon with a man's form and the wings and tail of a dragon, and finally as the terrible Crowned Dragon, breathing out flames as he menaced Athariel, captain of the heavenly host. In the last picture of the sequence he was depicted falling defeated into the Pit of Perdition, which was represented symbolically as a monster's head with fuming jaws that gaped to receive him.

She gazed on this picture for a time, and then turned to the Book of Being, where Orendyl's more detailed description of the Pit was to be found. "I beheld in my vision a realm of everlasting darkness," he wrote, "presided over by demons of hideous aspect, neither beast nor man. In that place there is a bastion of mighty towers and walls, the Citadel Perilous, wherein dwelleth the Great Deceiver and all his demons. It is founded upon the brink of a pit of eternal flame. Into that Pit of Perdition the condemned are sent, to endure forever the torments that the demons devise for them." The accompanying illustration showed a fortified tower rising above a gaping chasm from which curls of smoke arose, while the Crowned Dragon along with many grotesque demons drove cowering men into the abyss. She set the book down again. Was it simply a nightmare? Or had Orendyl truly received a vision of Valdur's realm? His account of Heaven was much like that given by Welessan the Wanderer, though less detailed—and Welessan's vision of the planetary spheres had proven remarkably accurate. Was Perdition also real then—not an imaginary place of eternal damnation, but an actual place in the material realm that Orendyl had glimpsed? And if so, where might it lie? One tradition made the black star in the constellation of Valdur the Portal of Hell, but that might be mere fancy. The scene described by Orendyl, however, could have been in a real world within Entar, Valdur's stellar empire. Perhaps the prophet had glimpsed the distant past of the empire's old throne-world Ombar, planet of the red star Utara? According to Mandrake, one side of that world was forever turned away from its sun. A place of "everlasting darkness." As for the demons, sorcerers could use shape-shifts or glaumerie to appear as hideous monsters—and the Archons had been sorcerers beyond compare.

She leafed on through the worn and dog-eared pages, then froze at one particular illustration: a woman battling the Crowned Dragon. The artist of this volume had for some reason chosen to include an apocryphal image in the canonical Book of Doom. She stared at the woodcut in dismay. The iconography was traditional: the Tryna Lia wore a crown of stars and stood upon an upturned

crescent moon, brandishing her Star Stone while the dragon reared
up with wings outspread, spitting fire from his jaws. Auron and old
Ana had both told her the future was fluid, that it was not irre-
versibly set—and yet there it was, before her, inescapable. No warrior angel would come again to fight the foe. That battle was in the
past, never to be repeated. It fell to her now to take the champion's
role, not wait along with others to be saved.

Her throat hurt when she swallowed, and she felt chilled and hot
in waves. She set the book down and slumped against the pew in
front of her, dozing from sheer exhaustion while those around her
thought that she prayed. With the loss of consciousness her
glaumerie faded: anyone who lifted her hood now would see the
face of a young woman and not an elderly one. Still she slept on,
insensible of her danger. She dreamed of—or did she see in
truth?—this same chapel in long-ago days, with robed knights and
monks kneeling in the pews. One was a young man of angelic
beauty and earnest expression, with shoulder-length hair of ruddy
gold and wondrous eyes of almost the same hue. A knight and
prince, he was then: freed from the torment of his early boyhood,
to live a life of honor and proud service untroubled as yet by shades
of a still darker future.

No, it was too much: she could not endure it. She cried aloud in
pain against the vision.

She hardly felt the hands that shook her, trying to wake her: it
had all become part of a fevered dream that she could not escape.
She was lifted, she dimly sensed, and carried; then there followed a
long time of darkness. She heard someone moan far off, and then
nearer; then she realized it was her own voice. And faintly, from
some distant place, there came another voice that seemed familiar,
though she could not match it with a face:

"It's she, all right. Ailia! We've found her at last."

THE CITY SEEMED STRANGELY HUSHED and subdued as evening fell.
The people, having obtained what they needed at the market
square and shops, did not linger in the streets but hastened home.
By day it was not possible to tell how many of the citizens had fled
their homes, but at night the emptying of Raimar became apparent.
Once the whole of the city would have been lit with the warm yellow lamplight glowing from its windows, but now many pockets of

darkness revealed that at least a third of the people had left. More would certainly follow them in the coming days if the news did not improve. All of Raimar seemed to cower in expectation of a deadly blow.

Jaimon Seaman stood gazing out the open door of the abandoned house that he and his extended family had taken over for their own use. He had gone to the harbor that afternoon to glean what news he could from the crews of the merchant ships. Two rival powers were now fighting for supremacy in Zimboura: yet another man who claimed to be the God-king, and his rival, a sort of desert prophet called the *Zayim* who worshipped a goddess, of all things. Ambassadors had been sent to Zimboura, to both sides, but it was not known how they had been received by either one. If only the two new tyrants would content themselves with fighting each other, or if one would ally himself with the western lands to defeat his rival! Then there might be peace. But uncertainty filled the voices of the sailors, and fear was in their eyes. Some ships had been attacked at sea, looted and burned. Whoever now controlled the Armada had no fear of the Commonwealth.

Jaimon turned and went inside, wondering whether he should share what he had learned with his family. It seemed that he was fated always to be the bringer of ill news: years ago it was he who had advised them to flee Great Island and seek refuge on the Continent from Khalazar's fleet. He decided to say nothing yet, and only speak of other things. His sister, Jemma, was in the kitchen soaking a cloth in the washbasin, and he went to stand at her side.

"She still hasn't awakened?" he asked. Jemma shook her head. Wringing out the rag, she returned to the sickroom and he followed her. Their aunt sat next to the bed, not taking her eyes off its occupant. For a moment Jaimon and Jemma stood motionless, gazing at the unconscious figure. The girl's eyes were fast shut and deeply shadowed, and her skin was waxen-pale. From time to time she moved restlessly, her hands twitching on the coverlet, but she did not wake.

Jemma took the seat next to Nella and handed her the cloth. "There, Ailia, my love," the older woman murmured, placing it on the girl's forehead. "That will cool you down a bit." She spoke knowing that her daughter would not answer: it was as if she sought to reassure herself with her own words. Jemma watched her ministrations with anxious eyes.

Jaimon remained standing, staring down at his sick cousin. She had been his close companion during their childhood, even closer than his sister because Ailia had shared his yearning for adventure. They had played many games together, imagining that they were heroes in the faerie tales and old histories, and talked about the faraway lands that lay beyond the encircling sea. He wondered at times whether this kinship that had gone far beyond the bonds of blood was responsible for his failure to marry. He had never yet found a woman who understood him as deeply as Ailia had.

Looking down into her face, drained now of animation as well as of color, he remembered the light of eagerness and longing that had filled her eyes, and the delicate flush of excitement that would come to her cheeks when she spoke of her desire for knowledge and experience. He recalled her childlike delight at finding herself here in Maurainia—a wish come true, despite the alarming circumstances that had brought it about. And then, mere months later, she had disappeared from the Royal Academy, leaving him and all her family frantic with worry. None of them believed the explanation offered by the authorities: that Ailia had joined a secret witches' coven, and escaped after she and her fellow witches had been placed under arrest. The charge of witchcraft had been absurd enough; but even if it had been true, she would have run back to her family and not vanished altogether. They knew their Ailia. If she had left Raimar, Jaimon thought, it had been against her will. He had scarcely been able to believe it when Jemma and Betta had come to him with the news that she had been found. They had never given up searching the hostels on a weekly basis, hoping that Ailia might yet turn up in one of them, but with the passage of years that hope had begun to wither. How they had all rejoiced when that vigilance was at last rewarded! Then they had suffered anew as they watched her alarming illness progress: the high fever, and the terrifying delirium that had set her to raving of strange places and people they knew nothing of. It would be too cruel to find Ailia again, only to lose her forever—and without her even waking to recognize them. Her fever had gone down at last, however, and it seemed she was on the mend. Jaimon felt weak at the knees with relief. *Now,* he thought, *we will finally learn what happened to her.*

"She has changed," said Jemma presently.

"Ah, yes, poor thing. She's gotten so thin." Nella lifted the cloth and felt the girl's forehead.

"I don't mean that. Her hair is longer—long enough to sit upon. I suppose it could grow that long in all this time, but it's also more golden than I remember. It was more, well, mousy before. And I swear she's grown taller. If she were standing up she'd be taller than I am, and we used to be the same height."

Nella said nothing, and after a moment her niece got up again. "Well, I must go feed the hens," Jemma said. "And see if they've laid any eggs. Will you help me, Jaim?" She felt a need to speak to her brother alone, share confidences as they had done when they were younger. They went out the back door together, into a little yard where a lone horse was stabled, and a few scrawny chickens pecked about in a desultory fashion.

Jemma sighed as she opened the grain bin. "We're lucky to have these. Poultry are priceless nowadays. But I don't know how much longer we will be able to feed them, Jaim. Grain is getting terribly expensive, and we need it for the cart horse. What if we had to flee the city?"

He nodded. "I know it's a great temptation to kill and eat the poultry, but as Uncle Dannor says, better a few eggs than one meal of meat. I'll see if I can find some food for them." He stooped to pick up two brown-shelled eggs. "Though if they don't lay more we'll surely have to kill them."

Presently Jemma spoke again. "I am so glad Ailia is back safe with us again, and feeling better. And yet—everything still seems wrong, somehow! I'm afraid, Jaim. It's not just the wars, and the talk of invasion—there have always been wars—but now there's *that*, as well." She raised a hand, pointing. They both looked up at the night sky above them, wondrous and terrible with its shower of many long-tailed comets. "Some people say this means the world is ending."

"I don't believe in portents and prophecies," said Jaimon, as they returned indoors and placed the eggs on the kitchen table. "I don't think the comets mean anything at all. They're just a natural phenomenon," he declared, following his sister into the sickroom.

"What's that?" said Nella, looking up as they entered.

"We're talking about the comets," said Jemma. "But, Jaim, what if

one of them fell to earth? It would be like the Great Disaster again."
She shuddered. "Whole lands burning up. Comets are made out of
fire—"

"Ice," Ailia murmured, moving her head from side to side on the
pillow.

"What did she say?" Jaimon asked.

Nella hastened to the girl's side. "Something about ice—perhaps
the fever's back?" She felt Ailia's brow. "No, she's just a little warm,
but will you get another wet cloth for her forehead, Jemma?"

Ailia stirred and spoke again. "Comets are made out of ice—not
fire."

"She's raving again," said Jemma.

Seeing the tears gathering in her niece's eyes, Nella turned brisk.
"Just get me the washcloth, please."

"I'm sorry, auntie—it's the worry getting to me. Poor Ailia being
so ill, and folk going on about the end of the world—" She swallowed a sob. "I wish it really were the End Times. Then we need
only wait to be delivered by the angels. I wish that someone *would*
come, and fight for us."

At that moment Ailia's eyes fluttered open, and they all fell silent
as she lay staring upward. Her gaze shifted from the ceiling to their
faces, and recognition dawned in her eyes. "Mamma? Jaim, Jemma—
is it really you? Or am I dreaming still?" she murmured.

Nella took her hand and held it close. "We're really here, love—
you're back with us again. Oh, we have been so worried, Ailia!"

"Why am I in bed? Have I been ill?" Her head tossed from one
side to the other, and her cheeks seemed more flushed than before.

"Yes, dear, but you're better now," said Nella. "Here, have a sip of
this—" She held a cup of water to the girl's cracked lips.

Ailia tried to drink, but choked, and that set off a fit of coughing.
"Where am I?" she asked as soon as she had breath. "This isn't
home. What is this place?"

"It's a house we have—well, you might say borrowed, since its
owners have abandoned it. Lots of empty houses in Raimar these
days. But, well, never mind that."

"Raimar," Ailia said softly. "I had forgotten. I was thinking this
was the Island."

"We found you in a hostel, in the city. You were suffering from
fever, and you have been asleep or delirious for nearly two days

now. How are you feeling, love?" Nella asked, placing a woolen shawl around Ailia's shoulders.

Ailia looked up at her foster mother and essayed a feeble smile. She was still pale from her illness, except for the two spots of color in her cheeks, but her eyes seemed more clear. "I feel . . . so tired, so weak—as if I have been running, but I don't know from what." She coughed again and pulled the shawl closer.

"But wherever have you *been* all this time?" Jaimon burst out, no longer able to restrain himself.

"Been?" Ailia looked at him for a moment with blank bewildered eyes. Then she sank slowly back onto the pillow.

"I can't remember," she whispered.

┌─────────┐
│ **4** │
└─────────┘

Fire in the Sky

"*AVATAR. HEAR US.*"

The voices entered Mandrake's mind, disturbing him as he lay half-asleep and half-submerged. As his eyes slowly opened he believed, for an instant, that he lay in his own watery cavern beneath the Forbidden Palace, in his own world; but then he noted the pale light coming from above, which illuminated the pool and revealed its floor and sides to be smooth, not rocky. Then he remembered: he was reposing in a heated pool in the pleasure gardens of Temendri Alfaran. His armies had taken that world without a struggle—or so they had reported, for he had not been present during the assault, and had arrived to find the moon-world already conquered and the Emperor fled. As he roused and looked about him he saw three familiar figures apparently suspended in the water, a claw's reach away. Elazar and Elombar, and Naugra the Regent. He opened his jaws and lashed his tail with displeasure, causing the pool's surface to boil and froth. *These invasions of my privacy are intolerable,* he rebuked, showing his great teeth.

The three visitors, being incorporeal images, showed no fear. The Naugra-image said, *But Lord Prince, we bring you important news. We have dispatched many flying ships and firedrakes, in your name, to subdue Mera. And we know Ailia is still within that sphere. Now is your chance to defeat her, while she is out of Arainia and cut off from the power it gives to her. This was the whole aim of your campaign in Mera—to lure her into a world where her powers are lessened! You lost your great chance when she was in your power, in Nemorah. Do not squander another opportunity!*

The dragon thrust his clawed feet against the pool's stone floor and surfaced, spouting like a whale. Above him the night of Temendri Alfaran blazed, as bright almost as its day: lit by swarms of stars webbed within blue and pale purple nebulae, and by the giant ringed world of Alfaran that at present filled all the eastern sky. Mandrake emerged from the pool, and shook the water from his wings and mane. "I have done as you desired. I came to Temendri Alfaran to seize the throne from Orbion Imperator, only to find him fled. My journey here was futile, even if you did claim this world for us. And in any case, did you not desire me to go to Ombar next?" He roared as he spoke, and strode away from the pool into a grave of flower-trees. Their blooms were fading, falling to the ground, for this region of the dragon-world was approaching its autumn. Many of the ephemeri, the plant-creatures that flew like birds, were also falling to earth: surrendering their brief winged lives, to be transformed into seeds. The sight of their impotent fluttering made him melancholy.

The three ethereal images followed him, floating in the air like ghosts. "We would have had you go to Ombar first, and leave Temendri Alfaran for another day," Elombar said, drifting at his side. "Orbion is aged and ailing, and not so great a threat to you as is the Tryna Lia. In my sphere there is a power that can make you more than Ailia's equal, should you choose to draw upon it. A sovereign power that is not confined to the sphere of Ombar, like that of Arainia, but can enter into you and go with you anywhere in Talmirennia—even Arainia itself. But you must come here and accept it first. I shall await you in the old city of the Archons that lies near the zone of shadow, along with Elazar. You have long desired to meet with us in person, you say, and you shall have your wish. But only if you come to Ombar."

"You are not Archons," the dragon rumbled. "The Old Ones are long dead."

"Well, then, you have nothing to fear from us. Why do you not come?" said Elombar.

"I do not fear you!" he bellowed, stopping short and half-unfurling his wings.

But he lied.

"I am glad to hear it; but the longer you delay our meeting the more it appears that you are afraid. The armies of Ombar await your command. We have slain all those in our world that defied us or would not own you lord: none will now dare to disobey. But the Morugei would behold their ruler with their own eyes, and your followers in Mera also await you: both those that are in open rebellion against Ailia, and others that bide their time in secret. We have prepared for your coming for many centuries. Come, and take what is yours!"

Had the Morugei not seen him? He thought he recalled processing through a street in one of their worlds shortly after he agreed to claim his title, in human form, hailed by clamorous hordes—but had that truly happened? Now that he had learned to wear draconic shape all the time, his memory of his human life was growing curiously blurred. Sometimes he felt as though his dragon-form was not only imposing its strange senses and appetites on him but actually taking on a will of its own, causing him to be more than ever estranged from himself. Might a day not come when he was no longer Mandrake at all, but a creature entirely different in mind as well as in body? It was a troubling thought. But for the moment the dread of human frailty overpowered all other fears.

So: at last he could meet the "demons" face-to-face, instead of discoursing with their ethereal phantoms. It was no bluff: they would not make the invitation if they could not indeed assume the material forms they projected. He had but to go to Ombar to confront them at last, learn who they truly were. Was this their answer to his many challenges? He had accused them of attempting to deceive him, and of hiding their true forms from him, but now if he did not accept their invitation it would look as though *he* were afraid of them. They lost nothing by refusing to come before him, for it was not shameful for them to fear *him*—the Avatar, the incarnation of the rebel god, commander of demons. It was he who lost face by appearing to avoid them. He would be shamed into going to Ombar—and what then? Did they believe, perhaps, that their physical presence would intimidate him? Or had they something more drastic in mind? A projection could do no harm: to work sorcery on another, one must be present in the flesh . . . But no, that was nonsense. They would not hurt or kill him even if they could, for he was their precious Avatar, and central to their long-laid schemes. No doubt this was but their way of bringing him to heel. One thing was certain: they were no mere illusions as he had hoped, nor were they lowly goblin-servants of Naugra's. The goblin-race had many magical skills, but they consisted for the most part of glaumerie and other kinds of trickery. These two were shape-shifters, from the strange forms they took: and only the greatest of Nemerei could wield that power. It was plain too that they did not truly fear him, despite the power he wielded; and that alone was cause for him to be afraid.

"I will go to Mera first," he said at last. "The Valei *will* see me, but only after I have proven myself as Avatar—a conqueror come to claim his realm." The figures bowed and vanished from sight, leaving Mandrake to ponder all that had been said. For now they and he shared a goal, but what would happen when Ailia and her forces were vanquished and he turned to pursue his own course? They must be destroyed, whatever manner of creature they might be.

He was not yet so far gone that he did not feel some unease at the speed with which this solution came to his mind. A warrior he had been for centuries, but not a ruthless or casual killer—a trait he considered primitive, and despised in others. No, his killings were always necessary, done in his own defense. For the meantime he had no choice but to accept the aid of his mysterious allies, although he would not go to Ombar—at least not yet. He would avail himself of the armies and flying fleets they had given him, the goblins and firedrakes as well as his own Loänei protectors, and go to Mera. That should be enough to aid his victory, without any recourse to the unknown and possibly perilous "power" in Valdur's ancient throne world. Once Ailia was a threat to him no longer, he would seek out the fugitive Emperor and take the throne of Talmirennia from him. But before he embarked on the task of ordering his stellar realm, he would at last make the journey to Ombar—to rid himself of these allies, who could all too easily turn into rivals once their mutual foe was destroyed.

"OUR ARMY HAS COME AT LAST from Arainia. The Nemerei sent them through the desert portal," said Lorelyn as she and Jomar descended the grand central stair of Yanuvan. "They will protect the people here when Mandrake's followers come. This time there are more of them, and some have had experience of battle. That will make all the difference, I think."

"Good. I'll leave the Arainian commander in charge, and you and I can go search for Ailia." Jomar replied.

"We must take the Star Stone with us. Have you got it?"

"Yes, of course. I've been carrying the thing with me everywhere. Someone would be sure to steal it otherwise: to the Zimbourans it's nothing but a gem." He reached into an inner pocket of his red silk vest and drew out a little cloth bag.

"It's in *there?*" Lorelyn asked, awed. "You just walk about with—*it* on your person, like that?"

"Why not? I haven't touched it—I've no wish to have visions, or whatever it is the Stone does to people." He opened the drawstring of the bag and they both peered in at the Star Stone. The radiant light that filled it in Ailia's presence was gone: it might have been no more than a large cut diamond, though an exceptionally clear and flawless one.

"She oughtn't to have left it behind," said Lorelyn. "Things go terribly wrong for her when she doesn't keep it close."

Feeling uneasy, Jomar closed the bag and returned it to his vest pocket. "Don't say that! She probably just didn't want to risk losing it, or have it fall into the wrong hands. Is there a dragon free to take us to Maurainia, or are they all fighting?" he added, changing the subject.

"I've asked them to send us some help. It worries me that the enemy probably knows about Ailia leaving, too. What if they track her down? I know she's got her magic, but as the Nemerei say, even a sorcerer must sleep—and she's all alone with no one to guard her." They walked out of the cool halls of the fortress into the glare of the vast open plaza. Kiran, who was standing a few paces away from the entrance with Wakunga at his side, gave Jomar a mischievous grin.

"Hail Jomar! The Zayim, it appears, is a great magician as well as a warrior. You can conjure whole armies out of empty air." He bowed deeply.

Jomar gave him a weary look. "What are you babbling about now? You *know* I can't do anything like that."

"Ah, but you already have. An army has been seen appearing out of the old stone gate in the desert: the one shaped like two winged stone beasts. One moment there was nothing, the witnesses say: then a whole host of fighting men came marching through the gateposts—out of nowhere. There were witnesses to this miracle, and the soldiers' tracks are still plain to be seen in the sand on one side of the gateway—but on the other side, nothing."

Jomar groaned. "The army didn't—oh, blast it, I can't explain. But I didn't conjure anything!"

"Of course not. It is the fulfillment of the prophecy. The army of Heaven follows the arrival on earth of the Morning Star's daughter," said Wakunga. He too looked amused. "The Bird of Heaven has come also," he added.

"The what?"

The shaman pointed. An excited crowd had gathered around a clump of stately date palms at the edge of the plaza. In the crown of the tallest tree, nestling among its luxuriant fronds, perched a large bird whose plumage shone with all the colors of flame. "It flew through the gateway not long after the army appeared," said Wakunga. "They say it is a sign from Heaven."

"It's Taleera! She's come back!" Lorelyn cried, recognizing Ailia's protector and friend. She ran to the base of the tree and called up to the firebird. "Taleera—hie! Down here!"

Taleera was plainly enjoying the attention of the onlookers: as they gazed up at her she literally preened, fanning out her brilliant wing coverts and dabbing at them with her beak. She answered Lorelyn's hail with a long trill, a lovely liquid sound like water bubbling from a spring.

"What did it—*she* say?" asked Jomar, wishing the T'kiri would take her human form and speak in plain Elensi.

"She says she heard about Ailia, and has come to help. And Auron is here too." Lorelyn looked about her, then called out again at the sight of a short, portly man standing in the crowd. He appeared to be of Kaanish descent and elderly, with a balding head and long white beard. But it was a mere disguise. This was Auron, an Imperial Loänan and trusted servant of the Celestial Emperor. He wasted no words when he saw them approach, but met them halfway, making urgent gestures with both arms.

"Come," he said. "Falaar told me what happened. He remained in the battle, where he is sorely needed, but Taleera and I will help you to find the Tryna Lia."

"Right. Just let us get our weapons and some food, and change our clothing," Jomar said.

"We will await you here."

Jomar and Lorelyn began to walk back toward the fortress, Kiran following. The ambassador from Maurainia met them in the main hall.

"If I may trouble you, my lord—" he began, addressing his words to Jomar. The latter kept on walking.

"I'm leaving," he said over his shoulder. "You will have to talk to someone else while I'm gone."

"Leaving? But you cannot leave! You are the ruler here." Ambassador Jevon stared at him, incredulous. "Where are you going?"

"To look for my friend." Jomar turned to Kiran. "Here, you! Take over for me. Since you think it's so amusing to be a leader, you can just try it while I'm gone." He marched on without a backward glance.

"I? A king?" Kiran laughed. "Whatever is Zimboura coming to? Well, I must work on my royal swagger." He headed for the throne room, walking with an exaggerated rolling gait.

The ambassador, left to himself in the hall, stood shaking his head and muttering to himself the words that he would later repeat to his sovereign: "These people are mad. Utterly mad!"

AILIA'S STRENGTH SLOWLY RETURNED AS the evening deepened. Assisted by Nella and her Aunt Betta, she managed to sit up in bed without feeling faint. But the gap in her memory remained, sharply dividing her present from her past. It seemed to her that she stood on the brink of a black yawning chasm, gazing at its remote and inaccessible far side. The bridge that had once spanned it, and by which she had come to this side, had fallen and been lost to its depths.

"We never gave up hoping you would come back to us," said Jemma. "I used to dream about it. Some folks said you were dead, lost forever. But deep down, I kept telling myself you were alive still, and would return from wherever it was you had gone to. I wish you could say where you've been!"

"So do I. It's very strange," said Ailia, "to be missing a great piece out of your life. And rather frightening."

"You really remember nothing?" Jaimon asked.

Ailia closed her eyes and thought hard. "Nothing after our arrival here in Raimar."

"That was four years ago," he said. "I've heard of such things— people losing their memories after illness, or a bump on the head. But usually they forget everything. You've not forgotten us, or the Island."

"Yes—it's as if part of me doesn't wish to remember something, for some reason. I believe I have read about such things: soldiers and other people who suffer or see terrible sights, and then lose all memory of them, though they can still recall the rest of their past. It's as if their minds blot out that one thing in particular, to save their sanity." Ailia sat quietly, her eyes still shut, trying to summon up that lost fragment of her life. She was surprised that she did not feel more afraid. What could have happened that was so dreadful her mind did not choose to recall it? But whatever it might have been, she was whole and unhurt, and healthy again: and it was comforting to be with her family, even if they were not in their proper home. "Supposing you told me what you know—I understand there isn't much, but we might piece something together. Or it might jog my memory," she suggested. But she did not speak with any urgency.

Jaimon cleared his throat. "Well, as we said, you were taken by the authorities—so we were told—on charges of witchcraft."

"But I wasn't, was I? It doesn't sound like me." She gave him a little smile, which he returned.

"Of course not! We all knew that part was nonsense." He approached her bedside and stood gazing down at her. "The other people who came to us wouldn't say where you were either—they just went all mysterious when we asked."

"Other people?"

"They were an odd lot—beggars and villagers mostly, but they all claimed to know what had been done with you. They said you didn't run away at all, that Zimbourans had carried you off. But they insisted you got away from the Zimbourans, and you were safe somewhere. Old Ana said the same."

Ailia gasped. "Ana—"

"What is it?"

"When you said that name, I saw—a face. An old woman—"

"Yes—the wise woman from the mountains. Most people here have heard of her, though she doesn't come into the city much. But she came to us a few months ago. She told us she'd seen you and said you were all right. But she wouldn't say where. We didn't know whether to believe her or not. Do you remember now? Anything?"

"I—I'm not sure." Places, people flowed before her eyes in a bewildering torrent. She could not fit names to most of them.

Aunt Betta intervened. "Don't pepper her with questions, Jaim. Let her get her strength back first."

"Tell me," Ailia said. "What has been happening here? Have you stayed in Maurainia all this time? I expect I was dreadfully worried about you too—wherever I was."

"Dannor and your Uncle Nedman came over to join us, when things got rough," Nella explained. "And Jemma's husband came later. The men are all working down on the wharves, except Jaimon. He's signed on to sail with the Royal Navy, and will be leaving in a few days."

"Not that the navy is much use anymore, with the enemy coming by air," said Jaimon. Betta made a motion with her hand to hush her son, but it was too late. Ailia stared at them.

"By air?" she repeated. "You mean—flying ships?"

"Yes. The Zimbourans' new weapon against us."

"But this reminds me . . . I remember something about them—"

The others exchanged sharp glances. "What do you remember?" Nella queried. There was an odd, intent look in her eye as she leaned forward.

"A word." Ailia struggled to grasp the elusive images. "*Ornithopters.* Ships that fly on wings like birds . . . I think—I think the Elei made them."

Jaimon nodded. "You used to tell us old tales of the Elei and their

flying ships when you were a little girl. That's what you are remembering, I expect. But these ones aren't faerie tales: they're real.
We see them flying overhead all the time now. People scream and
run at the sight. No one knows how the Zimbourans learned to
make them: some old-timers out in the countryside say it must be
done with black magic, but most say they've simply learned the
trick of flight from watching birds. Magisters at the Royal Academy
have been trying to do that for years. One nearly succeeded, but
the wings of his air-craft kept breaking off—"

Ailia said, "Zimbourans may be flying in them, but others devised
those ships, a very long time ago. The tales I told you were true."

"How do you know that?" he asked, puzzled.

"I—just *know*."

"There now—that's enough," said Nella, turning suddenly
brusque. "Let her rest. Her memory is quite likely to come back on
its own if she takes her ease, and isn't too troubled."

She shooed them all out of the room, then followed, closing the
door gently behind her. Jemma retreated to her own room, while
Jaimon went into the kitchen to join the two older women.

"You must tell her, Nell," he overheard Betta say in a low voice.

"Tell her what? That I and Dannor have lied to her all these
years?"

Jaimon stepped forward, and they both swung about to face him.
"Look here, if you know something about all this, you must tell the
rest of us. What do you mean by 'lying all these years'? Has it anything to do with Ailia being taken away from us? Is she in any sort
of danger? Tell me!"

Betta turned to her sister-in-law. "He's right. The time for se-
crecy's long past! Those people in the flying ships may well be looking for her. What if she's in danger? She has to know the truth!"

"But now, Betta?" Nella remonstrated. "When she's been ill, and is
so weak? Why frighten her? We can hide her, and keep her safe."

"And if they aren't her enemies? What if they want to help her?
We'd have no right to keep her hidden then. We must tell her, and
let her decide what she wants to do."

"In any case," Jaimon added, "you can at least tell me this secret,
whatever it is. I don't like being kept in the dark. Do you mean to
say you know where Ailia has been all this time—and what happened to her?"

"No," Betta said. "We don't know, Jaim." Her eyes went to Nella again. "But we can guess. If you won't tell him, Nell, I will."

Nella stood for a moment with eyes downcast. Then she said, "Come outside, so Ailia won't overhear. And fetch Jemma: she ought to hear as well."

She led them into the hens' yard, where they all faced her: Betta stern, the two younger ones confused and uneasy. For a long time Nella said nothing, but stood twisting her apron in her work-coarsened hands. Then she spoke, almost blurting the words: "There was a shipwreck, many years ago. On the south shore of Great Island."

"Yes, of course we've heard of it," Jaimon replied. "I used to pester you to tell me more about it when I was a little boy, remember? You older folk were terribly close-mouthed about it."

"I'm not surprised: for the wreck, you see, was all covered in gold. At least we think it was gold: hundreds and hundreds of yellow plates were stuck all over the hull, like fishes' scales. They are probably still lying in cellars and smugglers' caves all over Great Island. Oh, yes: we never told you young ones the whole truth of it. Very strange it was—a wreck like any other, we all thought at first. But the pieces of the ship that washed ashore were all golden. They must have been wondrous rich folk went down with that ship—and yet no ever came looking for them, which was odd. And old Jeb that lived down on the shore, he alone saw the ship before she sank. He swore up and down that he saw that ship sailing through the sky, like a ghost-ship out of the old tales, before it was struck by a thunderbolt and fell down, into the sea. He wouldn't have anything to do with the wreckage, gold or not. Said it was unlucky. Many came to believe him, and they hid or buried what they'd salvaged, and never spoke of it again."

"Jeb! Wasn't he the town drunkard?" said Jaimon.

"He wasn't drunk that night. No doubt that ship *was* sailing the sky—for it must have been the same as these flying vessels we've seen since. Though I still don't know why no one ever came to claim its wreckage—or the babe."

"The babe!" cried Jemma.

"We found her on the shore with the wreckage. Just a tiny child she was then, barely old enough to talk and toddle. But her little dress was all embroidered with stars in thread of gold. We kept that dress for years, in case her kin ever came to claim her, and then finally we threw it away. You see, we'd begun to think of her as ours, and we didn't want Ailia herself to think otherwise. I couldn't have babes of my own, so for me she was like an answer to a prayer. If she'd found that dress, she might have started asking questions we didn't want to answer. What was the use of it? All her folk must be dead, or they would have come looking for her."

"But if Ailia came off a *flying* ship, then who is she? Why, she could be anybody!" Jemma gasped.

"So I've said before, Nell—if that really was gold thread her clothes were worked with, she must be a lady. Maybe even a princess!" said Betta.

"A princess!" Jaimon snorted. "Of what country? If anyone were missing a *princess* we'd surely have heard of it!"

"So I said." Nella nodded. "And so I say still."

"But she must be told the truth." Betta's voice was firm. "Her folk may be looking for her now, Nell—these people in the flying ships may be her blood kin."

"Yes, it is possible. But let us tell her when she is stronger. Not now." Nella's voice had changed its tone: no longer firm and defensive, she was almost pleading. She turned from the others and went back into the house, signaling an end to the discussion, and after a moment they followed her. No word was spoken. The two older women were too steeped in memories, and the young people too full of wonderment at what they had learned, to say anything at all.

"So she's *not* our cousin," said Jemma at last in an undertone to her brother. "I can't quite believe it with a part of my mind, and yet—it does make sense. She always was different from the rest of us, somehow. Not so much in looks or anything, but in the way she thought and felt. She didn't fit, with us or with any of the Island folk."

"What do you mean?" responded Jaimon, not troubling to lower his voice. "Didn't fit? She was part of our family! I don't care where she came from. She's *ours* now. You only have to look at her face to see how glad she is to be with us!"

His sister looked long at him. "You were always closer to her than to me," she said presently. "Oh, don't worry, I'm not jealous or anything silly like that. But the two of you had such a lot in common. I think of all of us she felt closest to you. It was very hard for her when you went away to sea, Jaim."

"I know. And I thought about it a good deal. I knew she must be lonely, and I wrote to her whenever I could. Perhaps I shouldn't have gone."

"Nonsense. Of course you should, and Ailia would say the same. She knew it was the thing you wanted most in the world. She'd have gone away herself if she'd had the chance. I only said that, Jaim, so you'd understand how she felt. And how would it have been different if you had stayed?"

Jaimon made no reply, but an astonishing answer resounded through his mind. *We might have married. Cousins do, sometimes. And now I know she's not even my real cousin . . .*

Jemma watched his face again, then said: "I suppose she hasn't really come back to stay with us, after all. She'll want to go back to her own folk, whoever they are. The ones in the winged ships."

"Her own folk? But she's not Zimbouran," objected Jaimon. "She doesn't look at all like one. If she came off a Zimbouran sky-ship then perhaps she was a prisoner, and all her own folk are dead." He ran a hand through his sandy hair, leaving tufts of it standing upright, and said, "The Zimbourans—what did Ana and the others say about the Zimbourans? That they had tried to capture Ailia . . . Why? Is she important to them for some reason? Enough so that they took her prisoner twice, and are trying to find her once again? If so, we must hide her from the flying ships."

"Or perhaps Ailia is right, and the Zimbourans aren't the only ones that build such ships," said his sister.

"But who else could build them?" he argued. "They're not from this Continent, and all the other lands were conquered by Khalazar."

"I don't know, unless . . . Oh, Jaim, you don't suppose there are still Elei left in the world? So many other strange things have happened . . ."

"Elei!" he snorted. "Does she look like an Elei?"

"I don't know. What did the Elei look like?"

There was another long silence, which was broken presently by the sound of the front door and two voices, a man's and a child's. "Ah—there's Dannor back from the wharves," Nella said. "He will be so glad to hear that Ailia is recovered!"

The voices came closer, and Dannor Shipwright entered the room, along with a small blond boy who began to jump about in excitement when they told their news. "She woke up! She woke up again!" he cried, and before they could stop him he ran into the sickroom still shouting.

"Lem?" said Ailia, smiling and putting her feet on the floor.

"No, that's Dani," Jemma told her, stooping and putting her arms around the child.

Ailia blinked. "Baby Dani—but of course, it's been so long, I had forgotten Lem would be much bigger now."

"Lem is with his papa, down on the docks," Dannor said, sitting down on the bed beside her. "He wanted to stay and watch the ships. How is my girl?" he asked, laying a work-roughened hand on Ailia's shoulder. Dannor's demonstrations of affection were never effusive, yet Ailia could sense his love for her now—*As if I can feel his thoughts*, she realized.

"Much better, Father," she said, putting her hand on his.

He smiled. "Father? You always called me Papa before."

She looked confused. "So I did—I had forgotten."

"She can't recall anything of where she's been. So don't be bombarding her with questions, Dann, she's had quite enough of that for one day. And speaking of work, I should get our supper," Nella said. "What there is of it."

"We were paid today," Dannor told her. "Ned gave me his wages to pass on to Betta. We can go to the market later."

"If there is anything left to buy."

Nella's plea to Betta and her son and daughter had been accepted, by a wordless consensus: nothing was said of Ailia's origins and the wreck of the flying ship. They continued to speak of commonplace things. Then Dani ran to Ailia and looked up at her with bright brown eyes. "You talked when you were sleeping."

"Fever dreams," said Jaimon, meeting his aunt's eye.

"We listened to you talk," added Dani.

"What did I talk about?" she asked.

"Lots of things. Stories. You had a dragon who was your friend, and you lived in a castle. And the castle was in a star. The Morning Star. You told stories when you were sleeping. Will you tell some more now you're awake?"

Jaimon frowned. "Don't pester her, Dani! Run along now."

"Oh, let him be!" Jemma intervened. "Goodness knows we could all use a little fancy these days, life is that grim. Here, Ailia, I'll brush some of those snarls out of your hair. It got dreadfully matted when you were sick."

Ailia leaned back and tried to think of what she had said in her fever. The dreams were still there in her mind, vivid as any real memory, fantastical as any faerie tale. Some of the images disturbed her. But as Jemma combed out her tangled hair with firm capable hands, Ailia was composed once more. She began to talk slowly. Jemma listened along with her eager son, never interrupting, nor did her hands cease their soothing motions.

"The Morning Star . . . It's very beautiful there. It's always warm, because it is so near the sun. And the mountains there are taller than the ones here. And there are wonderful creatures—like the giant birds called rocs, that could carry off an ox cart if they chose. But all the beasts there are tame. And there is a great city, and a palace with glorious gardens." Her voice grew soft and dreamy, her eyes widened as though she looked at things none of the rest of them could see. Jaimon, who stood near her, found himself staring at those eyes with a kind of wonderment: he had always thought them beautiful, but now that beauty had an alien quality he had not noticed before. They were so very large in her delicate face, and the violet-gray coloring of the irises (who else had he ever seen with *purple* eyes?) and the faint pattern of pale rays within them, like starbursts—these things struck him as utterly foreign, even unearthly. Was it the years of separation that made him see Ailia as if for the first time, or was it Nella's unsettling revelation? *It's true—she's not one of us, and she never will be.* He continued to study her, fascinated and disturbed. Who and what was she, this beloved stranger in their midst?

Ailia went on: "And the sun rises in the west and sets in the east. And the moon is blue—"

She stopped short, startled, as her aunt gave a sudden cry. "Why, whatever's that?"

They all looked out the window. Above the roofs a fiery red glow flared briefly through the clouds—and then another appeared, away to the east. Betta exclaimed again: "It's not lightning. It's like fire in the sky—"

Ailia sprang up, and then reeled against Nella, who supported her. "An enemy is here," the girl gasped. "A terrible enemy. I—I *feel* it." She moved forward, swaying slightly, then stood very still in the center of the room, her fists clenched and eyes shut, as if she were praying.

They heard a rushing sound overhead, a flapping as of tremendous wings. Red light flared through the windows, and shadows leaped along on the walls. Jaimon ran to the nearest window. "There's a fire up the street—I can see the smoke and the flames—" He headed for the door.

"Don't!" cried Jemma. "Don't go out there, Jaimon!"

"They will need help putting out the fire—"

A great clamor erupted from the streets outside as they followed him to the door—all but Ailia, who remained where she was. Over the rooftops the shape of the domed High Temple appeared black against a red glow.

"Fires! There are fires everywhere!" shouted Jaimon.

Looking up, they saw something moving rapidly through the ascending smoke—a black, flapping shape. Then Jemma screamed. "All the ships in the harbor are on fire! I must go there. Lem is down on the wharves, and Arran—"

Jaimon pulled her back inside. "No—it's too dangerous! It's an attack of some sort. But how are the Zimbourans doing it?"

Ailia, still standing alone in the main room, flung her arms up toward the ceiling and gave a cry. Nella ran to her while Jaimon kept watch at the door. Suddenly he gave an exclamation.

"What is it now?" cried Nella.

"Rain! An absolute tempest, out of nowhere—it's sending up clouds of smoke and steam. I can't see a thing—"

"It will put the fires out," Ailia whispered. She was panting and haggard, as if wearied by some great effort of body or will.

"Let us hope so, but they are burning very fiercely," Dannor said. "What could have done this? Burning pitch perhaps, cast down from the air—"

"Firedrakes," Ailia said. Her eyes widened in horror, and she spoke in a low voice, as if to herself alone. "There are firedrakes in Mera!" She clutched at her head, swaying on her feet. "I remember now! It has all come back to me—the war, the enemy—"

"What?" said Betta, turning her distraught glance from the door to her niece and back again. "What's that you say?"

But Ailia said no more. Her face drained of color, and she fell sideways into Nella's arms.

5

The Monster in the Dark

JOMAR, LORELYN, AURON, AND TALEERA stood together on the shore of a lone island, more rock than earth, with a thin band of trees lying between the sea and a mountain with a bleak, bare summit. They had been journeying for days, always high up in the sky so that they would not be seen by the people below—for the Merans had not beheld a dragon in many centuries, and the sight of Auron would have terrified them. By day he wrapped himself in cloud-vapor, flying blind and relying on sorcery to find his way. By night he went uncloaked, and his passengers could see below them islands of the Archipelagoes, and the glitter of the moon upon the waves. Taleera went with them, alternately flying on her own and resting upon the dragon's broad back with Jomar and Lorelyn. On and on he had flown, swift and tireless as a footless alerion in the wind-world of Alfaran. When at long last he grew weary, he had descended to this small and sparsely inhabited islet and lain coiled atop the stony mount while Taleera roosted on one of his horns, and Jomar and Lorelyn slept propped up against his warm flank, sheltered from the wind. The climate had grown much colder as they passed northward. At daybreak they walked down the mountain, Auron and Taleera wearing human form, to speak with the Kaanish inhabitants on the shore.

There were perhaps fifty of them, and none had been born in this place. To its dreary shores they had come as fugitives after the fall of Kaan, and here they eked out a wretched existence, dwelling in caves at the mountain's foot and in lean-to shelters of cut boughs and driftwood, gathering shellfish and auks' eggs and anything else that they could find for food. Yet they would rather live and die in this desolate place than on the warmer isles of the south where the Zimbouran conquerors still reigned. Of what was now occurring on those islands they had no knowledge, but though years had passed they still feared to return.

"The Zimbouran lords killed and pillaged and burned," they told the visitors. They seemed more comfortable talking to Auron, who wore his usual Kaanish form. "Entire villages were destroyed, and the island governors and their families slain—those who did not flee. The Emperor of the Archipelagoes is dead, some say, and others tell that he lives on in hiding. We do not know which tale is true."

"Have you heard what happened on Jana?" asked Lorelyn in Kaanish, moving to stand beside Auron. "The island nearest the holy isle of Medosha?"

"I know of it," one elderly man said. "The governor there was spared, for he surrendered without a fight. But he was imprisoned, and many of his people were slaughtered. And Medosha has been desecrated. The Zimbourans have felled its sacred groves, and built themselves houses on the holy ground."

"But the monks of the One Faith?" Lorelyn pressed. "What about them? Have you heard anything?"

"Nothing particular concerning them," the man replied, "but I know that the Zimbouran governor's first act was to put all priests of faiths other than Valdur's to the sword. None escaped."

Lorelyn turned away. She could see Abbot Shan's face so clearly in her mind: bald, lined, kindly and patient. To her young eyes he had always seemed ancient and wise beyond imagining, but she realized now that he had likely not been so very old: no more than sixty years of age, perhaps. He *should* have lived to a venerable age; his wisdom and gentleness should not have been taken from the world. She had felt such certainty that she would see him again, that he was indestructible, permanent as the earth itself . . . The view of sea and shore before her faded in a mist of tears.

Jomar went and put his arm around her. "I'm sorry," he said, his voice gruff. He needed no translation to know the cause of her grief.

"I knew," she said in a voice drained of all expression. "I always suspected what their fate was, I just didn't want to admit it to myself. I let myself hope while . . . deep down, I knew." And then suddenly she sagged against him and began to weep. He could find no words of comfort. Instead he tightened his hold on her, so that her whole weight might rest against him, and he ran a hand over her bright hair. Auron and Taleera did not go to her too, but discreetly walked away and let them be. In that moment Jomar realized that words were not, and never had been, needed after all. As Lorelyn's stormy sobs turned to sharp tremors, then eased into silence, his hands caressed her shoulders and head, conveying his love to her through his touch.

A long time later they both sat and gazed out at the waves beating on the stony shore. They did not have to say what was in both their minds. It was not the wordless mind-language of the Nemerei that moved between them, but an older communing that predated both it and any form of language: the understanding that expresses itself through tenderness of look and gesture. Whatever happened from that moment forth, in life or in death upon the field of battle, they knew that they would never again be apart.

THE SKIES WERE CLEAR AS Auron and his companions flew on across the ocean: but as night fell again and they neared the coast of the Continent, a mass of clouds appeared ahead of them. It was strangely concentrated over one small region of the coastline, rising before them in an abrupt barrier, and making a thick gray roof to cover the land immediately below.

"This isn't just weather," Jomar shouted as they flew above its buffeting winds. "It's magic, isn't it? But what's causing it?"

He is right. There is some sorcery at work here, Auron said to Lorelyn and Taleera. *But whether it is a device of our enemies or not, I cannot say.* He dived down through the cloud layer, and they saw the ocean below them again gleaming dully like dinted pewter, and a dark coastline ahead with the shadowy peaks of mountains, and lower down a faint scattering of light where Raimar lay. But as they drew nearer they saw large patches of glowing red, like beds of coals—and were those columns of black smoke rising above the city?

At this point Taleera, who had been flying above them, came flapping down over their heads. *'Ware firedrake, Auron!*

A gout of fire flared out through the sky ahead of them. The firedrake itself was invisible in the blackness.

"Look! More!" Lorelyn pointed as other red flares appeared. "They're attacking the city!" Another parabola of flame burst from a firedrake's jaws, this one lower down, just above the roofs of

Raimar. Auron flew faster, and presently they could see fires breaking out on the ground, looking tiny and unreal as they thrust eager
tongues upward. The gold leaf on the high temple's dome reflected
the ruddy glare.

"Can't we help them?" Lorelyn stared down in horror at the
spreading conflagration as they flew over the city. Part of the royal
palace's roof was burning, and one wing was already a black shell
with flames streaming from its windows. But steam was also rising
in white plumes, for a heavy rain was falling: it gusted into their
faces and soaked their clothes. Auron's wet scales gleamed like a
fish's in the light of the fires.

Someone summoned rain clouds to put the fires out, Lorelyn thought as she
clung to Jomar's waist. *Not enemy sorcery, then . . . Could it be Ailia? Is she
really here?*

At the sight of the huge Imperial dragon, one firedrake pulled out
of its deadly stoop, fleeing toward the mountains. Auron did not
pursue it, but turned on another that had flown right down to street
level and begun to harry the people there to and fro. It could not
be helped: Auron would have to be seen now, or else leave these innocents to their fate. Lorelyn and Jomar clung tighter as Auron
dropped toward the street, flying between the buildings as if
through a natural canyon. So wide were his wings that their tips
nearly brushed the walls of brick and stone to either side. He
skimmed low over the panicked crowd, raising another terrified
clamor. The black shape of the firedrake wheeled around at the end
of the street, an immense shadow against the burning buildings, and
came hurtling back at the crowd. In the same instant its red eyes
saw the approaching dragon, and a spurt of flame burst from its
jaws. The two riders crouched low on Auron's neck as the huge
creature swept toward them. Finding that its flames could not
pierce the Loänan's quintessential shield, the firedrake roared in
frustration and swerved away. Auron flew after it and pounced on
its back, biting and clawing, and Lorelyn and Jomar recoiled as
much from the brimstone stench of the monster as from its wildly
beating wings and sprays of poisonous blood. The barbed tail
lashed through the air, and Lorelyn ducked and shoved Jomar in the
back, forcing him down, as it went sweeping over both their heads
like a boom.

One of Auron's claws tore the right wing of the firedrake. It shrieked and flapped awkwardly away, its rent wing trailing loose shreds of webbing. It strove to climb skyward, but the wing folded and the beast plummeted toward the harbor, where its fires were quickly quenched. Steam and foam rose up in a towering column where it went down, and it did not rise again.

Auron, his fighting blood now thoroughly roused, made as if to return to the main battle. And Lorelyn had drawn her sword. Her grief for her beloved monks had strengthened her: had given her a desire not so much for vengeance, as to make certain no other should die or suffer loss at the enemy's hands. She rejoiced at the chance to thwart her foes of their prey. But Taleera flew down and lit on the dragon's head, her feathers flattened in the wind of his great speed, and screeched in his ear. "No, Old Worm! You must go to ground—set the humans down safely, before you return to the fight. We will search for Ailia in the meantime, and help her if we can. Since the enemy is attacking the city, they must also suspect that she is here."

The dragon heard and assented. Soaring high over Raimar, he headed for the dark and empty fields beyond its outskirts.

AILIA STOOD IN THE STREET looking on the charred shells of houses. Even now, hours after the fiery assault, the stench of smoke was heavy on the air. Fringes of icicles hung from exposed and blackened roof beams, and the burnt rubble of the collapsed stories beneath them had yet to be cleared away. When at last dawn had showed gray at the windows, Ailia and her family had gone out to survey the latest damage: the buildings that still burned, the golden dome of the temple wreathed in the gray smoke and steam rising from the ruins. They knew they had much to be thankful for. Uncle Nedman and Jemma's husband and eldest son had turned up after the first night attack, covered in soot and bruises, but alive: they had fled the wharves as soon as the enemy appeared. But most of the Royal Navy ships had been burned beyond repair. The Valei's flying vessels had done their work—and the firedrakes also.

Many people by now had seen the latter quite clearly, and though the ones who had not (Ailia's foster family included) were inclined to think the witnesses had mistaken winged ships for flying monsters in their confusion and terror, Ailia knew better. Once again she was burdened with knowledge. When she had first arrived in Arainia, Mandrake had sought to deceive her with a carefully crafted illusion, making it seem that she had never left Mera and that the events in the Isle of Trynisia had merely been a dream. This time she had been the author of her own deception, albeit unconsciously: her fever-stricken mind had banished the more painful scenes of her immediate past to some dark concealed chamber, from which they had broken forth only with the threat of danger. With full memory all the fears and sorrows that had racked her mind came back to her. The bliss of forgetfulness had passed. Once more she was conscious of her sorcerous powers, and her dread of them. Once more she looked back on the bleak, black days in Zimboura, the grief of Damion's loss still fresh and searing; the turmoil of hate and fury and desire for revenge that had filled her nights and days with misery. And all the time people speaking of her as if she were a goddess! Had they only known what sort of a goddess she might have become! She shuddered now to recall the things she had been capable of in that dark period. Mandrake had called her a monster, and he had not been far off the mark. With the powers at her disposal she could have wreaked such havoc on the rebels of northern Zimboura that future generations would look back on it and tremble. She could have used her weather-magic, withholding rain and then sending down lightning bolts to consume the parched land with fire. Or she could have sent rain—weeks of it, swelling rivers from their beds to turn plains into lakes. Or created cyclones that would strike at her command, tearing towns to matchwood. She could have taken draconic form, striking her foes with claws and jaws. She herself trembled at the thought of it. Had that in fact been Valdur's intent? To take Damion from her in order to drive her to such savage acts of vengeance?

She gazed at the ruins now in silence. The air-ships had begun to appear months ago, according to her family: the first were sighted on the eve of Trynalia, the winter solstice festival. Her enemies must have chosen that date on purpose, as a provocation. For Trynalia was also the high festival of the Elei's prophesied ruler. Dark curtains hung at every window until midnight, and then the door of each house was flung open wide to welcome the Tryna Lia, while the light shone out to be an aid to the Princess and her forces of Light as they fought the Darkness. In the villages a young girl dressed up as the Princess, with crown and scepter, and went from house to house expelling the demons of darkness. Thinking of these old rituals reminded her once more of what she was, and this was unwelcome; but it also gave her an idea. Slowly and thoughtfully she walked back to the house. There she found her family talking in hushed tones, so as not to be overheard by the two boys who were playing upstairs. Their worn, frightened faces filled her with pity and tenderness. Though she was grateful that her family had been spared, she wondered what dangers still faced them—dangers from which she might not be able to protect them. Mandrake and his fellow rebels had no doubt learned of her flight from Zimboura, and were attempting to find her before her own allies did. They knew there were but two places where she was likely to go in this world: the island where she had been raised, and the coast of Maurainia where Ana and her Nemerei dwelled.

"It's a great blow to us," Jaimon said to Uncle Nedman. "There's no doubt about it. So many of our naval vessels were in the harbor when the attack came. There's no point in my signing up now."

His father replied, "Those ships were useless anyway. To fight these devils we would need ships that fly, like theirs. It's almost as if they did it from spite."

"Everything's wrong," said Jemma. "This is more than a war. It's something bigger and stranger, and even more dreadful. Do you think those comets are a coincidence? They were a warning!"

She began to sob quietly, and her husband put his arm around her. "Steady on, lass," Arran urged. But his face was as pale as hers.

Ailia could bear it no longer. "Don't be afraid," she said, stepping forward. "It's true we have enemies, but we also have friends and allies."

They all stared at her. "Who?" said Jaimon. "The Continent stands alone now. We've no allies left in the world."

"Unless you mean some sort of divine intervention? Are cherubim and seraphim coming to our rescue?" her uncle asked, raising his grizzled brows.

"Cherubim, anyway," said Ailia, and the merest trace of a smile flitted across her lips. Then she turned serious again. "The comets aren't omens. They were disturbed from their normal orbits long ago, by Azar and Azarah, and are just reaching us now—"

"Azar and what?" Nella asked, bewildered.

Oh, I forgot—the Maurainian astronomers haven't discovered the seventh planet and its sun yet. "Never mind. It's just as Jaim said: they are a natural phenomenon. I'm sure of it."

They continued to gaze at her in puzzlement, and she said no more. *I am a danger to them, and to everyone here,* she realized. *The enemy might have attacked anyway—they may not know I am in hiding here—but it doesn't matter. I am the cause of the whole business—simply by being what I am. In any case, I must go—I have wasted enough time here. I must find Ana and the other Nemerei.* Perhaps, she thought, the Valei had attacked in order to force her out in the open, rather than remain in hiding and see innocent people harmed. However that might be, her days of concealment and her brief respite of ordinary life were over. The thought tore at her heart. More than ever she hungered to return to that old life with her foster family, and not only for the illusion of safety it would bring. She felt a great love for them, and a fear of what might yet befall them. "Listen to me, all of you! I have had an idea. You must put out all the lights in the house tonight, or else hang thick cloths over the windows, just as though it were the Dark Days festival. And tell all the neighbors to do the same, and spread the word throughout the city."

"But why?" asked Jemma, surprised.

"That way our enemies won't see the houses so clearly, when they come again tonight. There will be no lights to guide them. But I must leave," added Ailia. "It's the enemies of my people that are waging this war."

"Your people." Nella gasped.

"I remember it all," she replied. "Everything. Where I came from, who I really am. It has come back to me."

Nella shot an agonized look at Dannor before turning back to Ailia. "Ailia. I'm so sorry, so very sorry not to have told you before—"

"That I am not your child? Don't trouble yourself about it. You saved me from a very great danger." She laid a hand on Nella's shoulder and added, "Mamma."

Nella looked relieved, then remorseful again. "You can't go calling me that now. I've no right to it. We never did see your real mother, nor any of your folks. They must have drowned when the flying ship went down in the storm. Nothing could live long in such a sea."

"I lived," she replied. "And my mother did escape the wreck. I—know it."

"But how do you know?" Jaimon asked, stepping forward. "Have you seen your other family? Is that where you went when you disappeared? Where is this land of yours?"

"Farther away than you can imagine, Jaim. My people have kept its location a secret for centuries." She took a deep breath, and then continued. "They will be looking for me—but so will my enemies."

"The Zimbourans?"

"The Valei, the Darklings. Not only Zimbourans worship Valdur. There are other races more powerful still, that have allied themselves with the last rebellious Zimbourans. It is they who attack the city. They may know, or suspect, that I am here, and that is why I cannot stay any longer. I must go back to my own folk. I can't go home immediately though, since I have no way of getting there. I must find a place to hide until my friends find me. But not here." Leaving them all gaping at her, she went to the front door and took her travel-grimed cloak from its peg on the wall.

Jemma, Nella, and Jaimon rose and followed her. "Ailia, you can't leave us already, now that we've found you again!" said Jemma. "Where would you go, anyway?"

Ailia stood with cloak in hand, considering. There were the tunnels underneath the Academy that had given shelter to the Nemerei. But these were no longer secret or safe. If she went to Mount Selenna she might take refuge in Ana's cave, and could search for the old woman as well. "I think I will go into the mountains. I can't tell you exactly where, but I believe I can find those people who came to you—Ana and the others. They are friends, and can help me in ways you can't. I'm so grateful to you for all that you have done for me—in these past few days, and before, when I was a child. You—you'll always be family to me." She slung the cloak about her shoulders. "But I can't stay with you any longer, and there are things I must do, things that are terribly important."

Nella said, "We can't let you do this. If any harm came to you we'd never forgive ourselves!"

"And I would never forgive myself either, if harm came to you because of me," Ailia replied.

"Then we will come with you into the countryside, to keep you safe," offered Jemma.

"But you won't, Jemma dear: you will only endanger yourselves. Think of Dani and Lem. It's no use going on about it: so long as you are with me you will never be safe."

"But you can't just disappear again, and leave us all wondering what's become of you!" Jemma wailed. There was a sound of running feet, and the two boys darted into the hall.

"Mum, what is it?" Lem cried. Then Dani noticed Ailia standing at the door, and gave a wail just like his mother's.

"She's going away again!"

Ailia looked at them all, her heart torn asunder. How could she explain the whole truth of the matter to them? Celestial dragons and gryphons, and sorcerers, and other worlds . . . They would think that she had gone mad. "I promise I will come back to you, or send word, as soon as ever I can," she vowed, feeling wretched, knowing that the promise might never be kept. But their safety must be her first concern.

Jaimon sighed in resignation and joined her at the doorway, pulling on his boots. "All right, then. I can see there's no point in arguing with you. You know more than you're telling: I could always read your feelings in your face. But you'll at least let me come part of the way. Come along—I'll give you a lift to the Range in our cart."

She wavered a moment, reluctant either to accept or to refuse. Without another word he pushed past his family and strode out the back door, heading for the stable.

Nella followed her nephew into the yard, watching as he led out the thin, tired-looking horse from its stall. "Jaimon," she said. "You don't hide things well either. I can see how it is with you and Ailia. You love her: you always did."

"As my cousin, yes." He began to put on the horse's harness.

"But now that you know she's not your own kin, your love for her has changed. Hasn't it? Your mother has noticed too." Nella took a step closer. "But Ailia's not for you, lad. Wherever she may be from, she's quality. That *was* real thread-of-gold on her little dress—and look at that white cloak she's got, and the gown she had on when we found her in the hostel. They're both of a finer weave than anything you'll see in the city. And notice too how she carries herself, and how she talks: her speech is more refined now. She's a lady, Jaimon, and not one of us anymore. You must accept that."

He made no reply, though his hand paused in the act of tightening a strap. Backing the horse up, he made fast its harness to their small two-seated cart and then led it by the reins into the street. Ailia came out of the front door. She now carried a rolled-up blanket, and was followed by Jemma with a basket. The rest of the family came behind. Jaimon helped Ailia into the cart, then Jemma handed the basket up to her. There was a loaf of bread in it, and some dried meat and fruit, and a couple of eggs—for the hens had begun to lay regularly, granting them a stay of execution.

Jemma and Nella lingered by the side of the cart. "You'll be careful to keep warm?" the latter urged. "Remember you've been ill."

"Yes: I am used to warmer climates, so I expect I catch chills and fevers more easily. I will take care."

Nella withdrew, and Jemma stepped forward. "I shall miss you, Ailia. Finding you again is the only good thing that has happened this past year. It has all been so dark, and so frightening; but I felt when you came back that things had begun to turn around, somehow. I do wish you'd stay!" she said, tears starting in her eyes.

"I wish I could." Ailia leaned down to kiss her. "Goodbye, Jemma dear. I hope we may meet again."

Jaimon shook the reins, and they drove away.

In the streets people still clambered through the ruins of burned-out buildings, like wasps swarming around a damaged hive. Ailia averted her eyes from the sight. Then her cousin drove into the back roads, and on through the muddy and rutted paths of the countryside.

"Where to?" he asked presently.

"To Mount Selenna, please."

"And you'll find old Ana and her friends there?"

"I—don't know. I hope so."

Snow still covered the mountain's higher slopes, so that the season seemed to reverse as they ascended. Presently the lightly winding track became too slippery for hooves and wheels. Jaimon stopped the cart and Ailia dismounted, clutching the basket and blanket. She turned and looked back up at him. "Thank you."

"Are you sure you're all right?" he asked.

"I'm not *sure*," said Ailia, "but at least it will be safer here. There is a cave in the mountainside where I can stay. And you will be safer too. Just remember to tell everyone to put their black curtains up tonight."

He hesitated, and it seemed to her that he was about to say something more. For a long moment they contemplated each other's face. Jaimon saw a woman at once familiar and mysterious, for whom he felt both the affection of their early youth and now something new and deeper. He yearned to protect her, to cling to her and prevent her from ever again disappearing out of his life. Ailia saw a man who had once been as close to her as a brother: but their long separation and the knowledge that he was no longer her true kin made her see him anew. Though he said nothing, she knew what he offered her: not only love but peace and security, the opportunity to vanish once and for all into the ordinary life she had once resisted, and now craved as a starving person craves food. But it could not be, even if circumstances allowed it. She did not truly love him, not in that sense; and to cleave to him merely for what he represented to her would be a betrayal of them both.

"No," she said softly, when he made as if to speak. "No, Jaim, please."

He closed his mouth again, and looked long into her eyes. After a moment he gave a smile, and a slight nod of his head. Then he withdrew his gaze, and drove the cart away, and Ailia was alone.

She trudged the rest of the way up the slope—she was still weary from the effort of conjuring the nightly rainstorms, and the steep climb seemed to take forever. Every turn of the path was poignant to her, for this was the way Damion had come when he met Ana for the first time. She walked, perhaps, in his very footsteps. If she remembered correctly what he had told her, the cave entrance was up near the summit.

She saw it at last, a black gap in the mountainside, icicles fringing its entrance. Stooping, she went in, her breath steaming in the chill air. All that was left of Ana's domicile was some smashed bits of wood and broken crockery. She did find a few things the vandals had not seen fit to take away: an iron cauldron, and a brazier, and an old moth-eaten brown cloak of Ana's. There was also a soiled little sketchbook with exquisite studies of animals, birds, and plants. She pored over it as she huddled by the brazier. The birds and butterflies looked ready to fly off the page, the rabbits and mice soft and furry, the berries and nuts good enough to eat.

"Oh, Ana!" she whispered longingly. "Where are you? You can't be dead too—you *can't* be."

At a soft sound she looked up from the book, and gave a start. A gray animal had slipped inside the cave mouth: for an instant she thought it was a wildcat, and then she saw that it was too small. It was not wild at all, but domestic. It made a beeline for the brazier, and curled up with the air of one who owns the place, and began to groom its bedraggled gray fur.

"Greymalkin!" she cried. The cat mewed in reply.

It was Ana's beloved pet, her "familiar" as she had called it. The old woman had taken the cat with her when she left Arainia, passing through the ethereal portal. Ailia felt as though she had been reunited with a long-lost friend. "Greymalkin," she said again, holding out her hand. The cat turned to her and sniffed at her fingers, then returned to licking the damp out of its coat. Ailia went to the supplies she had been given and found some dried haddock, which she offered to the cat. Greymalkin accepted it graciously, but not ravenously, as a starving stray would. She looked well fed. Did that mean Ana was still caring for her, and was perhaps not far away? She reached out again to stroke the cat, and Greymalkin began to purr, a low contented rumble. But even her comforting presence could not drive all the pain and worry from the girl's mind. Ailia felt Ana's absence as an aching hollowness within her, and Damion's too. It was here in this cave that he had been born, to the mountain woman Elthina and her lover, a man of the city who desired to reestablish the old order of the Paladin knights. When he had died young with his dream unfulfilled, Elthina had been inconsolable. She had vanished forever from Selenna, the place of their first trysts, leaving her son in Ana's care. The wise old Nemerei woman had placed him in the monks' orphanage at the Royal Academy. Was he truly an orphan, as he had believed himself to be, or did his mother yet live? Why had she never come back to seek her son?

She must be dead, Ailia thought. *And my mother also. They would not abandon their children so long. It was a dream I had that night in Halmirion, no more. I did not truly see my mother.*

But what, then, of the ring that had so mysteriously appeared on her finger—the royal star sapphire ring that should still have been in Mandrake's palace in Nemorah, where she had cast it off?

She could make no sense of these mysteries, and her thoughts turned to other and more troubling things. Mandrake and the threat he presented loomed large in her mind, like a mountain that dominates a landscape. The mere thought of fighting him still filled her with dread. If only she could remain here, take up the works of Ana in her stead, learn to make plasters, balms, and potions to assuage the hurts and ailments of people and animals. To use her life and powers to heal, and not to harm.

She loosened her hair from the tidy knot in which it had been confined, and removed her outer clothing. Then she rolled herself up in her blanket and lay down, closing her eyes. The darkness seethed before her eyelids, birthing images. She seemed to see the passage of many eons in her mind's vision—barren landscapes, boiling magma, turbulent seas. Mountains reared up and crumbled again like sand dunes; forests sprang like green mold from a mire, flourished briefly, and sank back again. Stars flickered into being, dimmed, and died like candles. In all this cosmic tumult living creatures were not even visible: they teemed and bred and perished like the smallest of unseen germs. She felt herself as one of these: a tiny mote of matter, her existence confined to a time that was less than the blinking of an immortal's eye.

Then the scene changed. She saw now as mortals see, from a point of vantage closer to the earth. She beheld ferny jungles like those of Nemorah, and scaled creatures crawling through the murk of an unimaginable antiquity. There were beasts that resembled the Tanathon, long-necked and large-bodied eaters of plants, and other, more fearsome creatures that went on strong, clawed hind legs and fed on flesh. And then, without knowing how she knew it—the intelligence was passed straight to her mind from some unknown Other—she understood that this was not Nemorah but the Original World, from whence the ancestors of the Tanathon came. This meant that among these cold-eyed monstrosities were humanity's own distant ancestors. As soon as she thought this, a new image came into her mind of a creature with a long low body that crawled through the mire on four legs, like an immense lizard: dun-colored and leathery-skinned, armed with teeth like curved daggers. The blood of this creeping thing was in her. She had seen it: the reptile, the monster that laired in the deepest regions of the self, and she recognized its vestigial presence within her mind. The primal source of anger, aggression, greed, desire—all of it sprang from this: this beast of a bygone age, that fought and killed and devoured its way through its brief and brutal life. Though its kind was long lost, still its pattern was imprinted deep within the living bodies of her race—a heritage from the most ancient of days, and an atavistic influence that warred continually with all higher impulses.

There was no denying it. No human being was free from this original taint: but in sorcerers such as she and Mandrake, its influence was vastly increased by the temptations of an unnatural power. *Mandrake was right. We are both of us monsters.*

Ailia opened her eyes, and sat up with a sigh. She could not hope to sleep now. For the rest of the night she huddled in her blanket, holding Ana's purring cat in her arms, and staring out into the darkness beyond the cave's entrance.

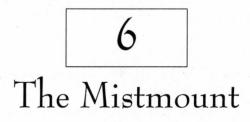

The Mistmount

"Do you suppose Ailia was never here at all?" Lorelyn asked.

She and Jomar sat at a table in the corner of an inn's dark and smoky common room. On their tin plates sat heels of bread and some pickled herring, while Jomar drank watery ale out of a dented tankard. In the present situation the inn's owner could provide no better fare. They had combed the city looking for news until their feet ached, and their spirits were lower than ever before. The common room too had a dismal air, with so few people there: those who had not fled the city feared to leave their homes. A few young and middle-aged men, their hands and faces smudged with ash and their eyes red-rimmed with fatigue, sat nursing tankards at a table by the fireplace. They spoke together in low voices of the damage from the burning. Last night's attack had not been anything like so deadly as those before it. The people themselves were apparently responsible for this: somehow, the word had spread that everyone should drape their windows, or avoid using any lamps or candles at all, to prevent any light showing after nightfall. Some said that it was the king who had given the command, others that it was the Supreme Patriarch, while still others credited some mysterious un-named source. At any rate, the tactic had apparently confused the airborne enemy, who on returning to wreak more havoc had dis-covered only darkness where the betraying lights of the city should have shone.

The two visitors discussed the matter among themselves, keep-ing their voices low. "Could it have been Ana? She would have known what to do. The king certainly wouldn't know how to pre-vent an aerial attack by night," said Jomar.

"Perhaps. Or it might have been Ailia," suggested Lorelyn. "The rain might have been her doing as well. I hope so, because that would prove she really is here." She glanced up from her meager meal as Auron and Taleera entered the inn's doorway in their human guises.

"No luck?" asked Jomar. The dragon-man shook his bald head as he and Taleera sat down on the bench opposite their human com-panions.

"It's worse than the needle in the haystack," said Lorelyn. "Ailia might be in disguise—a glaumerie, perhaps, or even a shape-shift. There are spies of Mandrake's here who might recognize her, after all. If she didn't happen to notice us, we would pass each other in the street and never know. At least I wouldn't, nor Jomar. I suppose you two would see through her illusion."

"We might," agreed Auron. "But Taleera and I have not felt any sorcery in this area for more than a day now."

"We must find her, and soon!" Taleera said. "Our spies say that Mandrake is coming to Mera—may even have arrived. Ailia must leave this sphere, and go to Arainia where she is stronger!"

They all fell silent as the true difficulty of their errand came home to them. Into their silence intruded the voices of the inn's other patrons, discussing the events of the past few days: the houses and other buildings destroyed or damaged, the people killed or missing, and beneath these things the growing sense that some still worse calamity lay in wait. The comets were discussed, and their possible role as portents; holy scriptures were cited, in particular the prophetic Book of Doom, together with old bits of folklore handed down by the speakers' rustic ancestors. The fear in the room was as heavy and penetrating as the smoke from the fireplace.

"Can't you use those magic powers of yours to find her?" Jomar asked Auron presently, in an undertone.

Auron shook his head. "Again, there are too many of the enemy about. Otherwise we might try contacting the Nemerei conspiracy here, and ask if they had seen her."

"If the conspiracy still exists," said Taleera. "Without being able to speak through the Ether, we can't even know if there is anyone here anymore."

"There were the tunnels where they gathered," said Lorelyn. "I know where they are: I've been down there."

"But those tunnels are no longer secret, you say. The Nemerei would not meet in them now," said Auron.

"I know! What about Mount Selenna?" asked Lorelyn. "That's where Ana used to live."

She had forgotten to lower her voice, and one of the men by the fireplace overheard. "Selenna? The Mistmount? You're not thinking of going out there, are you?"

"Why not?" said Jomar.

"Not everyone who goes up there comes down again, the country folk say. It's an unlucky place. They tell stories of faeries and black witches. Not that I'd have believed such tales once, but nowadays—who can say? Witches and flying ships—the world's gone mad. They say it's the end days, and I begin to think they're right."

"And there's a new witch up there on the Mistmount too, I hear," said another man, looking up from his tankard. "Someone saw her only yesterday. Reckon she's taken the place of old Ana, since she died."

"Died?" said Lorelyn in dismay.

"Well, they don't rightly know what became of her. Ana's not been seen in ages. She was old as the hills, any road. Were you looking for a healing potion or some such?"

"Well, not exactly, but—this new person, she's not one of the black witches?" asked Lorelyn.

"Don't know. She lives all by herself, they say, not in a coven. But I still wouldn't go near her, not for no potion nor anything else.

You'd best stay away from these conjuror types." He went back to his drinking, while the four companions looked long at one another.

"Could it be Ailia?" Lorelyn whispered, giving voice to their thoughts.

"It might be—but what on earth would she be doing on a mountain all by herself?" Taleera said.

Jomar drained his tankard and stood up. "Well, there's only one way to find out. Let's go and see."

THE MORNING AFTER HER ARRIVAL, Ailia had her second visitor.

As she was boiling the water for her morning tea in Ana's cauldron, there came a sound of shuffling footsteps outside the cave entrance, and she looked up quickly to see a figure standing there: hunched and misshapen in its ragged clothing, with head lolling to one side and restlessly moving arms. The man moaned as he looked in at her, and she thought for a moment that he had come to her for some healing potion. Then as the moaning continued and rose in volume she found she could understand him, as if the sound were a form of speech. His thoughts came through, like rays of sunlight shining through a fog.

How do you do? she heard. *My friends and I heard about you from the village folk. You've been spotted, did you know that? The new witch of Selenna! You're being talked about, here and in the city.* He took a staggering step closer to her. *You're one of us, aren't you—a Nemerei?*

"Yes," admitted Ailia after a moment's hesitation. "You're—Ralf, aren't you? Ana told me about you. You're a Nemerei too."

He moaned again. *That's right. It was she brought me into the Conspiracy.*

"Won't you come and sit down?" She indicated a chair, her hopes rising. "I have been trying to find Ana, and the rest of you. Tell me, have you seen her lately?"

He did not move, but stood returning her gaze. Then he began to make mournful, braying sounds. *You didn't hear then? Old Ana died five months ago. Since her return she had grown weaker and weaker. She spoke a few last words to us at the end. She was taking her leave of us, she said, because we could now manage on our own—at least until the Tryna Lia came. She said she would go into the Ether so that her essence would become a part of it. That is how the old archmages chose to die, you know: so their mortal bodies would be one with the Ether rather than the earth. And she went to the old Standing Stones out in the countryside, the two great tall ones that form a gate—to the faerie world, as the local folk say. She stepped between them, and she vanished, and she has never been heard from since.*

The daylight seemed to dim. Ailia sat down abruptly in one of the battered chairs and put her face in her hands. "I—didn't know. I suspected she had died, but I hoped it wasn't so." Despair filled her, and sorrow too. She had so wanted Ana's comfort and advice, the benefit of her ages of wisdom—but now she realized she had also wanted simply to see the old woman again, to hear her gentle voice. "I—loved her very much."

He came and sat down by her feet, looking up at her. *There, now. She was very old, you know, far beyond most mortals' span of years, and she was really very calm and peaceful at the end. She did not die ill or in pain. She simply felt she had done all she could for the world, and she was ready to go and leave the rest of the task to us. We're all still here. The Patriarch talked the king into banning followers of the Nemerei ways, and offering rewards to anyone who turned us in, but they never could catch any of us and now that there's a war on they've lost interest. So you see, you're not alone. And there is still hope. Ana may be gone, but she told us we would have help. The Tryna Lia will come, she said. In fact, she may already be in our midst. She is human, the child of Earth and Heaven, but she has great powers and will protect us all, and lead us to victory.*

His facial expression was contorted and unreadable, with eyes rolling in different directions. But she felt the joy in his words, and the mix of awe and wonder. His simple belief filled her with anguish. What to tell him? He was a Nemerei, but like all the village folk he no doubt believed the Tryna Lia was an incarnate goddess, a being whose victory against the present darkness was a certainty. How to tell him that her victory was not assured, her mind filled with doubts? Perhaps she should say nothing at all. But no: Ana had prepared the way for her, had promised these people she would come. She could not betray the old woman and all the work she had done here.

"Yes, I know. She spoke the truth." She stood up again and walked out into the sunlight, feeling its warmth on her face, breathing the fresh air. Then she turned to look back at him. "I am the Tryna Lia, Ralf. I have come to help you." *If I can,* she wanted to add, but refrained from doing so. Let him and the others have the hope they desired.

He lurched to his feet, crowing and flailing his arms about. *Your*

Highness! This is wonderful! Ana said you would come to Maurania. And when I heard of you—a mysterious woman, come to live on the mountain in Ana's old abode—I did wonder if it might be the Tryna Lia, and so did many of the others. That is why I came—why I said these things, hoping that you would confirm them and declare yourself. I must bring these tidings to the Nemerei—they will be overjoyed—

Yes—her admission would at least give them courage and strength to carry on. But was their trust justified? "You may tell them I have come, so long as the enemy doesn't get to hear of it. Are you all safe, Ralf? Where have you been hiding?"

Many places. We give shelter to one another, and warn our fellow conspirators when danger approaches. We used to use the mind-speech to do this, but now it seems the enemy has Nemerei too. I have been spying about the city, trying to learn what our Zimbouran friends are up to.

"Oh, Ralf, do be careful. They've hurt you before, haven't they?"

Don't you worry about me. No one wastes time on an idiot like me these days. They've got bigger fish to fry. There was no bitterness in his statement, only amusement. *And I daresay it's of no concern to you, great as your powers must be, but you might like to know that some people were asking after you at an inn down in the city—the new witch of the mountains! I don't know who these people were, but you might want to leave Selenna for a while, just to be safe. The other Nemerei sent me here to find you—it's taken us a while to hear of you, now that we daren't talk mind to mind all the time. If you like, we can take you into hiding with us.*

"Thank you," said Ailia. "But—" She hesitated. "I really should be going back to my own place. To Eldimia—Ana told you of Eldimia, didn't she?"

She told us it was a real place. To some of us she revealed where it lies, but not to all—knowing that some even of the Nemerei could not accept such a thing. But she told me. His arms whirled like a windmill's vanes. *The Morning Star! It is incredible, but I couldn't help but believe. A person would have to be mad to tell such a lie as that, I think, and even someone who was not a Nemerei could see that old Ana was perfectly sane.*

"Then you know I must go back there, and muster my forces, if I am to be of any help to you. Because, you see, it's not I who will save you, but the army of the prophecy—the brave fighting men of Eldimia. Will you tell the Nemerei that, Ralf, and say I'm sorry I can't join them here?"

The man dropped his arms and made a lowing sound, rolling his eyes. It translated into Ailia's mind as: *Oh—that's a pity. We would be glad of your presence in our midst, Tryna Lia. Particularly now that Ana has gone.*

Ailia looked at him sadly. "Yes, I miss her terribly. And I will miss her even more in the coming days."

As will I, he said. *She was always good to me.* He turned and shambled off with his awkward, lurching gait. *I must go now, and inform the others. I am so glad you have come at last, lady! Now I know that all will be well.*

She watched as he headed down the hillside, then looked at her feet as she felt a furry flank rub against her ankle. Her first visitor was with her still, and she was glad of the company: Greymalkin had an uncanny way of sensing when Ailia was unhappy or ill at ease, and would nuzzle her face and purr. However, Ailia's spirits were slowly recovering. The dark vision of the night before had filled her with despair, but its power had now begun to fade, like a nightmare that loses its terror in the light of morning. She closed her eyes, recalling the troubling images. She had seen the ancient reptile and, in it, her own tremendous capacity for evil. But that, she now realized, had been Mandrake's undoing. The fact of his own darkness had driven him to believe he had no hope, that the beast within was too strong.

The Vor was the darker side of existence: the chaotic nature of the universe, the brutality of wild creatures, the destruction wreaked by whirlwinds and earth tremors and volcanoes. But it was not evil. It merely was. It was in her because she was a part of the material plane, because her body was akin to the bodies of beasts and in its every cell and fiber it remembered its ancient ancestry. But the Vor was also a source of strength at need, and it could safely be called upon once it was tamed, contained, and known for what it was. She might yet subdue it, and not be consumed by it as Mandrake had been. She must accept with humility this essential stain upon her being, where his pride had been wounded and his mind turned to bitterness and despair. The dragon could be tamed. She could win the victory that had eluded Mandrake, who had feared and loathed the innermost self, and so succumbed to it in the end and become what he sought to reject.

Ailia opened her eyes and looked around her. The night's steady rains had washed away most of the snow, and as the earth beneath was uncovered she saw that spring's banner was already well advanced. Snowdrops and crocuses grew in clumps like nosegays among the fallen leaves, still redolent with autumn's fragrant decay, and in sheltered places at the roots of the trees and under the overhanging crags, the first daffodils raised their white and yellow trumpets. Farther in, on the forest floor, the scilla made blue spreading drifts. She called the flowers by their old Island names: maiden's-tears and meadowstar, faerie-horns, morningjoy. The tree branches too were budding. Nothing could resist the summons of the sun. Even where its light did not reach, its warmth did, and in the deep secret places of the earth seeds changed to seedlings, and animals stirred and woke from hibernation, seemingly none the worse for their winter's interment. The dead silence of winter still reigned over the night, but in the dawn bird calls had begun to chip at that silence, and as the sun mounted the sky their twitterings turned to full-throated song.

During her sojourn in Arainia's hotter climes Ailia had forgotten how very beautiful the early spring was, and how miraculous it seemed after the long winter. She breathed in the moist air, and began to feel the stirrings of a corresponding change within herself, a waking to new life. Not the same life, not the old one she had known here in Mera, and that her fleeting loss of memory had sought to reimpose. That had gone forever. But different hopes lay now within her, like a bud curled within its leafy case. "Ana! Oh, Eliana, where are you?" she whispered. She could almost see the old woman, with her pale clouded eyes and her neat white hair, sitting in the chair within the cave's entrance and smiling. She could almost hear her voice. "You are here," Ailia said. "You haven't gone, not really. There is something of you still in this world."

Around her all was still, save for a pair of nesting robins flying to and from their new home in an old oak, and the soft wind stirring in the boughs. At her feet Greymalkin sat and purred with content.

JOMAR, LORELYN, AURON, AND TALEERA hastened uphill, the birdwoman grumbling at each turn of the old stone road. "This miserable human form!" she panted. "I don't know how you endure it. *Walking* everywhere—if I had my wings I'd be there by now—" She paused for breath, staring about the mountainside. "There's no one here to see. Perhaps I could risk taking my own shape—"

"I wouldn't," Auron said. He was puffing himself, and his plump face was flushed. "There may be hunters hereabouts, or Valei spies."

"And we're nearly there anyway," said Lorelyn.

Suddenly the bushes at the side of the path rustled, and a girl with tangled red hair and smoldering green eyes emerged and confronted them, barring their way. "If it is the white witch you are looking for, then go back! I warn you, don't come here again—and tell all the other villagers to keep away too." Her eye rested for a moment on Jomar and Auron in puzzlement. "We have warned you before. Selenna is ours."

"We aren't villagers, as you can plainly see," Auron replied. "The white witch, as you call her, is our friend. And the mountain belongs to no one."

"Now get out of the way," added Taleera, "if you don't want to be hurt. You can see for yourself you're outnumbered."

"I am a witch!" the disheveled young woman cried. "I do not fear you, even if you are Nemerei." But she retreated a step as they advanced.

"If you are a witch, then whom do you serve?" demanded Taleera. "Are you aligned with the white arts or the black?"

"Good or evil," she said, her lip curling. "You see all things in those terms. I serve one who decided to seek after the knowledge that was forbidden, that others would deny him. Even though it meant that he was outcast forever afterward, he took that path knowing the consequences to himself. The echo of his great deed still rings throughout the universe, and his name became a banner for generations of humankind. We bear his name, for we carry on his noble aims into infinity. And for this we too have been reviled— we *Modriani*."

She's quoting from somewhere, Lorelyn thought. At her side Auron was nodding his head. "Ah yes, the Modrian cult. Black witches. I have heard of you."

"But this is nonsense!" exclaimed Lorelyn. "You're talking as if Modrian-Valdur was some sort of hero. He was the monster, the Fiend who brought war to the worlds—"

"He brought change," countered the girl in a proud voice, "and suffering and sorrow are the birth pangs of change. There is no victory without pain. You know that."

"But he caused *others* pain, not himself," Lorelyn argued.

"So that they might grow. And in any case, as a god he was beyond pain."

"Are you are in league with the Zimbourans?" asked Auron.

"Of course," the witch replied. "They are our brethren, fellow servants of Modrian-Valdur."

"And you spy on the Nemerei for them, perhaps?"

She made no reply, but did not deny Auron's charge either, and the triumphant smile did not leave her lips. "Then you are twice a traitor, whoever you are," said Taleera. "To your homeland, and to the Tryna Lia."

"Tryna Lia!" she mocked. "You had better seek your savior elsewhere—if she *is* that woman who dwells in the Faerie Cave, as rumor has it, she has no power to match our Master's. I have spied on her, and she has not even seen me."

"But you didn't dare go near her, obviously," said Jomar.

Her smile dropped away. "Our allies know of the white witch. We have sent messages to them. They are coming for her, and will take you too if you don't leave at once." She drew herself up. "Go now, or we'll destroy you and all your Conspiracy. Modrian's day has come. They tried to imprison him forever, the other gods: but his new Avatar is here. His winged ships own the air. And when he conquers the world he'll punish all those that did not serve him."

"And reward those that did?" said Auron.

"The world will be our inheritance," the girl replied, with the fierce confidence of the fanatic. "You will see."

"Oh, this is too silly for words. We're wasting time, standing here and debating!" Lorelyn drew out her sword and brandished it. "Come along then, if you want a fight. Otherwise, leave us to go our way in peace."

The girl took one look at the bright adamantine blade, her green eyes widening. Then she turned in a whirl of red hair and dark cloak, and fled back down the mountainside. Lorelyn sheathed her sword again. "So much for her."

"She will be going to alert the other Modriani," Taleera said.

"Let them come," retorted Jomar. "They're not real sorcerers, just a lot of ignorant idiots. Where is this cave of Ana's?"

Lorelyn looked up the mountainside, and then pointed. "There, below the peak—I think that must be it! That sort of crack in the rock, do you see?"

She started up the path again, and the others followed her. But when they drew closer to the cave Jomar laid a hand on her shoulder. "There's someone there!"

They all halted, and stood staring at the narrow opening in the hillside. A figure stooped at its mouth, tending a small fire there. It was wrapped in a hooded cloak, torn and threadbare.

Lorelyn gasped. "Ana? *Ana?*"

The figure stood upright, and then they saw that it was taller than Ana. They hastened toward it, and as they drew near they recognized the face in the hood.

"Ailia—we've found you at last!" Taleera cried.

She pushed the hood back and smiled. "Oh—I am so glad to see you! I was beginning to wonder if you would find me."

"Well, you did make it rather difficult for us." But Lorelyn was beaming with joy. She ran up to her friend and hugged her. "You were being spied on, did you know that? One of the black witches of Modrian—"

"Yes, Ralf came back here to warn me about her. He saw her as he was walking down the mountainside, and spied on her in turn." She nodded at the ragged beggar man who was emerging from the cave mouth behind her. "You remember Ralf, don't you? He is still with the other Nemerei, and is going to take them a message from me."

The man tossed his head and bellowed. *I'm not fast as couriers go,* Lorelyn and the two in human guise heard, *but I'm reliable. I really should start up a business.*

Ailia smiled, and turned back to her friends. "And I found my foster family again, Lori. They are all safe—for now. I am sorry to give you such a chase. I came here looking for Ana."

"You've found her?" asked Jomar.

"Yes. She is here." Ailia gestured at the mountain, the woods, and the range beyond. "Here where she belongs. In this place, and in us."

"Ah." Auron exchanged glances with the others. "I understand."

"Perhaps not completely," the Princess said. "I didn't really understand either, at first. I grieved for her, but now . . . I really do feel that she is with us still." Her voice softened until they could barely hear it. "And Damion too."

"Ailia, you must come back with us! Why did you run away like that?" said Lorelyn.

"I wanted Ana's guidance. The Nemerei and the Loänan—they wanted me to use my powers to kill." Ailia looked away.

"And you didn't want to. Oh, Ailia—"

She shook her head. "No! I *did* want to! I was so full of rage, for Damion's sake, that I might have done anything. I would have been a light, as the prophecies said—but a burning light, like a thunderbolt that falls from the sky and blasts the earth. I decided that I mustn't fight until I could do it without hate."

"The time to fight is now, whether we are ready or not," Auron said. "The enemy moves. Temendri Alfaran is taken."

She cried out in dismay. "Taken! But what of the Emperor? He was not slain?"

"No, he escaped, taking the palace of crystal and the Dragon Throne with him. We do not know where he has gone. But Talmirennia and its peoples have suffered a terrible blow."

"Ailia." Taleera stepped forward. "Mandrake is coming here to Mera. He's launched his first assault, and Arainia is next. The Loänan say he's put down all the Valei who won't obey him, killed the rebels, and seized control of their empire. And it's much larger than we ever imagined."

Ailia hid her face in her hands. "Yes: I must face Mandrake, and soon. He and I must meet. The longer I delay, the longer this war will last."

"But—if he wins—"

"He mustn't win. I will have to use all of my powers. And I once hoped never to have to use them for violence. And . . . I won't lie to you: I still fear him. Mandrake tempted me when I went to his world. With power and—and other things." She looked directly at them again. "I almost gave in to him. That is the truth, which I couldn't find the courage to tell you before. But I am ready to come back with you now," she added. "Whether it came from Ana or not I don't know, but I believe I've found the answer I was seeking." She turned to Ralf. "Would you Nemerei please tell my family down in the city that my people have found me, and I am leaving the country now? Tell them I will come back someday, if I can. And could you ask one of your members to look after Greymalkin for me?"

The man squawked his assent and shuffled off down the hill. "He will take no payment," said Ailia. "He says the Nemerei see to his basic needs, and he requires nothing else. Now I will come with you."

"Good! Things are moving, Highness," Taleera told her. "And we must move too. The enemy marches, and even now we may be overtaken. We cannot let him choose the battleground."

$$7$$

The War Between the Worlds

SOFILIA, QUEEN OF THE SYLPHS, stood in the royal gardens gazing on the revels of her court. There was no palace here such as humans built, and only a very few marble buildings scattered about the grounds; some were little more than roofs raised on pillars, to keep off the rain. The sky was a soft rose-pink, like a sky at the first blush of dawn, save that here that hue never left it. It was clear but for a few gossamer wisps of cirrus, very high up, while lower down there swarmed multitudes of flying shapes, delicate in form and tint as butterflies or wind-blown flower petals. These were her people, gliding and soaring freely on their fragile-seeming wings. They came to earth to rest and sleep, and take their food, and work: but there were no roads and little foot traffic in this world, save of the very young or very old. All others traveled through the pathless air.

In the royal gardens this world's never-ending summer reigned: the grounds were such a mass of flowers that in most places the underlying turf could not be seen. Pink, crimson, scarlet, and wine-red were the predominant colors, and in and out among the huge blooms went those of her people who were taking their ease on the earth. The women wore long loose garments of a weave fine as the cirrus clouds, and their wings flowed behind them like diaphanous capes. The men and the infants wore only cloths about their loins. The latter, with their absurd tiny wings that could not yet bear their weight, laughed and played together and gazed longingly at their elders in the heights above.

The queen felt alone, cut off from the happy scene before her. For many moons now she had been ill at ease and apprehensive. She had been first to throw in her lot with Ailia, declaring her support for the Tryna Lia in the Emperor's hall on Temendri Alfaran. Her example had swayed many of the other peoples, convincing them to turn against the Loänei Mandrake and his disturbing allies. But in offering to stand at Ailia's side, Sofilia was aware that she had made a weighty decision on behalf of her people—these same innocents now at play in the sky and among the flower beds—and that harm might yet come to them as a consequence of that decision. They would not condemn her, even if harm did come; for the sylphs looked to the coming of the Tryna Lia as did all other peoples in whose veins some human blood still ran. But this knowledge did not allay her growing unease. This morning she had awakened with a premonition of disaster that she knew was no mere lingering dream. Like all the sylph-folk she was a Nemerei, and her extra sense was forever attuned to the vast web of the Ether, feeling in it every least tremor of power and thought. Yet without any specific warning, she did not know what action she should take.

And so it was that she felt a sharp stab of fear, and yet no surprise, when a discordant chorus of cries shattered the peace around her.

Looking up, she beheld many black shapes descending from the dome of the sky. Sylphs were abandoning the air in fright to seek cover among the gardens and forests below. But the black shapes were swifter, and from their jaws sprang a withering flame. They tore through the butterfly swarms of her people and sent them tumbling earthward, like blossoms shaken down by a storm.

Firedrakes!

She leaped up, her own two sets of nacreous wings quivering as they spread to their full span, yet knowing even as she moved that there was nothing she could do, that her worst fears had come to pass. This was the price. The Valei had sent the firedrakes to re-

venge themselves upon her, and all those whom she had pledged
her life to guard.

THROUGH THE SKIES OF MERA Auron flew, with his three human riders and Taleera. A thin crescent moon hung above him: as the blue
of day surrounding it swiftly deepened into black its white smile
began to shine more brilliantly. There were other dragons flying
here in the upper limits of the atmosphere, gleaming in the light of
moon and sun.

Ailia, sitting behind Auron's head, greeted the celestial dragons
by raising aloft the Star Stone. Its white radiance made the celestial
orbs above her seem to fade. The dragons trumpeted in joy, and
spoke to her in her mind also. One of them, she was pleased to
learn, was Gallada, the young Imperial dragon from Temendri Alfaran. *Highness!* The dragon spun about and flew above them as an
honor guard. *We are glad you have returned at last.*

As am I, Ailia replied. *The people below have need of your help, Gallada.
There are firedrakes at large over the land.* She looked down at the dense
cloud, and realized that their enemies could use it now as cover,
through which firedrakes and sky ships could attack without first
being spotted. *There are many Nemerei down there also, and the enemy seeks
to destroy them all. Please help them!*

We will. Many Loänan are now on Numia awaiting your command, Gallada replied. *We feared some of the enemy had slipped through our net. But Your
Highness and your companions must go first to the moon, and bathe in the springs
there to cleanse yourselves. Then on to Arainia! It too is in danger.*

They flew into the Ether, through the luminous tunnel of a
dragon-way, and out again. Ailia was glad to be amid the stars once
more, though she knew their seeming serenity was an illusion. Wars
were being waged amid these silent constellations even now. *Ar-
chons of the stars, if you are truly still there, if you love the empire that you made,
then come to its aid now,* Ailia pleaded in her thoughts.

Numia was beneath them now, not above, and with the sun behind them it shone at the full. As they dropped toward its face it
changed slowly from the familiar moon into a pale gleaming country. It was a desert, however, and nothing in it moved or lived.

"This was once a world," said Auron. "It saddens me to see it.
Where those dark sprawling patches are, little seas once rolled and
shone in the sun; on those mountains and plains were forests teem-

ing with life. And there were cities also." They soared over a gray-white plain. Craters gaped below them, brimming with shadow. "The Disaster destroyed it all, and now Numia is barren and life-less."

Ailia felt anew the sense of desolation she had known when Auron brought her here after the adventure in Trynisia. On over the devastation wrought by the comets of the Disaster they went, and presently they came upon a strange sight: spots of bright color blooming amid the gray wastes. As they dropped lower Ailia saw these were great tents of gold and crimson: a war camp had been set up here on Numia. Many creatures moved in its midst and bathed in the springs that lay near. Auron alighted at the edge of the camp and the three humans jumped down from his neck. A strange motley crowd greeted them: human Nemerei, dragons, and cherubim. Two of the latter stood at attention on either side of a large flat-topped boulder, like guards: they both looked very much like Falaar, save that the one on the right had the talons of an eagle on its forefeet and no feathery crest between its pointed ears, while the one on the left sported a pair of curving horns like a he-goat's. Upon the rock a third cherub sat as if enthroned, bolt upright on his haunches: Girian Vaulyn, king of the cherubim. His great head was leonine in shape, but it more closely resembled a statue of a heraldic lion than the true beast: broader in the face and shorter in the muzzle, with a solemn and regal intelligence no beast can show. The sockets of his eyes were deep and dark, but as she drew closer Ailia saw the glimmer of the ancient eyes within them. His mane was dressed in close curls, like the beards of kings in old An-tipodean carvings; his folded wings, with their plumes the color of beaten bronze, rose high behind his shoulders and trailed down his back like a royal mantle; and on his head he wore a golden crown.

Ailia addressed him with respect, as one ruler to another. "Majesty, there is great need in Mera for your aid. I thank your war-riors for their efforts on our behalf, but I implore you to send some of them to help the people there." She looked up at the western continent of that world, plainly visible as it slipped toward the vast shadow of night. "If the city of Raimar falls, so will Maurainia."

"I will send as many as I can. But most are still engaged in fight-ing the enemy out among the comets," replied King Girian. Even in the thin air of Numia his voice sounded deep and resonant as a temple bell. "The firedrakes are more numerous than we had thought. And thou knowest what will befall that world, should the comets reach it."

Ailia glanced up at the terrible missiles with their long white tails. If even one struck that fair, fragile blue globe, it would cause destruction beyond imagining. She lowered her gaze to the dry, dusty ground and rocks that surrounded her, and she trembled. "The enemy is everywhere. But innocent people are already dying in Mera; even the most valiant deeds of the Wingwatch here will be of no use to them, if they are abandoned now to goblins and fire-drakes."

"Be assured, we will do all that we can, *Trynel*." Girian Vaulyn turned his kingly head and roared a command at his people. Several cherubim took wing at once, rising up into the black sky, eager as hounds to the hunt.

She bowed her head to him, and then turned as a familiar voice called her name. Her father had stepped out of one of the silken tents, and was hastening toward her. "At last! I was so afraid for you!" Tiron exclaimed, as he took her in his arms.

"Forgive me, Father," said Ailia, clinging to him. "I didn't mean to make you anxious, but I fell ill and even lost my memory for a time. I have recovered; and I won't ever leave you again."

"There, my dear, do not reproach yourself. I am only glad that you are safe." He took her by the hand, and led her away to the tent.

Lorelyn and Jomar went meanwhile and sat with a few of the Ne-merei, watching the dragons and cherubim bathe their many burns and wounds in the steaming waters of the springs. Some were too badly hurt even for the healing waters to restore, and the anguish of the cherubim who could not return to the battle was pitiful to see. The Archons themselves had made these creatures to defend the worlds from harm, and for them to be prevented from carrying out this noblest of duties was a blow worse than any hurt.

Lorelyn said presently, "The enemy will attack Mera again—and Maurainia too. Our allies can't be everywhere. And poor Ailia can't do everything either. We need flying ships of our own!"

A Magus replied, "Flying ships would need salamander scales, and wool and silk, to protect them from firedrakes."

"And our soldiers on the ground need protection from drake-fire too," Jomar said.

"But the supply of fire-resisting wool and silk and scales is exhausted everywhere in Talmirennia. The salamanders, unlike the other children of the Elementals, never left this sun-system. They exist nowhere else in the Empire."

"But there *are* still salamanders living in Arkurion? Couldn't we go there, and ask them?" Lorelyn addressed these questions to Auron, who had come padding up behind them in his dragon-form. The Loänan considered a moment, his great golden head cocked at a thoughtful angle.

I have not projected my image there in many an age, he said. *They do not communicate much with outsiders now. And it may be that the enemy has spoken with them and corrupted them. I would be surprised if that were not the case. Yet, I will project to them—and you should too, Lorelyn, for you can give testimony of the suffering of your world. Ailia is too weary to use her power, but as her close friend you can speak on her behalf.*

Can we not go there in person? she asked, curious. *Then Jo could come too. And I have always wanted to visit Arkurion.*

I am afraid not: for even my power could not long protect us in that world. Only the salamanders can live there. Any other creature that entered it without sorcerous protections would die a speedy death.

IN HER FATHER'S TENT, AILIA sat on a pile of embroidered cushions near a warm brazier. "You must rest, daughter," Tiron said.

"I've no time for it," said Ailia. "The prophecy said that I must lead the celestial armies into Mera."

"You have done that already."

"I have?" she asked, puzzled. "What do you mean, Father?"

"You went to Mera, and the host of the Wingwatch and the Arainian army followed after you. It is a much larger army this time, and aided by the fighting dragons and cherubim who will no longer hold back from battle. They will meet the Valei there, and deliver that world." He sat down beside her and put his arm about her shoulders. "Your role is fulfilled. You had but to inspire them, and lead the way."

"There are still so many places where I should be!" she said. "Back in Arainia, to reassure the people—and in Zimboura, to comfort the people there and help counter Mandrake's following—and up in the

void, helping the Loänan and cherubim to move the comets . . .
The Great Powers should have sent a dozen Tryna Lias, not one!"
She sprang up again from the cushions. "Father, is it true that there
are many more of the enemy than we knew?"

"It appears so. The Morugei have been made to breed in great
numbers, to provide fighters in their own civil wars. They have
learned the craft of battle for centuries, and perfected it, by slaying
one another. This did not reduce their numbers, but rather
strengthened them as a race, for the strongest and fiercest survived
to breed again. And now they no longer fight one another, but are
united against us under their Avatar. The firedrakes too are greater
in number than we had realized. This battle of the comets is but a
skirmish in a larger war that has been long in the planning—so long
that the roots of those plans go back to the Archons' time. All of
Talmirennia is now under siege. Firedrakes have assailed the sylphs'
world, and set fire to the cities of the dryads in the forests of Falnia."

Ailia was appalled. The sylphs under attack! This was indeed a
blow: and as for Falnia, most of the beings in that world were beast-
folk, centaurs and satyrs and harpies, that lived out of doors; but the
dwellings of the dryads were very wonderful. Because no dryad
would fell a tree for its wood, they made their houses by inducing
trees, through sorcery, to shape themselves into living halls and
chambers, winding trunks and boughs together to make the roofs
and walls. Some of these trees were of sequoia height and girth, and
the edifices they formed comparable in size and grandeur to the
temples and castles of humanity. It had taken hundreds or thousands of years to create these great houses, and would require as
many years to replace them. "The sylphs and the Falnians look to
us now for succor," Tiron went on. "And in many other worlds the
peoples that gave you aid and support are suffering in consequence.
The kitsune ambassador, Hada, returned to his people to try and
help them. But we hear now that he was slain, and many others with
him."

"Oh, no—no! Hada was a dear friend of Auron's: he will be
grieved to hear this. And Orbion is both wise and skilled in sorcery—if he could not face the Valei, but had to flee, then what
hope have I?" She passed a hand over her eyes. "We need more
armies, Father."

"There are no more armies, and there is no time to train Talmirennia's peoples to fight and kill. This war is not upon us; it is already well under way."

"And I have been wasting what little time we have by wandering about in Mera," said Ailia, distressed. "I so wanted Ana's help and advice—I even persuaded myself that her spirit had somehow reached out to speak to me. I really have been a little mad these past few days. I am sorry." She slumped down among the cushions again. "But I know what I need to do. I was not asked to fight whole armies, but only one person, whom I *can* defeat. If their Avatar is gone, then perhaps the Valei will lose their will to fight." *But will they?* she wondered. *Now that there are so many of them, and they are all filled with fear and hate?*

"My dear child." Tiron laid a gentle hand on her arm. "I would help you if I could. In the meantime, rest. There is a little travel pouch there by the brazier, with food and water—a little ambrosia too, though I am sure you don't need it—"

Ailia took his hand in both of hers and held it tightly, then stood up again. Going over to the pouch, she lifted it by its shoulder strap. "Thank you, Father. But I would like to go for a walk instead. I need air, and quiet, and to be alone for a little. Perhaps things will seem a bit clearer to me then."

She walked past the borders of the encampment, treading a flat stone surface that proved to be the remains of an ancient road. She followed it without knowing why, letting it take her down through the gray waste until, coming to the edge of a precipice, she saw it descend to the floor of a crater beyond, and run arrow-straight to a rocky hill at the center in the form of a causeway. And on that hill rose white walls and high needling towers that touched a chord of memory.

It is the same castle I flew over with Auron years ago, when he first brought me here, she thought. *What was it like, I wonder, when Numia was a living world?* She gazed in fascination at the Archonic structure: it seemed to draw her to it. From her travel pouch she drew out the small flask of ambrosia, removed its silver stopper, and put the flask to her lips. As she swallowed the liquor and replaced the vessel, her vision began to dim, and over the fading scene before her another was placed, like and yet not like, an image out of some bygone age.

The sun and stars still blazed together in the sky, but it was no longer so black, nor was the land so sere and gray. It was filled with vivid colors, with forests of emerald, indigo, and heliotrope. Only the cliffs were pale, plunging to the crater below. But a dark gleaming lake, reflecting sun and stars, covered its floor. The islet in the center glowed like a jewel upon black velvet, with greens and vermilions, and on its summit was the pearl-white palace.

She descended the winding cliff path and crossed the causeway, looking up at the white towers that were now ablaze with light against the dark sky. The great doors were flung wide, and the vast space within filled with a soft, pearly radiance. Many people stood before the palace, tall people arrayed in glorious many-colored cloaks that seemed to Ailia's wondering eyes to be all woven of feathers: scarlet, green, saffron, and violet, no two alike. Then one woman spread wide her arms and Ailia saw that her cloak was attached to her elbows and wrists, and fashioned in the likeness of two great bird wings. As she stared, the woman leaped into the air, followed by one or two others; and to Ailia's amazement their pinions held the wind and lifted them on high, so that they glided with the grace of swallows over the trees and across the lake.

A figure appeared in the doorway, some sibyl of the moon-folk it must be; not only her robe was white but also her winged cloak, and her hair flowed silver down her back. She stood gazing serenely into the night, and following her gaze Ailia saw the planet Mera, with her vast disc all blue and mottled with clouds, even as it appeared in Ailia's own time.

Then the sibyl spoke. "Welcome to the fane of Elnumia," she said in a clear mellifluous voice. She was addressing not Ailia, whom she could not see, but the winged pilgrims.

Elnumia—goddess of the moon. So this was where the Archon of Numia had made her dwelling! It was the moon palace out of the old tales, radiant as the little world in which it lay. The beauty and the wonder of it filled Ailia with delight. But this quickly turned to sorrow. The day would come when its light would be put out, and the groves and gardens on its islet be replaced with gray dust, and the crater-lake drained dry as an emptied goblet. And the moon-people too would be all gone from Numia, perished or fled.

Ailia moved past the sibyl at the doorway, and entered the palace.

It was as bright within as without, its main hall faced like its exterior with blue-white venudor, gleaming like a cave of ice. Great columns held up the roof, shining with their own pale light, and among these walked the moon-folk in little groups. Their soft foot-falls—on the moon one did not tread so heavily as on the larger worlds—and their hushed voices were the only sounds to be heard. On a dais at the far end a great marble throne—too large to have been made for any human ruler—sat empty. But beside it Ailia saw, drifting transparent on the air, an ethereal figure. It had the likeness of a woman, unnaturally thin and tall, her ghostly body swathed in trailing white garments. Her shrouded head was bowed in an atti-tude of mourning. None of the mortal beings within the hall seemed able to see the apparition; at any rate they paid it no heed. But as Ailia approached the dais, the woman-form raised its veiled face and spoke to her.

"Thou art welcome," the figure said in a whispering voice. "I see thee, Tryna Lia, visitor from the future age. I too am not truly here, but am outside of time."

"I saw you once before!" Ailia exclaimed. Whose was this pro-jected image?

"Yes. I can show myself only unto thee."

"Please—who are you?" Ailia asked.

"I am she who reigned here long ago. When my world was as thou seest it here, full of life and color. Thou knowest what those that dwell herein do not. Thou hast seen what will come." The face-less figure gestured to the throne. "Seat thyself."

"Lady, that seat is thine," Ailia replied.

"But for this time I give it thee, for so it pleaseth me. I pray thee, be seated."

Ailia complied with some difficulty, for the throne was tall and deep, and she felt like a child clambering up into its elder's chair. Looking along the length of the great hall to the open door she saw Mera blue and radiant in the dark sky. And as she sat there, all of a sudden she recalled the prophecy that the Tryna Lia would be throned upon the moon.

"That is Elmera's world," the apparition said. "It escaped the cat-aclysm that laid my Numia waste. Thou seest now how my lands once appeared. But the enemy of the Light dispatched Azarah to bring discord to the heavens. It sent the comets flying toward the inner worlds, and this my satellite realm was destroyed, and Mera came near to utter destruction. It may not so escape again. And Arainia too is in peril." A vision filled Ailia's mind. She saw all the world of Mera turned to burned and blackened desert under Numia's glow—lifeless as the moon above it. Then Arainia and its moon also came under the siege, and she recoiled in horror from the images she beheld: the forests withering, the oceans turning to ice, under a sky reddened with dust and fumes that shut away the sun.

Was the being warning her to keep on fighting? That if she did not go on with this war, Mera—and Arainia—could end as Numia had? And these worlds were not alone in their peril, for she saw now in her mind the tree-cities of the dryads, the age-old bark and fresh greenery of their living roofs and walls alight with wildfire. She saw a world of blending blue and purple hues of hanging mists and still waters: the world of the Tarnawyn, and it too was overrun. The beautiful creatures bounded through the woods, tearing the vapors asunder with their horns while the mist drops flew from their white coats like scattered diamonds. Barguests—huge black dogs with red eyes—pursued the unicorns while jubilant goblin-hunters followed. Then Ailia beheld a place of strange high mounds and columnar shapes all riddled with holes, thousands of holes set close together, so that the red-brown, rock-hard stuff of which the mounds were made resembled a honeycomb: and in and out of these openings there came and went in torrents hundreds of six-legged creatures like ants. She might have thought they were ants indeed, for she could get no sense of scale; but she saw the strange, furred heads that were more feline than insectlike, and knew these to be myrmecoleons, ant-lions, each bigger than an ox. They were swarming out of their mounds to attack an oncoming army of goblins and ogres and great trolls. The queen, a majestic creature twice the size of her drones, stood looking out of the highest opening atop the nearest mound. The armies were fighting to protect her, but they had no weapons apart from their claws and jaws. "These are not glimpses of the future," the apparition's voice said to her as the last image faded, "but things that are happening now. Those beings pledged their allegiance unto thee, and now they suffer for it. Do not fail them!"

Ailia bowed her head. "I understand," she said.

The scene swam before Ailia's eyes, dissolved into a mass of blended color that wavered and faded away. She blinked. She still sat the throne, but the pearly light was gone: the palace was once more a bone-white shell hung with gray gloom. She had actually wandered in body as well as in spirit into the old Archon ruin. Elnumia—if it were truly she—was gone. But a whispering voice lingered on the dusty air. *Seek thou the lands of Elarainia in her sphere. She will give thee power to defeat thy foes.*

Slowly Ailia climbed down from the throne and walked out the great door.

ARKURION'S SURFACE WAS LIKE A cauldron of molten metal, harshly brilliant, semiliquid and seething, all a rich yellow in color. Auron's and Lorelyn's ethereal forms skimmed over luteous flats and bubbling lakes of lava. The light of the huge white-hot sun shrieked out of the blazing sky.

If we were here in the flesh, Auron said, *and without any shielding magic, we would swiftly die of the fumes. And the glare would burn your eyes out.*

Why is everything so yellow? asked Lorelyn.

It is all made of sulfur. It rains acid instead of water here too—most unpleasant. But the salamanders like it. Their bodies are thickly plated to keep out the acid and the burning rays of the sun.

Why do they bear wool, then? Doesn't it make them warmer?

No, the wool has a cooling effect, in fact. The sun strikes only its upper surface, and does not penetrate down to the lower layer of the fleece, thus keeping the heat away from the body.

As they flew by one caldera it erupted, spraying a geyser of caustic liquid into the livid clouds. The world's entire landscape was a molten mass of yellow sulfur flats and reeking pools. The cones of the volcanoes would soon collapse and new ones form: the surface of Arkurion was perpetually shifting and reshaping itself. Lorelyn wondered what it would be like to inhabit such a place—a landscape with no permanent points of reference, where nothing ever lasted. What effect might that have on the salamandrine mind? Suddenly the steaming lake nearest them began to froth and churn in one spot. Out of the surface a yellow snout appeared, and a wet glistening back; and then the whole creature hauled itself ashore. The salamander was about twelve feet long and lizardlike in appearance, with a squat build and tapering tail, four stumpy legs, and a long narrow head. Lorelyn noted the thick fleece of what looked exactly like sodden wool on its back.

The creature spoke in a hissing voice, and in their heads Auron and Lorelyn heard the words: *Who are you? Why do you project your image here, Loänan? And why do you bring a human with you?*

Friend, we have need of your aid, Auron said. *Mera and Arainia are in danger. Valdur's servants threaten them.*

The outer planets—ugh! So far from the sun, so chill and inhospitable! Though it is said they have some very pleasant regions deep down, near their molten cores. The salamander glared at the human with round dark eyes like hemispheres of smoked glass. *So do their peoples flee here? Will we now have to compete with humans for living space?*

Lorelyn shook her insubstantial head. *Oh, no. I can promise you that.*

Are you certain? Who could resist such a lovely world as ours—the warm and fragrant air—the beautiful lakes?

Lorelyn, trying hard not to laugh, assured the creature that the humans would not colonize the sulfur planet. *We couldn't live here. We only came to ask you for your help.*

Still the salamander seemed suspicious. *You would draw us into this war? We are not fighters, and will not ever leave our world. Indeed we cannot live anywhere else. We would perish of the cold.*

We don't ask you to fight. But once before you shared your wonderful wool and silk with us, and your cast-off scales. We need to fight the firedrakes that are besieging our worlds, and not all our warriors are Nemerei.

My world is not threatened. The salamander moved toward its fuming pool again. *The fates of yours do not concern our people. Your battles have never affected us, for humans and goblins and dragons cannot dwell in Arkurion and have no use for it. And so it is even now. No comet is aimed at us. This is not our war.*

Auron said, *Can you be so sure? The Valei may yet find a use for your people, and enslave them. Firedrakes could survive in this world. You do not know the Darklings as I do.*

You cannot say for certain that they will enslave us. What is certain is that if we give you aid, then we will be the enemies of your enemies. They will have reason to harm us. You have heard of the fate that befell the sylphs, after their queen allied herself with your Tryna Lia? The burnings and killings in that world and others were meant as a warning to all the rest of us. Only if we keep to ourselves will we be safe. The salamander began to submerge.

Lorelyn wished Ailia were there: her skills of diplomacy were sorely needed. Lorelyn was accustomed to fighting with weapons not words. She tried to think what Ailia would say. *But we need your help. If your world were in danger, we would give you whatever aid you asked.*

You would? The creature's voice was skeptical.

Yes, truly. That was the whole reason for Talmirennia—the Old Ones didn't want all the worlds to be isolated and separated, but part of a larger whole. So we would come to one another's aid in times of need.

The salamander lay still with its head just above the surface, like a crocodile. There was a long pause as it considered. Then it said, *I will speak to the others, and see what they say. We have no rulers, such as you humans have. But I will tell my kindred what you have said. We will let you know our decision in a few days.* It dived into the bubbling pool and was gone.

Auron and Lorelyn looked at each other. *You have done all you could,* said Auron.

She nodded. *I suppose so. There are some who'd say we should take their wool and silk by force, because the need is so great. I am sure the Nemerei would find a way to come here, and fight them.*

You are right in that. Sorcery makes all things possible.

But I don't feel right about it. And I know Ailia wouldn't approve. Still . . . whatever will we do if they don't help us?

Continue the fight without their aid, said Auron, *and hope that they see our cause is just, and relent. But we are getting ahead of ourselves. First we must wait and see what the salamanders decide. Let us return to our bodies, and offer what help we can to our friends in the meantime.*

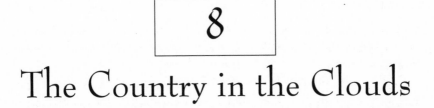

8

The Country in the Clouds

"WHY? WHY DOES SHE RETREAT?" Mandrake roared in his dragon's voice. "The fate of Mera lies yet in the balance. The Emperor is too weak to defend his realm and title. Now is the time for her to accept the throne he offered. Why then has she retreated to her own world, and to the wilderness? I have been to those lands: there is nothing there."

The red dragon stood on the frozen face of the largest comet, protected from the bitter void about him by an enchanted bubble of air and warmth. Above him Arainia shone, suspended over an icy cliff and limning it with the light of her rings and her blue orb. The dark forms of firedrakes circled in the black sky, scarcely visible save when they eclipsed the stars or scudded across the planet's gleaming disc. With Mandrake stood a small company of his rebel Loänan, including the monarch of the earth-dragons, Torok. Elazar and Elombar were also present in ethereal form, drifting before his face.

The latter said, "Our spies say that she has gone to seek the Archons of that world—her mother in particular."

The dragon gazed up at the ringed world. *Might there be Archons living still? Even I have not seen all that there is in the cosmos . . . But no, I have seen all there is to be seen in Arainia. Had there been any Archons dwelling there I would have found them.* "No, she knows the Old Ones are gone from Arainia. And her mother perished while delivering her to Mera. What could be of greater importance to Ailia than fighting on in Mera, or seeking and claiming the Imperial throne? I should go to Arainia myself and see."

"What would be the use?" said Elazar. "Lord Prince, it is to Ombar that you must go, to take the throne of Valdur. Then you must seek for Orbion, to seize the Dragon Throne. You cannot fight the Tryna Lia on her own ground."

"Hear him, Mandrake!" growled Torok, stretching his scarlet-scaled neck toward the Dragon King. "His counsel is good. Let the Tryna Lia cower in her own world if she wishes. We can take all of Talmirennia for ourselves meanwhile."

"Not yet. First I want to see what my adversary is about. She knows that I can take the Dragon Throne, yet it does not seem to trouble her. Of course, the safety of her world and people means more to her than any throne—and she can always fight me for it later. Yet she seems to feel that she can defend Arainia even without her army and her Nemerei, whom she has sent to liberate Mera. Why? What is it she hopes to find in Arainia that gives her so much confidence? Perhaps she has learned of some relic or talisman that might aid her in the battle to come?" The dragon paused, and then turned to the two demons. "Should your plan fail, may I suggest another? I am sure you would enjoy smashing Arainia into oblivion, but what would you say if its virgin forests and fine cities were instead to become home to your goblins and the other Valei? Would it not be an even greater triumph than mere obliteration, if the Elei were to see their beloved world overrun by the enemy? Why should we not take that world for our own?"

Elazar answered, "You do not understand. The powers in Arainia will be ranged against us, should we go there. The Archons—"

"Not again," said Mandrake. "Powers there are in that world, without a doubt, but I do not believe them to be Archons. They are Nemerei, many of them great ones, but none a match for me, and the armies you have given me. Whatever Ailia's hope may be, it is in vain. She will not drive me away a second time."

"But Arainia is the seat of Ailia's strength," the demon countered. "That is why she has gone there."

"All the more reason to deal with it first, and its ruler too. Cut off the head and you have little to fear from the body. Come, are you afraid? Let us go to the moon at least, to Miria. It will be a better base for our ships and our firedrakes than this airless mass of ice. From that point of vantage we can commence a siege of Arainia."

AILIA STOOD GAZING ON Hyelanthia, the Country in the Clouds. The table mountains that made up this fabled Arainian land were so huge and high that they blended into the sky itself, swathed about with cumuli that looked hard and heavy as marble—more solid, indeed, than the distant summits they enfolded. The largest plateau was enveloped in a single cloud, its heights invisible. The Place of the Mother, the Elei called it—where the goddess Elarainia was believed to have held her mystical court. And held it still, according to some. The Queen of the World reigned in spirit, they said, with her divine court about her. Was this, Ailia wondered, merely a local myth? Well might the early Arainians imagine that cloud-clad height to be the earthly home of a deity. Or had an Archon ruled there long ago—the very same Archon who became Ailia's mother? The "gods" of this world had been real, after all, living beings of flesh and blood who had practiced long-forgotten sorceries, altered their forms and toyed with the stuff of life itself.

It was good, at least, to be in her home world once more and in a warmer clime. She had exchanged her heavy clothing for a thin white gown with short sleeves, and her hair was bound in two braids that were snailed and pinned at the sides of her head, leaving her neck bare. The air was languid and sultry, with only the mildest of breezes blowing in off the sea; the sun was eastering in the deep blue sky above, where the Arch of Heaven hung like a visible celestial equator. High overhead hung a great comet, one of those sent by the enemy. It had not yet been turned, for it was well guarded. Inside its icy recesses Mandrake's most dangerous servants waited, preparing to strike at the world. Rumor said that Mandrake himself was there, and so the Arainians feared the comet, calling it the "dragon-star." Seeing it, Ailia felt her resolve strengthen.

"I must go to Arainia at once," she had told her guardians on Numia. "The vision I had was true, and I must follow it. But I will not go to the city. Wherever I am, there the brunt of the assault will come. I can draw on Arainia's power as easily in the wild places. I will go to Hyelanthia."

"But Highness—you will be in great danger," Taleera had objected.

"No greater danger awaits me there than in any other place," said Ailia. "And there are Elei living near the forest of Ardana. It is my mother's country."

"You must take the Wingwatch with you—" her father began.

"No, the Wingwatch must stay here, to turn the comets. I will take only a few friends with me. And I will have other allies there, I think."

"The Talmir," said Falaar. "The Great Powers."

"Perhaps," said Ailia. "Or it may be that the Fairfolk will reveal some inborn skills we never guessed at. I will certainly not be alone." Despite her determined words she had felt depression and fatigue like a poison seeping into her body, and she saw everything filtered through a veil of weariness. Everyone, she knew, was looking to her for inspiration, comfort and strength. They took life from her like plants seeking the sun. If only there were someone to fill *her* with strength!

She now returned her attention to the heights of Hyelanthia.

Somewhere, in the midst of those concealing clouds, the Archons had planted forests, where nothing should have been able to grow: ambrosia trees and others unique to those impossible elevations. The cloud-forests had long since died, but traces of them remained to this day. The Elei in this land had shown to Ailia a piece of amber carried down to the lowlands by a waterfall. It was of a rare, crystal-clear variety, which the finder had carved into a perfect globe. In its depths a fossil flower of elder days bloomed eternally, pale petals still spread to the light. That blossom had grown in the gardens of the gods, they said, when the Old Ones were still in Arainia—when the dragons were just beginning to fly between the stars—when her own race had not yet arisen. All of human history had yet to unfold when it first opened and breathed forth its unknown, lost fragrance. What other wonders had that long-ago land held, that myths knew nothing of? Ailia craned her neck, staring up at the plateau of the goddess. As she gazed, the cloaking clouds parted in one place, and she saw a lone pinnacle of rock: on it there gleamed in the sunlight, like inverted icicles, what looked like several towers or obelisks of adamant. Then the vaporous rift closed once more upon the pinna-cle, and the crystalline shapes were lost to sight once more.

The goddess . . . Elarainia . . . *My mother* . . . How to separate the lore from the flesh-and-blood woman? Had she truly been an Ar-chon, and if so, did she live still? Had she returned to this place where she had once lived in human form? In the southern face of the easternmost plateau there was a cave screened by a wide water-fall, and behind its cool curtain lay a floor of soft moss: Elarainia's old dwelling place. But it was abandoned still, and Ailia had found nothing there belonging to her mother, save a little pile of stones and seashells that might or might not have been left by her long ago. Some of the Elei here remembered her, but they had little more to tell Ailia than she already knew: that Elarainia had lived alone, that she had been accompanied more often by animals than by her human beings, that she knew all there was to be known about the wild plants of the forest and their various properties. Though Ailia had never been to this place, still she felt that she be-longed here.

The south shore was very like her winter retreat, she thought. The Eldimians had tolerated the yearly removal of her court to the Winter Palace, a castle of coral on an atoll in the Havens, in order

to give Ailia a respite from the rainy season. She had loved making
the annual journey. The royal yacht, *Sea Star*, was the size of a
galleon and equipped with every conceivable luxury, sporting tall
leaded windows in place of portholes, and decorative carving and
gilding throughout her elegant, spacious cabins. The figurehead
below her bowsprit was a golden-haired woman with a star upon
her brow, a design repeated on the white sails whose flaglike flapping and rustling lulled Ailia to sleep at night. When the *Sea Star* anchored in a harbor her masts were hung with lanterns, and feasts
and revels were held upon the decks with musicians and players,
and acrobats to swing and leap in the rigging for the passengers' enjoyment. Now Ailia looked back to those carefree days as if to some
ancient epoch of the world.

She began to walk along the white sands of the beach, right to
the very edge of the sea, as if the answers she sought lay there. It
stretched before her, seeming to contain in its sweeping expanse all
possible shades of blue. The Meran seas she remembered seemed
always to have been murky green or gray, borrowing the blue of the
sky only on clear summer days. But these waves might have been
stained with indigo: even their churning bubbles were blue. As they
had peeled back from the royal yacht's prow Ailia had always half-
expected them to leave a stain upon the white hull. And she recalled how the fishes called serras would surface in front of the
ship's bow wave, and spread wide their enormous wing-shaped pec-
toral fins just as the smaller flying fish of Mera did, riding upon the
same wind that drove the *Sea Star* forward. And there were the
Arainian dolphins—great, green, frilly-headed fish, as intelligent
and playful as the warm-blooded beasts of Meran seas, for whom
they had been named by the human settlers of this world; and the
charming "sea-dogs," little web-footed creatures like a cross between an otter and a sea lion. Sitting in the bow with her neck
craned eagerly forward, like a second figurehead, Ailia had happily
watched these and other wondrous creatures of the Arainian sea for
hours at a time.

But here, closer to shore, the waters were the green-blue of
turquoise. Flocks of trilling seabirds swarmed above them: the little
kingfisher-colored halcyons that were native to this ocean, and
built floating nests of seaweed upon its surface during the calm
spring months. In the shallows the sea grew transparent, and then

she could see through to floors of white sand, or the marvel of rainbow colors that was a barrier reef. For Arainia's riot of life did not end at the shore, but continued in another form, as sea-forests and fantastical gardens whose hues rivaled the brightest flowers on land: blazing scarlets, and purples and vermilions; delicate fans such as a court lady might carry, waving to and fro in the gentle currents, and groves of fluted columns crowned with plumes, and shapes like fanciful trees or stags' antlers. About the reefs swam fish of such exotic shapes and tints that they rivaled the corals themselves. Farther out in the bay islands rose, themselves formed of coral, but so thickly grown over with plant life that no trace of their foundations could be seen: they might have been solid mounds of vegetation. They clustered together, so close that their overhanging trees made green galleries above the narrow channels between them, and the leaping dolphins sported beneath a roof of leaves.

Each morning her mother had swum in the sea, it was said, joined by frolicking sea creatures. Elarainia had first been seen by the Elei coming up out of the waves, and the tale had been spun that she had not merely been bathing but had magically emerged from the sea fully formed, a goddess taking flesh to walk on land. Ailia stepped into the shallows. The water was warm as a footbath, the white sand smooth and yielding beneath her tired soles. This was the very womb of the mother-goddess, the source of all native life in her sphere. Another time Ailia might have dived into its clear sapphirine depths, to swim among the coral gardens and bright shoals of fish. But not today. A sense of urgency filled her. She looked up at the great comet again.

The battle of the comets was still being fought. Some the Wingwatch had sent sunward, and some they had pointed toward others yet held by the Valei—much as sailors might fire a captured ship and set it on course to strike another vessel of the enemy's fleet. But all of the turned comets had still to be defended, lest they be retaken by the firedrakes and aimed once more at Mera and Arainia. Thus each capture meant fewer warriors were available to guard the worlds themselves. Ailia wondered if this might not have been Valdur's plan. The one who had sent the comets flying toward the inner worlds had plotted their courses thousands of years ago; but that same power had surely known also that those worlds would have defenders. Had this celestial bombardment all been merely a grand bluff and distraction from the foe's true aim—not to destroy, but rather to invade and subjugate Mera and Arainia? And did Mandrake now follow that same plan, consciously or unconsciously doing Valdur's work? With her army fighting to deliver Mera, there were few soldiers left to protect her own world.

Only some great power, greater than army or Wingwatch, could come to Arainia's aid should an invasion occur. The apparition in Numia had spoken of Elarainia—had it meant that Ailia's mother indeed lived still, or had it referred to the planet itself and the strange enchantment that dwelled within it—that had helped Ailia to drive Mandrake away once before? She wondered if it was strong enough to repel an entire attacking force. She would not know until the attack took place.

The enemy may come soon, thought Ailia. *They must know I am here. But better that they find me here than in the city. The people there cannot defend themselves as well as the Elei.* She fancied there was a slight stress in the atmosphere, a hush of anticipation, as though the world itself was waiting for her to do something, perform some incantation. She felt that if she only knew the right spell, or the right action to take, Arainia's wealth of life and beauty would be saved from destruction.

She left the shore and began to walk inland, into the cool green groves of the forest that the Elei revered as the creation—more, the manifestation—of their goddess. Everything in it—the huge towering trees, the plants, the animals—was holy to them. There were many wondrous Arainian beasts in these groves: star-spotted pantheons, allocameli like donkey-eared dromedaries, the trogodryces whose antlers grow down rather than up, the argasills that resembled antelopes but for their long, toothy jaws, and boreynes with their curious fin-shaped dorsal humps and inward-curving horns. There were the beautiful bagwyns with their horselike manes and tails, and hoofed leucrottas with long badgerlike heads and ridges of sharp bone in place of teeth, and enfields like tall attenuated foxes, and the magnificent cats called calopuses, whose heads bore sweeping horns. There were many creatures unlike any the Merans had ever seen: the shaggy su, for instance, which carried its young on its back with its broad tail spread over them like a parasol. Most wonderful of all, though, were the giant aullays. In shape they were not unlike horses, though maneless and with tails shorter in proportion to their bodies; but from their upper jaws projected mighty curved tusks, and trunks that groped the canopy above them for food or restlessly winnowed the air. Ailia had read of these beasts in Meran bestiaries, and knew from the accounts (long dismissed by Merans as fable) that the aullay is as much larger than an elephant as the latter is larger than a sheep, but her first sight of the beasts years ago had still stolen her breath from her. There was no living thing in sight now, though, save for a dragonish-looking lizard that was basking on a mossy boulder. It was about the size of a croco-dile, and in any world but Arainia would probably have been a dan-gerous beast. Its scales were green, shading to blue on its back, and on its head was a reddish excrescence that shone in the sun like a jewel. It returned her gaze blankly, not stirring from its sun-warmed rock.

Ailia walked on. She yearned for the serenity this temple of trees brought to her Elei kin. Had her mother ever walked where Ailia now set her feet—or climbed the trees? In this forest it was possi-ble to traverse many leagues without ever setting foot to earth, so densely interwoven was the roof of boughs and attendant vines that roofed it. The upper tier of branches was a world unto itself, where birds as bright as flowers flew singing with sweet voices, and mimic dogs sprang like acrobats from tree to tree, clinging to the boughs with handlike paws. The Elei had added bridges and ladders of hempen rope and the occasional platform, rather like a hunter's "hide," for the use of those who harvested the sweet perindeus fruits and others that grew high in the canopy. Ailia had learned to walk the tree-ways, and though she dared not emulate the gymnastic feats of the Elei and the natural climbers, she found that she could get by quite well without needing to alter her form. For now, though, she was content to walk beneath the trees, in their cool scented shade. In addition to the many fruits, there were the trees from which grew the great hanging fleeces of cottony fibers that the Elei spun into thin white cloth for their garments. But the Fair-folk did not love only those trees that fed and clothed them. There were some that bore bright-hued and fragrant blossoms all the year, and there were groves of "singing trees" whose stiff leaves chimed one against the other in the slightest breeze to make a delicate music. Some of the trees bore leaves that were not green but crim-son, or blue or gold or purple, so that the tropical forests in places had an autumnal splendor of variegated hues, and the sun stream-

ing down through the foliage gave it the brilliant translucency of a
stained glass dome. Other trees brought forth what appeared to be
uncut gems: solidified globules of a saplike liquid that hardened
when extruded into the air. Each had a different-colored sap, so that
there were tree-rubies and tree-amethysts, and emeralds, and diamonds glittering among their boughs.

Walking through these jeweled jungles, Ailia thought of the
winter-dulled woods on the slopes of Selenna that would soon bear
their own glory of pale-tinted blossoms. Always her thoughts
turned back to Mera these days. And then, even as she brooded on
the fortunes of its people and of her army, a small shape darted
across her path—a gray-furred creature, familiar yet at the same
time unlooked for in this place. She blinked and halted, staring at
the stand of crimson bushes into which it disappeared.

*That's odd—for an instant I could have sworn it was Greymalkin! But I left
her behind in Maurainia. I'm just tired, that's all: seeing things that aren't there. It
is high time I rejoined the others.*

"THE ELEI HAVE BEEN WONDERFULLY welcoming," Lorelyn said to
Jomar. "They don't seem to understand that we're bringing danger
with us."

"Does this lot even know what danger means?" Jomar asked.

The interior of their guesthouse resembled a fine mansion, with
pillars and ceilings carved from a pale stone frosted with little white
crystals. Lamps suspended on chains shed a warm white-golden
light. The visitors walked down the glittering halls, many of them
frescoed with scenes of Elei history, or of gods cavorting with fabulous beasts. At least they had once been believed to be fabulous,
those hoofed and fishtailed hippocampi, and chimaeras, and the
like. But the Elei had shown their visitors a nearby cave in which
was preserved the fossil skeleton of a creature with a horned skull
and hoofed forelegs, tapering behind into an impossible fishtail in
place of hindquarters: a creature seemingly suited neither for land
nor sea. The singular outline of the beast was preserved in the form
of a shadowy film surrounding the bones. Another strange creature
had been found inside a cloven rock not far away, this one a serpent
with wings. No serpent of any kind lived in this world, and the
wings, attached by a keeled breastbone to the sinuous ribs, were
those of a bird: the impressions of feathers were still plain to be seen

in the stone. According to the Elei these lands, and the plains beyond Hyelanthia, had once formed the bed of a primeval sea. The inhabitants of that sea, and some winged beasts that had perished and fallen into its waters, had been entombed in the sands that later became solid stone. The fossil oddities could not be natural, but they were also too ancient to have been the work of any human sorcerer, and so through their mute witness the existence of the Old Ones was proven.

The guests passed on through a set of doors inlaid with gold, into an antechamber and then on through a doorless opening screened only by a curtain of vines. They emerged on the slope of a low green hill, one of a range that rolled about the feet of Hyelanthia: the city of the Elei. The Fairfolk did not want their houses to intrude upon the landscape, out of respect for the goddess. And so they had delved deep into the earth to make their dwellings, carving chambers from the living rock within and decorating them with the gems that they unearthed as they dug. At least the Hollow Hills would offer the Elei some protection against the assaults of the Valei, Jomar reflected. Apart from the great green mounds there were no other houses anywhere to be seen, nothing to provide an aerial assailant with a target.

Between the hills and the sea lay the forest. From its depths groups of Elei were returning from their daily harvest of fruit, root, and herb: a sweet smell as of incense came before them as they walked, for in addition to foodstuffs they had been gathering spices. An Arainian bird called the cinomologus lined its nest with these, and the gleaners had found an abundant store in a vast rookery high in the trees. They laughed and danced as they came, and their voices, deep and high, were raised in song. They were always singing, these pure-bred Elei: while they worked and while they played—as if music was to them like breath and blood, intrinsic to their very being. It was the heritage of angelic forebears, they declared, who continually praised the Divine. At the cavelike doorway of the largest hill several men and women in ankle-length white robes had gathered. They appeared to be waiting for someone—their returning kin, perhaps? There were Nemerei among them: Lorelyn could feel their power from here. Suddenly they all bowed and curtseyed deeply, and when she turned she saw Ailia coming toward them through the trees.

"Ailia! Hullo!" Lorelyn called, jumping up and down and waving. Ailia waved back.

Among the Elei stood a tall woman whose pale silver-gilt hair flowed back from a face fresh as a girl's and wise as a crone's. Ailia had nearly shattered protocol by curtseying when she first met Lady Jihana, so awed was she at the sight of this ageless, pure-bred Elei. Now the woman came to meet the Tryna Lia with a graceful flowing motion, and dipped her own shining head. "Highness, you honor us with your stay."

Ailia replied: "Lady Jihana, I thank you again for your hospitality. I believe you are one of the great Nemerei in this land?"

"I have command of magic, it is true. For the task to come, though, greater powers than mine are needed. I understand the enemies from Mera are expected to come here."

"They are. They may wish to claim your country as their own."

"And why should they not? If these Zimbourans desire land," said one of her household, a curly-headed youth who looked no more than sixteen, "there is plenty here to spare. I do not see the difficulty. We can share it with them."

"You do not know these people. They cannot content themselves with a little, as you do. They will take all, and leave you nothing." Thoughts of raped and pillaged Shurkana and Mohar filled Ailia's mind, and her voice shook a little as she spoke.

"But why?" the youth persisted.

"There is no *why*," Ailia said. "It is what they do to those they conquer."

"You mean," said one of his elders, "they are not, like us, beings of thought and reason."

"They are thinking beings," she answered, "but they do not think as you do. And they will bring with them the Morugei, who are children of Valdur and follow his ways."

"Perhaps, then, we can teach them all, and make them wiser." The fair youth turned to the others, who nodded in agreement.

Jomar leaned close to Ailia and spoke in a hissing whisper: "These people are doomed. *Doomed!*"

"No," she answered in a low voice as they took their leave of the lady and her retinue and walked off together among the green hills. "There is still hope, while there are Nemerei among them."

There was another power in this place too. It throbbed in her mind, a background noise as immense as the sound of the sea or the rushing flow of the wind. All sorcerers who came to this land experienced strange visions, like waking dreams. The Fairfolk claimed that the source of the enchantment was the goddess herself.

"The Elei told me they believe some Old Ones still live deep inside in the forest," Lorelyn remarked at length. "I don't think that can be true, but is there some sort of Archon magic that lingers here, do you think? I can feel—*something*—in the land, all around. So did Auron and Taleera: they went off to see if they could find its source."

"Yes, I feel it too. Look!" Ailia held her ring hand up. The star sapphire on her third finger blazed with light—not the light of the sun pooling in its blue deeps, but an unnatural radiance that came from within. "There *is* some power here. I have never seen the gem glow like this," she said.

Suddenly Jomar gave a startled exclamation.

"What is it?" asked Lorelyn.

"Oh, nothing—I'm just overtired, I think," said Jomar.

"But what made you yell?"

"Nothing—it's just that I thought I saw something. But I didn't."

"Are you certain?" asked Ailia.

"It can't have been what I thought it was. I was thinking of the Valei coming here, and what they might do to the Elei—whether they might make slaves of them. It got me to thinking about the days when I was a slave in the work camps, and how we always had to be on our guard for lions at nightfall. And as I was thinking that, I looked over there at the forest's edge and I thought I saw—"

"What?" Lorelyn asked, moving close to him.

"A lion. In the bushes—only it couldn't have been, not here. It must have been one of the Arainian animals. The light's beginning to fade, and it tricked my eyes."

Ailia looked thoughtful. "Perhaps not. It's like my seeing Greymalkin in the forest, just now. I was thinking of her, too."

"But that's what the Elei say!" Lorelyn exclaimed. "About the Archons: they say you can still summon them here. And that they can take any form. Remember, if you think hard enough about something that thought can go into the Ether. Maybe they can hear it—"

"We're all tired, that's all," said Jomar.

Ailia got up and walked in the direction he had indicated. "Was it here, Jomar?" she asked presently, standing beside a dense mass of undergrowth.

He followed. "Oh, for Valdur's sake. It was just my eyes playing tricks—"

And then his words died, at the sight of the huge paw prints pressed into the earth beneath the bushes.

"So I *did* see something, then! It wasn't just my imagination. An Arainian beast . . ." He squatted by the tracks. "That's strange. They *look* like lion prints."

"But they can't be," said Lorelyn. "Not in Arainia. It can't be a Meran lion. It must be an Archon, or something!"

"Let's follow them, Jomar, and see where they lead us," said Ailia.

"All right—but be on your guard, both of you."

"I will alter my form," said Ailia. "I have that power now." *Mandrake taught it to me,* she thought but did not add. "Perhaps I can follow the scent."

Ailia toppled slowly forward and put out her arms as if to break her fall. But when her hands touched the ground they were no longer hands. A huge lion stood there in her place, golden mane rippling over mighty shoulders, tail lashing. She—*he?* Jomar thought—turned and loped off, nose to ground, following the tracks.

They all walked alongside the prints for a short distance, but found that they ceased halfway across a clearing. The lion raised its shaggy head and snuffed the air.

"I don't understand it," said Jomar. "The ground isn't any different here, and the paw prints don't get shallower or anything. They just stop. As if the brute vanished into thin air."

Ailia changed back to her own form. "The scent just stops too. There's magic here, Jomar. I can feel it."

"But what's the point of it all?" asked Jomar, standing.

"It's almost as though our thoughts had some sort of influence here. We think of things, and then we see them. But whose is the sorcery? Not the Elei's: they wouldn't do such things without telling us." *Archons,* she thought. *It could be. The stories said they were shapeshifters. If my mother really was one, might there be others lingering in this place? Might she have returned?*

"I don't like this," said Jomar. "I think we'd better leave while we can."

"Just a little longer," said Ailia. "I feel as though we're *meant* to be here, somehow." She could scarcely contain her excitement now.

"All right," said Jomar. "Just don't anybody think about firedrakes or nuckelavees, that's all."

As they walked on, Ailia reached out with her extra sense, but could detect no danger here: only the same feeling of expectation, as though the whole planet held its breath. She reached out to the living world around her. *What is it?* She cried out silently. *Speak to me!*

A soft sound made her turn. She gasped, then made a quick gesture to the other two, pointing to the far side of the clearing.

A figure was walking there: a tall feminine form with long curling nut-brown hair. They could not see the face from where they stood: the woman was turned slightly away, looking into the forest. She was wound about with garlands of wildflowers, pink and white and red, and her slight green shift was patterned with them. A wreath sat upon her head like a crown. Ailia called out, but the woman did not answer or look their way. With a cry Ailia ran toward her. She turned at last, and the Princess saw a laughing girlish face. And then the figure was gone: she did not slip away into the woods, but vanished, as though she had never been. But when they approached the spring that bubbled from the earth where the woman had been standing, there was the print of a bare foot in its damp margin.

"Well," said Jomar, "was anyone thinking of *that?*"

Wordless, they shook their heads. Ailia thought of the face that had turned to her: it was not like a human face, nor yet an Elei's: it was at once knowing and innocent, wild yet benign. "A nymph," she said at length. "That's what it was. A nymph out of the old myths. They were a kind of Elemental: nereids and naiads, oreads and hamadryads."

"Were you thinking of them?" Lorleyn asked.

"No," Ailia replied. She stood for a moment thinking, then she called upon her power again and took a bird's form, a great golden eagle. Beating her wings, she soared up over the tops of the trees.

"I hate it when she does that," Jomar muttered. "*Is* she Ailia now, or a bird? I don't understand it."

"She's Ailia *and* a bird," Lorelyn replied. "You don't stop being *yourself* just because you change shape, Jo."

A hundred feet above them the eagle circled, drew in its wings, and dived. Just above the ground it changed its shape, and Ailia dropped the remaining distance to land light as a dancer on her toes. "No—there's nothing to be seen. No nymphs, no lions."

Jomar looked doubtful. "You might have missed them. The tree-canopy is thick."

"There are lots of gaps in the foliage. And an eagle's eyes are very keen, even in this dim light."

They walked back to the Hollow Hills together. The sun sank in the east, and the forests drowned in blue shadow. Lanterns bloomed like stars in the trees, twinkling on high boughs along the airy tree-paths to guide the last of the canopy-harvesters home, and lower down, to light the paths of the forest floor. These "lamps" were in fact vessels of sweet nectar that the Elei hung on chains from the branches. After dark each attracted its own little galaxy of pyral-lises, the four-legged fireflies of Arainia, and their compact, lumi-nous swarms served as beacons for wayfarers after dark. But on the heights of Hyelanthia an aureate glow still lingered, and the clouds about the goddess's plateau turned to lambent gold, making it look more than ever like a place of magic. Ailia's gaze kept returning to it. She could no longer endure its unsolved mystery, and as she looked at it a plan took shape in her thoughts.

I will try to see the past as I did in Numia, she decided, *even though I sup-pose I won't succeed here. No Nemerei has ever been able to glimpse Hyelanthia in its golden age: it's as though it's somehow forbidden. But I have to try. I might be allowed to see, to learn something—some power to aid us now . . .*

Parting company with her friends, she returned to her lodging for her warm clothes, then went to pluck a ripe fruit from a Tree of Life that grew near the foot of the Hollow Hill. Food-of-the-gods: perhaps its potent amber juices would vouchsafe her a vision. She placed it in the pouch at her side, and then climbed the hill's green slope to its summit. Auron lay there, coiled like a snake around the base of another tree, with his bearded chin resting on his tail. Taleera slept on a bough above, her head under her wing. "Will you fly me up to the heights, old friend?" Ailia asked the dragon. "I would like to attempt another vision of long ago. To see the gods, as they were, in their own land."

It has been tried before, he reminded her gently as he uncoiled himself.

"But not by me. Perhaps whatever has been preventing the other Nemerei will permit me to do this, if it will help me in my task? I must give it a try, at least."

Neither of them said any more, but an understanding that was not even mind-speech passed between them: the knowledge that Ailia's request was also a statement. She could now take a dragon's form and fly to the heights if she pleased, but chose not to, just as she had not taken draconic shape to flee Mera. She would not tempt herself with such power. Auron bowed his head to the ground—not merely to make it easier for her to mount; there was in the gesture a hint of the draconic obeisance. Drawing up the skirts of her robe, she scrambled onto his proffered neck, seating herself in the midst of his mane. Grabbing hold of his horns, she clung tightly as he crouched, then leaped skyward.

The ground dropped away with dizzying speed. Then the horizon tilted as he banked, gliding low over the land. Auron flew into the warm upward thrust of a thermal, and rose within the bubble of heated air in a slow circling climb, as though ascending a spiral stair. Before long they were level with the tablelands. Auron flew closer, until all the sky ahead was full of towering rock faces, sculpted by wind and erosion into vast numinous shapes. Far below, through rifts in the clouds, lay the roof of the great forest—like the coral-forests that grew upon the seabed. For this gulf of air *was* a sea, and the plateaux were islands: they rose above the cloud-layer as islands rise from the deeps, while waves of vapor broke upon their stony sides and were flung upward like sea spume. For a moment Ailia had a curious sensation, as though she were seeing the view from another's eyes. This realm of sky and soaring stone was the true world, it seemed to her, and what lay beneath the clouds merely a lowly, secondary realm, at whose very bottom humans and other creatures crawled about like crabs on the floor of an ocean, never knowing of the glorious spaces so far above them and beyond their ken . . . Auron soared higher—higher. The sky seemed to deepen above her—and, wondrously, more stars came shining through it.

The plateaux lay below now, amid the cloud-foam of the airy sea. Ailia looked down at gray rock, stark and still beneath the dark blue sky. Nothing lived here on the heights anymore, and the air was thin and cold: she was reminded of the desolate terrain of Mera's moon. Crystal glittered in the sun, forming grid patterns, interconnected oblongs and squares with here and there a lone, upright tower. Loose fragments lay strewn between them on the rock like broken glass: the foundations and rubble of fallen houses of the gods. Ruby towers, crystal pillars, ramparts and bridges like spun glass lay beneath her. These, then, were the buildings of the Archons, this world's original inhabitants. She studied the ruins with eager curiosity. But they revealed little of their makers—there were no statues or monuments to show what the builders had looked like. Some of the structures did not even seem to be proper buildings—glassy obelisks, hexagonal columns, globes, hemispheres, and pyramids that were solid right through. Most were made of gemstone or of adamant.

Auron flew low, then alighted on a spur of rock. The air here was hard to breathe, and Ailia had to alter the rhythm of her lungs. Before them lay a vast open space, paved with white stones in a circular pattern. A rounded column of clearest crystal reared up from its center. Ailia dismounted and stood looking about the place. Even had the Archons left images of themselves, she thought, would these have been of their *true* forms, or only shape-shifts they had assumed for their amusement?

Beyond the plaza of the column was a great oblong hall built of the same white stone. She made for it, and as she approached its high doorless entrance she gave an exclamation.

For a brief instant she thought they were alive: those tall, pale, slender figures enthroned amid the crystal columns. They had plumed wings, and slender hands resting upon their draped knees, and many wore diadems upon their long-haired heads. But all, crowned or not, had a lordly air. She felt that she had trespassed into some solemn council and shocked them all to silence with her uncouth intrusion—even though the passage of a few seconds had shown her that these were mere statues, not living beings as she had initially supposed. So here at last were images—and as she had expected, they were not true likenesses but only adopted shapes. The Seraphim, the Winged Ones, had delighted in combining the human and avian forms. She walked closer to the nearest figure. Like all the others it was seated on a raised throne, its wings spread to either side. These, and their implied ability to fly, seemed almost an extension of the exaltation that showed in the carved face. There was a curious atmosphere of expectancy in the great hall: the figures sat erect, heads raised as if listening, or awaiting something—some unknown event—with an ageless patience.

She went back outside to rejoin the dragon, who had not entered with her. "Auron, I feel I am closer to the Old Ones in this place, even if they are gone. I can't quite explain it: it is just a feeling. Thank you for bringing me here. And now—I will see whatever I am permitted to see."

She drew out the food-of-the-gods and bit into the smooth golden skin: and before she had consumed even half of the sweet flesh she began to feel the light-headedness that precedes an enchanted vision. She knelt down upon the cold stone and closed her eyes.

9

The Queen of the World

WHEN SHE OPENED HER EYES, Hyelanthia was enveloped in white.

A cloud had descended upon the plateau where she knelt. She could see no sign of Auron. Slowly she stood, and as she did so she realized that her form was ethereal: she could see and hear with perfect clarity, but there was no other sensation. She began to walk straight ahead, placing one phantom foot before the other, moving but feeling nothing beneath her feet. It was as if she walked through a thick fog, or as if she were wrapped in wool. From time to time some stirring of the upper air shifted the vaporous mass through which she advanced, and a pale pearly radiance tinted its whiteness. Or else she would look up, and suddenly through the blank space

above her she would catch a glimpse of the sky, with perhaps a scal-
loped edge of cumulus showing starkly white against its deep blue;
and then the gap above would close once more.

But presently she was aware of a looming darkness ahead that
shaped itself into trees: a stand of tall leafy trees that showed gray
through the white shroud. Then the air moved again, and the
whiteness turned to the thinnest of sheer curtains, and was all
blown away, and she found herself looking on the ancient past.
Upon the once barren summits great forests reared, all wreathed
about with the clouds that passed over and through their close-
growing boles. The nearer groves were green as an emerald's heart
within, but the cloud-vapor that streamed through them like mist
veiled the further parts in shades of pale gray. Through the arches
and oriels formed by the winding boughs and billows of foliage, she
glimpsed far-off spaces with still more branches and leafy masses,
nebulous and dim. Her desire had been granted: she had been
vouchsafed a vision out of the far-off past. This was the gods' own
country, part heaven and part earth. Here the winged people
dwelled, and the Trees of Life grew. Perhaps one of the pale blossoms starring the green boughs was the very same that was prisoned
within the Elei's amber globe . . .

Ailia sent her ethereal form forward, through the trees. Here in
the steep forests among the clouds many wondrous creatures lived,
unlike any in the world below. A large bird perched on a high
bough, a mere silhouette in the gray mist like a shadow projected
on a screen: but it was no bird, despite its feathered wings and tail,
for when it turned its head its profile was that of a lioness. After a
time she came upon a large body of water, wider than any mountain tarn: almost a little sea. The trees grew down to its edge, and
its surface was smooth and tranquil. As she looked down into its
depths, she saw the sky repeated there, its dome inverted. Across its
reflection went a blur of white, too swift for cloud, and with a shape
out of the oldest tales: a horse with wings. She glanced up at the
real sky with a gasp. There was the winged steed: as she watched,
it descended, its legs unfolding, reaching down for the earth. It flew
low over the placid lake, so low that it approached its mirrored
image, and she thought for a moment that it would settle on the
water like a swan. But it flew on toward shore, touched the ground—
was for a moment cantering, its wing beats matched to its beating

hooves. Then it halted, snorted, arching its neck and furling its long white pinions against its flanks. No earthly steed ever matched this creature for beauty, even the faerie mounts of the Elei: it was like a poet's dream of a horse.

As the sky-horse stooped to drink at the mere's edge a ripple spread in wide circles far out on its surface. A woman's head rose up, her fair hair floating about her. Then she dived, showing a bare white back and shoulders—and where her legs should have been, a long glistening green tail. It was scaled and finned and shaped rather like a fish's, only the tail fin that slapped the surface as it went under was horizontal, like the flukes of a whale. A daughter of the undines, perhaps—or was this lake home to the water Elementals themselves? In this long-ago time the mer-folk might not yet have come to be. Or, for that matter, human beings, or horses. These could be eidolons summoned out of the Ether; or creations of the Old Ones, living dreams of what would one day be.

She longed to stop and ponder these marvels, but she made herself journey on. At last the trees thinned, and the clouds gave way, and looking over the cliff to her right she saw far below her the rolling waves of the long-vanished ocean, where in her time forests and green plains spread. Ahead of her towers reared up out of the whirling whiteness, pale and pellucid as though carved of quartz: cupolas and minarets, with multifoliate windows of many-colored glass like great luminous flowers. She had come to the city that she had seen from Auron's back. There were the strange spheres and obelisks of precious stone: and they glimmered now, not like venudor with its strong steady radiance, but with lights that came and went, and danced and flickered as if alive. She was reminded of the glow she had seen within her star sapphire ring.

But her attention quickly shifted to the glorious beings in the city's white streets. They were as beautiful as Elei, but very much taller, and wonderful to see. For they were seraphim: each had a pair of wings feathered like a bird's, white or bronze or golden, crimson or peacock-colored, and they were robed in loose garments of many hues that fell from their shoulders in long and flowing folds. A few wore garlands upon their heads, of leaves or flowers. Some looked like women and some like men, but many had a hermaphrodite appearance, as though in assuming their forms they had not troubled themselves to choose one gender or the other. Shapeshifters beyond a doubt: though they all seemed to be young, the wisdom of countless ages showed in their eyes. The auras of many were visible, flickering about them like flames and crowning their heads with light.

Some of the seraphim went about on foot, while others flew overhead on their great pinions. There were many cherubim here also, of all kinds: one was unlike any that she had never seen before, with the face of a man whose kingly beard blended into its lion's mane. All around the otherworldly beings their city shone like diamond and ivory, its gleaming courts and towers half-enfolded in streaming clouds. It was a vision from the very morning of the world, when the oldest of all races reigned and took what forms they pleased. Tears rose in her eyes. She had seen many images of angels in books and in temples since her childhood, but *these* were no mere likenesses in paint and paper and stone. They were alive, although their forms were crafted by sorcery: the Archons had molded living flesh as others carved wood or stone. Yet theirs was a beauty like that of the flower in amber: unchanging loveliness that could never fade because it was outside the dominion of time.

The Archons paid no heed to her. They were of this age, and she was not. With an effort she turned her attention back to the city. At the far end of the plateau a palace stood, its towers rising gracefully into the air, its crystal walls many times higher than those of her own palace of Halmirion. At its entrance were luminous pillars of white venudor. She walked slowly toward the exquisite structure, half-expecting it to melt away into nothingness as she approached, or else retreat like a rainbow or a mirage. But it stayed in place, and soon she could glimpse through the doors that were thrown back invitingly a softly glowing interior like that of the moon Archon's palace in Numia.

She passed the threshold, and stood within the entrance hall. A sweeping staircase climbed upward, and she ascended it slowly, drifting like a dreamer. She emerged at its top into a great hall, its ceiling of carved and gilded marble high above her head. She kept thinking that she saw figures out of the corner of her eye, but when she turned there was never anyone there. She also thought she heard voices, but they were indistinct and never came any nearer. *It reminds me of the Ethereal Plane,* Ailia thought. *It has the same feel to it some-*

how: real and yet not real. Is this truly Arainia in olden days? Or have I left the world behind altogether, and entered the Ether?

A new sound intruded on her consciousness—a familiar sound, so strange in this setting that she spun around. There in the corridor stood a little gray shape. As she stared at it, the cat mewed again loudly.

"Greymalkin?"

The gray cat turned and trotted away, and Ailia saw that it was semitransparent, as if like her it was not quite there. She made haste to follow it. The cat darted up another winding staircase and then strolled toward an open doorway, out of which a warm light flowed, flickering. Ailia stood still upon the landing.

"What are you really? You're a projection too, aren't you?" she asked the cat, who was now sitting and waiting for her in the doorway. "Are you an eidolon?"

The cat blinked its emerald eyes, and answered within her mind. *Whatever that may be,* it replied enigmatically.

"But why do you take that shape in particular?" Ailia asked. "The shape of Ana's cat? To show me that you're a friend of hers, and are on her side? Or is it merely a form you chose at random from my past?"

The cat yawned. *You ask many questions,* it said, closing its eyes. *All of them the wrong ones.*

"I don't understand."

The cat opened its eyes again. *There—that is better! To admit you do not understand is the first step toward understanding.*

"But—"

Your mind is like a cluttered room—full of things you do not need. Empty it, clear it, be still inside like a cat lying in the sun.

"Empty my mind?" repeated Ailia. "Can that be wisdom?"

No. But it is the beginning of wisdom. The cat rose and walked sedately away from her, its tail in the air. *You cannot fill up a vessel that is already full, can you? If you would be filled, then empty yourself. But know that I am no mere image. I was with Eliana in Mera and in Arainia.*

"Greymalkin!" she cried. The cat turned, and fixed her with its unwinking eyes. "I thought it was Ana's idea of a jest, to say you were her familiar. Her demon servant. But that is what you are, aren't you: a good demon, a faerie, a spirit."

Power radiated from the small animal, a pulsating aura. *I am,* it said. *At least, I am that which your people would call by such names, though I would not myself use them.* The tone was amused, tolerant. *I have been a dragon, and a hobgoblin, and a sphinx dreaming on the sands. I have been an eagle flying through the clouds and a glowworm glimmering through the night, and a salmon swimming in the ocean deeps.* The cat curled its tail around its feet. *I have been master and jester, hermit and dancing maiden. I have been many things, Princess. And it was I who comforted you in the cave.*

"But why in this form?" she persisted, puzzled. "When you could take any other, even a human form? Why did you choose to appear as a cat in Mera?"

Because I wished only to observe, not interfere.

"Are there many like you in the Ether? Did the Archons really go there, do you know—or did they all die out, as some say?" she asked.

The gray cat yawned again. *Keep asking questions. One day you will ask the right ones, and get the right answers.*

"You really are an infuriating creature," said Ailia with a rueful smile.

Then she heard her name being called, in a woman's clear and melodic voice. Turning, she saw another ethereal form ascending the stairs: a woman cloaked in green. Her face was young, but her long hair was white as snow. As Ailia gazed on her, the woman's appearance changed: she became small and shrunken, old and stooped.

"Ana!" Ailia gasped. "Ana!"

The old woman smiled. Like a damascene fabric whose pattern changes in different lights and angles, her form shifted from old back to young again. She stood tall and slender now, pale hair streaming down her back, her beautiful face solemn. "There is so much danger ahead, my dear Ailia. But I am with you still."

"Ana, I thought you were dead!" Ailia ran to her. "You were in the Ether all this time? But what must I do now? Tell me!"

"My dear child, it is not for me to say. The answers that you seek are there, in that room." She pointed. "Go in. You are expected."

She vanished, and the cat with her. Left alone, Ailia hesitated for a moment; then she entered the illuminated room. It was a large white-walled chamber, decorated with jeweled mosaics. On a marble hearth a fire burned, casting its glow on the walls, while lamps like enormous pearls in wall brackets added their pale steady light.

But her eyes were on the woman seated by the window. She was slender and tall, clad in a mantle of blue worked with silver stars, and a white robe with long trailing sleeves. Her unbound hair flowed in a cataract of molten gold about her, like a second mantle: a light played upon it that did not come from fire or lamps. On her head was a circlet of silver. Fresh and fair as her face was, it was still not the face of a young girl. Beyond its serenity other things could be glimpsed, in the deep eyes and upon the pale brow. Sorrow, and gravity, but also joy and love. It was the face of a divinity, and yet still Ailia saw something of herself there.

Her breath caught in her throat as she recognized the woman. "Mother," she said.

Elarainia held out her hands. In one bound Ailia crossed the intervening space and was on her knees before her mother's chair, reaching up with imploring hands, half-fearing that the glorious figure would fade away . . . But the knees in the soft folds of the white gown were solid and real as she laid her cheek to them, and the hands that stroked her hair were firm and gentle and alive.

"My daughter," said the soft voice.

Ailia lifted her tear-streaked face. The eyes looking down into hers reminded her of her star sapphire ring: the irises were a pure, clear blue, with pale rays surrounding the pupils. "Oh, Mother, how? How can you be here? Are you alive, or are you a spirit?"

"I am and always was a spirit. I was a woman in your world for a time, and then I returned. Do you not see, daughter? I have never belonged to the mortal plane."

Ailia looked up into the young-old face, and understanding flashed through her. Angel—goddess—spirit: the words flickered through her mind. "You were never human, is that what you are saying? You are—something else. An Archon, you are an Archon. But then you can help me, for I came to find the Archons—"

"The Archons are here. The angels, the gods, the fairies, the eidolons—the El. All of these are Archons. For the Old Ones are not what you have thought: a mortal race, like the dragons or humanity. Spirit and not matter is our true nature. We did indeed remove to the Ether, but we also came *from* it long ago, entering the worlds of matter—and so legend says that we forsook Heaven. But though we have intervened in your history—even loved and taken mates from among mortals—our true home is the realm of quintessence, and to it we all must return."

Ailia murmured, "My mother is an Archon. My mother is—"

"A goddess?" said Elarainia softly. "Some still call us by such names, even now."

"Then—what am I?" Ailia whispered. "Am I not human?"

"What do you call human? You hunger for life and knowledge and love. Is this not what it is to be human?"

"Return with me, Mother!" pleaded Ailia. "Come back to the mortal plane! Elnumia sent me to seek you. I need your help—the war—"

"The Archons will not go to war again," her mother replied. "We cannot force the mortal creatures to live as we wish them to. However it may hurt us to see them suffer as a consequence, we must let them be. But I will be with you in spirit. Indeed I have never been far from you, child. But once before we warred among the worlds, and your cosmos was nearly destroyed. You were born to lead that fight in our place: a child both Archon and human. It was through my aid that you summoned the power of this world before, and you can do so again. For I am the Archon of Arainia, its world-spirit. Not its ruler: rather, I *am* Arainia—it is to me as your body is to your spirit. Once I took a mortal form, when I loved the man who is your father—for he had called upon the goddess many times in his life. But I could not have stayed long in that form. I yearned for the Ether, and my world needed me." She paused. "To the high El, the Elyra, the bright-burning stars are the purest things in the Lesser Heaven, and the planets mere dross. But we Elaia loved the planetary bodies, with their lakes and seas, their earth and air. We played on the winds and reveled in the waters, and marveled at the stones and the soil. Best of all we loved the gems, for their inward structure of latticework recalls to us the pure harmonies of Heaven. You saw the solid domes and spires of diamond and ruby and emerald, there on the plateau? To us they are like mansions, or rather refuges: for the Elaia desired at times to cast off their fleshly forms, be disembodied, and enter the gem-lattices as pure quintessence in order to know peace again. For that reason we made the Star Stone, a perfect crystal: it has so flawless a form that even the highest among the El are drawn to its depths.

"It was an old conundrum of theologians, was it not: how many angels may gather upon a mote of dust? But within that small gem innumerable hosts are housed. When you bear it, you hold in your hands a little Heaven. The light that burns within it is quintessence, the sign of our presence. The bird of fire, the Elmir, is our symbol: we send it forth from time to time as a token. For the Elmir, in the old tales, is made up of many birds flying together as one. So it is with the El. We were not always many and apart, but are like rays broken from a single light: the Source of all things. Before the treachery of Modrian and those who follow him, we were undivided.

"But even when our radiance does not shine forth from the Stone, it is still a potent thing. For it is more than a magical gem: it is the emblem of the One, the oldest and greatest of powers, by which all things were made—the El included. The Power that dwells in the Empyrean, beyond matter and Ether: the High Heaven that existed before either of the lower Heavens came to be. It was for this reason that the Elaia crafted the Star Stone in a far-off world long ages ago: as an act of worship, and a reminder of the beauty of the One that lies in all things. For as the Stone's many facets gather the pure light of the sun and render it in rainbow hues, so is the creation a manifestation of its divine source. Every star, every tree, every pool, every cloud, every flower, every living beast and being that ever was—all these things are true expressions of the One Power, for it is infinite. Beauty, purity, strength, love: all come of it. But the creation is not itself perfect. Being mere matter shaped from chaos, it contains also the lower things: pain, and cruelty, and sorrow. That is why its symbol is the Vormir, the devouring serpent. It is not evil in itself: it merely is. But it conceals, by its very nature, the higher truth. That truth comes to the mortals of the material plane as if filtered through many obscuring veils, so that at times the good seems lost, or merely a part of the chaos that masks it.

"But that is not true of the Star Stone. It is pure, and has no flaw: a reminder to all who behold it of their origins outside time, and the One they can no longer see."

"I understand," said Ailia. "But the magi of Arainia believe that I must wield the Stone somehow, to conquer Valdur. What is the Stone's power, Mother, and how must I work it?"

"The Stone is not a weapon, child: it is your protection. When you wear or carry it the El are with you, and no evil can touch your mind. It has no power to affect the material plane, nor can it save your mortal frame from being destroyed. Its only power is that which it wields over your heart and soul: a reminder to you—and all mortals—of the pure and sacred realm from which your spirits came, and to which that part of you still belongs. Do not lay it aside, even for a moment! Valdur desires to take this consolation from you and from all mortal-kind, and bind it to his own brow once more as a trophy of your defeat and ours—for he has not the power to destroy it. And its benign influence no longer affects him: his heart is hardened against it."

Ailia sat with eyes cast down for a time, absorbing all these things. At last she said, without glancing up: "Why did the El leave the mortals, if they were at the mercy of matter? Why did you not stay to help, and instruct them as before?"

"The Elaia had to leave this plane, Ailia. We were becoming too drawn into its affairs. There were Valdur's followers, of course, taking and using as they pleased, seizing worlds for themselves and enslaving their peoples. But the truth is that all the El were growing too attached to this realm, and to the mortals themselves. Especially we Elaia, the El who love matter. There was too much interference with the living creatures—under our reign they could not *grow*. Now we manifest only when asked to by a mortal, and only when all the El are in agreement that it is both right and necessary. I could come, you see, because the Elei summoned me. I could not have come on my own. That is the way the Pact works—it can be broken only at the invitation of a mortal. We cannot call to them—they must call to us first, and then we may answer.

"If any of us should choose to dwell for a time in the Lesser Heaven now, then that Archon must take on mortal form. And if we should wish to remain there, then we must become mortal in truth, and know death. For this plane is now to be for mortals only: our claim on it is ended."

"Ana—she is one of you?"

"She is. Eliana is the Archon of Mera—Elmera, as she was once called—and Greymalkin is one of the many minor Elaia spirits that serve her. She took a cat's form long ago for her material incarnation, but she has taken many others."

"So she said." A shadow touched Ailia's heart then, and she looked up. "And you say Valdur is an Archon too."

"Valdur was lord of the Elyra, the high Archons. After our war he was imprisoned within his own sphere, a self-consuming black star. Athariel, the great Elyra whom you call the Archangel, fought him in the upper air of Mera many eons ago, and struck the Star Stone from his diadem. Valdur fled then, forsaking his seraph form for that of a mighty dragon, while the Elyra pursued him across the Great Night. From star to star they sped, and world to world, until at last the Dark One retreated to his own celestial domain. There Athariel fought him one last time, and cast him into the depths of his black star. There is no escaping such a place: it is a void within the void, devouring light and matter. He cannot ever leave Vartara—the Pit, as you call it—either as quintessence or in material form. But his thoughts can still enter the Ether, and the minds of mortals. And he has many servants who are his limbs and tools in Talmirennia, while we are bound by the Pact we created and swore to uphold." The goddess's voice was low and sad. "It is not for us to intervene, even now."

"And yet I am allowed?"

"You asked me long ago, since we cannot descend in strength to save their worlds, if there was no other way to save mortals. Do you remember?"

"Remember?" Ailia frowned, searching her thoughts. "Now that you say it—yes, I *do* recall saying something of the kind, once. But when was it? Where?"

"It was here—in Hyelanthia. In this old city, long ago. It was then, as we stood together, that you asked me that question. And do you remember how I answered?"

She rose and went to the window and Ailia followed her. Evening had fallen, and Hyelanthia's many towers gleamed amid the wisps of cloud, as though they floated on air—all blue-silver under the light of Arch and moon. Ailia saw a slim and graceful form on the stone terrace below, looking out over the sea of clouds: it was her mother, or one as much like her as to be her twin. But this figure had wings of white edged with gold, and she was much taller. Her fair flowing hair bore a chaplet of lilylike flowers, and her gown was white. At her side stood another form, but this one was insubstantial as an ethereal projection: a wavering woman-form with just a hint of wings, like a pale reflection of the goddess at whose side she stood.

"You and I," said her mother in her ear as she watched. "This is a scene from long ago that you see, from a time before you learned to take a material form."

"I remember now," Ailia whispered. "When I asked my question you said to me, 'There is one way, but that I would not have you take—'"

Elarainia finished. "'For it is doubtful, and hard, and fraught with many dangers.' Yes, I said that. But still you were resolved."

"So—I *chose* my role." Ailia was filled with wonderment.

"Yes. In that time you were very curious about the human race, for you had no living things in your moon-sphere then. Nor had I any humans yet in my world."

"My sphere." *Her* moon, her own sphere of Miria, shining high above . . .

"We are El, you and I, and El are drawn to the things of the material plane. In particular we love shapes that are perfect, and spheres are the most perfect shapes in nature. There are here few circles or straight lines or cubes such as we conceived in our minds when we were in the Ether. And so we were attracted to suns and moons and planets for their shape, and sent our power across the Ether to fill them.

"You were fascinated by the little moon that came to be called Miria, and because it is near to my planetary sphere you and I became close. Mortals would later call us 'mother' and 'daughter.' And so we indeed came to be later, when you agreed to be born human. But before then it was but a manner of speaking. You were my celestial handmaiden as Elnumia is Elmera's."

Ailia stared down as the pale apparition of herself spoke, gesturing with a transparent arm at the moon. "It is strange to see it thus," Elmiria said, "as a thing separate and distant, and not a part of myself. Still, I would know more of this plane."

The winged goddess answered, her voice the same as the woman Elarainia's and yet not the same. "If you would move among mortals, in their worlds, then you must first become as they are. You must be born."

Ailia and Elarainia watched their own images from long ago in silence. Then her mother laid a hand on Ailia's shoulder, and spoke to her. "This was the task. Of all the Archons you alone were willing. Your chosen celestial sphere was small and would not suffer for your absence. You offered to be made flesh. And out of my love for you I chose then to be your mother in the material realm, having found for you a mortal father both kindhearted and willing to call on my name.

"You did not go alone, however."

"I didn't?"

"Long ago I brought you two companions from the mortal realm to dwell with you in the Ether, since you were so interested in humankind. One was an infant born to a mortal man and an Elaia who had taken human form. The Lady of the Grove—for so the humans called her—dwelled in the material world from choice, for she was not yet ready to forsake Mera and those who had called on her there. But in those days many feared the Old Ones, and they warned of the perilous faerie woman of Selenna who would cast her spell on any mortal who entered her domain. There was one who had no such fear, however, being of the Elei blood; and he made many pilgrimages to the Mistmount to pay homage to the powers that lingered there. The man was a knight who lived in Maurainia during the time of the Interregnum, and he desired to restore the order of the Paladins after it was dissolved by the theocracy. He continued to wear his armor, in defiance of the clerics' edict, and he rode about the countryside giving aid to all who called upon him. But he was captured, and tried and executed: the last of the Paladins. Elthina grieved for him, and in bitterness she forsook the mortal world. And she brought her infant son with her into the Ether, and gave him to me."

"Elthina! Damion's mother!"

"Even so. I took the child, and he grew in wisdom, living among the Archons as one of us. But because he was half-mortal, he could not stay with us on the Ethereal Plane. Only when the priest of Valdur struck him with the sacrificial knife, ending his mortal life, did he return to us. We bore him away into the Ether and translated his body, and in the Ether he must remain. For he is fully an Archon now, his human side taken away.

"As for your other companion, she was a child whose Rialainish mother was murdered after the Disaster by her kinsfolk, for consorting with a demon—as they believed. Her lover was, in truth, an Elaia in man's form. He too called upon me to take his mortal child, who was then but two years old, lest she suffer the fate of her mother. And she too was translated to the plane of the Ether, and you delighted in her company and Damion's. When you chose your mission to the mortals, they both swore to return to the material plane to be your protectors. But they had to return to the world in which they had been born, and to the age they were when they were taken from thence: to be helpless infants once more. That is why Lorelyn was aware of her Purpose, and Damion was not: she entered the Ether at an age when children are first growing aware of their world, and then she reentered the plane of matter at that same age. And so she was able to recall just a little of her existence here—just enough to remember that she had an important mission, a reason for her return. But she knew no more than that: the rest was lost to her child mind. And Damion, who left and then reentered the material realm as a mere babe, could remember nothing at all of his ethereal sojourn nor the mission he had sworn to undertake. The mind of a babe cannot hold such things. When you were born you were the same: you knew nothing of your former life upon the higher plane.

"Damion was sent to the Faerie Cave on Mount Selenna, to be cared for by Eliana Elmera, who yet remained in material form in her world because the Nemerei there had summoned her. And Lorelyn was sent to the Isle of Jana, not far from the resting place of the Scroll of Bereborn.

"And then you were born, Ailia! Ah, I can never forget that day when I knew *two* hearts beat within me, and felt you grow strong and begin to move! What a joy it was, to feel life for the first time as a mortal mother feels it!" She smiled, remembering, then turned grave once more. "I fled with you at last, knowing our enemies sought you to take your earthly life from you. I had surrendered the power to move between worlds at will, and the Gate of Earth and Heaven was closed for the safety of the mortals. So I crafted a winged vessel for myself, such as the Elei made in olden days, and hid it away until the time should come when I had need of it. But the firedrakes and soldiery of Valdur pursued me into Mera, and there I had to leave you, drawing my foes after me, retreating at last into the ethereal plane. For I could not remain in the mortal realm: my chief task there was done. And now you are grown, and need me no longer."

"I so longed to stay with my foster family in Mauraina, Mother!

To be one of them again. I thought then I needed them as a refuge, but I suppose I also remembered my desire to be a mortal in the mortal world. They were everything that I wished to be. But now what must I do?" Ailia asked.

"That I cannot tell you," replied Elarainia, stroking her daughter's face. "Oh, how I have longed to touch you like this! It is not permitted that I should direct you on your path, for demigoddess though you be, you are now half-mortal, and so by the Pact I may not interfere. But come with me now, my daughter, and be at peace for a little while . . ."

IN THE END AILIA SPENT a long idyll with her mother, for no time would elapse in her own day and age. They entered the undying worlds of the Ether and walked them together. And her mother spoke to her of the Archons' plans, that she herself had long forgotten.

"The Elei call upon Archons and live among us, but do not ask anything of us," Elarainia said. "And that is why we linger in the great forest. But we cannot remain there forever. And the Elei will vanish over time, as fewer Archons mate with humans: their descendants will wed Merei instead, losing their powers. That much of what Mandrake told you was true: they are a doomed race. In the end they will be merely a memory—but a memory that endures, of what a human being *can* be. This is what we intended."

Ailia listened, never speaking or straying from her mother's side. There was no sky in this ethereal country where they walked: instead the pure quintessence glowed above them like a golden mist. Within it soared flights of unnumbered seraphim, their forms illuminated by the radiance above them—like flying insects that, caught in a sunbeam, appear bright as sparks of fire. And even as she gazed on them Ailia saw them all come together, drawing into a tight swarm that assumed a distinct shape: a gigantic fiery bird. Its eyes blazed like stars, its wings and the feathers of its tail were like the plumes of flame that rise from the surface of a sun. It sang with one voice as it flew, like a choir in unison.

The Elmir. The One-Who-Is-Many.

"Before the material plane was fully formed," her mother said to her, "it was all of one substance, like the Ether. Within it lay the stuff of everything that would come to be: stars, planets, living creatures, lifeless stone, water and air, all the natural laws that govern them, even time itself. But as yet this stuff was all of a kind, uniform, unvarying. We who had awakened within the Ether looked on this new thing that had been wrought, and thought it good. But it was only the beginning. The balance had to be broken, the harmony altered, the primal unity turned to division, in order to bring forth many different things."

The celestial music changed: from a single divine melody it split into many different parts, a pattern intricate as a fugue. Another eidolon appeared in the sky, a dark green shadow winding sinuous coils about the Elmir's body. Ailia recognized the figure of the Vormir as she had seen it so often portrayed in art, combining with the figure of the Elmir to form the ancient symbol of the *Elvoron*. The divine bird and the earthly serpent were at enmity, it seemed to her at first. But presently it became apparent that what looked like a battle was more like a dance: the two figures were so evenly matched that they created a balance. Spirit and matter were as one. "But different as these things might seem," Elarainia continued, "beasts and beings, trees and rivers, mountains and clouds, shining suns and dark voids—all come of the first Substance. Every thing is connected to every other thing by that common origin—yes, even the Ether, for the lower plane was formed out of quintessence. Only Valdur would set himself apart, deny the bond that goes back to the Beginning. And because he cannot destroy the realm of Spirit, he has turned upon the realm of the Vormir, altered and distorted matter to his purposes, tormented its poor creatures—knowing that this causes still greater hurt to the El."

The music shattered into a jarring discord. The shape of the serpent changed: it became more monstrous, darker, grew fierce fangs and clawed legs. It tore at the form of the celestial bird, and even bit at its own coils in its madness. Ailia cried out in horror. At last the two struggling figures faded from her sight. Now as she gazed upward she seemed to see a light within the glowing quintessence above, a brightening at its zenith like a sun in a sky, which made the rest seem dim by comparison. But there was a blot upon the light, a cone of shadow cast by some obstruction near its center. Little motes of living light were circling about the central luminosity, but all that passed within the obscuring penumbra were darkened and consumed.

"He would cast his taint over all things. But it cannot ever be truly as he desires," Elarainia said. "For all are One: that unity stems from the Beginning, and what was cannot ever be altered."

Then all the things around them faded: the illusions and eidolons and semblances of material forms were gone, melted back into quintessence once more. And Ailia too felt herself at one with the surging power of the Ether, like a bird gliding on the wind's back, or a dolphin that rides upon a wave: she became a part of what surrounded her, of the light and the bliss, joining her voice to the countless others that were once more raised in perfect unison.

Sometime later—days or centuries, she could not have said— Ailia found herself alone in an ethereal landscape, without knowing how she had come there. Music flowed from somewhere—was it a harp, perhaps? She followed it, into a garden where fountains played amid billows of flowers. The music came from here—many seraphim had gathered together, and some other curious figures. All had human bodies, but one had six arms branching from his torso, while another had the figure of a woman but the head of a tawny-furred cat. At her sandaled feet crouched a creature with the jaws of a crocodile, the mane and foreparts of a lion, and the squat hindquarters of a hippopotamus. It rubbed its scaly muzzle against her knee and she stroked it absently, as one might a pet dog. Another being stood apart from the rest, a faint ethereal figure clad in flowing robes with just the hint of white wings rising in graceful arches from its shoulders: like her own ancient, semicorporeal self, only this figure had a masculine form. As she watched, the being began to sing softly:

> The crown jewel of the god of Night
> Was from him wrested long ago,
> And fell upon a hallowed height
> All mantled round with ageless snow.
> In that same land a fair folk dwelt,
> Who saw from far the radiance bright
> Descend upon the mountain-spire,
> As though a star did there alight.
> In wonderment they journeyed forth,
> And to that summit high and cold
> Climbed up, and knelt before the Stone,
> And raised a temple roofed with gold.

But fate o'ertook that elder folk:
They passed away, and now their prize,
The light divine, in chamber deep
Lies hid beneath the circling skies.
The stars above with sleepless eye
Watch o'er that temple, for the rule
Of all their bright celestial realm
Lies with the hand shall claim the jewel.
A prince of Night, and moon-maid pure
Who shall depart her orbéd throne
Shall war for it; and one shall fall,
And one take Heaven with the Stone.

As Ailia listened, she wondered whether the seraph's song might be an old one—or did the Stone indeed still lie on Elendor, while she had not yet been born mortal; was it the ancient past, or present, or future through which she now moved? *None of these*, she told herself. The Ether was outside of time, and a spirit was bound to no age of the mortal realm.

She gazed long at the scene; and presently the music ceased, and the El began to disperse through the garden. The ethereal figure too turned away, his bowed head coming up so that she saw his face. She stood motionless. The figure's radiance drained from it, and the glory of the wings became a luminous mist upon the air, vanishing away; what remained was a human form.

Ailia gave a cry and started forward. "Damion! *Damion!*"

But he did not seem to hear, nor see her. And then the whole of the scene faded from her sight, along with the ethereal realm. Someone was calling her name repeatedly, and shaking her by the shoulder. The voice was Lorelyn's.

"Ailia! Ailia, wake up: the enemy has come!"

10

The War of the Wood

SO THIS IS THE TRYNA Lia's own sphere, Syndra thought as she passed through the ethereal rift into the air of Miria. She had never before entered the moon-world, for the Nemerei of Arainia had not yet learned to use the dragon-ways when she dwelt there. Blue fields and isolated groves of lunar trees stretched beneath her: behind her the tall white pillars of the dragon-gate marked the rift, and on a hill beyond rose the white towers of the empty Moon Palace. *I feel no Power in this place: no immanent presence. Is it true, then, that its world-spirit has left it, and is incarnate in Ailia Elmiria? That her mother is in truth the Archon of Arainia?* Her gaze shifted to the ringed world that shone in the blue-black sky above. She had persuaded herself at first that the Tryna Lia and her mother were charlatans, and made this her argument for opposing them. But now she acknowledged the kernel of thwarted ambition deep within her as the true source of her fury and hate. Ambition, and wounded pride, and envy: these had led her on the road that parted her from the world of her birth. For a moment she felt a faint twinge of yearning for the blue orb above her, the sorrow of the exile. Almost it seemed that the planet called to her. But she warded off these thoughts by reminding herself that she was a traitor to its people now. They would surely punish her severely if she were to surrender. And as for the Archon and her half-mortal daughter—what welcome would they give to the Nemerei magus who had repudiated them, and schemed for Ailia's destruction?

No matter. I have aligned myself with greater powers than theirs. . . .

She spied the transformed Mandrake coiled upon a knoll below, with Torok and some of their other allies, and she began a long circling descent through the air. She traveled, as was her fashion now, in a chariot drawn by wyverns. She wished to soar through the sky as dragons did, so that she might look down from a godlike height upon the lands and peoples below. But she had not yet mastered shape-shifting, that most difficult of skills, and she would not consent to ride upon the back of a Loänan. She must fly by her own power, and no one else's; and since the dragon-form was denied her, she had found her own way to ride the wind. The chariot was in fact a sort of wheelless gondola that hung on two mighty chains from the harnesses of the winged reptiles, dangling beneath and between them as they flew side by side. Indeed, it took no small amount of sorcery to command the fierce creatures, and keep them from fighting one another.

The wyverns lowered the rocking chariot to the ground, then settled with loud flaps of their leathery wings to either side of it, hissing and snaking out their long necks. She stepped down onto the blue turf and approached Erron Komora, who stood nearest to her. He also was gazing up at Arainia.

"In that sphere dwell those who long denied me the knowledge and the power I sought," Syndra said as she went to stand by him— for she had told herself this tale so often that she had begun to believe it. "They will all learn a sharp lesson at my lord's hand—especially she who is named for this little moon, and thought to rule all the stars."

The Loänei lord turned to her and spoke in a low, confiding voice. "If Morlyn slays the Tryna Lia, we will have nothing more to fear. And then we will have no more need of *him*. We can reign in his place, Lady Syndra: you and I. Your power is growing. In time you will have your desire: you will be worthy even to be the consort of a Loänei. But the Prince is of no use to you now. He has grown mad, and no longer takes a man's form. I, however—"

Syndra looked at Erron with contempt. "What is this you are saying? Do you think *you* could rule Talmirennia?" she said.

"I speak only of ruling my own people," he said, "and freeing them from a ruler who has lost both his true form and his wits."

"And your ambition would stop there? With the Tryna Lia and the Avatar both gone, and the Emperor dead of old age? But you will never sit the Dragon Throne, Erron Komora. You have not the power to keep it."

"And Morlyn has?" he returned, his tone peevish and biting.

"He and I. Yes, in one thing you are correct: my sorcery is growing stronger by the day. Have you ever been to the grotto of Elnemorah, Loänei?" Syndra inquired. "No: for you would fear to go there. There is a power that dwells in that dark place that no man can endure. But I have gone there, and seen with my own eyes the image of the world-goddess carved into the black, volcanic stone: the stone that once was fire. She has a woman's shape, but is fanged and clawed like a beast, and wound about with the coils of serpents and with tongues of flame. She was there, Erron, before the Loänei, and before the Dragon Kings: long, long before her image was hewn out of the rock by human hands. She rules all the living creatures, and the molten fires deep in the earth: they rise at her command and destroy all in their path. But after the burning rivers cool, they turn to soil and green things grow in them. For that is her nature: like the creeping thing that hatches its young and then devours them, she is life and death in one. Virgins were sacrificed to her in ancient times, to stay her wrath. But the old goddess does only as she wills."

"What of it?" he demanded, though something in her look made him a little afraid, and he backed away a step. "She is no longer revered in Nemorah. The people there have forgotten her. Did you think to call on her for aid?"

"She can still be summoned," Syndra replied. "I did call upon her, there in the grotto, beseeching her to send her power into me. And she did, Loänei. I left that place filled with a new vigor and potency such as I have never felt before—as though my veins were filled with fire, like the earth's. I knew then that I too could give life, or destroy it, at my whim. I called serpents and wyverns to me, and they obeyed. And you would have me for your consort? I am beyond you, Erron Komora, as the sky is beyond the earth. And so too is the throne that you would claim." She drew her robe around her, and turned away. "Summon your Loänan allies, and go back to Nemorah, and I will say nothing of this to Mandrake. I know that you are only a fool, and no threat to me or to my lord. But trouble me again with your folly, and I will not be merciful."

He retreated, and she walked toward Mandrake: but the red dragon did not look once at her, only lay gazing pensively at the world above him, with its lands and little seas half-swathed in cloud. With most of Arainia's Wingwatch in its skies or flying ceaseless patrols within its icy rings, the few Loänan who had been stationed here on the little moon-world had fallen easily. They had expected the full brunt of the attack to fall on the mother-world, and the flights of savage firedrakes and rebel Loänan had taken them by surprise. Even so, the outcome might have been different had the firedrakes fought alone. Loänan hated these creatures, abominable distortions of their race. But the true dragons had no wish to battle other Loänan, and their reluctance to engage with their treasonous kin had weakened their resistance. Those few not injured in the initial encounter had been forced to flee to Arainia and alert the others there. Their warnings would do little good. The Valei had won for themselves a base from which to mount the further assault on Arainia: already a small force of Morugei and their human allies, commanded by King Roglug, had journeyed in flying ships to the southern shore of Eldimia where no army existed to resist them.

As Mandrake waited a huge firedrake came flapping over to his position and settled beside him. The firedrake was much larger than the red dragon, but even its fierce and bestial mind acknowledged his authority. Mandrake was more formidable in any form he chose to wear than the firedrake could ever hope to be, and the latter knew this.

"There were not many, Lord Prince," the great black beast said, little spurts of blue-edged flame flickering between his tusks as he spoke, "and most are fled by way of the portal—save for a few that were sorely wounded, and cannot fly. May we not kill them?" His talons flexed, and his mighty jaws opened wider.

Such an act, Mandrake thought, might well turn some of his Loänan allies against him. It had been difficult enough to persuade them to act in concert with the fire-breathers. Even Torok looked uneasy, shifting from one clawed foot to the other and darting side glances at the firedrake from his slitted eyes. "No; for we may need them to bargain with later. Leave them be for now." Mandrake dismissed the firedrake and turned back to his contemplation of the planet. It gleamed before him, like a globe of blue glass that he might reach out and take in his taloned claw. *Ailia is there,* he thought with a stirring of the blood that was half-wariness, half-anticipation. *So near . . .*

He turned again as two figures took shape in the air a wing length away. Elazar and Elombar loomed up before him, robed and crowned in fearful majesty: they had made their ethereal images huge to match the size of his dragon shape. "I say again, Avatar, that is a perilous place," said Elazar, pointing to Arainia.

"Too dangerous for demons?" Mandrake mocked. "I thought you were immortal, and impervious to harm?"

"We are. You are not," replied Elazar. "And you are central to our great campaign. I tell you, many Archons are in Arainia—all those on the side of our enemy. Have you not yet felt their presence?"

Mandrake *did* feel something, a vast oppressive power from the planet above, such as one might feel from a lowering thunderhead. The Archons . . . *Could* it be? His old suspicion stirred again. *The Archons are returning from the Ether, they did not die out after all, they have merely been waiting to come back and take the worlds for themselves again . . .*

A slight tremor ran through the red dragon's vast and powerful frame. His mastery of Valdur's magic was not complete: he had asked for aid only, not surrendered himself altogether. For that he must go to Ombar, to the old seat of the dark Archon's strength and the bastion of his ancient reign. Mandrake's fear of that place had not abated. There, he knew, the grim citadel that had been Valdur's during the great cosmic war still stood in the shadows of eternal night—its obsidian throne sitting empty, waiting to be filled again. Valdur's essence lived on in his star, the demons said, but was imprisoned there: no material form could be his ever again. It was for any claimant, now, to take that throne and rule as lord of the Valei empire. Why then did he hesitate?

Elombar said, "You know that Ailia is an Archon's child. Her mother is the ancient ruler of that sphere, and has passed on her authority to her daughter to command the Old Ones still dwelling there. The man Damion is one of these, for he also is the offspring of an Archon. His mother was not mortal."

Mandrake turned on the apparitions in anger, displaying tooth and claw. "These are the same lies that were spoken in Zimboura. Damion is dead!" he snarled.

"No. His mortal nature only was destroyed. It was but one half of his being. He lives now as an Archon, greater than he was before. And he can be summoned by any mortal to return."

Mandrake was silent, pondering this. If it were true, then he had gained another fearsome enemy. And yet he was also aware of a curious paradox: the murder of her beloved Damion must have been the chief grievance and cause of Ailia's animosity against Mandrake.

By returning from what had seemed to be his death, Damion removed that cause. She no longer had reason to hate the Dragon
Prince. It might still be possible to effect a reconciliation, and thus
free himself of the need for the demons' protection. The possibility
of regaining his cherished freedom beckoned and tantalized him.

The demon spoke on. "Ailia has countless allies in Arainia: there
she is stronger than you. Unless you call upon the Deep Power that
was Valdur's, you cannot face her in that world. Only call it, and
you will be greater than any mage of any race—impervious even to
iron, like the cherubim, for the power of Valdur is that of the Elyra,
the star-lords. Ailia could not stand against you then, not though
she called on all her strength and her mother's also. For Elarainia is
but an Elaia, one of the lower Archons, and was never Modrian-Valdur's match."

He trained his ethereal orbs on the dragon, but Mandrake made
no move and gave no sign that he had heard. His mind was already
mapping out plans of his own. "Very well," the Dragon Prince said
at last. "I will not go. Let the Valei try to assault her if they wish. I
understand Roglug has already led a force there by flying ship. But
I will not seek to drive her forth nor overpower her. So long as it is
clear she dares not face me, I have already won. If she wishes to
fight, why then she can always break our siege—and leave behind
the planet that grants her power. But I will not meet her again on
her own ground." And he wondered, as he spoke, if they guessed
that he lied.

BY SLOW DEGREES AILIA CAME back to herself again. Opening her
eyes, she looked up at a face directly above her own: an angelic
face, surrounded by a nimbus of luminous golden hair. She croaked,
"Lorelyn . . . ?"

"Oh, thank goodness you're with us again," the girl said. "Auron
brought you back here: you had been in the trance a long time, and
you were quite cold. Are you all right?"

Ailia nodded and sat up. She saw that she had been lying on the
ground atop a Hollow Hill, while Lorelyn and Jomar knelt at her
side; the girl's fair hair was shining in the light of the torch that
Jomar held. Auron was there too, lying with his chin on the ground,
while Taleera perched on his back. Ailia stood up with Lorelyn's
help; she felt drained and a little light-headed still, but also exhila-

rated. "Mother—Damion," she said, as soon as she could speak. "I *saw* them, saw them both."

"Saw them? Where—in the past?" Lorelyn glanced in puzzlement toward Hyelanthia, its heights lost now in darkness.

"In the Ether. They live on, in that realm, and can project their images from there. My mother met with me in the past, and I saw Damion too. He is safe, Lori. We haven't really lost him." She debated telling what she had learned of Damion and Lorelyn's parentage, and of her own. But how to tell this girl standing before her that she had been born in a bygone era, that her mother was five centuries dead—and, moreover, that she was the child of a being from the Ether? *Not now—I cannot tell her now.* This was not the moment: she must wait until she had Lorelyn alone. Privacy, and a little space of time, would cushion the impact of the revelation.

"But will *we* see him ever again? Jomar and I?" implored Lorelyn.

"Perhaps. I can't say. I had only a quick glimpse of him myself." At the memory longing filled her again. "I'm sorry—I can't speak of it now. I will tell you all I learned and saw, later; for now, I am just glad to know that he wasn't destroyed."

They walked back down the hill together, Jomar and Auron following on foot and the firebird flying ahead. Ailia still felt oddly disconnected from her body, and had to lean on Lorelyn's arm. "While you were up there, we saw the most extraordinary show of lightning on Hyelanthia," Lorelyn told her. "The flashes just went on and on, lighting the clouds up inside. Auron says he didn't cause it, and that your trance might have been responsible, though he wasn't sure. But it stopped when he carried you away from there. And the enemy was frightened."

"You say the Valei are here."

"Yes," Jomar told her. "No firedrakes yet, but goblins and Zimbouran rebels from Mera. They've taken some Elei captive."

Ailia forced herself to stand upright. "But how? How did they come here? I expected firedrakes, rebel Loänan—but not a land army, not yet. There are no portals here."

"They must have come by flying ship. They're not a huge force, but they're beginning to advance through the forest now, and we're going to go spy on one of their scout camps. Can you come with us? Taleera will lead the way."

She followed them away from the hill and into the forest. They crept quietly along the tree-lanes, keeping within the shadows while the firebird flew before them, her bright plumage glowing with its own light. Thick curtains of vines brushed against them, covered in aromatic blossoms, but no bird or small forest creature screamed to betray their passage. The creatures of this world waited in blissful ignorance of the disaster about to descend on them, knowing nothing of danger. Presently her human friends halted, while Taleera dropped down onto a bough, and Ailia glimpsed a glow among the trees about fifty paces ahead. There a campfire blazed, surrounded by a dozen or so large burly men and a few goblins. A small group of white-clad Elei stood at the edge of the firelight, watched by spear-wielding guards. Over the fires stood a makeshift spit, and on it hung an antelope's carcass. It was, or had been, a bagwyn: the flayed hide and the head with its proud sickle horns lay on the ground not far away. Ailia and her companions could smell the meat roasting, and hear the men jesting and talking among themselves. ". . . Stupid thing didn't even run away. Didn't even run! Just stood there looking till we shot it. I tell you, this place is paradise."

Ailia went rigid as she listened. Hatred stirred in her—hatred for the captors of the innocent Fairfolk and slayers of the helpless animal, the defilers of this beautiful land. Hatred for the humanity that linked her to them. But then the emotion appalled her, and she took several deep breaths in an effort to purge it away. The Zimbouran men could not be blamed for yearning to flee their own troubled and impoverished land, she reflected, as her mind calmed and the tension in her body eased. *They must be stopped. But my quarrel is not with them, it is with those who led them here.* She spoke to Taleera and Lorelyn using the mind-language. *I think you will all have to draw back and leave this to me. Two swords are not enough against these brigands. I will have to call on a great Power to aid me, and you might be harmed when it is unleashed. Will you all go now and have a look for the enemy's main camp? We need to know how many there are. I will stay and free these Elei.*

As they departed with great reluctance, she began to draw upon her sorcery.

IN THE CAMP THE ZIMBOURANS' mood was merry. Since the downfall of Khalazar and the coming of the new God-king, they had lived in the midst of a wonder-tale come true. First, there had been the ride in the marvelous flying vessels of the goblin-folk, who despite their hideousness were gifted with great magical powers, as might be expected of the offspring of genii. And now they had made landfall in a place of plenty beyond the world they knew, that the goblins told them would soon be theirs to rule.

The Morugei fighters prepared for battle, honing their notched swords. But their mood also was light. Goblins and trolls were creatures of the night, well able to see in the dark, and so anticipated an advantage over Ailia's people in combat after sundown.

"When the Elei are slain," King Roglug gloated, "it is everyone for himself. Today this land, tomorrow all of Arainia. With the Princess gone, they will not have the spirit to fight us!" The men cheered. This land where beasts were tame and birds sat on the bough waiting to be shot, where the precious gold and gems that only the wealthy could afford in Zimboura were in abundance—all theirs.

"Our old hearth-tales spoke of a faraway country," ventured one of the Zimbouran soldiers. "The Land of Wine and Honey. It is green and fruitful and runs with many fountains and streams, and jewels grow on trees, and the animals come at your call to be slaughtered."

"Ah, that's the right of it," agreed another. "My old grandmother told me about it too. No one ever goes hungry there, and no one ever gets sick, and nobody needs to labor for his bread. All can take their ease, while genii wait upon them and fulfill their every wish. When Khalazar talked about this Eldimia place, I thought: Ah, he's spinning that same old yarn to fool the simple folk. Promising the mobs paradise, so they'll not rise up against him! But now it turns out he wasn't lying after all. It's *true*, and he would have delivered it to us exactly as he said he would. Those stinking rebels that threw him down and murdered him, they've a deal to answer for: but we shall avenge him. We shall take this land, and we'll not let any of them near it. That's punishment enough."

The first man nodded as he inspected the roasting carcass. "The natives must all be killed or driven out first, but that shouldn't prove too difficult. They've no weapons and there are no real fighters among them. Once they're gone we'll cut down these forests, and plant ourselves some crops, and set up our own settlements."

Roglug grinned. "Why bother to build your own? Why not take *their* cities, and live in them? Much easier that way."

"We would have to fight hard to conquer cities," one man said doubtfully.

"Ah, you don't know Arainian cities. They have no protecting walls or fortresses, no cannons and catapults. And their people are poor fighters."

"But who will rule us?" the man asked, still in a tone of uncertainty. "This new God-king?"

"Naturally." Roglug shrugged his hunched shoulders. "He brought you here, didn't he?"

The other hesitated. "I had hoped we might be free, now that we are in a new land."

Another man snorted in derision. "Bah! Let him rule if he wants to, and his heirs too, just so long as we and our children get to live off the fat of this land." His companion said no more: the appeal to Zimbouran practicality had won.

The Elei captives, an elderly man of perhaps two hundred years and a few young women, continued to stand and sit quietly where they had been herded together, in the shadow of a tall upstanding boulder. Presently the old man spoke to his captors. "We will share this land with you and with your children," he said, "but you cannot drive us out altogether. The Mother is our guardian, and she will not suffer such things in her sphere."

One of the guards struck him and he staggered back into the arms of the young maidens, who cried out in fear. Never had such treatment been meted out to the people of Elarainia. "Your time is over," the Zimbouran snarled, standing over them with his hand on his sword hilt. "Over, do you understand? Your people will be destroyed. This land has been given to us. The Queen of Night and her daughter cannot defeat our god. He is stronger than they are."

"That is so," said a woman's voice. A figure appeared at the edge of the firelight, clad in a dark cloak: its hood overshadowed the upper half of the speaker's face, so her eyes could not be seen. Roglug recognized Syndra, the Elei traitress. She had come as she promised, to offer them her guidance and knowledge of this land. "You shall have all you want of Arainia, and so shall the Morugei also. Their revenge has been denied them for too long. But if the Tryna Lia is found here you must leave her to us: to my lord and me.

Even the goblin-wizards can do nothing against her. Ailia's power has grown too great."

"You believe she may be here?" asked Roglug, throwing a quick nervous glance around him.

"I know that she is. My powers tell me so. Prince Morlyn and I will seek her out as soon as it is light, but until then you must all remain close to the camp. There are evil spirits in these woods, the gods of our enemies. Those who stray may never return."

For a long time no one spoke, as the chilling effect of her words took hold. Then one small and wiry goblin sprang up from the fireside, squealing in terror. "I saw it! I saw it!" he cried.

"Saw what? What's biting you?" the Zimbouran captain demanded, turning on him in irritation.

"That tree, over there—I was looking at it, and suddenly I seemed to see—"

"What? What?"

"A woman—" the goblin spoke in a tone of fearful wonder. "Not a tree, but a woman tall as a tree, with long dark hair. A hamadryad: I've heard of such things. There are gods that live in trees, and can take human forms." He shivered. "She was looking down at us—she was angry."

A silence fell. The huge trees rustled and murmured like a thousand whispering, conspiratorial voices. The small goblin clapped his hands to his ears. "Stop! Stop it! They say, *Go away! Go away!* I *hear* them!" he screamed.

"He's gone mad!" shouted the Zimbouran.

"No—there is some enchantment in this," said Syndra. "You cannot feel it, Zimbouran, but we Nemerei can, and the goblins also."

The goblin wailed on. "Something stirs in this forest—a Power—I feel it: so vast, so strong—"

He broke off, cringing, as Roglug approached. "Enough of that, now! We've got our own sorcerers, and the witch-woman: they are more than a match for any spirit!" he shouted. But the goblin-king was not as full of aplomb as he appeared. The Avatar was not with them at the moment, and though Roglug feared him, he also looked to Mandrake to strike terror into their enemies' hearts. It was he who had delivered this paradise to them. But why had he not come with the army as he promised, to fight the beings rumored to dwell in this fearful place?

He looked up through the dark tree boughs at Hyelanthia and recalled the strange and terrifying display of lightning atop the tallest plateau this evening, illuminating the great roiling clouds that hung about it. "A storm," he had then said, dismissive. But it had occurred only on the one plateau—the very one that the natives said was sacred to their goddess. The native prisoners said that "she" was there—and "she" would be angered at the harm done her children. Who exactly was *she*? Not Ailia, surely—though the natives sometimes appeared to confuse her and Elarainia.

The forest . . . Now that the sun was gone, the forest seemed to change from a bountiful, benevolent place to one of dark secrets and unknown terrors. The smallest leaf rustle put him on edge. They said the Princess and her sorcerers could talk to animals. Was every night creature, every bird and burrowing thing, spying on them?

"There! Do you see?" howled the maddened goblin, pointing.

A figure had emerged from the deep shadow under the trees and stood there before them in the moonlight. It was a female form, young and slender, clad in a pale garment that fell to her feet and left her arms bare. Her hair was unbound and hung about her, and a fiery swarm of glimmering golden lights surrounded her figure and circled her head. These were in fact pyrallises, the little four-footed fireflies of Arainia, drawn to the power Ailia gave forth as to a light. They surrounded her like a living and visible extension of her inner aura. To the speechless men it seemed that the figure before them was robed and crowned with stars.

For a long time no one in the glade moved. Then one of the Zimbouran men lurched to his feet. "The goddess!" he croaked. "It's she! The Queen of Night!"

If he had shouted at the top of his voice the effect could not have been more dramatic. At once all the men were on their feet, yelling and cursing. The Elei also cried out, but in joy, recognizing not the Mother but her daughter, sent to save them.

Some of the men, led by their captain, moved upon her. But they moved like men in a trance. They feared this being clad in light. As they advanced, Ailia drew a step forward into the circle of firelight. Her eyes were unafraid, and drew into themselves some of the fire's leaping light, while in its glow her hair took on a fiery aureole. "I warn you," her clear young voice said, "you must leave now!" As she spoke Ailia sprang up onto the large boulder. And it seemed to her that the rock rang beneath her like a gong, sending out waves of power through the air. "I call on all Archons in this wood," she cried, "all powers of earth and water, fire and air. Naiads and hamadryads, nereids and oreads, I call upon you now! I call on the Mother also, to lend us her aid!" For a moment Ailia stood motionless.

Nothing happened. "So we have you at last," said Syndra, emboldened. She walked toward the boulder, casting back her hood so that her beautiful face shone pale and cold under the stars. "Mandrake and I. He is here, did you know? And he wields a new power that is greater than yours, greater even than Elarainia's."

The Elei gasped in horror at this blasphemy. "Syndra," Ailia said in a quieter voice, "you are a traitor to your people and your world. For these things you might yet be forgiven. Do not go further, and condemn yourself by opposing Elarainia. She is your mother also."

Syndra drew herself up. "I serve only the Dark One, whose incarnation Mandrake is even now becoming. I will reign at his side, as his empress, once he and Valdur are one."

"You love Mandrake," whispered Ailia. "Or so I thought. Would you wish such a fate on him?"

Syndra's gaze was stony. "You understand nothing. The union will not destroy Mandrake, it will only make him more powerful. It will give to him a strength even the Elaia cannot defy: a magic that cannot be bound, by iron or by law. The magic of the Elyra, highest of the high."

So that is why she is so confident, Ailia thought. *She knows she cannot defeat me, but she believes Mandrake will. And she knows that he is near . . .*

Syndra strode forward, her hands stretched out as if to seize Ailia. But from her extended fingertips quintessence began to flow, like blue and white forked lightning. It lapped about the sides of the stone on which the Tryna Lia stood, and reached its multiple tongues up toward her like hungry flames. "My powers also have grown since last we met," Syndra said. Ailia spread her palms, and the bolts crackled and faded away. *Mother, you promised I would have help!* she added in her mind as the Elei captives scrambled up to join her on the rock.

The Zimbourans were already fleeing in panic, but the goblin-sorcerers laughed at her. "She called on the Powers for aid! They must be hard of hearing!"

Suddenly the woods rustled loudly. Trees and bushes quivered, and their leaves stirred. The small goblin screamed again, "The trees! I told you the forest gods are angry! They're here, I tell you!"

Ailia stared into the forest along with all the others. The branches were tossing about as if in a storm, though there was not a breath of wind: it was as if the trees had come to life. And then she saw that they were full of mimic dogs. The usually gentle animals were leaping about from branch to branch as if possessed, hurling sticks and gourds down at the men below. They dodged.

"Shoot them!" bawled the captain.

At the same moment the bushes all around them stirred, and beasts began to emerge. Everywhere the invaders' panicked eyes turned there were horrors—or so the Arainian creatures appeared to their eyes. Vast slender shapes advanced out of the gloom, walking on legs as big around as saplings: camelopards, whole herds of them, like walking siege towers. Behind them came colossal aullays, dapple gray and chestnut-colored, flailing their mighty trunks and trumpeting in challenge; and then hordes of many other smaller grazing beasts: argasills, pantheons, thoyes, leucrottas, bagwyns, catoblepases, and boreynes. Creatures of Arainia that had never before shown violent intent, to human beings or to one another, now galloped into the clearing from all sides in a great stampede. Everywhere the men and goblins turned were horns and pounding hooves. The Elei cowered down on the rock in bewilderment, but Ailia remained standing. She might have been the goddess herself, surrounded by all her creatures.

For an instant Syndra stood silent, staring at her in hate, fists clenched and trembling. Then she flung her arms wide and called out. All the sorcerers felt the dark surge of her power and a luminous mist began to gather, shrouding her form. Her minions watched the glowing cloud spread, hoping for some great magic to deliver them. Instead it dimmed and dissipated, and Syndra was gone. Finding themselves abandoned, the remaining men and Morugei looked about them in terror, and prepared to flee in their turn. But it was too late. The hoofed beasts charged, a limitless cavalry, and after them followed the carrion-scavengers, with their fearsome claws and teeth. Lion-sized gulons, and lean pards and

calopuses came bounding out of the bushes, and fleet-footed enfields, and the alphyns with their great talons and muzzles tipped
with hooklike horns. Birds flew shrieking down out of the trees into
the enemies' faces. In the midst of it all Ailia stood stock-still on her
tall boulder with the Elei huddled about her, as on an island in a
flooding stream, as amazed as her unfortunate foes at what her pe-
tition had wrought. Then she understood. Her strong emotions had
spread to all the living things in the area, and they had responded with
this wild and uncontrollable rage, foreign to their own placid beast-
minds. "No," she whispered. "No, stop this! I never intended it.
Mother, let it stop!"

But the onslaught continued unabated, and against it the goblins
and men had no chance. Many were trampled and mauled, and the
few who escaped unscathed retreated from that place, utterly overwhelmed, as the din rose up to drown all other sounds under the
sky.

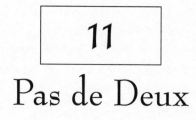

11

Pas de Deux

DAWN CAME AT LAST—FIRST to Hyelanthia's cloudy heights, turning
them red and then pale yellow, and then seeping down through the
forest's woven roof into the groves beneath. The light of the new
day shone there on scenes of battle and destruction: scattered
armor, lifeless men and goblins, and the carcasses of dead animals
also. They lay where they had fallen, on the trampled mold of the
forest floor, amid the ruins of crushed ferns and toppled saplings.
The campfire of the invaders had subsided to a bed of ash.

Lorelyn and Jomar had searched through the night for the landing site of the winged ships of the enemy, and returned with the

morning light to say that they had found it, but that only one empty craft remained. The survivors of the sorcerous attack had returned to their ships and fled into the void.

They found Ailia still slumped beside the boulder. She had not stirred from the spot since the violence ended, and she watched now with dull eyes as the Elei gathered up the fallen—beasts as well as men and Morugei—and bore them away. Their own captive kin had escaped unharmed. When the last of the dead were removed from the clearing, she rose and asked her friends to leave her alone for a while.

"Should Ailia be by herself like that?" whispered Lorelyn to Jomar as they complied.

"The enemy's gone. And she's strong enough now that nothing can hurt her, I think," said Jomar, pausing for a moment. He too was subdued by his first sight of Ailia's fully unleashed power. "If she needs to be alone, then let her have what she wants. *I* want to make sure no one's still lingering in the woods with a sword in hand. Will you come with me?"

"It all seems so peaceful," Lorelyn said to Jomar in a soft low voice as they walked away from the clearing. "As if nothing at all had happened, and the Elei and the animals were still living as they did before. And perhaps a day will come when it is all forgotten." *But Ailia will never forget,* she thought. She looked up. "What a beautiful bird that is, flying over there above the trees. Its feathers look like gold, though I suppose that's just the light . . ." Her voice trailed away.

In the sky above them, the bird with the golden plumage wheeled about and flew back toward the clearing.

AFTER THEY HAD GONE AILIA sat by herself on the stone, her eyes staring into the green forest—staring but not seeing. Her mind was sunk in unhappy contemplation. It had been necessary to protect her world, and the surviving intruders would tell fearsome tales of the perils of Arainia. But the violence sickened her.

She heard a voice call her name, and as she turned her heart seemed to still. Standing there in the grove before her was Damion.

He was not an ethereal image this time: there was no transparency about his figure, which seemed solid and real. He was clad in a plain white robe that fell to his ankles, and his feet were bare. The long slanting beams of sunlight that fell through the boughs touched his fair hair and surrounded it with a pale golden light. His blue eyes gazed at her, filled with a look of tender concern that she knew well. Amazed, she rose to face him, but though her mouth moved she could not form his name. "No," she breathed at last.

An illusion: it must be another illusion. It could not be the real Damion. He could not come again, for he was an Archon now and their Pact bound him. He had not been summoned. But he called out, softly: "Ailia." And then she wondered no more, but ran to his outstretched arms.

"Yes, I am here," he said as he embraced and held her. "I have been permitted to come back, to help you. The Archons know I am needed here. And you have been calling to me in your mind, night and day. That is as true a summons as any."

He was real, firm and solid, and filled with a living warmth. She buried her face in his shoulder, and realized that she was saying his name over and over again—just as she had said it in her dreams when she believed that he was dead. The pain that had lodged so long in her breast seemed to rise into her throat, and then break through her voice. "When I thought you were lost forever, I—I didn't know how I could live!" And with those words the pain was released at long last, dissipating into the air.

He released her, and then seeing that she was swaying on her feet, he took her hand and led her to the stone. She sat down upon it, and he seated himself by her side. "I am sorry to give you such a shock. And you were weary to begin with. I know what happened here in the night."

"I had to do something," she said in a low voice. "They would have hurt the Elei. But I didn't want to do it, and I am desperately sorry for the men who were killed. This is none of their doing—the Zimbourans, I mean, though I don't suppose the Morugei really chose to come here either. Their leaders sent them. The Zimbourans only wanted to escape their world, to live. And this is just the beginning. If Mera is to be freed, and Ombar defeated, there must be more fighting. More killing. But that isn't how you won your victory. You turned the killing on itself, by submitting to it, and you won."

"Not all victories can be won that way. But you're right that there might be another path to this peace you're seeking. Would it ease your mind at all to talk of it?" he asked. "Perhaps we can find a so-lution, together—"

She looked away from him again. "There is nothing you could say. I know I'm bound to my fate, and I am reconciled to it. But I am glad you are with me again, Damion." He said nothing, but sat with his arm about her, sharing her silence. Presently she spoke again. "I know what it is that I must do. I hate it, but I think at last I under-stand why it must be done. Ana told me long ago that I should not make the same mistake she did. That Mandrake is suffering, and may cause others to suffer, and when he was a true Paladin he would not have wished that to be. And if the enemy does come to control him, it will be a kindness to . . . free him."

The blue eyes turned to her, gently probing. "But still you hesi-tate to do it? Out of compassion—pity?"

"No—not pity." She could not lie to him. "You know the story of the philter, Damion. What you don't know is that I—felt something for him—long before that. Not as I feel for you, but . . ." She paused.

"You needn't say any more." He covered her hand with his. "I un-derstand."

"Do you? It was different, you see. With you, I felt the essence of you right away—your inner strength. You were so complete in yourself, so perfect, I had nothing to give you. I loved you for that completeness. With Mandrake, though—I sensed an emptiness, a need in him. I suppose I was lured by the thought of feeling needed, of being able to *give*."

He drew away from her a little, his face pensive. "I see."

"You don't mind?"

"Mind? Of course not. You feel what you feel, and it has nothing to do with me. Of course, given a choice, you would seek the one who needed you most. It is the way you are, Ailia. You could not do otherwise."

"But I do love you, Damion. I have from the moment I first saw you—only of course that wasn't really the first time: I recognized you, rather, from our time before—in the Ether—even though I had no living memory of it. And I will go back with you into the Ether, I promise, when this is over."

"You need not go," he said, "not if you don't really wish it. The Lesser Heaven is beautiful too, and you have seen so little of it yet." His voice grew softer. "You do wish to remain, don't you?"

Ailia closed her eyes. "Yes, a part of me does: the mortal part. I have been changed, by being born. A part of me will now be always yearning for this plane. It is very wonderful."

"Yes," he agreed, and his eyes dwelled on her, keen and intent. "It is."

JOMAR AND LORELYN RETRACED THEIR steps through the dense greenery, feeling anxious. Ailia had been alone for more than an hour now. If she were caught with her guard down, an enemy might yet harm her. As they neared the clearing they halted, hearing voices. Ailia was speaking with someone—but with whom? Jomar suddenly stiffened, listening. His eyes grew wide, then he plunged through the greenery. Lorelyn ran after him.

In the clearing stood Ailia, and with her a tall blond figure whose familiarity made them stop and stagger in their tracks.

Lorelyn spoke first, breathlessly. "Damion? Damion! Then it is true—you are still alive—"

Jomar stood staring. "No—it's just another of those illusions. Like the lion. We want him to be here, so we see him—"

"No. Neither is true." Ailia turned back to the Damion-figure at her side. "Once before you deceived me, using Damion's form. And you have done so again—but I guessed who you truly were when you spoke of the Lesser Heaven."

His form faded before their eyes, and changed: and there stood Mandrake. His face was thin, cadaverous, its pallor now of a sickly hue, the face of a man who has endured torment of the mind as well as of the body. He had allowed his nails to grow out into the long curved claws they tended naturally to become, and his eyes held a febrile gleam.

"I have come here," he said, "to offer you a last chance."

Jomar and Lorelyn rushed to Ailia's side, weapons drawn. But the Tryna Lia did not move. She stood regarding Mandrake with un-wavering eyes.

Mandrake in his turn looked at her, and his emotions rose again in a great flood, threatening to overwhelm him. He sensed a last chance for freedom, a last opportunity to avoid the path of de-struction that threatened them both. If only she would hear him! She was powerful, she could save him from the demons and their sinister designs. "I did not deceive you altogether," he went on.

"Damion does live. His mother was one of the Archons, and the Zimbouran priest was not able to destroy him. He dwells now in the plane of the Ether."

"Yes," she replied, her voice still level and calm. "I know, for I saw him there."

"So you know that your chief complaint against me is untrue. I did not cause your friend's death. And I will not harm these two either—" gesturing to Jomar and Lorelyn. "You will see that I bear you no ill will."

Jomar clutched his steel sword, wishing for his blade of pure iron. He could not counter any sorcery this warlock intended to cast. He had only words to throw at the enemy. "You still left us to die at Khalazar's hands. We have a score to settle with you, Lorelyn and I."

"Khalazar disobeyed me." He spoke to Jomar, but his golden eyes remained fixed on Ailia's. "He slew my goblin-guards and sent you to die—but he has paid for his misdeeds—"

"*You* haven't," Lorelyn interrupted, advancing on him with her blade of adamant.

"Lori—don't. Please. You are no match for him." Ailia raised a warning hand.

Mandrake continued to gaze at Ailia. "The prophecy is wrong, Highness. This will *not* end with the death of either one of us. It will go on—and on. If I am killed, the dragons that are on my side will seek vengeance, and the Valei will continue to spread destruction wherever they go. If you die, your people will fight me and my subjects to their dying breath. But there need be no contest at all, Princess. It is for you to say whether we fight. I cannot surrender to your side—Jomar there is not the only one among them who has sworn to destroy me. But if you were to come with me—"

"Then your allies would destroy me."

"No, they would not dare to defy me. I could keep you safe. Come with me, Ailia"—there was a new, imploring tone in his voice now—"I am alone, and I cannot trust any of the Valei. But we could rule the Empire together, wisely and well. You would have the peace that you long for."

Ailia said nothing. She felt that she saw him truly at last, exposed and vulnerable as a sea-creature out of its protecting shell: a being tortured by centuries of loneliness, starved for companionship, desperately afraid. She herself no longer felt fear, or love or hate for him: pity filled her soul now as it had Ana's long ago. And then she realized that she had unconsciously taken a step toward him.

At that moment a voice spoke in Ailia's mind: *You called on me, and I am here.* There was a great flash, as if a rift in the air had opened, and a white-clad figure stood there in the glade with them. Another likeness of Damion, or so it appeared. Lorelyn cried out as the figure strode toward Mandrake.

"Let her be," the new Damion-figure said.

It is you! Ailia answered silently. *At last!*

Mandrake stared at the robed man in hate and fear. Then he stepped back and reared to his full height, seeming to grow taller as they watched. He turned to Ailia. "Well, you may have changed and grown in power. But so have I!" As he spoke, Mandrake drew upon the dark power, calling on the demons for aid. *Help me . . .* He stretched out his hands, and as the sky clouded over and the light grew fainter he began to transform, becoming a towering shape of scales and gaping jaws. The red dragon.

"Ailia!" called Damion. "The Stone!"

Ailia reached into her pocket and drew forth the Star Stone. It shone like a fragment of the sun. Then she too changed her shape. Before the onlookers' eyes she became a form white as cloud and graceful as a gazelle, with a single horn like a spire of ice—the alicorn of the Tarnawyn, whose pearly spirals are founded upon a living gem like a Loänan's dracontias. But at the base of this horn's rising gyre was a glimmer of pale light: the white radiance of the Star Stone. It had become a part of her.

Lorelyn gasped. "She's beautiful!"

But the unicorn did not level her horn and charge. She turned and fled through the forest, passing easily between the close-growing boles of the trees. The dragon spread its wings and flew up over the canopy, pursuing her through the air.

"After them," said Damion quietly, and he too raced into the trees. Lorelyn and Jomar, recovering from their momentary stupefaction, followed.

At long last the trees thinned, and they found themselves on the shore of white sand. The unicorn had reached the sea's edge and turned at bay, her horn-gem glowing ever more fiercely. Surely she would fight now—or else the enemy would retreat in fear before the Stone, as he had done once before. But the dragon dropped out of the sky toward her, roaring. Ailia turned, and leaped into the water. In midair her unicorn-shape shimmered and changed, became the form of a dolphin that dived down in a graceful arc and splashed into the water. The dragon drew in its wings and dived after her.

Ailia sped over the wondrous branching shapes and turrets of the barrier reef and on into the clear deeps beyond. Diving down into a large rift between walls of coral, she waited as the Loänan swam past her, holding her breath. She could go for half an hour without breathing in this form, but then she would have to rise to the surface. Fish swam about her in bright, flashing schools. One large sargon-fish, his head topped by curving horns that gave him a regal appearance, passed within a finger's-breadth of her head. A sea-hog came rooting through the sea-herbage just as its earthly counterpart would on land: its barrel-shaped body was coated with scales and its tail was fanned like a fish's, but it had four stumpy clawed legs, and a snout from which tusks protruded like a wild boar's. Higher up, sleek black-and-white gerahavs darted about the coral caves with swift strokes of their wings, literally flying underwater; the wondrous birds that surfaced only to breathe, and never went ashore save to lay their eggs. She waited, watching all of these creatures with an anxious eye, but knowing as she did that they would show no fear of the dragon should it return, and so could give her no warning. She waited for many minutes in an agony of suspense, fearing to see the dragon's head appear in the gap overhead. But he did not come: only a pair of Arainian dolphins that glided out of the depths and circled above her, their round intelligent eyes gazing with open curiosity at this odd-looking intruder in their ocean realm—their namesake, had they but known it. At last she felt that her lungs were burning within her. She would have to rise and breathe.

DAMION STOOD AT THE WATER'S edge, waiting for the two adversaries to return. Lorelyn and Jomar hung back.

"If it is Damion—if he's really returned—why doesn't he help her?" Jomar said.

"I don't know! Fight, fight, Ailia! Why doesn't she turn and fight?" Lorelyn urged.

"What if she still doesn't *want* to fight—deep down?"

"But she must!"

Even as she spoke, the dolphin burst out of the water in a spurt of foam, leaping high into the air. Then in mid-leap it changed and became a swan, soaring skyward on white wings, graceful neck outstretched straight as a spear. The dragon too leaped out of the sea and sped in pursuit of the bird, talons outstretched.

"Ailia! Look out!" Lorelyn shrieked.

Too late: the dragon's claws closed on the bird's fleeing form, and then he flapped back to the shore, roaring in triumph. The friends stared, appalled, at the huddled heap of feathers on the sand beneath Mandrake's talons.

"Oh, no—no," Lorelyn breathed. "Not dead—"

Then there was a flicker, and suddenly the dragon was perched on the back of another Loänan. Its scales shimmered like mother-of-pearl, its wings were like white sails, its eyes blue as the ocean, its dracontias glowing with the radiance of the Stone. It gave a trumpeting cry and rose, dislodging the enemy from its back with a shrugging motion. The red dragon leaped aside, and then wheeled to confront the ethereal Loänan.

The humans watched in awe as the white dragon spread her wings and sprang into the air. "Oh, she's magnificent—but she really *has* changed this time. She isn't Ailia anymore!" Lorelyn exclaimed. But at the same time she thought: *Yes, she is. There was always more to Ailia than what you saw with your eyes. You are seeing that more, now.*

Land and sky whirled in a terrifying confusion as Ailia and Mandrake spun through the air interlocked. Then Ailia managed to break free and found she was hurtling through the air at a terrifying speed. The land rushed beneath her at a slant, the horizon crazily titled as she fought to regain control. A grove of trees rushed at her and she managed to clear it with a handspan to spare. Where was Mandrake? She moved her head slightly to the left, glad of the dragon's superior peripheral vision which enabled her to spy a pursuer without turning her head completely around. There was no sign of him though . . . Suddenly he struck her—from above, digging in his talons and closing his jaws in a vise-grip on her neck. He bit her throat, and the white dragon kicked out, scoring his underside with her claws in an action more instinctive than intended. He roared and released her. She looked at his blazing eyes, feeling the wild confusion of rage, fear, and pain. It was Mandrake she saw there, but also there seemed to be another presence in those eyes: more ancient, more powerful, but free of the terror and wrath that tormented the dragon's human soul. This other presence had moved far beyond such things. It was cold, passionless, guided only by some sense of purpose that she could not begin to fathom. Was this the primordial self she saw, the legacy of the reptile that lingered still in the man's mind, and was greatly strengthened by his shift to draconic form? Or was it something else—a driving purpose older still, older than all the worlds? The Power that reigned still from its prison in the depths of a black star? The slit pupils of the dragon's eyes seemed all at once to her like rifts giving onto a fathomless, inner darkness. She felt herself shrink from it. Her foe—Mandrake, or whatever now ruled him—took advantage of her momentary dismay to strike at her, raking her side with his talons. Then he turned and flew away toward the summits of Hyelanthia with their thick concealing clouds. After an instant of bewilderment she hastened to follow. He must not remain at large in her world. She plunged after him, into the dense whiteness that deepened to pearly gray and then lightened again as the sun showed through the other side.

Without warning, a giant dark shape appeared in the mist directly in front of her—a towering pinnacle of gray rock. She tilted her wings sharply. The wind shrieked in her ears as she flew past the grim gray shape, her near wingtip scraping the solid rock. Then other tall perpendicular shapes appeared, to right and left and straight ahead: dozens of rocky formations rising from the plateau beneath. She and Mandrake wove wildly in and out of them like swallows sporting around chimneys. The hunt became an ecstatic game—a race—a chase through high halls built of white feather-down, in and out of obscuring mists and around the colossal monoliths of granite that thrust up perilously through the veiling cumuli. Then they were both out into clear air and sunlight again: a view of the forest and plains on the north side of the tableland was revealed, a narrow view at first framed in scrolls of white vapor, then widening as they broke free of the clouds.

And now she could not help but feel what she had so briefly sensed before, when she had taken draconic form under the influence of the philter: the fierce wild joy of flight, the dizzy height above the earth, the howl of the wind and the feel of it under her wings. Beneath them spread the grassy plains, with herds of beasts vast as the shadows of clouds moving upon them. They saw a small lake coated in what looked like white lilies, but when they flew over it the whiteness arose in a flurry, and a great flock of caladriuses took to the air—not in fright like Meran birds, but in curiosity, flying along with the dragons so she and Mandrake were surrounded by a cloud of wings.

When the red dragon looked back at her, the black emptiness was gone from his eyes. They were bright as fire, challenging, fiercely alive. She understood then that he was not fleeing in fear but had led her on this wild pursuit on purpose, to make her feel her dragon's form, the strength and majesty of it, and the godlike freedom that it owned. His transformation had been deliberate, a challenge and an invitation to her to take Loänan shape as well.

Back over the tablelands they swept, until they could see the ocean spread out below them in a dazzle of sun. Ailia's friends watched from the shore as the dragons met and fought again, their necks and tails twined together, wings beating the air, mauling and biting one another's throats and flanks. Almost they seemed suspended there in the blue vault of the sky, nearly on a level now with the clouds. Then they broke apart and flew through the air, only this time the red dragon pursued the white, and they closed a second time, locked together, tumbling down through the sky. They dropped almost to the earth, broke apart once more, and rose— now flying with necks outstretched, wing to wing, no longer pursuing but soaring side by side.

"What are they doing?" cried Lorelyn.

Jomar said nothing. Once before he had seen a flight like this one: not a clash of two assailants, but the aerial dance of a he-eagle and she-eagle, meeting in the air above the hills in Zimboura . . . Higher the dragons flew, until they were only two flecks, red and cloud-white, against the dark blue dome. Then at last the red one vanished, like a flame extinguished by a breath: it had found and escaped into an ethereal rift, as a fox fleeing the hunters darts into an earthen holt. Would the white dragon follow?

Leagues above them it circled in the sky, its motion wild and purposeless as a piece of chaff caught in an eddy of air. Then it drew in its white wings close to its body, and dropped downward once more, disappearing into the blue expanse of the sea.

Damion watched its long plunge to the waves. Then he sighed, and turning to his friends he spoke to them at last. "We nearly lost her."

12

The Return

HE REMEMBERED WARMTH, A GOLDEN light, and what sounded like a chorus of countless voices raised in song: but these were perhaps only symbols, all that his material mind could afterward comprehend of the celestial harmony that was the Ether. Of the ordeal in the sanctum of Valdur's temple he recalled little, and nothing of either fear nor pain. There had been darkness for a time, that much he knew; and then into that darkness there had come the light, faint at first and then growing brighter as a flame grows. In the soft, golden radiance he had seen a shape appear, somewhere beneath him as it seemed. It was a man, young and fair-haired, robed in white and lying as if asleep upon a bed of stone. He looked down at it, uncomprehending, until at last he realized it was he himself that he saw—and no image of the mind, either: he was gazing on his own body, stretched upon the altar of Valdur. *Am I dead then?* he wondered. But still he felt more bewildered than afraid.

As the strange luminosity grew ever brighter he glimpsed the blind priest with the ceremonial knife still clutched in his hand, oblivious to the light that enveloped his figure; and the acolyte by the door gaping in blank terror, his face also lit by the glow. But Damion felt distanced from them, and from his own abandoned body, and from the world. After a time it occurred to him that the light was coming from his left, from a sort of rift or opening in the air. And through this he saw, as through a window, figures moving through a shining realm beyond: they were human in form, but beautiful with an unearthly beauty. Some were winged and some were not, but all were luminous as the land through which they moved; and they gestured to him, and called to his mind with sweet voices. *Come, join with us!*

Still he hesitated: though he yearned for that untroubled Ethereal realm, the bodiless drifting awareness that he had become was loath to leave his body behind—the one familiar thing in his altered world. As he lingered, a figure came to the opening, looking between the worlds: a woman's form, golden-haired and clad in a gown that glimmered like flame-lit emerald. Her white arms stretched out toward him.

I know you, he thought. *You appeared before, in my mind. Elthina . . . Mother.*

Yes, I am she who bore you and gave you mortal life, the being answered. *And I can give you life again, if you will heed me. Little time remains to you. Your bond with your corporeal form is fading, and soon your spirit will be gone: out of the world, out of my reach in the realm beyond matter and Ether. But this need not be. There is no return to the life you once had, but you can tarry upon my plane, translating your flesh to an ethereal form. The mortals who are born to Archons can do this. And then you can give aid to your beloved, who lives still on the lesser plane.*

Ailia, he thought. He need not perish, then, and pass altogether out of the world: he could still help her, in a new and different form. *Yes. Let that be my fate. Let my spirit remain within the Ether, and my body be transformed.* And as he thought this he felt no fear or regret, but knew only that this was in truth what he most desired. The place beyond the portal called to him.

As he watched, the light from the opening seemed almost to congeal and solidify, becoming a bridge between this plane and the next: and his lifeless body was bathed in the golden glow. His consciousness was drawn down to it again, engulfed in that radiance; and then in his new, quintessential form he rose up and left the altar, flying through the bright rift as a bird flies to freedom through an open window. It closed behind him, shutting out the world.

Gone were the grim sanctum and its dour occupants, gone the life of pain and doubt and misery that had been his lot, and all mortals'. He had entered the Ether. Twice before he had ventured upon that plane, but only to pass through the dragon-ways that wound through its brilliant expanse, as the tunnels of little burrowing creatures pass through the earth. Now he was suspended *within* the substance of the Ether itself. His mother was with him, and many other beautiful beings in ethereal form. Queen Eliana was there, drifting before him and looking as he had seen her in his vision of the past: slender and youthful despite her pale, silvery hair.

Majesty, he said, and bowed. She laughed.

There are no titles here, she said. *We are all Archons together. Yes, I am of the El too: I was not able to tell you before, but now that you are one of us no secrets shall be kept from you.* Then it seemed to him that she grew grave and sad. *I know what it is you lost to come here, child of Elthina,* she said. *I will give you such aid and comfort as I can.*

Then she and Elthina showed to him his past, scenes from his life on both planes as they had observed it, some that he had merely forgotten and others of which he had no memory at all. They showed him a man in knightly armor, clean-shaven with brown hair and eyes of clear and piercing blue. *Your father,* Elthina told him, and her mind-voice was filled with longing. *Arthon of Raimar, knight of the Paladin order.*

Longing also filled him at the vision. *Is he here in the Ether also?*

No. Sorrow filled her voice. *He has gone where the El cannot go: where mortal spirits dwell forever, far beyond matter and Ether both. I am parted from him for all time.*

Then so am I, now. At the knowledge he was overwhelmed with grief.

His mother hastened to console him. *Do not regret your choice, my son! It was the best choice, and good will come of it for you and others; and now I shall not lose you as I lost him, lose you forever and ever.*

She showed to him many other things: lives of other beings, and far-off worlds, some that were not unlike Mera and Arainia, some as strange as dreams. Now that he had been translated into ethereal form, he was free to go where he would upon that plane, through all the incorporeal worlds and realms that the El had shaped for themselves, like islands in its seas of quintessence. And he could also project himself into the material worlds, so long as he went unseen. As for time, it was no longer his master but his servant, and he moved back and forth in it as he pleased.

At last he came upon a world, without knowing where and when in Talmirennia it might be. It had a golden sky and a vast gold orange sun, and the lands that he saw below him as he soared through the air were dry and desolate: deserts of riverless canyons and wave upon wave of rippled dunes. Weathered pinnacles rose in ordered rows, like the towers of cities, and from steep cliff walls sprang arcs of stone that resembled flying buttresses, but were the work of nature and time. The rocks were tan-colored and many were oddly porous, so that they looked almost like petrified foam.

As he drifted onward, following he knew not what guiding sense, he came upon a structure that was not natural in origin: an ethereal portal. Two gigantic stone cherubim lay facing each other, and between their opposed forepaws the ethereal rift—which he could see, though no mortal eye would have spied it—was still open, as though it had recently been used. From the cherub gate a road led to the ruin of a real city where he saw, rising majestic into the morning, high turrets and monumental arches and pyramids larger than any ever raised by human hands, their foundations half-swallowed by sand. All were built of the same sand-colored stone. The largest structure of all was a roofless hall with a doorway framed by six stone columns, three to each side—a doorway through which an army might have passed. Lining on either hand the road that led to the door were statues on broad plinths, some partly crumbled away, but most still looking as though they had just been sculpted. In his birth-world of Mera these would have been figures from mythology, but here they were representations of real beasts and beings: winged lions and bulls, and cherubim, and lamassus and shedus, and lion-bodied sphinxes with the heads of men or women, or falcons, or rams. He descended to move between them, up the long aisle they formed, toward the hall. In the heat shimmer the colossal pillars at its entrance seemed to dance, swaying and quivering. Perhaps the whole edifice was but a mirage, and would fade away on approach . . . But as he moved toward the pillars they remained in place, and ceased to quiver, and grew firm.

But before he reached the door he heard a sound behind him, and turned to see a distant figure speeding through the trembling air. It was like one of the stone images come to life: ram-headed and lion-bodied, tawny-colored like the sand on which it ran. The creature snorted from time to time and tossed its curling horns, while its padded paws raised yellow dust clouds from the desert floor. On its back there perched a rider, his face veiled with cloth against the flying sand. He was spurring his strange steed toward the portal, but suddenly he turned and made in Damion's direction, as if he could see the Archon's invisible projection. Damion remained where he was, watching curiously as beast and man approached to within only a few paces of where he stood, and halted. The rider dismounted, and unwound the scarf from his head.

"Old One," he said. "I feel your presence in this place: I know you are here. Will you speak with me?"

It was a man whose grizzled hair and beard still showed a little of their original red-gold hue, perhaps three score years or more in age. But despite his gray hairs, he could not be any common mortal, or he would not have sensed that Damion was there. A Nemerei magus, he must be. His features were stern and proud, with a high-bridged nose and pronounced cheekbones, though the lines about his eyes and mouth gave him a sad and pensive look. His eyes were a grayish blue, clear and unclouded, and they looked directly into Damion's own immaterial ones.

"I am the one called Andarion in the world of Mera," the man continued. "I am mortal, but I carry the blood of Archons. We are of one kind, you and I."

Damion's astonishment grew. It was Brannar Andarion himself, the king of Maurainia in the Golden Age. But how could that be? "I am called Damion, Majesty," he replied, assuming a visible image as he spoke. "I had thought you were long dead. Or do I walk now in elder days, when you reigned still in that world? I have wandered far in time, but never before has a being in the past been able to see me."

"Even the Archons may not truly enter the past, but can only observe it," the king answered. "You are in the present age—the wave of time still in motion."

He seemed weary, and as Damion stared at him he went to lean against the plinth of one of the statues and brush the sand from his garments. His steed settled down onto the ground with a grunt, its horned head raised and its forepaws stretched out before it, looking exactly like one of its stone kin.

"What is that beast?" Damion asked.

"Do you not know?" the other asked, surprised. "You are one of the Elaia."

"I am half-mortal, like you," Damion explained. "Or rather I was. My former life was taken from me, and now I am of the El. But I still have much to learn."

"Ah, I see. The beast is a criosphinx," Brannar Andarion said. "Some of the Old Ones' creations live on here, where their ancestors were first formed through sorcery. This world is Meldrian, Lord of Thrones: one of the oldest of our Archon forebears' settlements. Here the Star Stone was made, and many other things of wonder. It was the seat of Athariel's power—that sun that burns above us is his star—and it became capital of the Archonic empire after Modrian's fall. As for me, I never died, but passed into the Ether five centuries ago to live among my Archon kin. I had grown weary of the human world, of wars and suffering and grief." A grimace crossed his lined face, as if at some twinge of reawakened pain. "On that plane time could not touch me, but ere long I began to visit other worlds of the mortal realm. I am a man, and never desired to be anything else. At last I decided to leave the Ether altogether, and live out the rest of my mortal life upon this plane. I have taken a wife from among the Elei people of a distant world, and there my home shall be until I die at last and pass on to the High Heaven. But I still choose to wander from time to time." His keen eyes dwelled on Damion for a moment. "It is curious that we should both come here, at the same time. This is no chance meeting. We were sent here to encounter each other, I think."

"To what purpose?" Damion asked.

"Perhaps that will become plain in time. Let us go and see the Meldraum, where Athariel sat in majesty—the model of all earthly kings." Andarion began to walk toward the giant pillared entrance.

"*Meldra um*: the throne hall," Damion translated, and he went with the king, walking soundless and shadowless behind him. He was curious to see the old kingdom of Athariel—the Archon for whom he had been named.

The Meldraum was nearly a mile in length. Its roof had not fallen in, for it had never possessed one, but was designed to be open to the sky. Here and there a giant carved arch bridged the walls to either side. On those walls were huge stone images that looked down on the small figures passing beneath.

"The work of the Elaia," said the king. "They took no corporeal form in this world at first, merely making images for their enjoyment."

"But how then could they make images, without bodies, and hands to wield the tools?" Damion asked.

Andarion smiled. "By a method most ingenious. The living things of this planet were not all made by the Old Ones. Some were here long before they came: that creature carved on the walls there, the scaled beast with neck and tail like a serpent's and long clawed legs: the *sirrush*, it was called. It lived here when this world was green and wet, full of growing things. There is also another even older creature in this world, called the *shamir*: a little worm that lives in solid stone. You saw the curious appearance of the rocks here? The worm eats its way through them, boring many small holes and tunnels. The insubstantial Archons bent their thoughts upon these minute creatures, and wielded them as the sculptor wields his chisels. They caused the worms to eat stone on command, and so carve out forms and shapes in it. These mighty halls were designed by the Archons, but made by the shamir-worms."

Damion gazed in amazement at the fine detail of the figures that neither hand nor tool had made. There were many seraphim, and cherubim in various postures of vigilance, standing or lying or sitting upright on their haunches. Two, carved in relief upon a wall, were depicted guarding a stylized tree laden with pointed leaves and round fruits. "The Tree of Life," Andarion said, seeing him look at it. "So the Old Ones called it, for they created a fruit that would refresh their material flesh and ichor when they ate of it, and also recall their spirits to the Ether from whence they came. It does the same service for their half-mortal offspring: we are attuned to the Ethereal Plane when we eat of it, freed from the bonds of space and time so that we may see things that were and things that may yet be. The Archons guarded these trees so that the mortals would not eat of the fruit, for it could cause those who were not of Archon blood to fall into endless sleep. When the Old Ones departed this plane, they gave that task to the cherubim. But in these days the food-of-the-gods has lost much of its potency, and any can eat it without harm." He traced the old carvings with his hand. "Lion-bodied and eagle-winged: these truly were living symbols, the creatures of Earth and Heaven. The form of the seraph is symbolic too:

it signifies a life lived between two worlds. The Elaia expressed their yearning for both matter and Ether by crafting such images, though when they took flesh they generally assumed a mere human shape. But their lofty kin, the Elyra, preferred the seraphic form, as it gave them human hands to use, yet also granted them the freedom of the air."

They walked on, until at long last they came to the end of the hall. Here there was a mighty dais, with a throne of carved stone upon a high plinth with steps leading up to it. The sides of the throne were lion-headed cherubim, and their wings framed its high back. The king pointed to the great statue that was seated upon it. It was crowned, and its sculpted wings spread from its shoulders to overshadow the throne. "There is the seat of Athariel, long abandoned: now only his image sits enthroned there." The wall behind was carved with many more images in bas relief, and there were words engraved upon it too. "The letters are alien," Damion said, perusing them. "I cannot read them."

"I can," Andarion said. "For I learned these old runes from the Archons themselves, their written language that was lost long ago. These words speak of the old war that was fought among the worlds, and also of the battle that is yet to come. The leader of the Archons knew well he had not won the final victory, and that Modrian's evil lived on and would wreak more woe in the mortal realm. He left behind this account, and for those who could not read it there are the images." He pointed to the carvings, and Damion recognized two figures right away: a woman crowned with stars, and a dragon menacing her.

Ailia and Morlyn, Damion thought.

It was as if someone had struck him a blow. The tranquillity of the Ether left him all at once, leaving him filled with dismay. "*Ailia!* I have forgotten so much while I was in the Ether! My friends, my world . . . This is the present, you say—the moving crest of time. That means the last war is coming soon."

"It has already begun," Andarion said. "No world is safe, not even my haven-home far away from here. I came here hoping to find some help or counsel in the former world of the star-lords."

"And Ailia is fighting now—and in danger still. And I cannot help her." He was filled with remorse at the thought of her, and of Jomar and Lorelyn, all of them believing him to be dead.

"You can. When we die we are called to be one or the other, we who are of human and Archonic descent. You chose not to pass away, but your only other choice was to be an Archon, and that means you are subject to the Pact that forbids you entry to the mortal plane. But if your human friends need you, then they can call upon you, so long as they are in full knowledge of what you have become. It may be that they have already done so and you have not heard their pleas, being outside of time. But if they have not, then I summon you, Archon, and any of your kind who hear. It is one of your own that we fight, Valdur, who was Modrian. Will you help us?"

"I will. With the powers now at my command, I can give you the help you need. That is why I died—to become more powerful than I was before. I did not fully understand then, but I do now." He turned from the carvings to look on Andarion's face. "I must go back to Ailia."

"So," said Lorelyn, "you came back here through the Ether, to Arainia. But you couldn't become human again until one of us called you."

They were sitting together on a stone near the shore, the two mortals staring at Damion in wonderment. He answered softly, taking the girl's hand in his: "Lorelyn—I really have returned, but this is not my home. I will do all I can to help you, now that I am here. But I am an Archon, and my place is the Ether. You must know, for you lived there once too. We knew each other before our life in Mera."

Lorelyn stared at him. Then she gave a gasp, put her hands to her head, and struggled to her feet.

"What is it?" cried Jomar. "What's happening?" He sprang to her side and supported her, as he had done on the island of the exiles.

"The Ether," she whispered. "I *remember*. Yes, I remember it all." Her head swam with visions of light and fleeting forms, faces and voices. She straightened, and turned to look at Damion. "We *were* together there: you and I. And Ailia too. And before that I remember . . . arms that held me, a gentle voice singing. My mother. And I remember my father taking me away, telling me how she died, telling me I would be safe now. But I didn't want to stay there, I wanted to go back . . . *Damion!* I know it at last! What I am, and what my purpose is. I knew it all along—I just forgot!" Joy filled her; the last words rang out in triumph.

But Jomar stepped back, and stood looking from one of them to the other. His emotions were a stormy welter, like waves colliding with one another. There was hope that he still did not quite dare to feel, that Damion had in truth returned alive—renewed anxiety for Ailia—and now this. When he spoke his tone was not so much demanding as imploring. "What are you saying, Lori? I don't understand. Is that really Damion? How can he have come back to life?"

"Yes, it's really he—not another illusion." Lorelyn laughed for sheer delight. "I so wanted to believe that Ailia was right, Damion, that you'd return to us!"

Jomar gaped at her, then approached the other man hesitantly. "Damion! I still can't believe—Damion?" He reached out, touched his friend's shoulder. It was solid, warm.

Damion took hold of Jomar's arms and looked into his eyes. "Yes, Jo—I've come back."

Relief flooded Jomar's mind at the firm grip of those hands, and at the sound of the voice—the same as the deceiving Mandrake's, but imbued with a very different personality, safe and familiar. The man was not his face or voice only, but his underlying essence. There was no mistaking it. Still, Jomar was full of questions. "But—how? How? We all thought you'd died."

"I am half-Archon. I never knew it before. Archons can't be killed, not altogether. My mortal self could be destroyed, but not my immortal one."

"Yes . . ." said Lorelyn softly. Jomar turned to stare at her. Then she asked, "Damion, do you know what is going to happen?"

Damion shook his head. "Archons don't ordain the future. We only foretell it."

"Isn't that the same thing?"

"No. Imagine a company of travelers who come to a range of hills, blocking their view of the country ahead. The people who live on the hills tell the travelers that the country beyond is full of difficult, rocky terrain: they can see it from the hilltops. Should the travelers be angry at the hill dwellers? They only survey the land from a higher point of vantage: they did not make it as it is. And neither do we shape the future. We see the way ahead, better than mortals can. But the path they take through that arduous terrain is up to them. There is no fixed road. The Archons simply foresaw a role that I could play, shaping events to come. They knew that Ailia needed protectors. It's why you and I were allowed to return."

"Return?" Jomar was still bewildered. His relief was subsiding in the surging storm of his thoughts. "Lori? What's he saying?"

Lorelyn looked at him: this man who had never flinched from any sort of danger, whose strength of will and body had borne him through ordeals that had destroyed many others. But now he looked to her almost like a child, his dark eyes troubled, his usual brusque confidence stripped from him. She felt a great stirring of love and tenderness for him. "Jo, he means I am half-Archon too," she told him.

Again Jomar stared from one of them to the other. Then he turned away.

"Jo? What's wrong?" Damion asked.

Jomar spoke without turning. "You're not human. Either of you."

"Why do you say that?"

"You aren't what you seem—you never were. And now you've been changed completely, Damion. Turned into something—*else.*"

"Jo, whatever I am now, I was born human. So was Lorelyn. And I haven't really changed—that much."

"So—is this just a shape you're taking at the moment? What do you *really* look like now?" Jomar demanded

"What do *you* really look like, Jo?" Damion smiled.

"I don't understand."

"Is this all you are—what you see in mirrors, your skin, your hair and eyes? Or are you something more?"

"I suppose you mean this soul you were always going on about when you were a priest." Jomar shrugged.

"Exactly. We are two souls, two spirits, each represented by a material form. But we are more than that. What you see now was never more than a part of me, never the whole. The same is true of you. Still, the El envy mortals. To walk freely through the material plane, to pick up a pebble in your hand, to own that reality, to know danger! Matter rules you, you say: but that also means it belongs to you and you to it; you *possess* it as no Archon can. They obey a pact that forbids them from interfering. Now I too am bound by that ban. That is why I could not reach out to you and explain to you what had happened. *You* had to come to *me*. I was allowed to send you dreams, no more."

"Yes, Ailia dreamed a good deal of you. But she called on you before, in Zimboura. And you didn't come to her," Jomar accused.

"It wasn't allowed. She still thought she was calling on a mortal man. For a summons to be answered, the summoner must understand that she or he is calling on an El." Damion started to walk back up the beach. "But we must leave this place. The Emperor has come to Mirimar, and has sent his Loänan guards to bring Ailia to him. Look—there is Auron, coming for you."

They watched the golden dragon gliding low over the white sands. "You can't just—grow wings, and fly there yourself?" Jomar queried, half-seriously.

Damion shook his head. "No—not here. The Pact limits what we can do on this plane. Ana could not get herself to Trynisia, and Elarainia had to build a flying ship to reach Mera. Come, now! Auron will fly you to Mirimar. I will go and find Ailia, and bring her too."

Damion watched as they walked reluctantly to the waiting dragon, then he walked on along the beach. He understood their bemused state of mind, for he too felt dazed by his transition. After the pure harmonies of the Ether, the world of sensation had been an assault: a roar of sound, a blinding light that only slowly resolved into shapes and colors, all of them devoid of meaning. The constant communion with the other Archons was gone, cut off; he was alone, a universe unto himself, lonely and afraid. Soon, he knew, even his symbolic of memory of the Ether would be gone, receding before the onslaught of the material plane.

But he would remember his mission. *Ailia*, he thought again. There was pain then, as his fingernails dug into his palms. Pain, fingers, palms—the words were beginning to come to him. *Man*, he thought. *That's what I am: a man.* He still staggered at times like a newborn foal, his own legs strange to him. He had not been aware of his first transition long ago, his infant's brain being too small and unaware to hold the strangeness, the confusion, the terrifying isolation of incarnation. He forced himself onward, seeking Ailia.

He came upon her at last, a mile down the shore. She lay where she had emerged from the waves, her body sprawled face-up on the sand, her bare feet laved still by the soft curling foam of the surf.

He stood for a time looking down at her. He suddenly recalled the picture he had hung over his bed as a boy, of the knight rescuing a maiden from a dragon. He wondered if this meant he had always known his destiny: to save Ailia from Morlyn.

Presently she stirred, and opened her eyes. "Was it only a dream?" she said aloud.

"It was real, Ailia. I am here."

She gave a cry. He knelt by her side, and took her in his arms, rocking her gently as if she was a child.

The terrifying, exhilarating flight and chase, the return of Damion—it had all really happened, Ailia realized. She gazed up at him: at his eyes blue as the Arainian sea, and shining with the same reflected light. Or did those irises gleam with their own inner radiance, like her enchanted sapphire? Her thoughts reached out to touch his, and knew his mind. It was he, her beloved Damion returned at last. And the other one—her adversary—had fled this world.

"Oh Damion, you came to me! You heard my call!" She embraced him in turn, holding him closely, while he stroked her hair. For a long time they rested in each other's arms. At last she drew back to look at him again. "I saw you, in the Ether—but you were winged there, like a seraph."

"I tried many new forms there. But here I will move among mortals, and for that the old form is best." He smiled, his dear familiar smile, but she sensed a sadness in it.

"Damion, aren't you glad to be back?" she asked, looking into his eyes.

"I am glad to be back with you." He put his arms about her once more, and helped her to rise. "You are safe, and so is Arainia—for now. But this war has only begun, and you must rest before we all meet and decide what is to be done next. Look: the cherubim have come to carry us home. We must return to the city."

EVERY BELL IN THE CITY of Mirimar rang, and every banner flew; people ran into the streets, living torrents of many colors that flowed and roared as the flight of dragons and cherubim swept high above them toward the palace. They were filled with joy: Ailia's retreat to the south had spared their city from the assaults of the enemy, and the Arainian army had also returned from Mera victorious. Mandrake had fled the system, and without his leadership his followers too had withdrawn. And now, to the awe and delight of the Arainians, the Celestial Emperor had also arrived, his palace of adamant descending out of the clouds to settle on the earth. Its crystal towers rose now from the broad fields to the north of the city, gleaming in the light of the waning stars and the Arch of Heaven: for here the day was not so far advanced.

The crowd awaiting the Tryna Lia in the great central court of the palace was smaller but no less joyful. The king ran forward and took Ailia in his arms as she dismounted from Falaar's back. Seeing his glad face, she knew with a pang that she must tell him the whole truth about his vanished wife. For now, she only listened to him. "The enemy is departing! They will not dare march against you again. And our forces have triumphed in Mera! But another, most amazing thing has happened," Tiron said.

"Yes—the Emperor is here. I saw his palace from the air."

"He has brought the Dragon Throne with him also. And a gift from the salamander-people of Arkurion: a veritable mountain of their wool and scaly hides. The Nemerei have it now, and are seeking to make armor from it for our soldiers."

"So Lorelyn succeeded! She told me she and Auron tried to persuade them."

"Yes. I only hope that the Nemerei will find a way to take away the odor: the materials smell like all the rotten eggs in all the worlds! But you must rest now, and get your strength back."

Ailia would not rest however, but went straight to the crystal palace with Auron to see Orbion. It was strange to see the familiar glassy walls and towers rising now from the once empty field outside the city. As she drew near to it, her eye caught a glimmer of white off to her right, and she turned to see the pale shape of a Tarnawyn in the midst of a little copse of perindeus trees. It was keeping pace with her as she walked, its head raised high on its long, graceful neck. There were scars showing dark on its flank.

"It has fled its world," said Auron. "The Valei are hunting its kind like beasts, for they have always hated the Tarnawyn. But the unicorns have portals of their own, and paths they can take through the Mid-Heaven. This one has come here to do you honor."

Then Ailia remembered what it was said of the Tarnawyn: that they appeared to rulers at the beginning of a reign, as a sign of

Heaven's approval and benediction. Did this creature, too, desire her to take the Dragon Throne?

When she entered the cloud-hung palace she saw that Orbion wore his true form, a great white dragon: his snowy-maned head rested on his foreclaws as he lay curled about the Dragon Throne. She walked onto the dais and into the circle formed by the great bodies of his Imperial dragon-guards, a huge living temple-space roofed and pillared with gold by their outspread wings and strong clawed legs. The cherub monarch Girian was there also, with his head and his wings bent low and his golden crown lying between his forepaws.

Auron followed her onto the dais. As they drew near to the old ethereal dragon he opened his eyes, and she saw that the blue orbs were sunken and dull. The Celestial Emperor raised his head with an effort. "Ah, you are come! I feared I would pass into the Ether before seeing you," he said, in a voice like the dry hiss of wind-blown sand.

Ailia knelt before the huge head, tears coming to her eyes. "Son of Heaven, please! Linger a while longer, if you can. We still need you—your wisdom and knowledge—"

"Loänan do not choose the time of their passing, any more than other mortals." The dimming eyes looked steadily into hers. "My time has come—indeed, I have prolonged my life with sorcery for as long as I could, in the hope that you would come to me. Before I go, I would see you claim what is yours. If you do so, all will be well. I know this: many things seem clearer to me, now that I draw nearer to the Empyrean." He laid his head down again and Ailia sensed his living aura waning.

"Don't go!" she cried in a panic. "Wait but a while—there is so much I would ask—"

"Take the throne." It was but a whisper, hardly audible now.

Ailia obeyed. Stepping forward, she went to the great golden chair and seated herself, her hands resting on the carved dragons' heads of the armrests. Orbion's eyes closed. A long tremor passed through the silvery body, and then the dragon lay still, his ragged breathing silenced.

"He is gone," said Auron gently. "We will take him into the Ether now."

The dragons raised their heads, beat their wings and gave voice to their grief in ringing, bell-like cries. Auron joined with them. The beating wings sent little breezes flowing through the crystal hall, and the majestic, booming chorus went on for many minutes before dying away. A throbbing silence filled Ailia's ears in its place. Then Auron cried, "All hail the new ruler, appointed by the Old Ones! Long live the Celestial Empress!"

The dragons cried out again as Ailia remained seated on the Dragon Throne. Looking toward the open door, she saw the unicorn standing there, its horn held high like a sword in salute.

SHE NEXT WENT THROUGH THE healing wards where the injured warriors lay, and spoke to them. Ailia had no healing gift, and all her other powers were spent; but her very presence caused many an injured patient to revive. But she was beginning to feel very weary herself.

She walked back out into the forecourt of the healers' building, and through the crowd of the patients' friends and kinsfolk. Many were talking together, but here and there she was aware of pockets of silence in their midst. One such cell of quiet centered on a girl who sat on a bench, her face cast down, white robes torn and dirty. Ailia recognized the face under the dark brown curtains of hair: it was one of the Nemerei she had met at Melnemeron. What was her name . . . ?

Kathia, that was it. "What is the matter, Kathia?" she asked.

The young Nemerei lifted a tear-streaked face, then made as if to rise. Ailia stopped her with a hand on her shoulder. "Oh—Your Highness, I didn't see you. But I have lost—I have lost—" Her face crumpled. She could not yet break through the walls of her sorrow's self-containment.

Ailia sat beside her. "Who are you talking about?"

"Lothar," she whispered. "My Lothar—he's dead! They brought him back, but he died—in there. I couldn't save him—I have no healing art." She began to rock back and forth. "I could do nothing! I wish that you had been there, Trynel. Then you could have raised him to life, as you raised your Damion."

"Is that what they are saying?" exclaimed Ailia. "I have no such power, Kathia. No one has. Damion is half-Archon, and when mortal children of Old Ones die they are able to linger within the Ether, becoming like their immortal kin. But for other mortals who die—no one knows what their fate is. They do not go to the Ether. It's said there is another plane above both Ether and matter, the Empyrean, and there the souls of mortals dwell with the Maker of all things."

The girl's dark head dropped to her white-clad knees, and the wash of her sorrow struck Ailia like a wave, bringing an echo of her own former grief. "You loved him." The head nodded, but the only answer was a sob. "I didn't know him well—but I know he was a fine, and brave, young man. I am so sorry, Kathia."

"I wish I had died too!" the girl whispered.

"No—no, don't say that! The pain is real—but it will not always hurt as sharply as it does know. I promise you it won't." But Kathia wept on, and Ailia could give no other comfort save the bodily contact of her encircling arms. The girl's anguish, like a fever, must run its course. At last Ailia rose, and leaving the girl to her circle of concerned friends, she walked slowly away.

Tiron observed this, and was troubled anew for his daughter. *She cannot detach herself from the pain of others,* her father thought. *Such a one was never meant to go to war. She has too much imagination. Wars are begun by those who cannot imagine another's pain. What will become of her?*

"Ailia's bodily weakness is no defense against temptation. If anything, the desire of the weak for power is all the greater," one of the Loänan had said.

"But it may give her more sympathy for the weak," Damion had answered.

The priest's reappearance had indeed filled the people with amazement, and birthed the rumor that the Tryna Lia had restored him to the realm of the living. Their awe grew with the mysterious manifestations that accompanied Ailia's return to Mirimar. Once again the land was awash in reports of visions and marvels. The Archons were drawing closer to the frail barrier that separated their domain from that of mortals.

On the next high day a service was held in Halmirion's Chapel of Elarainia Queen of the World, in thanksgiving for the deliverance of Mera and Arainia. The rites themselves were the same as always: water, the sacred element of the goddess, was brought to the chapel in vessels of crystal and blessed. Ailia and the sibyls then drank of the water, and the remainder was sprinkled over the heads of the worshippers to symbolize the fall of life-giving rain from heaven. But now these rituals held a deeper meaning.

The sibyls led a procession with the Stone into the Chapel, singing the Cherubic Hymn:

The stone approaches,
behold, the host of Heaven accompanies
the stone into the temple.

And suddenly the chapel was filled with luminous elusive forms: flying figures that swept overhead, pale robes and shining wings, along with the very real cherubim that marched before and behind the procession. The sibyls themselves were filled with wonder; trembling, they conveyed the sacred stone into the sanctuary where Ailia received it. The shining forms were seen to swarm around its light, like moths around a lamp, and the air was filled with a pale pearly radiance and a sweet ethereal singing. Many there claimed that Ailia too seemed radiant, as if her spirit showed through her flesh.

At the conclusion of the service the ethereal form of the Bird of Heaven flew up from the Stone and circled about their heads, singing with the sound of many voices raised in unison.

"IT DOESN'T SEEM REAL AT all, does it?" Jemma breathed.

Ailia's foster family had come to Arainia with the returning army, at the Tryna Lia's invitation. As they descended the ramp from their flying vessel they were ushered to an open carriage by a special escort. They wondered at the greeting Tiron gave them, and that he should be riding with them in the same carriage: this "king" who wore no crown save only the thinnest of silver bands about his brow, and who treated them with reverence, as though they and not he were royalty. They stared all around them as they rode, as well they might, for wonders were everywhere. Ambassadors of many worlds had come here with Orbion. In addition to the Fairfolk, there were dryads, sylphs, and satyrs, and woodwoses, or wild men, who were clad all over in thick hair like beasts. The Merans marveled at these; and at the dwarfs, or gnomes, with their inhumanly short and broad build; and at the still smaller pygmy people, whose height seldom passed two feet, and who rode upon goats and rams because they were too small to mount horses.

On they went, and still the wonders increased. A woman walked toward their carriage as they paused at a turning of the way, and they stared at her: she was tall as a man, with bronze-colored skin and dark hair dressed in rows of tight braids woven with leather thongs. She wore gold-plated armor over a short white linen tunic, and she hailed them with a great shout, holding aloft a wooden spear.

"A *Malija*, what you would call an amazon. They are from a world where women are the rulers and warriors," King Tiron said, smiling at their startled faces. "There are other peoples in Talmirennia that are stranger still, or so I am told: the Androgyni that are neither men nor women, for instance, and the Cyclopes that have but one eye apiece. And in some worlds, the creatures you call beasts have gained the power of reason. They have mated with humankind, producing offspring that can be either shape at will. Those fair ladies you see there, my friend," Tiron said to Jaimon, who was eyeing a bevy of black-haired women clad in garments of green and gold that shimmered and clung to their figures, "they seem to be human, but they are not. They are Nagas, and in their true forms they are serpents." The Merans hardly knew whether to believe him or not; but the unearthly beauty of the Naga women haunted Jaimon for many days.

And there were dragons too, and cherubim, and sphinxes and tengus, manticores and myrmecoleons. Even to the Arainians such sights were amazing. To these humble Meran folk it was as though they moved in the tales that Ailia had once told them. Jemma and Jaimon and their parents, and Nella and Dannor, rode on through the city streets in a daze. At Jemma's side her two little boys were all eager, straining eyes. At last the carriage took them through the gates of Halmirion, into its gracious grounds and on to the faerie palace itself on its high hill: and they were ushered by guards in splendid livery into the cool marble halls beyond. Nella felt small and shabby, and yet the grand people looked at her and her family in apparent awe. For they were the protectors of the Princess, who had twice given her shelter at need.

Into the hall of audience they went, staring up at the frescoed clouds of the ceiling. And they came to the end of the hall, where

sat a goddess on a crystal throne, with stars on her scepter and diadem and in her train. Her long hair flowed about her, and she had
a white gown on under her starry blue mantle. Nella scarcely recognized Ailia at first, and when she did she quaked a little. Had she
raised this girl, nursed her and cared for her? And made her do
chores, and tried to wed her to a fisherman? As she looked at the
Tryna Lia on her throne, Nella felt like the hen in the old folktale
who raised an eagle from the egg and then watched it soar aloft
among the clouds. She surrendered in her mind every claim she still
felt she had upon the girl, and merely gazed at her in wonder and
in awe. Jaimon too found himself acknowledging the truth at last:
She's not ours, and never really was. But then she looked down at them,
and smiled her old familiar smile, and they knew her again.

Afterward Ailia spoke with them all in one of the receiving
rooms. They laughed together, and cried a little, and then Ailia
grew solemn. "Now we must make ready for war. I would have you
remain here, where you will be safe."

"But isn't it all over now?" Jaimon asked. "The rebel Zimbourans
have been defeated, and we have been allowed into this world—"

"The battle in Mera was only a small part of a much larger war.
The Book of Doom spoke of the deliverance of your world only.
This conflict hasn't ended: it has only started. But don't trouble
yourselves about it now. Rest, and take your ease."

After seeing that her foster family were comfortable in their
guest rooms, Ailia went to the war council. Mandrake, it was reported, had retreated to his stronghold of Nemorah; his servants—
or his masters—had prevailed on him to go to Ombar for safety, but
he had resisted them, perhaps as he began to realize what confine-
ment and enslavement awaited him there. How long, though,
would his resistance last in the face of their constant persuasion?

"Now is the time to strike," said Auron. "While he is still in a position of weakness. For if he does flee to Ombar he will have the full
protection of the evil Archons—perhaps of Valdur himself. He
must not be allowed to go there."

Taleera grumbled, "All very well for these Archons! All they have
to do is watch. They've forbidden themselves to help, you say."

"But that is the hardest part of all," said Ailia. "What can be worse
than watching those you love struggle and suffer, and perhaps fail—

knowing you can do nothing for them? I think I pity the Archons the most."

THE NEMEREI WORKED FEVERISHLY TO create the new flameproof armor, the mail of overlapping golden scales, the shirts and trousers of close-spun silk to go underneath and the surcoats and mantles of wool. Over the visors went the dark eye coverings that the salamanders cast off with their skins.

"I can't see very well," remarked Lorelyn, peering through hers. "It's like looking through smoky glass. But I suppose we shall only need them when the flames are right in our faces."

Throughout the battle preparations at Melnemeron Ailia was curiously silent, pale and withdrawn. Damion watched her with concern.

"She hates battles, you know that," said Lorelyn.

"I know," replied Damion. But as he looked at Ailia sitting silent on her carved seat, the serenity left his face and eyes for the first time since his return. He knew her now for what she truly was, a spirit, and yet still he flinched at the thought of any bodily harm coming to her. For he had also learned, from his own experience, that suffering too was real.

"Well, I for one can't wait to get at Mandrake," declared Jomar.

It was decided that the host should be transported by means of the dragon-gate to the enemy's world. Ailia's knowledge of the land surrounding Mandrake's fortress was called upon in planning the assault. The human army would attack by land, and the dragons would engage Mandrake's Loänan in the air.

Ailia strove not to remember the courteous, attentive, gracious Mandrake she had known during her stay there. That man, she told herself, had been an illusion, false as any glaumerie; the true Mandrake was the one who had betrayed the Paladins, supported the murderous tyrant Khalazar, and was allied now with evil Archons to destroy Talmirennia. Even if Mandrake had been virtuous once upon a time, the enemy had transformed him into a monster and a murderer. If she grieved for him at all, it was for one who was dead.

"I do not hate Mandrake," declared Falaar. "He at least is a worthy adversary, and were that task not appointed to the Tryna Lia I would seek to kill him and win much honor thereby. But I shall do what I can. I was made for war," he said, spreading his great wings as he spoke. "Also, I have brought the Star Sward from Mera."

Jomar held up his iron blade with a fierce joy before giving it back to Falaar to carry: for its power would prevent any sky-ship or dragon from flying. The blade that could destroy the Dragon King! He was almost grateful to Mandrake for taking the role of Avatar. At long last the elusive, shadowy power that had mocked Jomar from behind other men's faces had manifested, taken on a form of flesh: now in Mandrake's person it could be challenged, assailed, slain.

THE DAYS PASSED—FOR AILIA all too swiftly—and the hour came at last when all was ready. The warriors donned their salamandrine armor. The dragons on the plateau of Melnemeron all prepared for flight, flexing their great venous wings. Those with human riders ensured that they had a firm hold and were not in danger of falling off. On Auron's golden back Ailia sat looking up at the deep blue sky above them, and the comets that now followed harmless courses thanks to the efforts of these celestial warriors. Their foes had retreated, following their leader. The first battle was won, it appeared, but a still greater one lay ahead. They would no longer endure the forays of the enemy, but advance upon his own fortress.

An ethereal dragon hurled her huge silvery body into the air, and spread her wings. Others followed: white, gold, blue, red, and green wings sprang open, flared and lifted their owners aloft. How wonderful it would be, if one were able merely to enjoy it! But Ailia's breath was coming fast at the thought of what lay before them.

At last her turn and Auron's came. He spread his wings and flexed them carefully, then crouched low like a lion about to spring. And they were off in a rush of wind, and the other dragons were no longer above but all around them. For an instant Ailia did forget her fear in the exhilaration of it all. She had never before flown with an entire flight of dragons: now she recalled those she had seen long ago, soaring above the peaks of the Holymount in Trynisia. All around her were beating wings and winding, sinuous bodies, as they swept around the mountain top and sped toward the Gate of Earth and Heaven.

After many centuries the Loänan were at last going to war. But the heart of their chosen leader was still weighed down with doubts.

Part Two

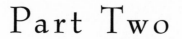

THE BATTLE

13

Nemorah

No one who had seen it in its former days would now recognize the Forbidden Palace of the Loänei. Most of the dragon-folk had abandoned it when news came of the defeats in Mera and Arainia, and the human servants had fled. Many of the Loänei that remained partook of the bliss-flower from the jungle, whose sweet perfume brought ease and forgetfulness to the mind: it had once been used for the ill and for women in the pangs of childbirth, but in the face of looming despair it had now become a mere drug. As they withdrew in mind and body from their fortress, the Morugei from Ombar had moved in, and invited others of their kind from the city; they had taken over most of the larger rooms. The once lovingly tended carpets were soiled, the tapestries torn, and the tall standing candelabra broken from much use as weapons in jousts playful and not so playful. In the pleasure gardens the wild native flora and fauna were invading and driving out the otherworldly ones that had been so carefully cultivated. The carp were gone from the ornamental pools, seized and devoured; the roses were reduced to tangles of bristling thorns, half-choked by strangling vines.

The formal throne hall looked much as it always had, save for a fine layer of dust upon all its furnishings. Mandrake sat in his throne, his claw-tipped fingers tapping a sharp staccato on the armrests as he brooded. He knew well that the ranks of his court were steadily thinning, as one by one his subjects deserted him. A few of his dragons remained: he was their Trynoloänan, and they would defend him with their lives. But he and they no longer inspired the fear they once had. New gods would soon appear from the skies, challenging Loänanmar's God-ruler, and already the people were abandoning the city. Mandrake was aware of this, but felt curiously indifferent. His mind was too taken up with other fears.

It was said in some old legends that no tomb for King Andarion had ever been found because he had not died, but had passed into the realm of the Ether to sit at the side of his immortal sire; and it was said too that he would one day return to Mera and continue his reign. Mandrake had dismissed this as myth and wishful thinking, spawned by the terror and uncertainty of the Dark Age; and now it was rumored that Andarion did live still, that he had returned. In response perhaps to his alarm at the reports, the wound inflicted by his father's sword long years ago had remanifested as a throbbing scar on Mandrake's neck. No matter that the weapon had been wielded by another hand: such had been the devotion of Ingard the Bold to his liege lord that he had seemed at times but an extension of Brannar Andarion's will, knowing the king's inmost desires and acting upon them when he himself would not. *And my father did nothing to prevent him,* Mandrake thought. *It was honor, not love, that stayed his hand from slaying me; he was glad enough to have another do the deed for him.* His face was still scored too with the angry red welts Ailia's dragon claws had left upon his dragon's countenance. Even his shift to human form had not banished these injuries, for his mind as well as his body had been wounded. The pain was far worse in his draconic form however, and as he could not hold any other shape so long as the two that were his birth heritage, he was forced to be a man. The burden of human weakness had again fallen upon him. Was this what Ailia had intended?

As he brooded, a form appeared in the air at his side. The Regent of Ombar gazed at him with narrowed eyes. "How long will you persist in this madness?" Naugra demanded. "I tell you the enemy is coming. You must remove to Ombar."

The clawed hands tightened on the armrests. "I have been to your world before," Mandrake replied. "I have no desire to return to it, now or ever."

"For your own safety—"

"Tell me, is what awaits me in Ombar any better than what awaits me here?"

"You still do not trust us, even now? We have stood between you and your foe."

"Out of the goodness of your heart," said Mandrake dryly.

"Naturally not—but your well-being is in our interests, all the same. To find another being with both Archon and Loänan blood in his immediate ancestry would be unlikely, and to create another would be impossible. You are unique, and were meant to be so."

Mandrake snarled, "I want nothing to do with Archons and their machinations."

"But we are rebelling against the dominant Archons," said the Regent. "Like you, we disapprove of their plans for the Empire. Our own masters parted company with them many ages ago."

"They have done their share of meddling. They ruled the Zimbourans through their offspring Gurusha, transformed humans into wretched goblins and dragons into firedrakes, raised them up as a fighting force to serve their own ends—"

"To thwart the Archon empire! Elmera, that you call Eliana, and her allies—and Ailia, the Archons' heir—"

Mandrake ignored the interruption. "And as you say, they planned my birth for generations—they foresaw the king's coming, and bred the Loänei sorceress Moriana so that Andarion should sire me to be your weapon in the conflict to come. We are their tools. The Archons are all the same."

Naugra's phantom eyes gazed steadily at him. "Say what you will, they made you, Mandrake—without them you would never have existed."

"Then I have them to thank for all that I have suffered," said Mandrake. "Enough of this. If I am your ruler, then you must obey me. Be gone! And remember, if I grow tired of this game I can always take my own life—and you will lose your precious weapon!"

"Do not linger here over-long, or the new Empress may yet perform that service for you." With that the Regent faded from sight.

Left alone once more, Mandrake got up from the throne and began to pace about. He had watched the converging ranks of the enemy in his crystal scrying globe. Perhaps the Archons had been right, perhaps he should have fled when he had the chance. But to Ombar—he shuddered, recalling darkness. He had spoken lightly of the world to Ailia, but he knew it to be a place of horror, its memory an evil dream. Still, Ailia and her army would hesitate to follow him there . . . What to do? His present, chosen refuge was no longer safe. The Tryna Lia could not command such power in

Nemorah as she had in her own world, but she had improved her skill with sorcery and she had many other sorcerers at her command. Surrender was not possible—not to foes who had sworn to destroy him, who believed him to be the greatest danger their Empire had ever faced. They could not even safely imprison him, bound with iron, lest the Valei rescue him. There was nowhere to flee to, no safe haven where he would not soon be discovered, save only for Ombar. No matter how often his thoughts pursued solutions, always they cycled back to Valdur's world as if compelled by some remorseless fate. It was a bastion, he acknowledged, defended not only by sorcerers but also by lingering Archonic powers. These would protect him—but to what end? They meant to make use of him, considered him their lawful property since they had brought him into being.

Presently a voice hailed him from the doorway. It was Syndra. Alone of the humans she had remained with him. Her black hair with its glints like witches' oils was unbound, pouring down her back, and she was clad in a long, loose garment of deepest red. The shadow of a smile was upon her lips. That smile, and something that hinted of gloating in her expression, unsettled him.

"What is it you want?" he snapped.

"No: what is it that *you* want?" she asked. "Tell me, and I will give it you."

"At the moment, I desire chiefly to be left alone," he replied.

"But you will never be alone, Mandrake," she said. "You never have been, from the first." She advanced with a soft rustle of her robe. "I know this. I was there when you were born—and before."

He stared at her. Had she partaken of the bliss-flower? Her eyes were fever-bright, her cheeks flushed. She laughed low in her throat. "Naugra is right. We endured the tyranny of the high Archons for centuries, but we could do them no harm. We could only harm their precious creatures, and for that we required a mortal servant to act on our behalf."

"Syndra—"

"I am not Syndra. I am Elnemorah."

Elnemorah: she named the old deity of Nemorah, the goddess of volcano fire who dwelled in the burning heart of the world. He backed away. Was she mad, drunk, possessed?

"I am the Archon of this world, who rebelled against my kind long ago. For that I was banished, prevented from returning in the flesh—until now. Now I have found a willing vessel. As for Ailia, she is a mere servant, a moon-spirit, the least of those whom we hate. Through her they act; yet through her sufferings they too can be made to suffer. You will kill her for us, our Morlyn." She reached out a long white hand, tipped with blood-red nails nearly as long as his own. Her mouth was red too, glistening with paint: it curved into a full smile as she gazed at him with her too-brilliant eyes. "Ah, it is good to be robed in flesh again, and free to walk this plane." He drew back from the pale hand. "But perhaps this form does not please you. I shall alter it."

And then it was Ailia standing there, with her soft hair and her great eyes turned up to him. He started and clenched his hands, wounding the palms with his nails. She smiled, and held out an arm graceful as a lily on its stem. She was still clad in the shift of ember-red: it slipped, showing the soft white sculpture of one shoulder and the dimples at the base of the throat. He was sickened at this blatant theft of another's face and form, and yet he could not tear his eyes away.

"You see?" Ailia's soft voice said. "I can be anything I wish, Mandrake—or that you wish. You have but to ask it of me."

She was so like . . . yearning called to him, irresistible as a current that seizes hold of a swimmer and pulls him out to sea. But then resentment awoke in him: resentment at being thus controlled, reduced to a mindless animal by an unsummoned instinct. The fierce pride that was all he had left now came to his aid. He averted his eyes with an effort of will greater than any he had ever called on before. Syndra, or the thing within her, wanted him bound to her just as he himself had sought to bind Ailia. But though he might owe his life, his very body, to the dark Archons, his mind he still jealously guarded as his own.

"Keep your ensorcelments for the enemy," he said in brusque dismissal, moving away. "I will have none of them." Sultry laughter greeted this statement, and by its sound he knew that she had reverted to her own form.

Mandrake swept from the room, striding swiftly along the corridors while his few remaining vassals fled before his dark-mantled figure and dead-white face. Once alone in his own quarters he slammed the door, and flung his mantle to the floor. Syndra was only a minor trouble. Most likely she had merely partaken of some potion that had maddened her. But the Tryna Lia: what must be done about her? Perhaps Damion Athariel had done him a service by returning and claiming Ailia. It would be easier now to kill her— kill them both. Jealousy and hate came now to his aid. He saw in his mind's vision the two of them together, and was able to feel the rage he needed—to fight them, to survive. Hate was an ally, the dark door through which power came. He clenched his hands on his robes, tearing them inadvertently with his claws. Then releasing them he went to the cabinet where he kept his ambrosia elixir, and on taking it felt the physical self recede and his mind detach itself with the old feeling of freedom. Lying down, he was removed from the events unfolding around him, and from the body reclining as if in sleep on the divan. He could look dispassionately at the drawn face with its ghastly pallor and vivid scars, at the red-gold hair tumbled about it in disarray. It was more distancing than looking at one's image in a mirror, for this was no shadow but the thing itself. He observed with detachment the slow rise and fall of the chest beneath the black silk robe, and knew that should the tenuous thread between it and his immaterial self be severed, it would be stilled forever. *And if it ends, will I end too? What of this conscious spark—will it continue, or be annihilated? And if it were annihilated, would that not be a release?*

Shaking off these thoughts, Mandrake decided that he would project himself unseen, and move among his few remaining courtiers. He must be desperate indeed to seek such pitiful company, but his solitude was unendurable. Too human for the Loänan, too dragonish to be among humans, all his life had been spent in limbo. He drifted from the room and down the halls, and no one fled from him now, invisible as he was. He moved among his people like a ghost, observing them, listening to their talk.

Presently he heard his name spoken, and he followed the sound of voices into the dreary empty space of the ballroom. Some Morugei were lounging there, including Roglug.

"We shouldn't hang about here. I reckon Mandrake's done for," said the goblin-king. "I'm leaving, at any rate."

"I won't shed no tears when he dies!" said another. "Let that Empress have him! Then we'll be free."

"Free," murmured the king. "Yes—they did nothing against us before he came. After he's gone they may let us alone."

Mandrake had heard enough. He fled back the way he had come.

All at once the demons were there, with him, one ethereal form at either side. Elombar thrust his bestial face close to Mandrake's. "You fool! Why do you not leave this place yourself and come to Ombar? You allied yourself with us, for good or ill, and now you must remain on our side, or be killed. Do you think the Tryna Lia will spare you? That we are helpless to stop you turning against us, so you can do as you will? We made you, you are ours."

Mandrake laughed, the sound harsh and humorless. "You are afraid now, Archon—if that is what you truly are? You fear that your weapon has in mind of its own, and can turn and cut you?"

"We shall see. The Empress has come with her army to destroy you. Depart and live, or stay and be slain: it is your choice, you think. But you are wrong."

They had entered his private chamber. The Archon pointed to Mandrake's prone body. And then he watched in disbelief as that body, apparently of its own volition, rose to its feet. It walked out of the door, and down the hall, and he heard it addressing the Loänei lingering there. The voice was his, but not the words:

"We go to Ombar. Prepare to depart. It is my command!"

Mandrake's ethereal form pursued his stolen flesh. And there in the high-roofed hall he saw his body begin to transform into a dragon's shape.

Horrified, he imposed his will upon it. The scales came and went on his face and limbs, talons and teeth lengthened and then grew shorter again. He returned to his body, and mastered it; but there was no longer any sense of absolute control. He felt that he was twice imprisoned: in this hated castle and in his own flesh that had been designed, deliberately bred by the Archon Valdur in order to be taken over—a tool, a thing to be used. He stared down at his hands, at the bones within the meshes of veins. He flexed his fingers with their sharp claws. They were his to command—*for now*, a voice seemed to say. *Only for now.*

"No," he whispered. The dragon-folk stared at him, and he straightened. "No—wait. We do *not* go to Ombar."

"But the enemy—they have come to Nemorah," began one Loänei.

"We will go to my castle in the sea. It is easily defensible." His eyes flared golden fire at them. "Obey me!"

*   *   *

AILIA LOOKED OVER AURON'S HORNED head at the sphere of Nemorah. The world lay beneath them, a huge dome of many tints: grassland, jungle, ocean showed as pale jade, dark malachite, and shimmering emerald. Clouds swirled across that patchwork of greens, pure white save in one place, where the whorl of a vast and angry storm could be seen upon the ocean's surface. As night's shadow advanced over the typhoon, tiny sparks of lightning flickered fitfully in the gray mass at its center, not all of it natural in origin. For this was no natural storm arising from sea and weather but a magical barrier, a gigantic citadel crafted by the Dragon King out of cloud and air. It did not advance as a true sea storm would, but remained always in one fixed position, and its central eye stood directly above the spot where his submarine castle lay.

Auron continued in his lofty orbit. Weightless here, he had no need for his wings, and the great translucent membranes hung half-furled at his sides. Her heartbeats quickened at the familiar sight of Nemorah. It was another Ailia who had come here before, who in retrospect seemed like an innocent child, naive and unsuspecting of what lay before her. Now she knew. From her height above the world, she marked the spinning mass of the typhoon and knew she had found her quarry. He *is there*, Ailia thought, and she felt as though her heart would burst through her ribs. She saw Damion astride his own mount, the cherub Falaar, and he looked back at her reassuringly.

"Now *we* are the attacking force!" said the cherub. "I cannot wait for battle to be joined. This is what I was made for."

Ailia looked across at Falaar's fierce hooked beak and savage talons, and realized that this must be true: they were designed for seizing and rending flesh. Almost she could pity his prey. Damion looked at her as though guessing her thoughts.

Auron gazed down with ears and nose barbels twitching, following the aerial battle far below. "They have engaged the enemy," he said at last.

"Then let us go," said Damion. "They may need us."

"We will have the victory!" cried Auron as he descended, burning the air with his speed. Falaar gave a ringing eagle-cry and followed him. Soon they were low enough to see the great clouds roiling and colliding beneath them, and the flying forms of dragons and cherubim plunging in and out of the ragged gaps between. In another few minutes they were level with the field of battle. Thunderheads reared high above, veined with lightning bolts, lit up by great fiery flashes from within. Never before had Ailia seen a storm from above the level of the clouds, and she was filled with awe even as she mourned what was taking place in its depths.

Dragons fighting each other! she thought, grieving, and she felt Auron's sorrow too. The firedrakes were evil, but for Loänan to fight Loänan was a terrible thing.

We have to fight, said Damion in her mind. *They gave us no choice.*

I understand, she agreed, unhappily.

They flew on toward the main battle. They were high in the sky still, moving above a gray-white cloud-plain under a starry sky of darkest blue-black. Two of the world's moons shone above them, bright-lit on their left sides: one gray and one golden in color. The only other light came from the bulking gray-purple cumuli ahead. When lit from inside, they flashed pale lilac, and every detail of them showed: crags and tufts and filmy strands spreading like roots in air. They were being buffeted and tormented by the great winds into strange shapes, top-heavy towers and bulging battlements, table-mountains with long streamers of mist blowing off their flat tops, mounds of wool slowly shredding to pieces and re-forming before her eyes. Ailia was reminded of the winter sea off Great Island: of the great shapes of the white icebergs looming up out of floating pans of ice. The cumuli were the bergs, and the flat plain of cloud between them the pack ice: in places it thinned and gave way to dark openings, just as the frozen pack gave way to dark patches of open water. She looked down into those deeps of air as Auron passed over them, but could see nothing below.

She felt the winds too, as Auron encountered them, often with as jarring an impact as if he had struck something solid. Sometimes he dropped as if an invisible floor beneath had given way and cast him into a pit. Often he was blown about so violently that the dragon had to pull his wings in and let himself fall like a stone, away from the gust that had seized him. The other winged warriors were suffering the same difficulties, she could see. Ailia clung as hard as she could to Auron's horns, for if she were blown off his back she would not be able to breathe, even if she took a bird's form to save herself from the fall. Only a dragon or cherub could live at these heights;

she had not learned how to take the latter shape, and dared not assume the former.

The storm was constructed like a fortress with concentric rings of curtain-walls, protecting an inner keep. The Wingwatch's aim was the same as that of any army besieging such a structure: to break through each barrier in turn, until they could overrun the keep. The dragons and cherubim could choose to overfly the storm and plunge straight down toward the central eye, and some had chosen to do so; but there the wild winds were strongest, the sorcerous guardians fiercest. Many losses had already been reported among those who had made the attempt. For the rest there was the task of breaching each ring of defense, until the enemy's ranks were depleted, and those at the center were forced to spread themselves outward to replace the fallen, weakening the inner guard. Peering ahead through all the gray fantastic shapes that barred their way, Ailia caught glimpses of bright lights, tiny sparks they looked from here, that came and went in an instant: they might almost have been the shining specks that appear before weary eyes, but she knew they were gouts of dragon-fire. The firedrakes were trying to attack the Loänan. It was not like the fights among the comets where the firedrakes had to enter the Loänan's envelopes of air in order to use their fire on them. Here there was plenty of air to feed the giant flames.

She understood now why the weather was in such turmoil. Two factions of Loänan were imposing their will upon the atmosphere: and as they dueled each other, the great winds they commanded clashed together, and created this chaotic turbulence. She tried to help, drawing on her own power to move wind and cloud, but could not bring any order into the airy melee: instead her efforts merely contributed to it. "This is no use!" she cried as they plunged into the middle of one thunderhead. A jagged bolt clove the air before their eyes, mere wing-lengths away: the gray darkness flared to white-purple brilliance all around them. Dazzled, they burst out through puffs of what resembled motionless steam into open sky again.

"We are seeking to move the storm out to sea," said Auron.

"But what if it strikes the coast instead? Hundreds of people might perish."

"We cannot turn the whole cloud-mass southward, nor east nor west. It is the nature of such storms to move in a northerly direction as they feed on the warmth of the waters beneath them. A contrary path would be unnatural, and would take more power than even we can command. The very atmosphere would have to be altered, with devastating effects in many other places. The winds of the world are against us."

"Auron, I know it is difficult to get *through* the storm ourselves, but if shifting it could cause more harm then let us not try it."

Auron gave a beat of his wings and soared skyward again, out of the grasp of the tumultuous winds. "You are right, Highness. We may risk our safety, but no one else's. My people will continue the fight to breach the walls of cloud and lightning, and win through to the storm's eye. For now you should join with your army, who await you near Loänanmar. There is still the matter of the people on land, who do not yet know their deliverance is near."

14

The Overseer

AURON AND FALAAR FLEW their riders to the old city of the Loänei downriver from Loänanmar, where a portal had been opened by Mandrake: the same through which Syndra had come when she first fled to this world. It now gave entry to the Arainian army. The soldiers had set up an encampment in the ruins, after Ailia warned them of the many dangers in the jungles beyond. None of them had ever ventured to the domain of an alien star, while a few had not even passed beyond the bounds of their home world. Jomar and Lorelyn were as filled with awe at their surroundings as any of the warriors fighting under their command.

Ailia was restless and uneasy. She had not wanted to return to this place, and not merely because of its sinister associations; there was a real menace in the air that unsettled her. She understood, now that her Archonic side had reawakened, why the jungles had seemed so hostile and threatening to her when she first entered them. It had not been merely because of their unfamiliarity, and the dangerous animals dwelling within them. The incorporeal powers that reigned over this sphere were aware of her and resentful of her intrusion. Was this what the invaders of her own world had felt in the forests near Hyelanthia? However she might feel, though, she must not let anyone in the camp sense it. As their leader, her duty was to inspire them with confidence.

She went to stand at the opening of the tent that had been raised for her, and looked at the sentries strung along the riverside. The tepid water was flat as glass, and opaque with silt; it was impossible to tell what lurked within it, and she had told everyone of the perilous river-dwelling beasts: the many-headed hydras, and the terrible guivres that resembled serpents with the jaws of crocodiles. Everyone was watchful and ready for an attack, from either the jungle's denizens or the enemy. The air steamed all around them, humid and dense, full of eerie cries from the tangled groves beyond. It was heavy, sultry, and the knights who were wearing their armor sweated and mopped at their streaming brows. The whole of the atmosphere was oppressive with heat and tension.

Yet beneath all the apprehension, Ailia was aware of a competing emotion: it felt oddly comforting to be in these same surroundings, but not this time alone, as she had been before. Now her dearest friends were here with her, and the Wingwatch and an entire army. The more mundane fear she had known before, the dread of being injured or killed, had gone. Ailia gazed at Damion where he stood in the open, his hair bright in the glow of the two suns as he looked around him.

"This is a terrible world," he said. "Do you feel it? The Vor-power is very strong here."

The Vor-power. "I saw it," Ailia said. "Our old ancestor, the reptile in the mire. I know it is in us all, the chief cause of our failings."

"In mortals, yes," Damion said. "All beings began as beasts, long ago. I was aware of the creature's presence within me. Even the Tarnawyn, the foe of serpents, began as cold-blooded creeping things themselves. The first unicorns were hoofed and horned as now, but their bodies were scaled, and they had heads like dragons. In fact, they arose on the same world as the celestial dragons. Tarnawyn and Loänan are close kin. But humankind is young, and closer to its bestial ancestors. Perhaps that is why I—and so many others—dreamed of slaying dragons. It was not the Loänan we hated and feared, nor even the firedrake, but the creeping thing that lies *within* us. I no longer need fear it, though: my link to it was severed when I became an Elaia. My dragon is slain forever."

"I think perhaps it need not be slain or conquered," said Ailia. "What if it could be tamed?"

"Tamed?" He frowned.

"Made subordinate to my will, but allied with it, so that I might draw on its strengths."

"That would be very dangerous. Mandrake too thought he could command the beast within, and he ended by becoming a beast." *And you came close to it,* he added with his eyes alone—not accusing, but gently warning her.

She looked down, not able to meet his gaze. "I am so glad you are back with us, Damion. Back *home,* as it were."

"It isn't really my home," he answered, his blue eyes growing distant. "I was never more than a sojourner on this plane. Much of the time it horrified me with its cruelty. I returned because I was asked to do so by you. But this is not my place, not anymore."

"You wish to return to the Ether?" Her heart sank within her.

"It is my true home." He saw her look, and went to put his arm about her. "And yours also. Will you go back there with me, when this is all ended?"

She looked up at him, and then down at her body, viewing it as if it were a separate creature and feeling a strange pity for it. It wanted to do all those things for which it was made: to live on this plane, to love, to bear children. To become an Archon again meant to abandon all that she had become through her incarnation . . . The mere thought filled her with sorrow. "I—don't know," she answered. "I had not thought of what will come after, if I live. I suppose I must return."

He turned to look away into the depths of the jungle. "Have you noticed how he's changing back again?" Lorelyn had said to her earlier. "The way he stands, and talks, and walks? He's becoming more, well, *Damionish.*" Perhaps he was. But as she gazed at him now, at the clean, comely lines of his profile, chin, and throat; at the blue of his

eye, at the way his fair hair grew on the nape of his neck, she
thought how all these things were the same as before, and yet he
was not. He was the child of an angel, and now a full Elaia; it was
curious how she had sensed that otherworldly quality in him from
the first time she saw him in the chapel, without knowing who and
what he was. Eons ago, as it felt to her now . . . He had returned,
and in a way he had not; it was the same Damion who stood beside
her, and not the same. He was farther from her now than ever before. She felt a stirring of anxiety. *Have I regained him only to lose him
once and for all? Or will I change too?*

Ailia lifted her face to the sky, as if seeking the hidden stars. *I don't
ask for life—I have loved the mortal son of an angel—befriended a dragon, and
ascended to Heaven on his back—lived as a princess in a palace—it has been
wonderful, all of it. Few have lived as I have, though they may have lived longer.
I asked that my life be a story, and I have had my wish. I will ask nothing more.
I will only do what I must do.* She still shrank from that destiny, that de-
creed she must be murderer or victim. But if it were the price for
this mortal life with which she had been gifted, then she would
pay it.

There came a sudden commotion from the far end of the camp:
shouts and yells and the sound of running feet. Ailia, grateful for the
diversion, hastened toward the scene with Damion following.
"What is it?" she asked.

"The guards have caught something," said a Paladin. "Some creature stole into the camp—one of your venomous beasts, perhaps.
I've never seen anything like it," added the man, looking a trifle
revolted.

A loud squalling filled the air and Ailia, recognizing the sound,
rushed toward it.

"Twidjik!" she cried, seeing the amphisbaena struggling wildly in
the grip of several men. "No, let it go—I know this creature. It
saved my life!"

They released Twidjik and he crawled toward her chittering.
"Sorceress lady—we heard you were coming again. Don't let them
harm us."

"No one will hurt you," said Ailia, kneeling beside him. "You are
safe here, Twidjik."

"We must stay here. We daren't go back—the Dragon King, he
grows more terrible each day—all go in fear of him. Palace people

have fled—the city is emptying—strange things are happening. We are afraid!"

"There, you can stay with me now," Ailia reassured him.

"Are you sure the creature is not a spy, Trynel?" asked one of the Paladins.

Ailia briefly entertained the thought that Twidjik might hold a grudge against her, considering her treatment of him while she was under the influence of the philter. But she decided against this. "Mandrake has other, better ways of spying on us," she said. "And Twidjik has given aid to me in the past, at great risk to himself."

She went back to her tent, Twidjik following. "Tell me, do you know what became of Mag and her daughter?" she asked. "The woman from the inn, who cared for you?"

"They safe, both. The woman send us through jungle to find you, when she hear your army come. She want you should know about Overseer."

"The Overseer?" The human ruler of the city of Loänanmar, deposed by Mandrake. "You mean he has come back?"

"Yes, yes—come with army. He wish to fight Dragon King, take back city. He has army, many many men. But not enough, we think."

"Do you know where they are now?"

"No. But Mag and her daughter, they know. Daughter has been with his people in jungle, in camp. She help cook food for them."

"I see. Could you take me to Mag?"

"Yes, yes. She want see you, very much. And daughter Mai can take you to Overseer. But maybe he not let you near. He very strict about who may come and go. Mag says he not believe in Tryna Lia, nor sky-army."

"Well, he should be glad to learn that we are real, for we can add our forces to his, and help him win back Loänanmar. That is why we are here: not only to conquer the Dragon King, but to free those under his rule."

"Very good. You come, then?"

"Yes. Lead the way, and I will follow. Is it very far?"

"Many days."

She smiled. "By foot perhaps, but not if my dragon friend takes us."

Ailia set out a dish of food for the creature, and then went to talk to her friends and the army's leaders.

"I can trust this messenger," she said. "He's Twidjik, the amphisbaena who helped me."

"What is an amphisbaena, Highness?" asked a knight who had not seen Twidjik arrive.

She smiled. "A sort of two-headed monster. Don't look so alarmed! He is quite small, and will be far more frightened of you than you are of him. He says he can lead me to a gathering of rebels, in another hidden camp in the jungle."

"You should take a company of soldiers with you, Highness," advised Taleera. "Just to be on the safe side."

"No—I think it will be better if I go alone. They might be afraid."

Auron said, "I will fly you there, and then go with you to the camp in human form."

"And I too," offered Damion. "They won't fear a small group, if we are unarmed."

Her other friends also wished to accompany her, but Auron advised against it. "As few of us as possible should go," he said. "And Jomar has a rather threatening aspect, and can be somewhat aggressive."

Jomar was about to argue, then realized he would only be confirming Auron's point. "Right, then. I'll fetch the Thing and tell it to lead the way," he said with a shrug.

"He's not a thing," reproved Lorelyn. "He's an amphisbaena."

"*Thing* takes less time to say." He headed off through the camp.

AURON FLEW WITH AILIA AND Damion on his great golden back, while Twidjik perched in Ailia's lap craning both his necks to look for familiar features in the landscape below. At last he indicated a place of many old ruins about ten leagues from their own encampment. All three of the Nemerei could feel the presence of iron in that place: perhaps it was only in use in tools and cook pots, or lay deep in the earth itself. But it hampered Auron's flight. He descended with some difficulty into the trees—their branches caught at the webs of his huge wings—and waited as his three passengers climbed down. "I cannot join you," he said. "The iron inhibits me from taking any other form, and the humans will be frightened of a dragon. I will wait here, and if you are not back in a few hours I will assume you have been captured, and come to your aid."

Ailia and Damion thanked him. Then they followed the amphisbaena through the jungle. Presently they smelled the cook fires of the camp, and heard many voices. The refugees from the city had gathered in a large cleared space, filled with the stumps of fresh-cut trees. Twidjik led them into the midst of the encampment.

Ailia saw a familiar face bent over one of the stew pots. "Mag!" she cried, rushing forward.

Hearing her call, the dark-haired woman started and looked up from the pot. "Lia, is that you? Lia!" she cried, throwing down her ladle and looking all about her. "Where are you?"

"I'm here, Mag—I've come back!"

The woman started to run toward her, and then she halted in bewilderment, looking full at Ailia without recognition. Of course: in her delight at seeing her friend, Ailia had forgotten that Mag had known her only in a glaumerie guise. The illusory "Lia" had looked altogether different, round-featured and dark of hair and eye. "It's I, Mag, truly it is!" Ailia said, going up to her. "I had to alter my looks before, but I am the same person you knew. Listen to my voice. It hasn't changed." Mag continued to gaze at her in wonder.

"Ah—it's true what they said," she murmured. "You are not at all as you appeared to be."

"I am sorry to have deceived you, dear Mag. But I was alone and afraid. If I had known you a little better then I would have trusted you with my secrets."

"Bless you! I'm not blaming you. It's only—it's a little hard to understand. But your voice *is* just the same. It's true, isn't it—what that little old man said about you?"

She meant Auron, Ailia knew. Mag had never seen him except in human form. "You mean that I am the Tryna Lia? Yes, it is true."

"Some of our old tales mention her. But I thought she was a sort of goddess."

"Not exactly. I am a sorceress, and I come from a world called Arainia. This is my friend Damion, who has also lived there."

"When we heard the rumors about your army, and the dragons and all, we sent Twidjik off to see if he could find you," Mag told her.

"I am glad you did. Mag, I wish you would come away with me—

you and Mai." Ailia's eyes shifted to a slender young girl who had emerged from the crowd, and now stood shy and wordless at her mother's side. "To my own world. They would take care of you there."

"Thank you so much, but I don't feel right about leaving with my people in this fix. Take Mai, if you'd be so kind. But I will stay."

"We are here to help your people, Mag. That is why we came. To help you, and to end the Dragon King's reign."

"I expect you'll want to meet with the Overseer, then. There are folk here who know where he is living in hiding. Mai's young man, for one."

"Young man?" asked Ailia.

"The boy she loves: Teren, his name is. He's a rebel, one of their army, and visits here to bring her food and give us news. He's here now, if you want to meet him."

MAI INTRODUCED THEM TO TEREN, who agreed to lead them through the dense groves to the rebel camp. The youth was as beautiful as the girl, with eyes of the same liquid brown hue as hers and skin like dark honey, and Mai clung close to him as they walked, gripping his hand in hers. Ailia felt a pang of unexpected poignancy as she observed this. Was it fear for these two young lovers that she felt, knowing the dangers they faced from the coming war, and the threat of loss and an end to their happiness? Or was it envy that they had this happiness, even for a little while, even to lose it at the last? She wondered if Damion felt any such regret, or if his altered nature was no longer sensible of such things. Casting her eyes down, she strove not to look at their guides, or at the fair young Archon who walked with her.

At last Teren stopped, challenged by a curious cry from deep within the trees. It sounded like and not like an animal's shrill scream, and as Ailia and Damion stood watching he returned a similar call. "The guards," he said to his followers, glancing back at them with his splendid eyes, that now looked to Ailia dark and wary as an antelope's. "They have heard us coming, and would have shot us with arrows had I not called right away. The Overseer will take no chances. He may not let you approach him, I fear."

There were rustling sounds to either side of them, but no figures could be seen through the thick screens of leaves and vines. Teren and Mai walked on. After fifty more paces one of the Loänei ruins could be seen: a beehive-shaped hill that had been carved without and hollowed within to form a fortress. At its low, dark door two Cynocephali in human armor stood guard. Both dog-men lowered their halberds threateningly, and showed their yellow fangs at the sight of the strangers. The guard on the left growled, but the one on the right suddenly spoke in Elensi, to Ailia's astonishment. "Strangers come," it said in a thick slurred voice. It was speaking not to them, but to someone inside the fortress.

An unkempt man in shabby clothing emerged from the damp dark chamber within and stood at the entrance, leaning against the side of the doorway and watching the visitors with a surly, indolent expression. Ailia stiffened when she saw his face.

"I know that man!" she exclaimed, turning to Damion. "His name is Radmon Targ. He is a robber and murderer."

"He is high in the Overseer's favor," Teren warned. "I would not object to his presence, were I you. It will not endear you to his master."

Ailia thought back to her days in Loänanmar, to the squalor and cruelty that had reigned there, in large part due to the Overseer and his thuggish followers. *What allies are we making here?* she wondered in dismay. *Will they turn the city into a place of misery again, this time with our aid?*

Radman leered at Mai, watching the youth beside her with one mocking eye as he did so. "Well, if it isn't the witch's daughter! You should stay away from that young lad, Mai-girl. He'll get you killed, traipsing all over the jungle with you. You can do better, my love." His baiting words were aimed not at the girl, but at the boy, who stood tall and protective at her side.

Teren would not be drawn, however. "These people wish to see the Overseer," he said in his quiet voice. "And if he knows what is good for him he will see them."

"They can help," Mai broke in. "They are sorcerers, both of them, and they have brought their own army from beyond the world."

"I know Brannion Duron does not believe in such things," Ailia hastened to add. "But we ask him at least to grant us audience."

Another person appeared out of the darkness within the doorway: a woman older than Mai, with slightly darker skin and long black hair bound in a single braid. It was apparent that she had been listening, for without wasting words she dismissed the guards, and then directed the strangers to follow her. Within the entrance there was a passage, lit at intervals with torches, and at its end a curtained doorway led to a large domed chamber that must lie at the heart of the hill. In it a middle-aged man with olive skin and a grizzled beard sat at a table reading a roll of parchment by candlelight. Ailia recognized the beetling brow and sternly cast features: she had seen them before, in a bronze statue of Duron in the city of Loänanmar. Here, it seemed, was the metal man-made flesh: but still the flesh somehow appeared to her as hard as the bronze, its features as unyielding and grim. This was not a man to cross, she sensed, and she remembered what Mag had told her of his violent victory over the theocrats years ago.

He spoke without glancing up. "Well, Jelynda, what is this you have brought me?"

Their guide bowed low. "This young woman would speak with you. Will you hear her?" she asked.

Ailia stepped forward. "I have come to warn you of a great danger."

"Silence!" cried Jelynda, scandalized. "One does not address the Overseer unbidden!"

The man Duron fixed his dark gaze on Ailia, then he waved Jelynda aside. "I will overlook the infraction for now. What danger do you speak of, girl?" he demanded.

"The Dragon King, whom you are planning to overthrow. He is not a beast, nor a figment of the imagination. Nor is he a god. He is a sorcerer, named Mandrake: a very powerful one."

"You say nothing that is new to me." He leaned back in his chair with a sigh of impatience. "Do you know how all this talk of gods began? In ancient days our people were vassals of a race called the Loänei, who claimed to be offspring of the creatures they called dragons. Our people actually worshipped these Loänei, who were mere flesh and blood like themselves—can you believe the foolishness of it? It was easy for the dragon-folk to feign godhood with the help of their sorcery. Oh, yes, I know well that sorcery exists. I forbade any mention of it in Loänanmar after I took the city, not because I myself disbelieved in it, but because I wished to discourage anyone from seeking knowledge of it. There must be no more false gods."

Ailia thought guiltily of the adulation of her own people in Arainia. Then she recalled the Overseer's bronze image in the square, and met his eye again. Whatever this man might say, he too had been an object of reverence in his city—and worse, of fear. "If Mandrake were here, he would say the people had been freed merely so that they could tyrannize one another."

Damion gave her a swift warning look, and she said no more. Brannion Duron took no notice of her comment, but continued, "A few years ago some of the Cynocephali fell into error, showing an unwholesome reverence for an exceptionally large and strong bull in the communal herd they were charged with protecting. Before I knew what was happening, they had begun to worship this animal, placing garlands about its neck and singing its praises. I acted swiftly, ordering my men to slaughter the bull and butcher it before the dog-men's eyes. This may seem a cruel thing to have done to the Cynocephali, but the lesson was for their own good."

In fact Ailia thought the lesson cruel to the bull, but she said nothing: there was little point in annoying the man. "We must destroy this so-called Dragon King," he continued. "So that we may be free again. It is not enough merely to kill the priests. The creature they venerate must also be removed. No longer will the citizens be forced to bend the knee as miserable slaves to a cult."

Ailia bridled for an instant, recalling the cruelty under Duron's reign: the rule of the strong over the weak, the abandonment of the ill and poor, the murderers like Radmon who went unpunished. But she recalled also her mother's words: "We cannot force the mortal creatures to live as we wish them to. However it may hurt us to see them suffer as a consequence, we must let them be." It hurt terribly to watch, particularly when those suffering were people she knew, like Mag and her daughter. But there was no other course. The Archons still preferred human tyrants, who could be cast down as Khalazar of Zimboura had been, to sorcerers whom mere mortals had little chance of defeating.

Duron said, "We must kill the dragon-sorcerer *first*. The conquest of the cult will be an easy matter without its deity to strike fear into people's hearts."

"Then you will need our help to deliver your world. We have sorcerers with us, and you have not."

Unexpectedly Duron smiled—a smile without mirth or warmth. "There you are wrong," he said.

From the shadows behind him stepped a tall figure, which un-hooded itself. Ailia nearly gasped. Here was yet another face that she recognized. It was Erron Komora.

"This man is an enemy—one of the Loänei!" she cried.

"I have never denied I am a Loänei," Erron replied. "I have offered Brannion Duron my aid to rid him of the Dragon King. It is Man-drake's fault that we Loänei have been discovered by the Loänan again, and are in danger of being driven into exile or destroyed. I do not believe the boasts of Naugra: they will not win this fight, and my people will suffer for it. But if we are freed from Mandrake's rule, we will live in peace with our Merei neighbors. You have my word." He bowed, but his black eyes stayed on Ailia's face.

"You believe this?" Ailia cried, turning to Duron. "He only wants power for himself. Mandrake said Erron wanted to kill his own fa-ther, and rule the Loänei. His plan was thwarted when Mandrake took the throne. He means to use you, and then take this world for his people, enslaving yours. If we help you, Overseer, Erron must go."

"I will not proceed without Erron Komora," Duron said. "He is of the utmost importance to my plan, for he can provide us with knowledge of sorcery and the means to defeat it. In return we will give him our numbers, thousands of willing hands to wield swords. He wants to be free of the dragon-cult that has oppressed his peo-ple as much as ours, and those Loänei who are faithful to Komora are too few in number to challenge the hierarchs now in power. After our victory is won we will part company, each going to his own people and lands. But the Loänei sorceries will not again en-slave us, never fear. Komora himself has promised that, or I should never have allied with him. We have followed his counsel, and made for ourselves weapons of iron." He stood, and for a moment looked as unbending as if he himself were cast of iron. At his side, they now saw, a leather scabbard hung. He laid his hand on the sword hilt that jutted out from it. "With these weapons we will de-feat our foe. And we can defend ourselves from any sorcererous treachery. We need no aid from you, but if you wish you are wel-come to join your ranks to ours."

The Tryna Lia and her friend asked for a moment to confer, and drew apart in order to discuss the matter.

"I think perhaps we should agree, and ally our forces with his," Damion said to Ailia. "That way the Merei in this world can say they won their own freedom. It would be better than simply delivering them."

Ailia said nothing for a moment. "It would be good," she said, "if they are able to say this. But the Overseer is more likely to portray himself as their savior, if I know him. When he reigned in Loänanmar before, he filled the streets with statues of himself. The same thing will happen this time. Even if he himself never strikes a blow in battle, the people will feel beholden to him, rather than give the victory to themselves. I do not want to see them as slaves, either to him or to the Dragon King."

"But if they must choose the less evil of two masters? Would you not say the Merei who commands no sorcery is the better one? Mandrake can send his human minions to seize all iron in the realm by force, and then reign supreme with the aid of his magic. But if the people do not like Duron, they can rise against him as they rose against Khalazar."

Ailia gave a reluctant nod. "You are right, as always. Let us go tell Duron we will join our army to his."

It was done: the people of this land and world were now a step closer to liberty. The cause was just. But what allies they had gathered to it: the treacherous Komora, and the cruel Overseer.

┌─────────────┐
│   15   │
└─────────────┘

Wind and Wave

MANDRAKE, RETURNED TO DRAGON-FORM, stood gazing out the wall of his palace—a wall that was all window, being constructed entirely of adamant. It gave on to watery green depths, where fish swam in gleaming schools only a wing's length away from him, while groves of kelplike weeds waved languidly in the gentle currents in place of climbing ivy. This was not a drowned castle, for it had never stood in air. The Archons had built their dwellings wherever they pleased, whether on land or on the beds of lakes and oceans. This one was set atop a sea-mount. There were long tunnellike corridors with clear walls that passed from one part of the edifice to the next, so that one might seem to walk through the deeps amid the rocks and corals of the seabed; and there were tubes filled with seawater that ran up through the air-filled chambers and halls, so that sea creatures might pass through them and amuse the occupants. After the Archons' time a Dragon King had made his dwelling here, and then in turn his Loänei descendants had taken the place for their own. Many dwelled here now, and they had furnished the halls to their taste, while dragon-lanterns of various glowing hues drifted about the high ceilings, serving for lamps. It was a safe fortress, for it could not be reached from the surface save by sorcery, or by dragons and other creatures capable of diving to these depths. Even the full light of day could not reach here, doubled in strength as it was: morning announced itself only by a feeble lightening of the green gloom beyond the window-walls.

Yet the security of his retreat did nothing to ease Mandrake's mind, which was troubled more and more with each passing day. In particular, he was disturbed by the increasing intrusions of mental images, ideas, and insights that were in some way alien to the rest of his thoughts—that had become, in effect, a secondary voice whose counsels were in frequent conflict with his own decisions and desires. The inner voice was not new: he had sensed it ever since childhood, and always assumed it to be a part of his own consciousness. But it seemed to have grown almost independent of late. There was a form of madness, was there not, in which one heard imaginary voices advising one to undertake strange and terrible deeds?

You are not mad, the voice said, or seemed to say. The dragon looked down at his shadow, cast on the stone floor by the living lantern above him. *I am a part of you,* it said in his thoughts, *far more than that shadow. I am deep within you, and without me you could not be. I am your strength. It is through me that you will be able to resist the sorcery of cold iron. Could you command such power on your own?*

Had it in truth been the "demons" who had manipulated his body in Loänanmar, or had it been some other, sinister agency? The same that promised him this unlooked-for mastery over iron? First his body, and now his will seemed to be influenced by some elusive other, whose power grew with the passing of each weary hour in this place. There was, he knew, another sickness of the mind that caused it to become divided—to become like two separate minds, each struggling for mastery. It was an alarming thought, but he dared not seek help. To appear weak before his allies could well prove fatal. The goblins dared not harm him, but the Loänei were another matter.

Erron Komora had fled his court—no surprise in itself: the young Loänei was not a skilled mage, and not one to stand firm in the face of danger. That was why he had delayed so long to destroy his own father. Mandrake could not say why he was troubled at this particular defection. He had disliked and distrusted Komora, and felt no regret at losing him. But the impression of impending disaster was growing on him.

You must go to Ombar, counseled the inner voice. *The Morugei are surer allies than the Loänei. They wish for you to live and lead them; not so the dragon-folk.*

Ombar again! No, he would not go there. He was safe here. The enemy hosts had not penetrated his weather-defenses, nor entered the deeps. He would remain in the dragon palace, and he would keep his current shape. His wounds had begun to heal with the passing hours, and it was curious how easy it was now to assume and to retain draconic form. Indeed, it was the human form that was becoming harder to take—as though his mind had begun to forget how to do it. That, surely, was a positive sign: if his Loänan magic were stronger, he would be able to repel his foes.

In Ombar it would be stronger still, the soundless voice persisted. *Better to go there now, than remain here waiting for your fortress to be taken. I can give to you the power that defies iron. But even that cannot save you, unless you go to Ombar as I command.*

The dragon began to pace about his glassy prison again.

THE TRYNA LIA AND HER friends returned to their own encampment—along with Twidjik, who had chosen to remain with Ailia, though Mag insisted on staying behind—and shared with the others what they had learned of the rebels. "It appears the people of this world are not helpless after all," Damion told the Nemerei. "But they mean to use weapons of iron, and that will hamper our own sorceries. Still, it would be a great triumph if they could win freedom for themselves."

"If freedom is what they will have," said Ailia. She was standing apart, gazing out of the tent's opening. Jomar looked at her.

"You don't sound very hopeful," he observed. "What is he like, this Overseer?"

"He is a tyrant," she replied. "He neglected his people when he was not being cruel to them. His rule was brutal. His servants were brigands."

"Well, maybe the people will depose *him* too in time," suggested Lorelyn. "Look at what happened to Khalazar."

"Not if we make a great hero of him," said Ailia. "They will never be rid of him, then."

"Still, it is better than being ruled by Loänei," Damion reminded her in his gentle voice. "They can rebel against a mere man; they have little chance against the sorcery of the dragon-people."

"Yes—of course, you are right," Ailia acknowledged again.

The other dragons and cherubim were returning from their aerial battle, flying into the twilit ruins like great gliding shadows. They were no closer to breaching the cloudy barriers of the sea-castle, though they had slain many of its defenders. But some of those had been Loänan, and the dragons were filled with grief and bitter self-reproach over the deaths of their kin.

"Torok was among the slain, I hear," Auron told Ailia. "He was a traitor to our kind, but I am sorry he is dead, and I am glad it was not I who killed him. And some of the earth-dragons who answered his call to serve the enemy were very young."

Some of the dragon-folk, they had learned, were still guarding the hill-palace in Loänanmar, having given up on the defense of the whole city. The few humans there were now in a panic, trying to arm themselves with pitchforks and scythes.

"I suppose we should take the city back," said Ailia. "People can't go on living in the jungles like this. They need to go back to their houses."

"Later, perhaps, we can meet with Duron's rebel army and march together," said Jomar. "Any Loänei left in the city will feel our iron, and flee. But Mandrake should really come first."

Suddenly Twidjik, who had retreated underneath the draped table in the corner of the tent, gave a cry and sprang out again. "'Ware danger!" he shrieked.

They all leaped to their feet, and Jomar with an oath turned the table over. A small creature, little over a foot in length, had somehow crept into the tent and underneath the table: a lizardlike creature, with beak-shaped jaws and four pairs of claw-footed legs. It scuttled on these, like a huge and horrible insect, nearly to Ailia's feet.

Ailia stumbled backward. "A basilisk!" she cried.

The reptile's beak gaped, preparing to release its deadly venomed breath. But in the next instant Jomar struck it with his sword, with such force that he cut it in two. Both halves wriggled sickeningly for a few moments, and then they were still, though the jaws of the creature continued to snap open and shut.

Ailia was very pale as she looked about her. "Are there any more? Those creatures are deadly!"

They hunted about the tent, but saw nothing. "It was alone, then," said Taleera.

"It might have killed us all. I didn't even see it come in," Ailia said, still shaken. "The poison could have killed everyone in the tent. Twidjik has saved us."

"Was it only chance that brought it in here, though?" Damion queried. "Or design?"

"The jungle is full of dangerous creatures . . ." Ailia began, and then her voice faltered. She looked down into the staring eye of the basilisk, and it seemed to her that it returned her gaze. Almost she was mesmerized by it. For an instant, as it lay there, she believed she saw in its expanded pupil the same dark intent that had shown briefly in Mandrake's. Could the same power that had mastered the sorcerer also wield dumb brutes like this? A power that was like her mother's in Arainia, but ruled the living creatures instead of merely influencing them? The world-soul of Nemorah was as malevolent as Arainia's was benign. Elarainia's daughter was a trespasser in another ruler's domain. Here it was Mandrake who could draw on a planet's power to augment his own.

A hasty search of all the surrounding tents unearthed no more basilisks or other venomous reptiles. That confirmed the suspicions of Damion.

"How likely can it be," he said, "that the basilisk would choose Ailia's tent to enter, and that it merely happened to approach her first? It was an attempt on her life."

"No one was seen anywhere near the camp," Jomar said. "The sentries would have caught a human intruder."

"Then it may well have been sent by sorcery. A Dragon King can command lowly creatures like these to do his bidding, simply by imposing his will upon them."

"Then," vowed Jomar, "tomorrow we move against the Dragon King, and put an end to this once and for all."

AT MID-MORNING THE FOLLOWING day Ailia and her Nemerei stood with the Overseer and his counselors on the white shore, looking out to sea. Great waves with tumbling foamy crests were rolling in, like the ranks of an attacking host, and the sky was filled with gray clouds rising leagues into the air: the outer wall of the great typhoon that protected Mandrake's retreat. It was a battlement that advanced like an army. The storm was shifting closer to the shore as it grew in size and strength, but still its eye protected the submarine stronghold of the Dragon King.

Since the enemy's fortress lay underneath the waves, their soldiers could not march upon it: they massed in the jungle instead, awaiting their orders to advance on the city of Loänanmar. The Nemerei, not being able to use their sorcery in the presence of so many iron weapons, had come instead with Ailia to assist in the assault upon the Dragon King. Erron Komora had provided them with a vessel, unlike any seagoing ship they had ever seen before: a crystal ship of the Loänei, built in olden times when they still had the craft of making and shaping adamant. These were the "glass ships" of legend that Ailia had read about in books, vessels that needed neither sail nor oar, but could be driven by the power of thought—so long as the captain was a Nemerei. And like the little glass-bottomed boats that the Arainians made to reveal the beauty of the coral reefs, so these crystal barques with their transparent hulls gave their passengers views of what lay beneath the waves. The Loänei of latter days could no longer take draconic form to dive in the deeps, and so had come to rely on these ships to show them the watery realms that once had been theirs. With such toys as these the descendants of the Loänan had at once amused themselves and at the same time reminded their human thralls of their masters' superiority. Also, the adamantine keels and hulls were indestructible. Such ships could not be stove in and sunk, not even if they were cast up on sharp rocks. Only a Loänei ship could face such a sea as this.

"Your weapons of iron must be left behind," the Loänei lord had told the Overseer. "Else we cannot sail the ship with our magic."

"How then can I fight the enemy's magic?" demanded the Overseer.

"No matter," Erron replied. "You could not descend to the deeps in any case. Our Loänan will join with those of the Tryna Lia, and drive Mandrake forth from his refuge. From the ship you will observe as this takes place, and you can employ any other weapons you may have. Spears and arrows tipped with flint or bronze, and swords of steel may be used. The ship will serve mainly to give the Loänan a platform on which to rest between dives—else they would have to return to land, wasting time. If you do not wish to come aboard, you need not. But I think you will prefer to tell your children and grandchildren that you were there in the battle."

Slowly they all waded into the sea and boarded the ship by the ladders that were let down for them. Once all were on board the Loänei captain sent his craft skimming forth upon the waves. It had no sails to be caught in the wild gusts and torn, and though it tossed about wildly enough, it could not be overcome by the strength of the waves that sought to push it back to shore. The glassy hull rode up each frothing green slope, and plunged into the watery valleys beyond, without any of the unnerving creaks or groans of stressed timber, and no water leaked into the chambers belowdecks. Ailia looked through its clear side, trying to keep her feet as it heeled and rolled. One moment she was standing above the waterline, and the next she was plunged into the midst of the surf so that she could see into the depths of the sea. An eerie, pale glow came from far below, as of some phosphorescent life dwelling there. But as the ship forged further and further into the storm, she saw that the glow came from the clustered lights of an undersea castle. Then as the ship drew nearer, all the lights vanished.

IN HIS FORTRESS FAR BELOW Mandrake observed the undersea battle. He had banished the dragon lanterns back to the Ether from whence they came, so that the adamantine castle should give no betraying glimmer to the enemy above, and it lay now in an oppressive gloom. The deeps above the transparent roof were filled with spinning shadows: dragons locked in mortal combat, some seeking to destroy him and some to protect his life with theirs. It was a battle of Loänan only, for firedrakes shunned water, fearing the element that quenched their flames; and the cherubim with their feathered wings could not dive to these depths. And so the balance here was tipped, for the Loänan that were loyal to Ailia vastly outnumbered his own rebels. He had erred in fleeing to the seabastion, and was caught now in a trap of his own making.

Two voices spoke within the Dragon Prince's mind as he stood there watching his fate draw ever nearer. They offered him power, and the chance for escape. He would perish here, they said, only if he did not accept their aid. One of these voices he recognized as the same entity that had spoken to him through Syndra. Elnemorah had truly possessed the woman, and now she was seeking to take his mind as well. The other was the old shadow-voice that had always been within him.

Only touch your mind to mine, Elnemorah promised, *and I can give you strength to drive forth your foes from my world.*

Hear her, the shadow said. *Power I give as well: power from the stars, greater than any earth-sorcery.*

It was true that the Archons had returned: not in full embodied might as in days of old, but as incorporeal influences that persuaded and seduced. The dragon paced about and tossed his horned head, like a horse tormented by stinging flies. He could deny them and perish in this prison, or he could submit and save himself, together with those few who remained loyal to him. His eyes turned to the glassy floor. In its center lay what seemed a round pool, but the water in it was seawater: it was, in fact, the main entrance to his keep, opening onto the depths. Being underwater, the castle could be entered only from beneath. If he fled now, he realized, his foes would pursue him and abandon their siege of the castle, leaving his followers here in peace. But for him there could be no escape without help. He stood still, shuddering, and eased the barriers about his mind. The earthly power of Elnemorah he accepted, and felt it enter into him. Energies seemed to flow toward him from the sea around and the earth beneath. But remembering Syndra, he did not surrender himself wholly: he guarded his innermost thoughts, the core of his being, from the Archon's grasp. As for the other, the dark one, he did not answer it at all. He would call on it, he decided, only at the direst need.

Now! I must leave now!

Mandrake plunged down through the opening and into the sea. As he swam beneath the castle and then rose up past its walls, he saw the other dragons battling in the green deeps, appearing to fly as their wings beat like fins in the water. Higher up, cherubim dived through the surface like seabirds after their prey. The Dragon King swam with great strokes of his tail and limbs, his Loänan clearing the way for him. But his hurts still weakened him and slowed his progress. He called out to the Power of the deep.

As Ailia watched far above, several of the Loänan who were fighting the winds overhead drew in their wings, and dived into the murky green depths. She saw other shadowy shapes surging to and fro, farther down. A great battle was being waged there. Dragons' auras glowed in the water's depths like sailor's-fire. Then her point of view was above the surface once more.

As Erron had said, the ship served a dual purpose, providing a platform for the winged beings to land on when they tired; particularly the cherubim, who unlike the Loänan were not at home in both elements. Time after time they paused on the decks to rest, and then dived again. The ship had come at last within the storm's eye, passing its inner wall, and the waves were no longer so high or violent. A wide space of clear sky was above them, with cloud showing around the rim of the sea, which had turned from the sullen gray of dull steel to gleaming emerald. Ailia stood once more above the waves, looking down on them. Presently the water on the starboard side began to boil: it turned white, leaped and heaved. A dozen red-scaled dragons burst through in a shower of spray, like breaching whales: but when they reached the apex of their leaps, where the whales would begin to fall back into the sea, the dragons' wings snapped open and carried them higher. They sought the sky even as other dragons surfaced in pursuit.

"Enemy Loänan," said Taleera, moving to stand next to her. "But where is *he*?"

As if in answer the ship rocked. They had struck something, some submerged object, and a shiver went through the ship from bow to stern. Ailia started, and the firebird flew up off the floor. "What was that? Did we hit a reef, perhaps?" the Princess exclaimed.

Paladins and soldiers ran down into the lower chambers of the ship, which lay beneath the water, and Ailia and Damion followed them. "There is something there—" a man called out.

And then the ship was struck again, amidships this time, almost turning over. Yells broke out. And those who had gone below saw what had happened.

The fleet was under attack. It appeared that Mandrake had used his power as Dragon King to summon forth the largest and most perilous creatures of this world's sea. They were attacking the Loänan underwater, and several were heading directly toward the ship. Up through the deeps swam a many-armed kraken, larger than the most monstrous of giant squids. Its saucerlike eyes bulged from its bulbous mottled head, and its tentacles trailed after it. From another direction there came a pair of ship-sized scolopendrae, rowing themselves forward with their many-jointed legs, the green subaqueous light glancing along their lobsterlike carapaces. And there were orcs and great sea serpents undulating their sinuous coils as a water snake might, and last of all a veritable fleet of aspidochelones, piscine in shape but armored like sea turtles, and larger than the largest whale. It was hard to grasp the true size of these beasts, with nothing in the green deeps to give any sense of scale. As they drew nearer they seemed to expand, growing terrifyingly, impossibly huge. The largest of the aspidochelones was the size of a small island. Ailia called on her powers to halt their advance. Once before she had linked her mind to an aspidochelone's and bent it to her whim, albeit unconsciously; but when she reached out now, all she felt was the same dark driving will that she had sensed with the basilisk. It resisted her, barring her from the animals' minds. They were possessed.

They strove to smash the adamantine hull, and failed; but the gigantic beasts did not retreat when they found their efforts fruitless. They butted their heads against the ship's sides instead, and drove up against its keel with their armored backs. The kraken meanwhile spread wide its tentacles and wrapped them around the bow, while a colossal serpent flung a scaly coil over the stern. Nemerei ran up to the decks, striving to keep their balance on the slippery wet adamant, and the Overseer's personal guard also ran up with spears and bows. The arrows could not penetrate the lapping scales of the serpent's coil, but with repeated blows from blade and spear they succeeded in severing two or three of the kraken's tentacles. The monster pulled back its remaining arms and withdrew. At last a bolt of fiery quintessence from one of the Nemerei sent the creature recoiling into the sea.

The serpent meanwhile menaced its attackers with its jaws, which were lined with rows of wicked inward-curving teeth. Quintessence only angered it, and caused it to snap and lunge at the source of its pain. The men drew back in fear. Then two cherubim alighted on the pitching deck, beating their huge pinions for balance. One had aquiline foreparts and leonine hindquarters, and the scaly tail of a serpent; the other resembled a lioness, but for her eagle's wings and the great horns upon her head. They attacked the serpent, striking at its eyes with claws and beak and horns, until at last it too retreated with a bellow. Its place was taken at once, however, by an aspidochelone and a scolopendra. They rushed the ship from opposite sides and rammed it by turns, sending it rolling now one way and now the other.

Beneath the water Ailia and Damion saw it all: the attacks of the monstrous creatures, the Loänan still fighting savagely below; the shapes of enemy dragons rising up from the towers of the sea-fortress, whose shape they could now dimly discern. It was as if they rode in a flying ship above a castle of the land—a castle ob-

scured by a thick green fog, through which they could not see the
enemy distinctly until he was almost upon them. So it was that they
did not at first notice the color of the Loänan that came up right underneath their ship, wings and limbs folded to its sides, swimming
with powerful strokes of its tail. Only as it approached the light of
the lamps aboard the ship did they see that it was red with a tawny
mane. Its slitted yellow eyes looked full into theirs, and then it
swam past.

As Ailia and Damion rushed back up the crystal stair that led to
the decks, the red form breached off the starboard bow. It did not
fly, but swam through the surf like the sea serpent, menacing the
ship. Then the Dragon King submerged and they saw him glide
below the keel. The vessel shook and quivered. The Overseer, over-
coming his fear, seized a spear from one of his men and hefted it
like a harpoon, watching the luminous churning wake of the dragon
circling them. The red back with its knife-sharp dorsal scales
reemerged, and he threw, cursing wildly as the spear hissed into the
water wide of its mark. He drew his steel sword and waved it about
impotently. The Dragon King dived, reversed, and lunged upward,
and such was the force of the sorcery that assisted his leap that the
seawater heaved up in a white fountain as if to follow him.

He opened his wings and flew skyward. *To Ombar!* his Loänan
cried. But Mandrake sheared away from them and flew toward the
distant coast, disregarding the wounds his foes inflicted on him, not
fighting back against the cherubim who hunted him like hounds
across the remnants of his dissipating storm. Out of the lowering
clouds long ragged streamers hung, looking to those below almost
low enough to touch. As the red dragon's upward flight pierced the
tattered clouds Ailia and her companions perceived that they
roiled, and then began to rotate. And then there was a long cloudy
tentacle reaching down, down, to the sea, touching the spire of
white water and making a column. More dragons rocketed out of
the deeps, and wherever one passed from sea to cloud, another
whirling pillar was formed.

Duron and his men went rigid. "Waterspouts!"

Only now, perhaps, had they truly realized the tremendous
power against which they had pitted themselves. Their craft rolled
helpless on the waves and the occupants were flung from one side
to the other. Two men fell screaming into the sea, and did not rise

again. The waterspouts surrounded them now: ghostly columns in
a vast hall floored with water, roofed with cloud. The funnels began
to twist this way and that, as their Loänan creators directed them.
Waves crashed over the bows of the crystal ship, and water began
to leak down from the deck hatches.

Ailia spread out her arms. In her right hand the Star Stone shone,
white and blinding, as she called on the power that stills the gale.
None of the enemy dragons dared approach her, so great was their
fear of the shining Stone. With no need to defend herself from
them, she sent her calming thoughts up into the roiling clouds, and
down into the depths of the sea. And there, even in the eye-wall of
the spinning storm, the force of the winds was lessened, and the
wild white crests of the waves bowed. The waterspouts writhed and
broke asunder, wisping away into air.

"Retreat!" Erron Komora bawled at his Loänei captain. "Go back
to land! The Dragon King has fled—we can do no more here. Let
us pursue him!"

The Wingwatch were already doing so—in long clamorous lines,
like migrating geese, they were hunting the fugitive dragons across
the sky. The Dragon King was still leading his Loänan westward,
toward the land. Mandrake had enveloped himself in cloud-vapor,
so as not to present a clear target to his foes, and appeared now as
a vast, gray-white, misty mass speeding through the heavens. With
a great effort of will the Nemerei and Loänei, working as one,
turned the adamantine ship about and sent it plowing back through
the gray chaos of the storm, following pursuers and pursued. Ailia
and Damion had already been taken up by Auron and Falaar, and
together with Taleera they joined in the airy chase.

$$\boxed{16}$$

The City of Dragons

THE PATHS OF MANDRAKE AND his allies, the Overseer with his rebels, Jomar's army, and Ailia's Wingwatch were now converging, with Loänanmar their common point—as if some ruling destiny led them there. Even as the Dragon King winged his way toward the abandoned castle on the volcanic hill—his last refuge in this world—and the Tryna Lia pursued him, the two joined armies of Jomar and Brannion Duron were at the same time drawing nearer to the city. Lorelyn had gone apart from the camp for a time, so as to avoid the influence of the iron weapons while she spoke through the Ether with the Wingwatch. She returned with the news that Mandrake had fled from his undersea bastion and was heading for the Forbidden Palace. The Nemoran rebels clutched at their weapons and shifted their feet, now that they knew they would have to confront their foe at last. Jomar noticed their unease. "You've come this far," he told them. "You might as well keep going. You can't get back on his good side now: you've joined with us, for good or bad. So let's be on our way."

Their task was not, after all, to give battle to him—that would fall to Ailia and her dragons and cherubim. Their part was to liberate the city, and that should be no great hardship, as there were no defenders at its gates and no land army of any kind to meet them in combat. In the past, Mandrake and his Loänei had relied overmuch on sorcery to protect themselves, and the new iron weapons would put an end to all such defenses. In worlds across Talmirennia worse battles than this were being fought, Lorelyn reflected. They had but to succeed in this campaign, and all other worlds would be safe.

Yet battle awaited them all the same, and not from any foe they had anticipated. As they approached the place where jungle gave way to plowed fields, there was a hissing as of many arrows in flight from the bushes around them. Men in the front ranks cried out and fell, while the rest flung themselves down or retreated in confusion and fear. In mere moments the attack was over. Many of the men lay dead, their chests blazoned with blood. Those who had not been struck down fled the scene.

"What is it? What happened?" shouted Jomar as the survivors pelted toward him.

"We don't know. The enemy attacked us, but we saw no one: men were stricken down where they stood, and died at once."

"Sorcery?" asked one of the Nemoran soldiers.

"No, it couldn't be," returned Lorelyn. "Not with all this iron. I am a Nemerei, and kin to the Archons: trust me, I know these things."

The rebels were not seasoned fighting men, but farmers and hunters who had killed only beasts, and men of the city who had never done either. Superstition was strong in them, despite the Overseer's teachings. They all had weapons, but most had no proper armor. They feared now to go forward, and only when Jomar and Lorelyn and the Paladins led the way would they follow, keeping always at a safe distance.

They came upon the glade where the stricken soldiers lay lifeless. Stooping to examine the dead, Jomar and the knights found that the bodies had been pierced not by arrows but by darts of a strange design: green, needlelike, tipped with no feathers at the end. The men had died even if only an arm or leg was struck, and none of their wounds was deep. It was clear that the darts were poisoned.

"As I thought," said Lorelyn at last, her voice trembling a little. "It wasn't sorcery. But why did the attack stop? Did they run out of darts?"

Jomar advanced slowly, sword and shield at the ready. "There is no one here now. Let's keep moving forward."

"We can't just leave them here," said Lorelyn, looking at the fallen men. "It's a jungle—there are animals—" She shuddered. "We ought to bury them."

"Later, perhaps," said Jomar. "We can leave guards here, with torches. All animals are afraid of fire."

There were many among the Nemoran men who were more than willing to remain behind with their fallen comrades, so great had their terror become. It was, Jomar thought, just as well: though he did not name them cowards, aloud or in his thoughts, he knew that these were the men who would not be able to stand firm in battle. City dwellers, no doubt, softer and more easily frightened than the others. It was not their fault, but they would be of small use in the fight to free Loänanmar. They might as well remain behind. He would take the less fearful with him to the siege.

Then even as the armies advanced, the foliage to either side of them stirred again, and more darts came whistling through the air in deadly showers.

"Get down! Throw yourselves down!" the Paladins shouted at the soldiers. They obeyed as the green needles rained down upon them, glancing off the armor of the knights. In the tangled groves beyond, shapes were moving: not men, but beasts.

They were being attacked by peludas. Most of the Nemorans had heard of these strange and terrible creatures from the deep jungle, but none of them had ever seen one. Ailia, who had read the old bestiaries in which forgotten lore of otherworldly animals was preserved, could have told her friends that the huge reptiles could shoot the quills right out of their spiny green hides: these were the strange darts that had slain the soldiers. They carried a venom in their tips, deadly and swift to act. The first wave of the creatures had exhausted their quills, hence the brief lull in the assault; now they had been replaced by others whose hides still bore thick arsenals of the natural weapons. Nor were the peludas alone in the charge. The jungle had come alive with terrible forms. One was so huge that it might have been a little hill, had it not been in motion: a hill from which a long serpentine neck thrust forth. Lorelyn gasped at the sight of it, recognizing the gigantic saurian from Ailia's description: the "tree-eaters" that came from the Original World. Their enemy, it seemed, had learned from Ailia's defense of Arainia. An animal army like that which had assailed her foes in the Eldimian forests was now attacking the Princess's own soldiers. In front of the giant Tanathon came many-necked hydras, and hideous two-legged lindworms with gigantic jaws opened wide. Behind them came six-legged tarasques with domed tortoiselike shells, studded with great spikes, impervious to spears and swords. And iron did not distress any of these creatures in the least.

Arrows sang through the air. A lindworm or two went down, and the Tanathon bellowed and tossed its long neck as the shafts sprouted from its thick wrinkled hide. But the peludas merely tucked their own snaky necks and tails underneath their bellies, and turned about like porcupines to present their bristling backs. More deadly spines lanced through the air. Amphipteres with bat wings and serpentine bodies and bird-like cockatrices came flapping down over the ranks of men, flying into the faces of the archers, though there were not enough to stop the barrage altogether. As for the tarasques, they could not be stopped at all. When attacked, these creatures simply drew their heads inside their shells and marched on. They advanced, relentless as great stones crashing down a mountainside, crushing with their clawed feet all that lay in their path, flailing their barbed tails. The air was filled with screams and shouted warnings.

But as they began to despair, there was a cry from above and Taleera flew into the face of one of the lindworms, pecking at its eyes. And then the cherubim were there, diving upon the monsters in fury. Finding their claws and jaws and beaks could not harm the quilled pelts and metal-hard shells, they surrounded the beasts and lunged in and out, until one of their fellows succeeded in thrusting a foreleg underneath the tarasque or peluda and overturning it. The bellies of the peludas were soft and vulnerable, it turned out, although the tarasques' were armored like their backs. But these creatures had great difficulty in righting themselves again, their six legs waving impotently in the air as they rocked back and forth like immense beetles. In the meantime the cherubim bit and mauled those legs, so that even if the tarasques did succeed in turning over they could not walk.

The human warriors, fatigued in mind and body, were able to draw back and regroup as this titanic conflict was taking place. Jomar gathered them together with the wounded in a safe position at the center, and they stood and watched in awe as the huge creatures warred with one another. The cherubim did not escape injury, and before all was over more than a few lay wounded or dying from the poison of the peluda quills, which worked more slowly on their larger bodies but still had the same deadly effect. At long last, however, the jungle denizens were all slain, rendered harmless, or put to flight. The Battle of the Beasts, as it came to be called in later days, was ended.

In the thick of the sonorous strife all eyes had been on the immediate scene. And few aside from the flying fighters had noticed the change of weather. Now as the soldiers and knights looked about them and caught their breath, all noticed that the sky had clouded over completely: the effect, perhaps, of the sea storm that had broken apart as it collapsed, sending the last of its winds and thunderheads sweeping outward in all directions. The surviving fighters, looking up, saw the day grow dark, almost night-black as they watched. The undersides of the clouds seemed to be swirling and bulging in places. A great wind struck the trees, making them sway and bend like bows in the hands of archers. With it there came a pattering on the leaves and the ground, not of raindrops, but of the last thing anyone present expected, and many of them had never seen: a fall of hailstones.

"'Ware sorcery!" shouted a knight, pointing skyward with a gauntleted hand.

The gray-black clouds above were now unmistakably rotating, and descending to the earth. Within that circling mass a dark and sinuous shape appeared, writhing like a serpent, its lower end reaching for the ground.

"Cyclone!" yelled a soldier, and others took up the cry. "Cyclone, cyclone!"

Such storms were not uncommon in this place, but none doubted that their enemy had spawned this one in revenge. There was panic in the ranks as the black funnel began to spew flying debris in all directions, showing that it had touched the ground. With a terrible deliberate motion it swung back and forth, devastating all before it, cutting through the jungle like a scythe through wheat and tossing uprooted trees aside. Fragments of splintered trunks and boughs whirled around it like a cloud of dust motes. The noise of it was high and keening, accompanied by a deeper rumble as it smote the earth.

It was less than half a league away, and advancing at great speed.

"It's coming this way!" Jomar yelled.

The Nemoran men were fleeing willy-nilly into the trees. The beasts had been challenge enough, but no one could stand before this new and worse manifestation of their enemy's power. They had provoked the wrath of a god, and now they were filled with a terror that verged on madness. As the cherubim took flight again, the rebels ran into the jungle. Meanwhile Jomar's fighters stood helpless, knowing that fleeing was useless and their only hope lay now with the warriors of the air.

RIDING HIGH ABOVE THE CLOUDS with the other members of the Wingwatch, Ailia and Damion and their mounts looked down through gaps in the canopy on the scenes of destruction on land. "We promised them they would be safe with their weapons of iron," said Ailia in anguish. "What are we to do? We cannot go to their aid with our sorcery—not with the iron present. Only the cherubim can fly down there, and they have no weather-magic."

"Fly above the windstorm," Auron answered, "and use sorcery to assail *it*. We are too high for the iron to hinder us."

They flew on, with the green sky above them and the clouds all torn and tumbled below. On flying down into that dense grayness they soon discerned beneath them a black pit, a hole sucking the cloud-stuff downward into its maw as though it were water swirling down a drain. Lightning flashed around it. Ailia shuddered at the sight. It was plain that the cyclone was a part of the sea storm, and had been spun off from it; but this could not be by mere chance. It was moving directly toward her land-bound army. Black sorcery had created it, and set it on its path of destruction.

But the Loänan were well versed in the ways of weather, and more than equal to the task at hand. As they overflew the storm they drew on the air, on the winds and the suspended moisture, using all their knowledge and magical skill to impose their will upon it. Ailia, sensing this, lent them all the aid she could. Together they commanded the cyclone, seeking to split the swaying funnel apart, to reverse and tame its winds. And they felt, as they reached out, a great power of pure malice resisting them. Again and again they struggled with it, and still it would not yield. The whirlwind had almost reached the scattered army.

"It is Mandrake," said Auron. "He is merely distracting the cherubim and the Loänan with these challenges, so he can escape to his fortress."

"No," Ailia responded, "not Mandrake. Or at least, not he alone. There is—something *else* there." Once more she felt the dread she had known when she looked in the Dragon King's eye, and in the basilisk's.

With all her might she asserted her own power, and slowly the malevolent other began to give way. It was not destroyed or defeated; it merely withdrew, as if its purpose all along had been only to make her use all her resources and weaken her. And she was weakened: her breath came in halting gasps, and every nerve and muscle of her body felt strained. She slumped down into Auron's mane and held on to him with the last of her strength. And as the dragons swept down toward that terrible maelstrom, the clouds ceased their swirling, and the central pit began to collapse. In moments it became a mere depression, while the cumuli began to lose their angry shapes and pull apart, drifting away on the clear air. The victorious Wingwatch flew back down over the jungle, through which a broad swath had been cut: trunks of uprooted trees lay in rows to either side of it, like mown hay. But the funnel cloud was gone, itself destroyed; and it had not reached the soldiers or the city. Mere minutes after the attack had begun it was already ended, with the carcasses of the slain monsters lying amidst the wreckage of trees and shining drifts of hailstones the size of hens' eggs.

As daylight began to seep back into the sky, the embattled army looked on the devastation surrounding them and the Wingwatch flying low overhead, and knew that their side had won the victory—for now. But against whom had they fought? Not mere beasts, incapable of plotting designs and strategies; and the cyclone, though not unnatural to these climes, had surely been created by an act of wizardry. Mandrake, the Loänei, and the Archons of this world were variously blamed by the survivors.

"I don't understand," growled Jomar. "How can he do these things? With all this iron in our hands? How can he use sorcery?" He turned to Auron, who had transformed to human shape.

Auron replied, "But the windstorm was not entirely sorcerous. It might have begun with magic, but all Mandrake had to do was set it on a course that brought it to your army's position. It wasn't magical when it reached you—just a storm."

"But the animals—what about them? They had to be controlled, and sent against us. When they came close to our iron weapons, shouldn't he have lost control?"

"He is right, Auron." Ailia spoke slowly and wearily. "This is a new magic he is wielding—star-magic, that can resist cold iron."

Jomar shook his head. "You'd think he'd have been weakened by

now, not strengthened. And I thought no human sorcerer could resist iron. Where is he getting the power?"

"Only cherubim and Archons have star-magic, haven't they?"
Lorelyn asked.

"No cherubim serve Mandrake," said Falaar. "Of that I am certain."

"No," Damion agreed. "This power is lent to him by Archon allies. He has accepted their aid. But it is not the power of the Archon
of this world, though I suspect Elnemorah has been helping him.
She is one of the planetary Archons that chose to rebel and serve
Valdur long ago, and her influence is still strong in this sphere. I see
it in the attacks of the beasts, which belong to this world and so are
under her command. But Jomar is right: once they drew close to our
soldiers' iron the will that wielded them should have failed. Elnemorah is still an Elaia, a lesser Archon like Elarainia and Ailia. Another, greater power is at work here."

EARLY THAT EVENING, WHEN AILIA had recovered a little, she and
Damion flew ahead on their winged mounts with the rest of the
Wingwatch while Jomar and the Overseer led their united forces to
Loänanmar. Taleera flew above the armies to watch for wild beasts
and other dangers.

Looking down over the city streets, the Wingwatch and their
passengers could see small figures running away in terror, pursued
as it seemed by the flying shadows of the dragons and cherubim.
Ailia and Auron alighted next to the temple while Damion and
Falaar settled in the central plaza. Other winged warriors flew to
high towers and walls and perched there. Then the armies came
pouring into the unguarded city gates, while the inhabitants gave
way before them. Many recognized the Overseer, and greeted him
with joy and relief—for even those who had suffered under his
reign feared him less than they feared the dragon-priests and their
terrifying living deity.

Ailia dismounted and went to the temple steps where Mandrake's
priests were in the habit of making their proclamations. "People of
Loänanmar!" she cried. "We mean you no harm! We know that you
are the slaves, not the friends, of the Dragon King and his Loänei!
Put down your weapons and join with us, and you will be free."

There was a rumbling as of thunder from the cloud-shrouded

heights of the hill, where Mandrake had taken refuge. But some other people emerged from their houses, looking at the white-clad figure in hope.

"Free!" one white-haired old man said. "We do not know what you mean by that. Many have promised us freedom in the past."

"We mean," said Damion, walking up the steps to stand at Ailia's side, "you will no longer live in fear of your rulers. You need give them no more tribute, nor worship them."

More people began to creep out into the open: men first, and then women with clinging children. They gathered in the plaza before the temple.

"Is it true?" asked a woman. "*Will* we live without fear?"

A robed man emerged from a side door of the temple, and pushed forward through the crowd. "The Dragon King is the only true ruler! These intruders are your enemies! You will be punished—"

Jomar silenced the priest with a sword point to his throat. "Quiet, you. We've dealt with your kind before now. Your bullying days are over." There was a hush as the crowd waited for some divine retribution, and then a murmur of wonder when it did not come. As for the priest, he fell silent as it became clear that his god was not going to deliver him. Lightning flickered fitfully in the roiling cloud that had engulfed the hill, but no bolt struck. "You see!" shouted Jomar. "He's no god! He's an evil wizard who has held you all captive!"

Some of the people seemed bewildered, and some were crying. They looked almost like frightened children, thought Damion. "Do not be afraid!" he called out in an encouraging voice. "We will help you. You will not be left on your own."

"Who are you?" The white-haired man cried. "What are you?"

"We come from beyond this world. I am called Damion, and this woman is Ailia, the Tryna Lia."

Some in the crowd surged back in fear. "We have heard of her. But is she not our enemy?"

"No," Ailia answered, drawing herself up with an effort. "I bear you no ill will, I promise. See, I have done nothing to harm you."

"I'll serve you," one man said at last. He stepped forth from the crowd. "I'll serve anyone who'll fight against *him*. He's the real enemy." He waved his hand at the sorcerous cloud on the hill. "Death to the Dragon King!"

The onlookers took up the cry, and it spread among them like flame. The fear of centuries was lifted from them all in a moment, like a stone that slips from its place on a ledge after stationary ages. Voices were raised, and fists, and many weapons as well, as the cloud wisped away and revealed the fortress on the hilltop.

"Let's go after him now—seek him out in his lurking place! He is only a wizard, and can do us no harm—this sorceress is stronger than he!" They rose up like a flood, and behind them came the Paladins and soldiery of the Overseer. The Wingwatch soared above. Only Ailia stood quite still, leaning on Damion's shoulder, her head bowed.

A small knot of people approached her. "Can you really do as you promise? Is your power a match for his? Will you calm the weather, and ease the earth's anger?" said a balding man with dark-shadowed, frightened eyes.

"Its anger?" inquired Damion. "What do you mean by that?"

"The Dragon King's power has only been over air and water until now. But it has always been said that he is truly a dragon of the earth, and his sorcery can command it also. For the past nine days there have been portents, of a kind never known here before. The earth quakes beneath our feet, and strange sounds come out of its depths: a growling, like a great beast, and a hissing like serpents. And the springs that we once bathed in are grown too hot to use— hot enough to boil meat—and a few have dried up altogether. He is turning the earth itself against us!"

Ailia and Damion exchanged glances. "What does this mean?" the Princess asked, moving close to Damion and speaking in his ear. "Earth-dragons have some limited power over stone and soil, it's true. But Mandrake has been far away under the sea, and all his power had been bent on the storm that was his protection."

Damion took her by the arm and led her into the great main hall of the temple. The Loänei and their human priests had not been idle: the vast chamber had been repaired, painted, and adorned with woven hangings, and the huge statue of the crowned dragon at its far end had once more been plated with gleaming gold, re- flecting in the tiled pool beneath. "His power has grown," Damion said. "He can use sorcery even in the presence of iron now. Perhaps his reach has grown as well."

"And only an Archon can defy iron," Ailia said. "Of course, he is part Archon as we are, but—as you said, even Elnemorah could not do it."

"Only the greatest of the Archons can command the star-magic," he said. "The planetary Archons and their lesser kin who dwell in the midst of the planets have no resistance to the magic of star-metals. We are all subject to it, save the Elyra who entered the stars and became one with them. Mandrake has gained the power of an Elyra."

"An Elyra." She was still for a moment, afraid. "You mean Valdur."

"The prince is the servant of Modrian-Valdur, and the channel through which his influence reaches into the material plane. Mandrake agreed to become the Avatar of the Valei, and now he is being consumed by the Power he summoned." Damion's voice was filled with pity.

"I don't think he meant for this to happen," Ailia said. "He believed Valdur was long dead, and no threat to him or anyone else. He wished only for protection from us."

"Valdur can work as easily through those who disbelieve in him as through those who believe," Damion replied. "Many are unconscious of his call, but they obey it nevertheless. And Mandrake was made to be his vessel. Perhaps he could not help but be seduced by him. In any case, this is the enemy we must now fight."

"Damion—I am, as you said, one of the lesser ones. I have no strength to fight an Elyra!"

"What of the Stone?" he asked. "It is a talisman that links you to all other El. Perhaps all you need do is wield it, and they will add their strength to yours."

Ailia considered. "Perhaps," she said at last. "I have it here. We will see what power it grants me. But my mother told me it was not truly a weapon."

There was a low rumble and the floor trembled beneath their feet, as if masses of steel-shod cavalry had just galloped past. Then the earth itself seemed to rock—back and forth, like a ship at sea— and then settle once more into solidity. Screams and shouts broke forth from the crowd outside.

"It's begun," said Damion. "We must act now, before he gains too much power from his master. He may not realize even now what he has become."

Together they walked back out the tall doorway. The crowd was dispersing in fear, and not because of the tremors alone. The hill with its fortress was wreathed not only in its customary white steams, but with black smoke as well, billowing up to hide the lofty towers from view.

"Is there a fire?" cried Ailia as Jomar and Lorelyn came running up to the steps.

The bald man overheard. "The fire is in the earth!" he answered. "We will be punished for listening to you! The Dragon King is angry, and now we will be destroyed!"

17

The Power of the Earth

LATER IN THE EVENING AILIA and her allies gathered in the court before the Dragon King's temple. From its gilded roof the battle-standard of Arainia now flew: it depicted the Elmir Triumphant, holding in its beak the writhing form of the conquered Serpent. The earth had grown quiet once more. But the fortress of the living god still lowered over the city, its towers enfolded in smoke-plumes rising from deep fissures in the hill's sides, and circled by sparring dragons and cherubim.

"That's our next conquest," said Jomar. "And the last, and hopefully it will end the war."

Erron Komora shook his head. "Few will follow you there. Not while Mandrake lives, as your dragons and cherubim say he does. And the Lady Syndra has also grown in power, so that the people here fear her as much as the Dragon King himself. She told me that she had turned to the earth-goddess for aid," he said, shuddering.

"Mortals who turn to evil Archons often live to regret it," commented Taleera.

"And we have iron. The armies must go together to the hill, and enter the castle. I will teach them the way," said Ailia. "Once they enter the stronghold with their weapons, they will weaken the enemy's sorcery."

"But Mandrake is impervious now to iron, you say," Taleera pointed out.

"That is true; but Syndra and the Loänei are not, and neither are his rebel Loänan and the firedrakes. Even Elnemorah cannot resist it." They all looked up at the winged shapes wheeling above the fortress. "He will have to fight alone once his allies are rendered powerless," Ailia continued, her voice turning dull. "And our Wing-watch wounded him as he fled. Great as his sorcery has become, he cannot fight forever. Our Loänan cannot fight either, of course, with iron present. But the cherubim can."

"And will," said Falaar in his great trumpeting voice. It was clear that he took pride in the thought that his people should fight the final battle.

"So it will be Mandrake alone against the cherubic hosts. I am sorry, Auron," Ailia said, turning to the Loänan, "to deny your people this fight. But none of us who wield sorcery can take part in the battle. Mandrake must not be allowed to go to Ombar. With no cherubim on his side, nor any that can resist iron, he will grow weary, and his wounds will weaken him. He will need rest and sleep, and then . . . that will be the end." There was a catch in her voice as she said the last words, barely perceptible to most, though Damion heard it. He went to stand by her side.

"The prophecy says that you will triumph, Ailia," said Taleera. "But in this plan you propose, you have no active part to play. That cannot be right."

Damion said, "Perhaps Ailia has played her part already. By devising this plan, she will be the *indirect* cause of the Dragon Prince's destruction. And this way the mortals will have a larger share in the victory than if we tried to win through sorcery."

"Yes," said Ailia. "They will have the triumph, not I."

"That is as it should be," said Brannion Duron. "This is, after all, our world and not yours." The woman Jelynda, who was standing close to him, laid her hand upon his arm in a manner both reverent and possessive. He did not smile, but responded to her touch with a casual caress.

Ailia averted her eyes from the pair, only to find herself looking instead at Lorelyn and Jomar, who had also put their arms about each other. She had seen their love grow over the past weeks, from small and subtle signs to more open displays of affection. Even as she rejoiced for them, the sight gave her the same heartache as had the love between Mai and her Teren. The boy had survived the battle in the jungles, but he would likely take part in this new campaign as well. How could Ailia ever face Mai if her lover died, since the campaign was of her own devising? And were Lorelyn and Jomar also doomed?

THE KNIGHTS AND ARMED REBELS, together with many of the people of the city, advanced to the foot of the volcanic hill and looked up. Its sides were sheer, its top lost in the swirling steams and smokes. Through these they glimpsed the path that Ailia and Mai had once taken, winding thin as a thread up to the cave mouth in the hillside.

Lorelyn went to stand beside Jomar. "Ailia says there is a tunnel inside that, and it goes right through the inside of the hill, and joins onto a passage that leads up into the castle."

"I don't much like the sound of that," he responded. "We could be trapped inside a tunnel."

"Perhaps with the cherubim attacking by air, the enemy's attention will be distracted from us."

He considered. "Perhaps. But we had better wait until it turns dark, just to be on the safe side."

After the setting of the second sun they began their cautious ascent, Jomar and Lorelyn leading with their knights while the soldiers of the Overseer followed in long files. The Overseer himself was not with them: he and Komora had disappeared before the march began. "Cowards," Jomar had said in contempt. "They know now that iron's no use against Mandrake, so they don't dare attack him again. They'll leave all the hard work and danger to us." Some of the Overseer's men also became afraid as they approached the cave mouth, and turned back. But most continued on past its steamy curtain, confident in those who led them. It was hot and dark in the cave beyond, almost stiflingly so: the walls were no longer merely dewed and glistening, but dripped and ran with moisture. The intruders panted and mopped their brows, and the knights began to remove some of their armor despite Jomar's warnings. When they came at last to the cavern and the pool they saw that the surface of the latter was bubbling like a great pot over a fire.

Lorelyn stepped close to the edge, staring. "Ailia said that the pool was hot like a steam bath, but not boiling. What has happened?"

"Look, my lady," said a knight, pointing. They could see a red glow coming up through a narrow crevice in the rock floor, and a heat like a forge at full blast smote their faces as they stooped and looked down into it.

"Fire—there's fire below," said Jomar. "Is this volcano coming to life again?"

"It's sorcery," declared Lorelyn. "I'm sure of it. Perhaps we ought to go back."

"If it's magic, then Mandrake is doing it to make us retreat," Jomar answered. He felt a rising impatience now that he was so near his quarry. "But he'll not do anything to endanger himself. He's only trying to frighten us. We should be safe enough." He rubbed the sweat from his brow. "Come along. Where is this stair that goes up into the keep?"

On they went, their weapons at the ready, up the rock stair to the door opening on the lower level of the castle. This they broke open with ease. There were a few retainers milling about the halls, and these fled at the sight of the invaders' swords and armor, save for a few who seemed to be in a sort of stupor, as if drunk. But there was no sign of Mandrake anywhere.

Presently Lorelyn found the great doors to the throne room and peered in. There was a red-robed figure sitting on the throne. She gave an exclamation as she recognized it.

"It's *she*—Syndra! The traitor!"

Jomar strode through the doorway, sword at the ready. "Where is your prince? Tell me now!" he shouted.

Syndra continued to sit the throne unmoving. Her loose hair spilled like black oil down her red robe, and her face was utterly serene. "You cannot prevail," she called out in a clear, unhurried voice. "The fires of the earth are rising. I summoned them, and they obeyed my command, for I have dominion over them. You thought to overrun a keep, and instead it has become a snare. Still, you may depart if you will, and go back to your Tryna Lia. Remain, and you will burn!"

Jomar stared. "So will you, you fool!"

She said, "No: only this mortal creature will perish with her body. I cannot be harmed."

He gaped at her. "What? What are you saying?"

"That isn't Syndra speaking. She has been possessed!" Lorelyn walked swiftly up the aisle and to the foot of the throne, and held out her adamantine blade. "Who are you? What have you done to Syndra?"

"I am the Archon of this world," said the red-painted mouth.

"Elnemorah," gasped Lorelyn, turning to look back at Jomar. "Elnemorah has taken her over. You see, Jo? That's why she's not afraid: the Archon knows *she* can't be destroyed!"

"We brought iron with us," Jomar said. "Even the earth-Archons can't resist that, can they? It stops their sorcery from working, just the same as any mortal magician's." He too advanced up the aisle, and as his Star Sword drew near the woman on the throne writhed and glared at him.

"It is too late!" cried Syndra's stolen voice. "The earth-fires have been awakened, and they rise now not by my power but in obedience to their own nature. You and your rebel allies can never retake Loänanmar now. The city will be destroyed, and its people must flee or perish. You brought this doom upon them."

THE TRYNA LIA AND HER counselors had taken an abandoned house in the center of the city for a temporary dwelling. It was one of the finer homes in Loänanmar, having once belonged to an ally of the Overseer, and its many rooms were filled with sumptuous furnishings of fine wood and gilt. The tall windows were open, letting in the sultry air. Ailia and Damion and their advisors sat around a table topped with marble, talking quietly of what must be done. The Overseer and Komora were not with them, having departed on some business of their own. Auron sat with them, transformed into human shape, and Taleera perched on the back of his chair. Falaar was outside, guarding the main entrance of the mansion.

Ailia felt light-headed with worry and weariness, and with the heat. No breeze came through the opened widows. She noticed Damion looking at her with concern, and made an effort to sit upright and keep her mind on the discussion, but what she yearned for was a long rest and sleep.

She had changed to a plain white robe, and she wore no crown save for a braid of her own hair, bound over the top of her head while the rest flowed loose down her back. Her only jewel was her mother's star sapphire: the Stone she kept hidden away in a deep pocket. As she sat in her gilded chair, she sighed often and twisted the ring on her finger.

"It is taking so long!" she said. "And with the iron we can hear nothing of what is happening in the castle."

"Falaar says the battle was going well when he fought there," Auron assured her. The cherubim were taking turns in fighting Mandrake, whose power was greater than any had expected. "As you said, the Prince cannot last forever. He is only defending himself now, not attacking, and his dragon warriors cannot come within the central court where he has taken his stand. The soldiers ring it about with their weapons." He laid his hand upon the back of her chair and leaned close to the Princess, talking in his most soothing voice. "It goes well, Highness. The final victory will not be long in coming."

"No victory awaits them or you, Princess," said a new voice. It came from the direction of the door, and everyone in the room jumped and whirled. There in the entrance stood a goblin, or perhaps a hideous man: its figure was clad in a somber dark robe, and its visage was wizened and malevolent.

"How did this person get into the building?" demanded Taleera, rising up in a flurry of feathers.

The great head of the cherub Falaar appeared at one of the windows. "He did not get in. The coward is merely projecting his image. See, thou canst look right through him."

"Who are you?" Damion demanded, rising.

"I am Naugra," the aged creature said, his dark eyes fixing each of them in turn. "Regent of Ombar."

"What do you want with us, Naugra? Say what you came to say and leave," said Damion.

"You are advised to go at once from this place, for while you stay you imperil the people's lives," the Regent said.

"And leave Mandrake to reign over them as a tyrant?" retorted Damion.

"It is better than allowing them to be destroyed. Elnemorah has possessed your traitorous Lady Syndra, who wished to be the con-

sort of the incarnate Valdur. She extended her power too far, and
was captured. Now she serves the goddess of this world. The hill
will erupt in flames and all in this city will perish. And the first to
die will be your friends, who are now caught within the hill-
fortress: unless you command them to retreat at once. I leave you
to ponder these things, and make your choice."

With that, he vanished.

Ailia, her face drawn, rose from her seat. "What am I to do?" she
asked.

Falaar fixed his great golden eyes on her. "We cannot halt our
campaign now. If we do so Mandrake will recover his strength, and
escape to Ombar. As for the warriors, it is an honor to die for the
light. Their souls and names will live on in glory."

"The people of this city aren't warriors! They are mere merchants
and farmers—and women and little children," she cried.

"The enemy knows thy heart is full of compassion. He expects
to make this work to his advantage—to make thee hesitate."

She put a hand to her head. "A moment—give me a moment, I
need to think . . ."

Ailia walked out of the house and into the high-walled garden
that lay behind it. Over the roofs of the city the volcano brooded,
black and ominous. It was full of the earth-magic: far below its base,
in its deep and hidden bowels, the fiery forces that had raised it up
were now awake again. In the dark green sky beyond all the stars
were out—including the one that burned red. The air was warm,
and heavy and oppressive, recalling another night that was scented
with the fragrance of roses. She paced to and fro beneath the stars.
*What must I do? Mother, are you there? Tell me what I must do! Archons, help
me.* But the stars were silent. *What will happen? How many lives will be the
price? Are they nothing in the scheme of things? Is that acceptable to you?* She
appealed to the sky. *The war will go on for centuries—perhaps millennia. The
goblins and others will always hate us—they hate us now more than ever.* She
recalled the words of Mandrake: *only if we unite will there be lasting peace.*
She longed for that vision of peace with all her heart, but it was not
to be.

The earth shook again, and the stench of brimstone was thick on
the air. Ailia's eyes turned back to the castle wrapped in its reeking
pall. Now she understood the enemy's plan. The rising fires would
drive all the human warriors from the fortress, and their weapons

with them. With the iron gone, the firedrakes and the enemy Loänan would be free to descend to the fortress, and assist Mandrake
in his battle. The only way to prevent this, as Falaar had said, was
for the soldiers to remain in the fortress to the end, and perish in
the eruption. Many cherubim would doubtless die too, as they
strove to keep Mandrake from fleeing. She thought of Teren and
the other young soldiers, and of Jomar and Lorelyn, and she trembled. *No! Our warriors must not win by becoming martyrs. It would be such a
horrible end. Let the cherubim leave off their fighting, and go save the soldiers instead. They alone can fly them to safety. The iron might be left behind, I suppose,
to hinder our foes from coming near their prince.*

But even as she thought this she knew it was no answer. Mandrake's human minions could simply gather up the swords and
spears, and cast them off the battlements. *It seems sorcery is the only answer, after all, and I must fight as the prophecy foretold. I will go with the cherubim, and help them and our dragons to defeat Mandrake.* But might there not
be some hope still, that Mandrake would listen to reason and surrender, rather than go with the firedrakes to Ombar? He had delayed going there thus far, and that meant he still resisted their
designs for him.

After a moment she became aware that Auron, Falaar, and
Damion were there with her, just standing still and silent a few
paces away, offering their presence as comfort. She faced them with
hands clasped before her, like a petitioner. "Damion," she said,
"would you take command of the army for now? I am going to try
and help Jomar and Lorelyn and the others—if you will take me to
the courtyard, my friend," she added, shifting her gaze to Falaar.
"With the iron, I cannot reach it by taking a winged form myself."

"I will bear thee hence," said Falaar. "But what canst thou accom-
plish there, Highness, if thou art wearied already, and iron is at
hand?"

"I have still one advantage over my enemy," said Ailia. "He is
hurt, and I am not. If he is not too far gone, I may even persuade
him to surrender. But I am going in any case, to do what I must."

LORELYN HAD GONE APART FROM the rest of the army into the castle's conservatory, so that their iron weapons should not cloud her
mind as she reached into the Ether. As she stood in the sad silence
under its shattered panes, among the withered potted trees, she

reached out and was relieved to hear a familiar mind-voice respond. *Lori,* Ailia called, *I am flying to the castle, with Falaar. You must get everyone out of the castle if you can—quickly! Take everyone up to the battlements. The cherubim will fly them to safety.*

"What about you?" Lorelyn asked. "Why are you coming here?"

There is something I must do.

"What thing?"

What I should have done before: fight my own battle, not leave it to others. Lori, please hurry!

Lorelyn ran back to the throne room where the fighting men and townspeople were assembled, and relayed Ailia's command. Syndra still sat her throne, but in the presence of so many iron weapons her possessor had withdrawn completely, and her face was haggard and white with terror. "Do not leave me here, I beg of you," she cried. "*She* will return, and claim me. I cannot resist her."

"Oh, you'll be coming with us right enough," Jomar replied. "You'll have to answer for your treason, for one thing."

"No—no, what am I saying? It is no use. You do not understand. You cannot win." Syndra rose, swaying as if she were about to faint, and leaning against their arms. Then swift as a snake her hand darted out and seized the dagger in Jomar's belt. He cursed and turned on her, sword at the ready; but she pointed the dagger's blade at her own breast. Before either of them could stop her, she thrust it in. "Free," she gasped as she sank to her knees on the crimson-carpeted floor. "*She* cannot take me again, ever. I am free! But he is not—he will be consumed—"

"Mandrake?" queried Lorelyn, kneeling down to support the woman's sagging shoulders and head.

"Your one hope, and his—Ailia." Syndra choked, her lips red now with more than paint. "She can kill him. Tell her—if she loves him she must kill him, before—before . . ." Her head fell back in Lorelyn's arms, its emptied eyes staring upward.

They looked at the lifeless form, then at each other. "What did she mean?" Jomar asked. "All that about loving and killing?"

Lorelyn shook her head. "I don't know. She always hated Ailia, and we never knew why, and now we never will know." She stood up again. "But at least she tried to *stop* herself, in the end."

"What will happen now?" Jomar demanded. "Will the fire still come up through the hill now that Elnemorah has gone?"

"Yes, I think it will. The Archon seemed to be saying that she had started something that can't be stopped—if we can believe her, that is. But do you feel how hot the floor is?"

He nodded. "It's probably best to take her at her word." Jomar looked down at the still body on the carpet. "Leave her. There's nothing to be done for her now. It's the living we must help. All these people have to be gotten out of the castle and onto the roof, just as Ailia said."

With some difficulty the Paladins herded the remains of the court together. Some of the people had tried to retreat through the tunnel door. But when they had reached it they had been forced to halt. Black smoke boiled from the entrance, past the shattered door still hanging on one hinge, together with an unendurable heat. Coughing, peering down the stair through the ashen haze, they had glimpsed a fiery glare. Molten stone had burst through the cavern beneath and was mounting the steps in a swift red flood.

Now Lorelyn confronted the mass of frightened faces. "Up the stairs, all of you, and onto the roofs! Help is coming, but you must do as I say!" There was no argument. They ran, with the Paladins flanking them and Jomar and Lorelyn bringing up the rear. They could not move as speedily as they might have liked, for those few who were unconscious from the bliss-flower had to be carried, and the fighters were burdened with their armor.

"Are you quite sure that everyone is here?" panted Lorelyn as they mounted the second marble flight. Even at this level the heat was overpowering, and it was difficult to breathe. Smoke was pursuing them up the staircase: the lower halls were on fire.

"We ran through the rooms, but all were empty," answered one of the knights. "Only the Tryna Lia remains, and the Dragon Prince. We saw them both in the courtyard."

"Ailia!" cried Lorelyn. But the iron shut her off from the channels of the Ether, and there was no reply.

THE PEOPLE IN THE CITY below watched in awe as the steams issuing from the hill's side grew dark under the moons, turning to smoke laden with ash. There was a sudden red flicker from the cave mouth, and then it spewed forth a fountain of liquid stone that blazed bright as molten metal. It cascaded down the steep slope, burning all it touched. At the same time, as if in answer, tongues of flame leaped in the sky above, and wheeling black wings obscured the stars. The firedrakes were preparing to rejoin the fight.

The Loänan all took to the air. Damion turned to the crowd that had massed behind him in the street and shouted, "Fall back! Fall back and save yourselves, and any people who are left! There is nothing you can do now but take the women and the children and run. The city is lost!"

He ran for Falaar, who had alighted nearby to deposit the soldiers he bore. "The firedrakes are circling above the fortress. I think they have come for Mandrake, to guard him and lead him to Ombar. We must stop them! But the townsfolk need our help too. There will be rivers of fire running through the streets soon."

"I hear," said Falaar, kneeling again so Damion could mount his back. "But I think we will be hard put to save the humans, and to defend ourselves also."

Damion peered downward as his winged steed climbed into the air. Cherubim were setting down their human passengers at the city's edge. "Lorelyn is there," he said with relief. "I hear her. She and Jomar will lead everyone to safety. But we must help Ailia."

"We will do so—but we must now fight our way through firedrakes," said Falaar.

THE LIGHT FROM THE CASTLE'S windows spilled into the pleasure garden at its heart, and there Ailia stood facing Mandrake. The wounded dragon was sprawled on the grass, wings askew, scaly sides heaving. His golden eyes were half-open, but showed no recognition as she drew near. He moved his head a little at the sound of retreating wings, as the cherubim carried the last of the fortress's occupants off the roofs to safety. "They are all fleeing, leaving you to your fate," said Ailia softly. "Change back to your own form, Mandrake, and we will carry you to safety as well. Surrender, and you will not be destroyed."

The dragon did not transform, nor answer her. His eyes had shut, and his breath came in rattling gasps. He seemed to be in a swoon. What if he could not be revived? Even were she capable of taking draconic form now, she could not lift another dragon bodily into the air. He would perish alone in the fiery cataclysm to come, a fate she could not wish on any creature. Pity filled her, and guilt too, as she gazed at the scarred and prostrate form. Had Mandrake not spared *her* life, when she lay sleeping in this very castle? Had he slain her then, he would not have come to this pass. Must she now return evil for good? To walk away from him was to leave him to the fires. Elnemorah, in seeking to save the Avatar, had doomed him—unless Ailia's friends could give him aid. She cried out to Auron and Falaar, pleading for their help. Then she realized that she could not hear any ethereal voices at all, even though the fleeing warriors had taken their weapons. She had been cut off once more, as if by a barrier. A barrier of iron . . .

There was a roar of star-magic from directly overhead, the over-mastering voice of cold iron, and with it came the sound of beating wings. She stared upward as a wyvern flapped down between the castle's towering walls, and settled in the courtyard. On its back were two riders, whose faces she recognized as they dismounted and came into the light of lamps and fires. Brannion Duron and Erron Komora. The Overseer bore his sword of iron at his hip.

"The great advantage of a wyvern," said Erron, as he tethered the hissing reptile to a tree with a length of rope, "is that it is a creature of nature, and uses no magic to fly. Iron cannot bind it to the earth, like a dragon, and sorcery is not needed to command it."

As they drew closer, the unconcious Loänan shuddered, but did not wake, and then the sorcery that held its shape gave way. It was Mandrake the man who lay there in the firelit garden, among the crushed rosebushes. The wounds of battle still covered him in this form, showing dark against his face and arms. He lay motionless, eyes shut, and face deathly pale. Ailia gazed on him with compassion—and another, stronger emotion that she could no longer deny. *We can end his suffering now, while he is oblivious to all that is happening,* she thought. *How easy it would be, and how kind! The doom would be fulfilled by an act of mercy. This must be how Eliana felt. But—she spared him. Was that mere chance? Or could it be that she was obeying destiny, and he was somehow meant to live?* In any case, she did not want Duron to win all the glory. Triumphing over the Dragon King would strengthen his hold on his people, as he well knew. He had not marched with his men, but had waited until Mandrake was weakened—until it was safe to attack him. He was a coward but would be hailed a hero.

The Overseer paused in the act of unsheathing his sword. "I see no dragon now, only a man." Duron frowned. "Our iron should make the creature revert to his *true* form, should it not?"

Erron looked scornful. "That *is* his true form. He is no Loänan. He is but a man who can take a dragon's shape. Did you not hear what Ailia told you? In this at least she did not lie: he is merely a Loänei sorcerer. As is this woman, this goddess as she likes to be called: Ailia too is powerless before your blade. But be swift! The fires consuming the castle will spread to this garden—and those below the earth are drawing near. Can you not feel how hot the earth is beneath your feet? Slay the Dragon King, and let us flee!"

"And when he is dead you will take his place, and rule this world," Ailia accused, moving to stand between Duron and his prey. "Overseer, Erron means to betray you once Mandrake is gone."

"Come, Brannion, never mind her," Erron said. "Kill him! We need not take the whole body with us, just cut off the head. It is all the proof you need of your victory."

"I had hoped for a worthier trophy than this: the head of a great dragon," grunted Duron.

"No matter. We will make a statue of you holding a dragon's head," snapped Erron. "Make haste! Pay no heed to the witch: she cannot stop you. She cannot use her sorcery with iron present."

Duron raised his sword. "Move away from him, woman."

"No."

"Move or I will strike you down too."

The hill rocked beneath them, and more fires broke out in the castle. The wyvern, wild with terror, swung its long neck to and fro and screamed. Then, beating its leathery wings, it sought to reach the sky, but was held back by its tether. Ailia looked up. The Wing-watch were engaged in fighting the firedrakes. She could not summon them by way of the Ether, with iron so near, and only a cherub could have saved her in any case: the dragons would be just as helpless as she.

Duron took a step toward her.

And then he turned, with shocking speed, and plunged his sword into Erron's chest. The Loänei man gave a hoarse, rasping cry and his hands went up to claw at the blade. Then his legs gave way beneath him, and he collapsed backward into the rose bushes, and lay still. Ailia stood aghast.

"I have not lived to so great an age," observed Duron in a calm and level voice as he drew his blade from the other's body, "by trusting traitors. Fortunately I need him no longer. Let that be a lesson to you, girl. Now get out of my way." And he began once more to walk toward Ailia and Mandrake.

She ran from him, and then, as he stood at the fallen Mandrake's side, Ailia lunged toward Erron's body and grabbed the jeweled knife from his belt. Duron caught the movement at the edge of his sight and turned to look full at her. "You think you can fight me with that little blade?" he asked, contempt filling his eyes and voice.

"No," she replied, clutching the hilt. "I have no such intent."

"I should really kill you too, for I see you are also treacherous by nature. And my people might come to worship you, as your own ignorant subjects do. But more important matters first." He turned to Mandrake, but kept an eye on Ailia.

She began to run again—this time for the wyvern, which was struggling frantically to fly away, maddened by the smell of smoke and the threatening fires. With one blow she cut halfway through the rope that tethered it to the tree.

"What are you doing?" screamed Duron, losing his composure at last.

She turned to face him, knife in hand. "Setting this creature free. If you want to live, Duron, then you will get on its back now and go. The wyvern is your only hope of escape. Go now, and take your iron with you!"

A ring of fire surrounded them now: the whole castle was aflame. Molten rock poured along the floors of fine marble, flowing from room to room, setting alight curtains and tapestries and furnishings of wood. The wyvern screeched and strained again at the rope, which began to pull apart at its weakened point. Only a few strands kept the beast from freedom: Ailia raised the knife to sever them. Cursing, Duron sheathed his sword and ran for the wyvern's saddle. The rope broke even as he made his desperate sprint, and he grabbed frantically for its trailing end. As the wyvern rocketed upward, flying away from the hilltop as fast as it could go, he dangled precariously from the rope, clinging for his life as he swung above the roaring conflagration. The two of them vanished together into the cloud of smoke and suspended cinders.

Ailia was left in the court. She threw down Erron's dagger: it was steel, thankfully, for no Loänei would ever carry iron. But she was still too weak to perform any sorcery. She called out with her mind, but received no answer: the Wingwatch battled the firedrakes high above, and their thoughts were a welter of pain and rage and confusion as they fought.

With a last effort she sought to center herself, to touch the dwindling core of her power and draw on it. But at the same instant there was a great gust of wind, fanning the flames in the burning trees, and she spun around to see the red dragon rear up behind her with flailing wings and eyes that returned the fire-glow, reaching out his claws to take her.

IN THE CITY JOMAR AND the others saw the great smoke-cloud billow upward from the hill, obscuring all but the angry glow at the summit, and the blazing torrents streaming down its slopes. The city was doomed: at the hill's foot the streams would slow but not halt, and in time its streets too would run with the fiery flood. A black snow of ash was settling on the roofs. Tearing their eyes from the dreadful sight, they set themselves to the task of guiding the fleeing citizens toward the city's edge. As for the castle, it was spouting flame and molten stone from every window. Then the whole of the keep seemed to blossom outward, walls bulging and toppling in ruin: as they fell they revealed the gaping red-lit crater that had appeared in the midst of the central court. The hill's peak had collapsed into a caldera, taking with it the keep's foundations. The tall pinnacled tower was the last to fall, wavering and bending and then at last bowing its proud head as it fell into the fiery pit and was consumed. The watchers saw the vast dark pall that hung above begin to flare with lightning at its top, where the roiling smoke blended with the low-hanging clouds.

"Ailia! Ailia!" cried Auron, as he set a firedrake to fleeing. "Where is she? Does anyone know what became of her?"

But in the next instant he had his answer, without needing to hear from his companions. A red dragon burst up through the smoke-cloud, wings beating the blackened air, straining toward the sky and freedom. It was Mandrake; and clutched in his front claws was the limp figure of the Tryna Lia.

18

Ombar

"NO! DON'T LET THEM! JO, he has Ailia—he'll drop her!" Lorelyn screamed, seizing her friend by the arm.

More than a dozen Arainian archers stood in the middle of the street, training their man-high longbows on the red dragon as he flew above the belching hill. He seemed to be having difficulty gaining height, weakened perhaps by the poisonous fumes within the reeking smoke-cloud. Beneath him the volcano sent forth swift-rolling scarlet tongues of molten stone mottled with black cinders, and in the fierce glow of these they could all see the small white figure clenched in Mandrake's front claws. Jomar, on the point of giving the command to his archers to loose their arrows, fell silent and stood staring up helplessly, seeing that Mandrake's stumbling flight would turn to a fatal fall, or else that he would let Ailia plummet to her death. But his wings continued to labor, and he did not drop his victim. As he won free of the smoke at last and climbed higher, several wheeling shapes descended to flank him—firedrakes, forming a long phalanx with the red dragon at the center. The Wingwatch observed this, but it was plain that they dared not interfere either, lest Mandrake let Ailia fall. A few moved to fly alongside the firedrakes, but the latter repulsed them with claw and flame. Higher and higher they flew, until the Dragon King, now a minute spot scarcely to be seen in the dark sky, was engulfed by the Ether and lost from sight—together with his captive.

Lorelyn's grief burst from her in a long wail. "No!"

Then there was a cry from the air above them, and out of the melee dropped a tawny form—Falaar. He descended in a flurry of wings, and alighted on the pavement, dropping into a crouch. Damion sat astride his furry back.

"Jomar—Lori!" he called. "There is molten fire pouring down the hill. It will slow when it reaches the level ground, but the city is doomed all the same. And some of it has already reached the river-bank—do you see the steam rising up? When fire and water come together, they will send out showers of embers into the air, that will set alight everything they touch. These wooden houses will burn quickly. Gather your men and flee as fast as you can. Some of the Wingwatch will stay to guide you, and try to save any who are caught by the fires."

"But—Ailia, what about Ailia?" Jomar shouted.

"The rest of us are going to her aid now."

As Jomar gave the order to retreat the cherub stood and spread his wings, preparing to depart. "Damion, wait!" exclaimed Lorelyn, running forward. "I want to go too!"

Damion looked down at her from the height of the cherub's back. "No, Lorelyn. I'm sorry, but it will be much too dangerous. You must understand: we are going to Ombar. That is where he has taken her. And the scales of battle have been tipped against us. He is stronger in that place than she can ever be, and it is well de-fended. There is nothing more you can do, friends! Stay in Nemorah and help the people here, or else take a flying ship back to Arainia. There is no use for armies where we are going." He and his mount rose with a roar of wind into the black sky.

The company ran back toward the edge of the city. There was a sound of many loud reports, as of cannon fire, and glowing bursts of ash and embers rained down upon them. The air was growing foul with fumes. "Why?" Jomar yelled as he ran, his voice rasping and hoarse. "Why would she let herself be taken like that? She knew she wasn't strong enough to face him yet! Now he has her!"

"Perhaps she was too tired to think clearly. But why didn't he kill her straight away?" Lorelyn shouted back.

"Because there would be nothing between him and us then. None of us dared harm him while he was carrying her. She gave him pas-sage to freedom. For all we know she's dead now—"

"Don't say that! Perhaps they will catch him in time—or perhaps she will come out of her faint, and fight back—" Even now Lorelyn could not let go of hope.

They pelted on through the street. On one side of them rose the black smoke of houses ignited by the falling cinders, while on the other a white bank of steam wisped up from the river, marking the progress of the lava stream: the waters were seething in protest as they mingled with the river of fire. Ahead lay a gap between the black and white clouds, but it was closing as they ran. They would be caught between the two fires. Taleera flew above them, keeping pace with them and uttering urgent trilling cries.

"We know, we know!" panted Jomar.

They sped on and heat smote their faces from both sides as they entered the gap. To the left a stately cypress tree in a garden turned to a sparking torch, and beyond it were roofs rimmed with flames. To the right the river boiled, and sent forth more bursts of liquid flame like burning pitch. They ducked their heads as they ran, and the firebird was forced to fly higher, out of range. Then they were through, they were safe at last. A rush of cooler air met their faces as they left the outer boundary of Loänanmar behind and raced on into the fields beyond, away from both city and river.

Great throngs of people had gathered here, faces red in the light of destruction, watching as all they had ever known shriveled and fell in ruin. Some were weeping, but most had fallen silent in despair. Jomar left them no time to mourn, but urged them onward. "I don't know anything about these fire-mountains," he said. "I can't say how far this will spread. We must keep going." He added in an undertone to Lorelyn, "Better that they shouldn't watch. Moving on will give them something to do."

Lorleyn moaned. "I *can't* just go back to Arainia and wait to find out what's happened—who has won. If everything is going to end, I want at least to be there when—when it all happens. Not standing about here or in Halmirion, biting my nails! Ailia is my friend."

"I feel the same way," said Jomar. But he was afraid now as he had never been in his life before. Ombar! He glanced up at the sky above the smoke-cloud, where the red star could be seen, the Worm's Eye and the pale star next to it with its unseen companion . . . The Zimbourans had worshipped Vartara, shed blood for it and the god said to inhabit it. And now Ailia was being taken to the world nearest that star.

He swallowed. "Couldn't we use that portal thing in the ruin?" he suggested.

"I don't know how," Lorelyn groaned. "And I can't fly a ship on my own either."

But as they marched on with the fire at their backs, a mind-voice spoke to Lorelyn: *Come with me!* She turned to see another huge golden shape descending through the air. Auron—and Taleera was with him also, hovering over the dragon's head. As he alighted, blowing their garments about with the gusts from his tremendous wings, Auron's great green eyes looked on Lorelyn with under-standing. *I am going to Ombar, and I will take you with me, if you wish.*

"Auron! Thank you!" Lorelyn exclaimed, running to his side.

You may have little to thank me for, but I feel as you do. We may as well end our days there as here; and though we cannot help Ailia, it may comfort her to know we are there. Come! But I fear Jomar must leave his iron sword.

Auron did not tell her that he had never yet been to Ombar. He had seen it long ago, from a great distance: lying between him and its parent sun, it had appeared to his eyes only as a black circle like a sunspot, a mole on the red eye of Utara. Auron would go no nearer than that to the world where Valdur had reigned—until this moment, when he no longer had any choice.

Reluctantly Jomar surrendered the Star Sword, exchanging it for one of steel. Then he gave orders to the Paladins, instructing them to accompany the people onto the jungle paths and urge them to walk on as far westward as they possibly could. There would be few dangerous beasts about, at least, with the smoke-stench and sound of the burning putting every living thing in the area to panicked flight. Auron waited as the dispirited crowd moved slowly off, and the two humans and the firebird settled on his broad scaly back. Once they were secure in their places he sprang aloft, sweeping high above the dying city and the spouting volcano, with its tall plume of black and blazing red, the pyre of the Forbidden Palace.

AILIA CAME BACK TO HERSELF by slow degrees, aching and bewil-dered. Beneath her was soft cloth over some hard surface, and the air about her was cold. Blinking, she sat upright and saw that she had been lying upon a black cloak, which was spread on the floor of a stone chamber. Two great rows of rounded columns marched along its length, their capitals lost in the darkness of the ceiling, and the floor was barred with their black shadows. On one side were tall unglazed windows set deep into the wall, through which a red light poured. The huge room was completely bare of furnishings and had only one door, and was lit only by that blood-colored light. For an instant she feared that it was firelight, and she was still in the burning fortress. But the chamber was too cool for that—she was shivering in her thin robe.

Mandrake stood in human form before one of the windows, his back to her, his tall robed figure casting a long shadow upon the floor behind him. He did not turn his head as she rose and approached him.

She too said nothing, but went to stand at his side, and she wondered at the view before her. The cloudless sky glowed dark crimson, as if with the last light of sunset, and in the west rose a great arc of lighter hue. In the next instant she understood what she was looking at. It was a sun—but a sun so vast that its swollen sphere filled nearly all the western sky. Before Ailia's eyes its dull red surface seethed and boiled, and immense prominences thrust out from it on all sides like tongues of fire.

Mandrake said, "There were once other planets between this one and Utara, but when the Worm's Eye aged and swelled up it engulfed them. The sun is expanding still. This world is doomed: Utara will one day devour Ombar, her only remaining child, before she herself withers and dies."

Ombar, she thought, filled with horror. *We are in Ombar. Why has he brought me here?*

Beneath the sun spread a vast city that borrowed its hue from the light. Ailia's tired eyes beheld great temples and arenas, bridges and aqueducts, ziggurats, massive courts, and triumphal arches. After a moment Mandrake said, "That city down there, it is half-dead now, but once it was full of life. The Archons built it: they lived here, and later were joined by the mortals who served them. Now only the slaves remain, living on like rats in the ruins of their masters' houses."

Though the city was inhabited, nothing stirred anywhere, neither beast nor being. There were no trees or gardens to be seen: nothing green would grow here. Beyond the city a desert stretched, dull red under Utara's light. Though the colors were warm, the wind blowing toward them was bitter: despite its nearness, the great ember of a sun above gave out little heat. Ailia already felt starved for other colors, especially the eye-soothing greens of vegetation and the blue of sky-reflecting water. The one small sea on the horizon was shrunken and stinking with salt, red-lit so that it seemed a sea of blood. The western sky, like all else, took its hue

from Utara: the red of a perpetual sunset. But the day here was always ending: night could not come to these lands. The domain of
night lay to the east, a looming darkness that did not advance.
Auron had told her all he knew of Ombar, which was not a great
deal, for few even of the Loänan dared to come here. Because the
world always kept one side facing its sun, neither side could be inhabited: one was too hot and bright, and the other too dark and
cold. But between the lands of the sun and those of the never-
ending night, he had said, there lay a narrow girdle of twilight, circling the world. In this shadowy zone were the cities, and the only
growing things in Ombar's sphere: swamp lands that bred the nuckelavees, bugbears, barguests, and other creatures that haunted humanity's oldest tales and dreams.

Ailia suppressed a shudder. She had seen the beasts of Ombar
that had been kept in Zimboura: the fighting beasts from the arena,
and the barguests that had been used as watchdogs in Yanuvan. All
had been slain after Khalazar fell, and she had looked on their
hideous and nightmarish carcasses in horror.

"Forgive me, but I had to bring you here," said the Prince. "You
would have perished in the fiery ruin of the palace had I not lifted
you up, for I could tell your powers were spent. And once I was airborne, the firedrakes surrounded me, and your Loänan also. The
latter would have wrested you from my grip, and then slain me. I
did not know what else to do but follow the firedrakes, and come
here." He shuddered. "I wished for it all to end, there in the palace
courtyard. I was not unconscious: I *refused* to use the iron power any
longer, to save myself or to continue fighting my foes. I decided
that I preferred to die. But, you see, I *have* been saved, despite my
efforts. Even my wounds have healed themselves. I cannot slay myself: I cannot die. There is a fate that governs me, and turns my
body against my will, and prevents my escape. I did not wish to
come to Ombar; yet here I am."

"Why did you not kill *me* when you had the chance?" she asked.

"I might ask you the very same question. Is it that you pitied me?
Or do you still wish to join me, and be free?" There was a little
pause as she tried to form an answer. Then Mandrake spoke again.
"You and I were bred to destroy each other. It is the reason we exist.
It may be that we have no choice. Long ago, when I lived in the
land of Marakor, I had a hedge-maze on my estate. It used to com-

pose my mind to walk along its convoluted paths—until I began to reflect on its semblance to my own life. Is there something beyond even the schemes of the Old Ones that holds us to a certain course? Do they merely serve a higher destiny, which even they must obey? In a maze there are no true choices, only the design long set out by the maze-builder. So long . . . I have been fate's slave so long. I wanted only to be free." He turned his head, suddenly, and fastened his eyes on hers: it was like gazing into endless depths of fire. "I thought, back there in the burning castle, that if I died it would at least mean I had been freed from destiny. But perhaps there is no freedom. Perhaps you and I, Ailia, have been moving toward an end that was foreordained from time immemorial. And—there is in me another power, a second personality that is taking command. I am no longer one person but two, and the parasitic thing within me is winning the conflict. I have done vile things without knowing why, obeyed commands that came from elsewhere. I believed at first that I was going mad. But I know now I was made this way. When I was born it was not a normal birth, and it seems I am not destined to die as others do either. When the moment of my death comes, it will not be the death of my body—that will live on—but of my mind."

"You're saying that you are possessed." Ailia took his hand, and looked deep into the dragon-eyes.

"There is something evil within me, a Voice. It has always been there, a part of me."

"No," Ailia said, "the Voice is not part of you. It comes from outside, from the dark place, Perdition. It is Valdur's voice. Do not listen to him, Mandrake. Be free of him. You have a soul, and that is your own, however your material body came to be. As to what you have done, I certainly cannot condemn you, because I too nearly became a monster." She told him what had happened in the forest of Ardana, when her fear and anger spurred the beasts into attacking the invaders.

"I did the same in Nemorah, with the beasts of sea and jungle," he said. "And like you, I was unaware of what I did. But your soldiers suffered all the same. This is what befalls when we accept the aid of Archons. We must resist them."

"I will help you if I can."

"Remain here with me." He closed his eyes, shuddering, and his fingers grew tight around hers. "I can trust no one save you. You spared me when I was at your mercy. Forgive my rambling a moment ago: I know it was not any dark fate that made you save my life, but your own free will. You were always compassionate, to me and to others." He opened his eyes and gazed down at her. "The Valei hate and distrust me. I can barely keep them all in check, and I need someone to guard my sleep. Not all of them want me for their ruler." His grip eased. "But if you will help me, watch over me, I can control them. And your world will be safe, and all others, so long as I rule the Valei empire and you command the rest of Talmirennia. Together, we can thwart destiny."

"But can you control the Valei, Mandrake? Or will they end by controlling you?"

He released her hand. "I can control them because I must. Our two empires can be joined in one." A trace of a smile flitted across Mandrake's features. "It would be a grand jest. Did it never occur to those scheming Old Ones that two adversaries as finely matched as we might come to admire each other for the very qualities we share?" But as he gazed out the glassless window, he grew somber again. "Here humanity's ancestors were brought, to be bred with demons, and over time become the goblins and ogres, trolls and ghouls. Loänan became firedrakes. Even some of the cherubim turned to the Dark One's side. For a time the Empire was ruled from this place—before the war. Before Valdur was defeated, and cast into the black star."

"Did Valdur—live in *this* palace?" The thought set her to trembling again.

"No. This city was Elombar's to rule, and this was his palace. The Archon of this world had his cult here, and demanded the worship from his slaves. Valdur chose to dwell in the Nightlands. Do you see that great avenue running through the center of the city? That is the road that led to his old fortress, through the lands of twilight and of the Night, to the Perilous Citadel."

Something within Ailia shrank back. "The fortress of Hell—does it truly exist? Does it still stand, after all this time?"

"I am told it does, though I have never been there. The central keep was made of adamant, and could never fall in ruin. His throne is still there, it's said, and his crown of iron. He came back to this place after Athariel defeated him in Mera and took the Star Stone from him. He left his crown here, and he changed to a dragon's form to fight the other Archons one last time—out in the void. They conquered him and cast him into the black star. But his slaves believe he will return in another form, and reclaim throne and crown. The Iron Diadem, the latter was called. Modrian used it to dominate Elombar and all the lesser Elaia in this world, for of course they could be cowed with iron. It was a potent symbol of his supe-riority." He paused. "And I must go there, to that Citadel."

"Why?" she asked.

"To destroy both throne and crown, to show his minions that there will be no return of their god. Also Naugra is there, I believe, and as Regent he too is a symbol of that hope, and must be cast down. Until these things are done, there will be no peace or free-dom for these miserable creatures. You need not come with me."

Her mind recoiled again, but she moved to stand closer to him. "I will go. I believe you are right, Mandrake—we *can* choose our fate, and not merely surrender to it."

"But we cannot go yet. I am weary, and so are you. Rest now, if you can. You will need all your strength and power. If you do not fear to take a dragon's form again, it would be best to do so for this journey. The Twilight is a perilous place, as are the Nightlands. There will be dangers on land and in the air, some that can creep on you unawares, so claws and scaly armor will serve you best. Much rests on our success. There is no tomorrow in this place, but change may yet come to it." And with that he bowed to her, and left the room by the door that she had seen in the shadows.

She remained, unable to tear herself away from the window, gaz-ing out on the city from the deep embrasure. And as she looked, it wavered before her eyes, and though she had taken no ambrosia, it was suddenly transformed in a waking vision. Seated colossi with faces worn away by wind and time became whole, their features ap-pearing out of stone and shadow, staring down in lofty arrogance. The city came to life, as did the barren land, re-forming and reju-venating as she watched in bewilderment. Shades of people, human and otherwise, thronged streets now smoothly paved. Surely this was a glimpse out of the past, out of the days of Ombar's glory when it had been the capital of Entar. Did Modrian reign on his throne in the great fortress-fane in the Nightlands? She thought of the majestic archangel-figure she had seen depicted in old books, slowly transforming into a demon, and then a dragon. So great a power, in visible form—the mere thought of it set her knees to shaking with a mixture of awe and dread. No, she dared not look upon him, even as an impotent phantom of the past.

High on one of the ziggurats a gong sent out its shivering voice. The crowds stirred and murmured, glancing back up at the palace. Ailia saw their looks of fear and her own dread increased. A figure strode out of one of the high doorways below, majestic and regal, and yet shrouded in dark raiment, only the eyes glowing. It looked up toward Ailia. *It can see me*, she thought. *It is not truly in this time, as I am not.*

The figure spoke. She saw the face now, and it was not comely but hideous, with cruel tusks protruding from its lips. A face shaped like a mask, with deliberate malice by its wearer, in order to strike fear into mortal hearts. *What think you, little sister, of my world?* it said.

"Elombar," she whispered.

The figure faded, until it was only a shadow on the pavement. *I will be great again*, it said.

"No," Ailia said. "Your sphere is dying."

I will be great again! the shadow roared at her silently.

Ailia's body trembled as her mortal flesh was overwhelmed, but deep within her the core of white flame burned unwavering. Out of that blazing light came her answer: "Your time is over. There will never again be a day when Ombar rules the Empire." She spoke with compassion now.

Hatred seethed in the shadow. *I will make the Empire serve me yet!* it hissed at her. *The Dragon Prince thinks that he can prevent it. But he is the very instrument through which we shall work our will. It is Valdur he obeys, and not himself.*

And it was gone, together with the images it had imposed upon her mind. The city was a broken, haunted shell once more. But she shook as she gazed on it, as if she had caught a deadly chill.

19

The Perilous Citadel

TIRON SAT IN HIS DAUGHTER'S apartments, his head in his hands. At his feet Bezni the mimic dog lay, her graying muzzle pointing toward the door. The aging animal spent most of her days now in this attitude, in which both hope and listless pining were mingled. *She waits for her mistress to return,* he thought. *As do we all. But will she? Even if Ailia defeats the odds that weigh against her and wins the battle, saving the Empire from destruction—will she survive the contest, or will she purchase our freedom with her life? Victory may yet be as bitter for me as defeat: all I desire is to have my daughter back again, Archon though she be.* He stooped and stroked Bezni's head, then straightened as a knock came at the door. "Enter," he called, and wished for the visitor to leave as quickly as possible. He had no desire for company.

The door opened, and a young woman entered, her brown eyes solemn. "Your Majesty," she murmured.

"Jemma, isn't it?" he asked, rising and composing himself with an effort. "How can I help you?"

She stood twisting her work-coarsened hands together. "My family and I were just wondering if anything had been heard of Ailia."

"No, my dear. There has been no word. But I have been selfish, I see: I forgot that I am not alone in my fears."

"It *is* dreadful to be alone at such times, sire. My family thought perhaps you might like to join us in our quarters, since there is nothing any of us can do but wait. We might at least wait together."

Tiron was moved by this forthright Island girl, with her simple kindness, and her emotions that showed clearly in face and voice. "Of course—you love her too. You lived with her longer than I did." It was some small consolation to remember that if he mourned, it would not be in solitude: that Ailia's life had touched many. And these Meran folk had many tales to tell of that life, of her girlhood and all that she had done and been before the burden of the prophecy fell on her.

"But perhaps you would rather be alone," Jemma said. "I am sorry I interrupted you. I'll leave now, Majesty." She made as if to go.

"No, I am glad that you came." He hesitated, and then he held out his hand. "And I will join your family. It is as you say: we can all comfort one another at least."

AURON AND HIS RIDERS BURST out of the Ether into the sky of Ombar through a rift that hung invisible in the air. Below them stretched the ocher-red deserts. He flew lower, skimming over cliffs, buttes, mesas, dried-up riverbeds, companioned by his own black shadow. It was like the Muandabi in its time of drought, Jomar thought as he looked downward—only worse, for the whole of this world was one great desert, its drought perpetual. Moharas had many tales of the final destination of the damned: he had never before thought of it as a real place, but now he believed he looked upon its inspiration. Ombar had only one oasis, it was said: the slender zone that ringed it with dreary mires under endless twilight. And it was no refuge, but a haunt of monsters.

Presently they saw ahead of them, red against the band of dusk in the east, the towering shapes of stone arising from the desert floor. These were not natural features such as they had seen in the desert below, but old crumbling pyramids and steeples erected by human or other hands, and the canyons that lay between were old streets filled with rubble and shadows.

"Ailia! Ailia!" Lorelyn cried, sending her thoughts into the Ether as they flew over the silent city. Auron and Taleera also called out. There was no reply.

"She is not here," said Taleera at length. "I am sure of it. Mandrake must have taken her into the Nightlands, for that is where the throne of Valdur is. He would not come here merely for the Valei's protection: that places him too much in their power. It is why he feared to go to Ombar before. His only choice now is to claim his realm and be their ruler."

"Then we too must go into the night," Auron replied, thrusting aside his own fears in his anxiety for Ailia. Was she dead? Had the fatal contest already been held? He beat his wings harder, increasing his speed.

They passed on over leagues upon leagues of desolate ruins, seeking the country of the night.

AILIA AND MANDRAKE MADE THEIR way slowly through the deepening dusk. They had flown as far as they could in their draconic forms, following the line of the ruinous road, but even a dragon must rest, and they had come down at last in the lands of twilight.

For a time they had walked on in human form, meaning to go as far as they could before they slept. But Ombar's gravity was heavy: it made each and every step a weariness, and now they had lost what remained of the road. The sun was not visible from here, its great orb now concealed by the horizon, and its red light did not touch the sky, which showed a dull blue-black above the mists of the mire through which they walked. They had to tread carefully. All around them the rank swamps and quagmires sprawled and steamed, adding their own wispy breaths to the dank air. The pale twisted shapes Ailia had taken at first for trees were fungal growths, she found, slimy to the feel and more pliant than wood. She shuddered, for they felt like soft clammy hands touching her. There were whole forests of these fungi, grown to huge and nightmarish shapes: colossal toadstools, round white globes like skulls half-buried in earth, bulbous forms glowing with their own sickly green light. And there were many dangers in these lands, Mandrake warned her. Barguests prowled the swamps, their eyes glowing like living coals, and there were great shaggy bugbears, and the hideous nuckelavees with their translucent hides. The nightmare creatures of Meran hearth-tales here were living, breathing beasts. Boobrie birds larger than moas stalked the shallows on stiltlike legs, questing for food with their cruel hooked beaks, while the scaly afancs lurked in deeper pools with wide, waiting jaws. The beasts preyed on one another, and occasionally on the Morugei who scratched a meager living from the marshy soil. Ailia and Mandrake toiled on, skirting the mires. They saw none of the larger beasts, but there were things like huge and hideous toads, with leathery wings and serpents' tails and fangs, that came leaping and flapping out of the slimy pools, and had to be fended off with steel weapons because neither of the sorcerers had any strength left for conjuring. There were eerie pale lights glimmering in the murk that might be marsh gas, and might not. Occasionally they saw another traveler, but in the feeble light it was hard to tell if it were a goblin or some other creature. Everyone in these twilight lands was a walking shade, and all of them avoided one another out of fear. Not only beasts preyed on the people here.

They came upon a small islet, damp and cold, and rested there in the unchanging dusk, building a fire and taking turns to sleep and stand guard. Ailia took the first watch. Gazing at the prince as he fell asleep, she felt a new wave of compassion for him. With his dragon's eyes covered by their dark-lashed lids, Mandrake's face looked fully human. He also looked more vulnerable—there were lines that one did not notice when the strange fierce eyes were open: the marks of stress and suffering. Even in sleep his face was unquiet. The muscles of it twitched and trembled, like the surface of a pool disturbed by its lurking denizens. Sometimes he would start, and seem to be on the verge of waking; but then he would fall back into deep dreaming again. At times his hands were raised, to fend off she knew not what horror.

She let him sleep for many hours before she woke him. Her own sleep was light and dream-troubled, and she was roused too soon from it by a noise that made her sit bolt upright with her heart beating hard. Mandrake was nowhere to be seen, and the fire had died down to a red-eyed smolder. At the edge of its sullen light crouched a creature: a thing with the batlike wings of a dragon, opening and closing as if in spasms of agony, and a dragon's scales and twitching tail. But its form was like that of a man, and it was draped from the waist down in some dark material. Ailia started at the sight of this hell-fiend, wondering in terror how it had come so near, and what had become of her companion. As the horned head lifted, she saw it had a man's face crusted with scales, and two blazing eyes weeping tears, which, in the reflected fire-glow, seemed to leave trails of flame. The monster moaned and thrashed about as if in pain; but its burning eyes did not seem to see her. And in the next moment she realized what this creature was.

Mandrake, she thought, sickened. In mid-transformation! It was a hideous sight. Was he turning from man to dragon? He was neither one nor the other, but a horrifying blend of the two, a thing utterly unnatural. "Mandrake?" she whispered.

"Help me," he said, and— "Stay away!" He drew back into the shadows, moving on all fours, his face growing more dragonish.

And then he moved forward, crawling on limbs that were still human in shape, despite their scales. What made it so horrible was that there was just enough of Mandrake remaining to recognize. The scales covered his face and neck like some scabrous disease of the skin; his mouth was lipless as a lizard's and seemed to be trying to fuse together with his nose into a muzzle. But the voice was his, and the mane of red-gold hair, and the body in the half-removed robe was a man's still.

"Mandrake," said Ailia, "it's Valdur! He is ensorceling you!"

The creature groaned and writhed. "I hear his thoughts! He is within me!" The voice came slurred through lengthening tusks. "Power—he promises me power—"

"The power enslaves you! Free yourself of it!" She made herself sit still, even when the scaly face came within a finger's length of hers, and the dilated eyes glowered into her own, perhaps seeing their hideous reflection there as well as her expression of alarm.

"Free," gasped Mandrake, seizing the word as a drowning man might seize a spar. "Free." And the monster withdrew again; his face and form were a man's once more. He collapsed at her feet, panting, and then sank into a swoon. She stoked the fire, and drew his head into her lap, watching over him until he revived.

THEY SET OUT AGAIN IN the morningless gloom, flying above the mires for as long as their borrowed wings could carry them. To fly in this world required a great deal of sorcery, and it exhausted them. Worse than weariness for Ailia was her awareness of Elombar's ceaseless malice. The Archon of this world could not destroy her, but his enmity beat against her mind like a fierce buffeting wind, so it was all that she could do to hold her dragon's shape. The air grew ever colder as they flew, and the sky darker, for it was covered now in clouds. Even had the sky been clear it would have been hard to see, for there was no moon to light the lands below. The forests of mushroom-trees thinned, and there were but a few fungi that glowed up through the dark. Some of the pale ghostly lights seemed to move. Mandrake told Ailia that certain animals in this place carried their own luminous markings, like fishes that dwell in the black sunless depths of oceans.

After many hours they found the road again, for here in the Nightlands it was marked by waystones of white venudor at regular intervals. These served only to mark the edges of the pavement, for venudor illuminated only itself: it could cast no light on its surroundings as a lantern would. After following the track of cheerless lights for many leagues, they descended to rest once more.

The clouds parted as they lay together by the roadside, and the stars came out. And now they saw Lotara low on the horizon, but it was still too distant to dispel the darkness, a pallid corposant. For the first time Ailia saw it, not in a vision or illusion nor in a spyglass, but with her own unaided eyes. From one side extended the vast prominence that was at its extreme end shaped, by invisible yet violent forces, into a fiery circle with a black void at its vortex. But something within was blacker still, a thing less substantial than a shadow—a Nothingness. There lay the Worm's Mouth, the black star that devoured light instead of giving it forth. Into that pit, it seemed, she and this planet and its sun and all the surrounding stars were falling. She reeled where she lay, and put out her hands as if to save herself from that dreadful fall. But no: the fear was baseless. Auron had told her that Vartara could not consume the cosmos. The black star trapped only those things that came within its grasp. To be devoured by it, one had to approach its very sphere.

When at last they were rested, they prepared to continue their journey. But Ailia could no longer summon the strength to take a dragon's form. Instead she disguised herself with a glaumerie that gave her the likeness of a goblin-hag; and Mandrake shifted into the shape of a great black firedrake, the better to approach Valdur's stronghold undetected. Then he took Ailia on his back and sprang into the air.

As he flew on, Lotara gave a cold blue illumination to the lands beneath, though it could do little more than limn the edges of the more prominent features. There were mountains looming ahead, capped with pale ice and snow, and the forests and mires had gone. Flocks of black creatures flapped slowly through the skies on membranous wings. Each bore a glowing red carbuncle on its forehead, which was used as a lure to attract its prey. As they flew, the creatures gave piercing shrieks that woke desolate echoes among the dark hills and valleys below.

Mandrake had been silent through much of the journey, speaking only when she asked him a question. *These are called vouivres*, he said in answer to her query. *They live in the farthest reaches of the Night-*

lands. Vouivres fly in the dark like bats, uttering cries and listening for the echoes. As they flew close to a group of the creatures, Ailia saw that they resembled wyverns, with long necks and two taloned legs. But to her horror they had no eyes. The scaly skin stretched over their long skulls had only shallow dints to show where the eyes might once have been.

Of course, the same thing happens to fish that live in caves, she said. *Without any light, they have no need for eyes and they lose them.* But still the creatures' gaunt eyeless faces made her shudder. They had achieved what the followers of Modrian-Valdur had once desired: they no longer beheld the universe in which they dwelled.

And even as she thought this, Mandrake flew over the high mountains, and they both saw in an enclosed valley beneath the fortress of Modrian-Valdur.

THERE WAS A VAST CIRCULAR wall, mountain-high and sheer, quarried from a black volcanic stone, with ten towers spaced along it that tapered at the top like great spikes. The curtain wall was pierced in one place by a gaping gateway that could have swallowed a lesser fortress. It had been carved in the likeness of a dragon's head with upper jaw raised to devour all who entered in. *The Hell Mouth,* Ailia thought, recognizing it from the old illuminations in the books of Meran scriptures. The inner bastion was a single tower of glass-smooth adamant that could be neither breached nor scaled. Gray as a ghost, it rose from a rounded plinth to a dizzying height, more than a thousand feet above the plain, like a challenge to Heaven. At the top it had the shape of a crown, a circle of ten sharp tines, and beneath this was an opening, tall and arched at the top, like a great window. It was utterly dark within, black as the sky beyond. In front of the keep's hemispherical base the ground opened up into the wide ragged mouth of an immense pit. As the keep's tower seemed to reach in arrogant majesty for the sky, so the pit seemed to plumb the deepest bowels of the earth. Ailia, looking down as they passed above it, could see no bottom. Firedrakes dwelled within its depths, clustering upon rocky ledges like bats and flying up now and again to hover about the towers of the fortress, warmed from within by their furnacelike bellies: they were among the few creatures that could long endure the cold in this place. Fumes rose from the hot heart of the world far below.

Here, circled by his demesne of ice and fire, the lord of the black star had reigned for thousands upon thousands of years whose passage was marked, not by the turn of seasons or days, but only by the alteration of the stars as Ombar pursued its tight orbit. That time of the year when Lotara was visible in the black sky above was a festival in elder days, though not one celebrated with any joy by the mortal creatures: many were sacrificed then as offerings to the unseen star that came with it. Slaves had been brought here by the millions, to work the mines in the pit, so there was always a plentiful supply for the altars. Far below, in the deeps of the pit, lay a realm where Elombar had once reigned in material form: a subterranean kingdom, hard and barren underlands where nothing ever grew, beneath a starless sky of arching stone. There the only light came from the molten fires of the earth, forever rolling about the rocky shores, and there multitudes had moiled in the stifling heat, until the lands above where stars glimmered and forests grew seemed no more to them than a tale or a dream.

Over the dragon-jawed gate in the outer curtain-wall ran in Archonic runes the inscription: *Who enters here comes not forth again.* When Mandrake translated it for her, Ailia remembered her dream on the Island. This place, this perilous citadel, was the foundation of all her oldest fears. It was the reason she had been afraid of darkness all her life long: this shrine to the Black Star of Modrian-Valdur.

Mandrake flew down toward the round inner ward. "We cannot fly to the throne room at the top of the tower," he explained as they alighted. "There is iron in it, the Iron Diadem, so we must take the long way up in our human forms. There is a stair within the central keep that we can take, but it must be reached from inside the pit."

"The pit!" Ailia looked in dismay at the yawning chasm only a few paces from where they stood.

"There was a path cut into its side in olden days, for the slaves to use. That is how he protected his fortress: nothing could approach him by air, and the ascent of the tower stair is long and weary. It will take us many hours."

They found the earthen path and walked down, mindful of the fathomless fall to their left. Ailia clung close to the wall and would not look, even though her powers could still protect her this far from the keep. The abyss itself horrified her. She could see the dark holes within its walls, mouths of mines that led into the earth, where countless slaves had worked and died. Far below were the stony shelves where the roosting drakes clustered. Occasionally one would fly up toward the pit's opening high above, turning a malevolent eye on the two interlopers, but Mandrake's power and Ailia's warded them off for now. At last the two intruders came upon a wide entrance that gave onto a narrow passage, and this in turn led to a stair of stone that wound endlessly upward.

For Ailia this was the most unendurable leg of the journey yet. In the lower stories it was still possible to make use of sorcery, and they changed to winged forms in order to make the ascent. But at last it changed from rock to adamant like thick, gray glass: they were inside the tower's base, gazing up at a stair that looked as if it were carved out of ice. And with each turn of the spiral flights they sensed a growing power above them, heavy and oppressive, thunderous with malign enchantment. Soon they could no longer use their own magic, and must climb the steps in human form. The treads were smooth and treacherous, and the central shaft plunged into shadowy depths. At first Ailia was comforted to think that she could still take another form lower down, before she hit the bottom; but then fatigue set in as the barrage of Elombar's hatred took its toll, and as her back and shoulders sagged she realized that she would not have the strength to save herself should she fall. From time to time they both rested, perched on the narrow stair, though they dared not sleep. Then up and on they went: step after step, turn after turn. Mandrake had to carry Ailia once or twice, but she could not do the same for him and had to pause when he tired. At such times, she noticed, the scales reappeared on his face: when he weakened, Valdur grew stronger. The only light was the blue glow of Lotara, seeping faint and cold through the pellucid walls. At last, after what seemed like days, the stair turned from adamant to stone once more: a black stone, like obsidian or dark marble. They were within the upper reaches of the tower proper. And still it went ever upward in the same tight turns.

They came at length to a landing, broad and flat, and Ailia flung herself down, too spent to go any farther. The prince also halted, leaning his aching back against the wall. They rested in silence, too fatigued to speak, for more than an hour. Then once again Mandrake lifted her in his arms, and holding her carefully he mounted the last coiling flight, emerging from it into a round chamber of stone. It was empty, but another short flight of steps at the far end led up through a square hole in the ceiling. "Rest here," said Mandrake, setting Ailia down and giving her his cloak to lie upon. "There is nothing that can harm you in this place. I will go on up, and see what is to be seen."

While Ailia sprawled upon the dark cloak he climbed the last stair, with a grim anticipation in which not a little cold dread was mingled. The straight flight brought him into a second chamber, far higher than the first: he could not see the roof at all in the wan light. In the eastern wall gaped the windowlike embrasure they had seen from below. The great height had made it look small, but it was wide enough for half a dozen men to pass through abreast, and more than twenty feet high. Through it showed the pallid peaks of the mountains, and the dark sky. All the room's interior was black, so that at first his eye could not distinguish details. Then dimly, by the dull blue light of Lotara, he saw high on the western wall the form of a circle surrounded by many rays: it was the shape of a star carved into the stone wall, black upon black. Beneath this insignia there stood a black throne, far too large to have been made for any mortal man; and in it there rested a tall crown of black iron, also too big for a human head, its circle of ten sharp tines imitating the shape of the tower. The crown of the lord of Vartara, still lying here where it had been abandoned millennia ago. In the front of the diadem there was a small round depression, the empty setting where the Star Stone had long ago been placed.

And on the steps leading up to the throne, muffled in a hooded sable cloak so that he seemed a part of the chamber itself, there sat a hideous goblinlike man. Naugra looked up as the Dragon Prince approached, his face showing pale within the hood.

"Avatar," he said. "You come back to us in Ombar, as I said you would. And you have delivered to us the Tryna Lia, and the Sovereign Stone."

"No," Mandrake answered. "I came back to perform another task. I did not expect to meet you in battle, Regent. A rat must be routed out of its nest."

He advanced on Naugra, but the other man did not move. He gestured instead toward the crown resting on the seat of the throne.

"The Iron Diadem. It has waited many thousands of years for you to come here. And now you may claim it."

"I do not want it. In any case, you may have noticed it would be a poor fit." Mandrake spoke in a dry voice.

"True. Modrian-Valdur favored a form that was manlike, but larger than any living man could ever be. But your mortal frame can be molded into many other forms, human and otherwise. And after you there will be others, children of your line, who will receive the Diadem in their turn. And like the crown the deathless spirit of Valdur will pass from one body to the next, owning each in turn and then setting it aside."

"Not if I cast your precious Diadem into the pit," said the Prince.

Naugra smiled. "But *will* you? We shall see. Take it up now, and see what doom befalls you."

THE LANDS BELOW WERE UTTERLY dark, the haunt of eyeless things. As they flew, Auron and his three companions peered ahead, trying to follow the faint line of the road marked with venudor as it wound through the range. At last they came over the mountains, even as Ailia and Mandrake had done before them, and they saw the secret vale and what lay within.

"The Perilous Citadel," Lorelyn whispered, averting her eyes.

"You know it?" asked Jomar, astonished.

"I've seen pictures, in old books. The Fortress of Perdition. I didn't know it was a real place."

"There is cold iron within the tower," said Auron. "I cannot fly to it."

Taleera, who had flown ahead with her luminous plumes shining like a lantern before them, called out. "You will not need to. Look, there is Falaar down there on the valley floor, with Damion."

They flew down and settled next to the cherub and the Archon.

"I knew you would come," Damion said with resignation as Jomar and Lorelyn jumped down and walked over to him. "Ailia and Mandrake are in the keep."

"What are we to do?" Lorelyn implored.

"Wait," said Damion quietly.

Jomar said, "Is there nothing we can do? For heaven's sake, you're an Archon—one of *them*—is there anything at all that you can do to help her?"

"It is all out of our hands now, Jo," replied Damion. "We cannot interfere."

"But if all our fates hang in the balance?" said Taleera. "It would be the end of everything if Ailia lost."

"No, not the end of everything," said Damion. "Not even the end of Ailia. Her spirit will survive even if her body is destroyed. But it will be the end of the Celestial Empire, of things as we have known them. And for mortals there will be no escape but death."

They looked at the fortress and tried to imagine what powers were striving there. The mortals felt that they awaited a battle of two gods, whose outcome would decide their own fates.

"We will not intervene," said Auron heavily. "If, as you say, all rests on Ailia now, we must trust in her."

"But how can we leave her to fight on her own?" cried Taleera.

"She will not be alone," said Damion softly. "Those who serve the light are with her, in the Stone and in spirit. There are still more of us in the Ether than the darkened ones."

"All the same," said Auron, "I will remain in this world."

"Auron," said Damion gently, "there is nothing that you can do."

"You say yourself that Archons do not see the future," said Taleera. "Auron and I are Ailia's protectors, and even if she no longer requires our protection we will continue to be present, though the only support we can offer is our love."

"And we're her friends," said Lorelyn, with a glance at Jomar. He nodded. "We're staying too."

"I can fly ye all to the top of the tower," offered the cherub. "Except Auron, of course. He must remain at a distance lest he lose his power of flight. Iron is nothing to me."

"Then let us go," said Damion.

He and the two humans mounted, and the firebird flew on ahead. Auron had to content himself with flying alongside them for as long as he could, then sheering away to circle the tower beyond the iron's range. Damion, Lorelyn, and Taleera could not use their powers past that point. And without the speech of the mind, most of the party could not now understand one another's tongues. Taleera knew Elensi, for she had spoken it when in her woman's form, but Lorelyn and Damion now heard from the T'kiri's beak only the fluid birdsong that Jomar had always heard. Falaar could not understand her either, and for the other four his own aquiline cries had no translation. As they drew ever nearer to the tower they could only meet one another's eyes with urgent looks, and make signs. Auron, moving in his restricted orbit, felt the moment when their thoughts were severed from his, and his anxiety grew all the greater.

The cherub rose steeply, his wings nearly furled to his sides, and flew right into the high black casement. For a moment the five companions saw only darkness within. Then something moved: two shadows that resolved themselves into the figures of men. Mandrake stood there, and before him was a stooping gaunt form that Damion, Taleera and Falaar recognized as the Regent of Ombar. Mandrake turned to face them.

"Where is Ailia?" Lorelyn demanded of him, holding out her adamantine blade.

"She is safe," the prince replied. "She is resting in the chamber below. I did not bring her here to do her harm, but to give her a last chance to join with me. The two of us together have the power to end this war. She need only consent to reign alongside me, and the battle of empires will be ended."

"Ailia would never agree to that! She knows the Valei are evil, and serve only Valdur. You're holding her prisoner!" Lorelyn accused. She brandished her sword, turning to look at Jomar.

But Jomar was silent. He gazed on Mandrake's face, which appeared whiter than ever before in the cold light, and he saw its long years of suffering as though they were engraved upon it. His anger and his hatred left him. He, Jomar, had known a life of pain and bitterness, and he knew how it could scar the soul; but this creature had suffered for centuries longer than Jomar had been alive. Much as he had longed to kill Mandrake, he suddenly felt the stirrings of shame. He asked himself, for the first time, how it was that he had come to fasten all his rage, all the blame for his travails and those of others, upon this one person. It was strange, he reflected, that Mandrake of all people should have taught him pity.

"Ailia and I *will* reign together," the prince insisted. "I brought her out of Nemorah, but she came here to the Citadel of her own free will."

"You cannot escape the doom," said Damion. "If you seek to avoid it, Mandrake, you will find that it overtakes you all the same. You can only reject the crown and the Power it serves."

Mandrake stared at him, pride and anger in his eyes. "I say I will avoid it, and this is the only way. By ruling those who would rule me."

"You will become a tyrant," said Damion. "Mandrake, whatever you have now become, you were once an honorable knight in Mera. Remember what you once stood for!"

Mandrake hesitated. If he drew on the dark Power now, he could defeat them all. But he did not wish to do so—he feared it too much. "Go now," commanded the Dragon Prince. "I will not destroy Ailia's friends. But I *will* fight you, if you force me. You know you cannot match my strength if I do call on the Power here—not even the cherub." He advanced upon them.

But as he stepped forward, he turned his back toward the Regent. The latter sprang up, and lunged at Mandrake from behind. Something flashed in his hand, swift as a striking snake. And then there was a blade of iron thrusting out through the left of Mandrake's chest.

All stood immobile: Ailia's allies, the stricken prince. Mandrake's eyes widened, and then he fell—toppling forward without a cry. "Well done," said the Regent to the staring intruders, jerking his blade out of Mandrake's back. "I had planned to wait until his guard slipped, and then use my dagger. But you have done my work for me, by drawing his eye away from me."

"You're mad!" Lorelyn cried in amazement. "He is your ruler!"

"No, not he. I am but removing an encumbrance from my Master's way." The Regent stood over Mandrake. "Now, Prince, you *must* use the Power or die. No sorcery of your own can heal you: summon it, and save yourself. Just one last time."

Mandrake lay gasping, eyes glazed, clutching at his chest. He seemed not to hear Naugra's words. The Regent stooped to hold the injured man, supporting his head—almost cradling him as he spoke in a low, gloating voice. "The Power—the great magic that no iron can master! It will save you. Call on it now, and heal yourself. For you know you must not die: you are the last hope."

He truly was mad, Jomar thought, incredulous. If Mandrake used dark sorcery in order to save himself, would he not then turn on the Regent and take revenge? The Dragon Prince's eyes were closed now, and his breathing shallow.

Then, slowly, he sat up. His eyes opened, glinting in the wan light. His face was no longer contorted with pain. Naugra, on the other hand, seemed to lose what strength had shown in his withered face. He appeared to shrink and shrivel before their sight, cowering low upon the floor and turning deadly pale. His eyes were suddenly bewildered: they blinked up at the figure towering over him.

The firebird gave a piercing cry. "Possessed! The Regent was possessed by the Dark One! And now the enemy's spirit has passed from him into Mandrake—can you not see?" Taleera, seized with terror and frantic at her inability to make herself understood, screamed at her companions, and then rose up in a flurry and dashed at their faces, beating at them with her wings and trying to force them back toward the cherub. They started, as if roused from a trance. Falaar, understanding what she was about though not the reason for it, retreated toward the embrasure and opened his own wings, and as the agitated firebird flew at them again, and again, Damion, Lorelyn, and Jomar ran for the cherub's back. He waited only long enough for them to find their places before spinning about and fleeing through the air.

The prince stood tall, and looked after Ailia's fleeing friends with a glance that, had they seen it, would have seemed colder and more inimical than any he had given before. The uncertainty and hesitation were gone. But he spoke to the Regent. "Your task is fulfilled. You were yourself but a vessel, though you did not know it. A vessel too weak and flawed to hold my full power. I take on a new one that is a more fit housing for my spirit." And showing now no sign of wound or weakness, he took up the dagger, and with it he struck the cringing Regent a blow to the side of the neck. Naugra crumpled before the blade and lay still.

The prince cast the weapon aside. Then he strode toward the throne, and, reaching out with both hands, he took up the Iron Diadem.

20

The Prince of Shadow

AILIA WAS IN THE DARK, alone. Filled with a growing fear she wandered aimlessly through great silent empty spaces that she could not see, feeling her way, looking for Mandrake, who did not answer any of her calls. She sensed that there was someone or something dogging her footsteps, but she could not see it in the darkness when she turned.

"Wake up, Ailia," said a voice.

She came back out of the dark dreams, and opened her eyes to find that waking reality was the same: darkness still surrounded her. She could just see Mandrake standing there above her, only a tall shade in the gloom; and then with a spasm of loathing and dread she remembered where she was. "Are you rested?" he asked. "There is a chamber above us. The throne room of Valdur himself. Come up, and I will show it to you."

She was not at all certain that she wanted to see it, but she took his outstretched hand and let him haul her to her feet. Up the short stair they went, and emerged into the black cavern of the room above. And there, as her eyes slowly adjusted, the obsidian throne and iron crown took shape out of the shadows. At the sight of them she recoiled. And then she saw the dead sprawled body of Naugra lying on the floor, wrapped in his dark cloak.

"You killed him!" she exclaimed.

"Of course," Mandrake told her. "He was a vile creature, and not to be trusted." He went to the high arched portal and indicated the view below with a sweep of his arm. She went to stand at his side. "Here was the seat of Valdur's reign in ancient days. Here he looked out as ores were mined and forged into weapons for his mortal armies, all at his command. They made automata in the shapes of men, brazen giants that could loose arrows and wield gigantic swords: armies no soldier could face, no valor could defeat. Can you imagine such a spectacle? And the Archons in their strange composite forms, neither man nor beast. You could see these things for yourself if you tried: you no longer require a draught of ambrosia to visit past and future."

She recalled the account of Orendyl, and the old woodcuts in the Kantikant. "I do not wish to see it," she said shuddering. "It is over, and for that we can be glad."

"No: it can live again, here and in other worlds. The glory of my new empire will be greater even than this!"

The fear that had been growing in her seized hold of her mind; in sudden horror she sprang back, away from the tall portal, away from Mandrake. "No—this doesn't sound like you! Not the Mandrake I know. You wanted an *end* to war. Valdur is doing this—tempting you, trying to take you. Resist him!" She shivered, looking at the great blue star hanging over the mountains and the black nothingness its fires embraced. "This is still his place, though he is confined to Vartara. He can reach you here."

Mandrake looked at her, a thin smile of contempt on his lips. "Fool," he said. "You speak of things you cannot possibly understand."

Ailia stared at him. He continued to look at her, with the pupils of his eyes wide and black, and the thin smile that was not his own. "So—now you know. It was time that we met face-to-face, Tryna Lia."

She touched his mind—and felt again the same dark dominating will she had encountered in Nemorah, that she had taken for the sorcery of its world-spirit. But Elnemorah was herself only a slave and a channel for its influence. The One was manifested in the Stone, and of it all things living or unalive were a partial expression; but this Power did not allow things to be themselves: it took and devoured them, and made them into images of itself alone. Syndra, Naugra, Khalazar, and now Mandrake, had been possessed by it utterly.

She cried out, her voice high and shrill: "Where is Mandrake? What have you done to him?"

"That creature has served his purpose. It was my intent that he should bring you here, where you and he are weak and I am strong. At long last I have a material form again. When I was cast into the black sun, it claimed only my corporeal frame. My spirit has lodged

here, in the bodies of my mortal Regents—bodies too frail to withstand my full powers. Unlike this body I made."

She regarded the black-eyed prince with something of
farewell—more, of grief—in her gaze. For it was a kind of death she
was seeing. "Mandrake, no," she whispered.

"Give me the Stone," he said, advancing.

"No." Again she retreated, throwing a quick glance behind her.
He was forcing her toward the open window.

"Give it to me. It will go in my diadem, where no mortal can ever
again lay hands upon it: the emblem of my triumph."

"No!" Turning, Ailia flung herself out the window.

Icy wind shrieked past her as she plummeted, prevented by the
Iron Diadem from taking any other form. But its influence would
fade as she fell, and she could gain the power of flight before she
hit the ground . . .

Then there was a thunder of giant wings, and the dragon was
upon her.

THE FRIENDS OF THE TRYNA LIA had gone to wait in the ward below,
gazing up at the grim tower.

"What is going to happen, Damion?" asked Lorelyn. "Was it
really—*he*? What will he do now?"

"I don't know," Damion said softly. "Only one thing is certain: no
power in Talmirennia can stop it now."

Lorelyn fell silent. Jomar looked up at the black sky, at the stars
that lay beyond Lotara and Vartara. It was true that these far-off,
glimmering lights embodied intelligences older than time . . . *I never
believed in you before*, he thought, *but I know now you really are there. Ailia
needs you, needs your help. Don't fail her now. Don't let anything happen to her!*
The stars gave no answer. For his ears they made no celestial music,
nor ever would. He tried again. *I thought I might be able to kill him for her,
and I was wrong: I know I can't. So you see, it's up to you now. If you're so powerful, then do something. Save her!*

"What is it?" said Lorelyn presently. "I keep seeing things all
around us—little flickers and flashes of light, and moving shadows—but when I look straight at them there's nothing there."

"It's beginning," said Damion in a low voice. "Powers are being
unleashed here that you can't begin to imagine."

"That is true," said a voice. They turned and saw the ethereal form of an old woman standing there behind them, her face lined and solemn. It was Ana; and Greymalkin was with her, standing at her feet. "You are brave to come here," the transparent figure said, "but you have done all that you are able to do. You can have no part in what is to follow."

"It is as she says." Another ethereal figure appeared, tall and majestic with gray-golden hair and beard. He needed no crown to show them that he was a king.

"Brannar Andarion," said Damion, recognizing him, and bowing low.

The others stared at the figure, and then back up at the keep. They realized that though they had proven strong in other battles, they were less than the lowliest foot soldiers in the war that was about to be fought here: above them were the great captains and princes in this struggle, the Archons of the elements, the worlds and the stars.

Suddenly they spied a figure standing in the black opening high above. It looked very small at that height, and ghostly, its long white garment fluttering in the wind.

"It's Ailia!" Lorelyn started forward. Jomar stopped her with a hand on her arm. "Ailia, Ailia! What is it? No, of course—she can't hear us, with the iron!"

Ailia leaped out of the embrasure. Her gown, its sleeves and hem tattered, flowed loosely around her as she fell headfirst through the air. Her long hair was unbound, flowing behind her. She looked so small, so utterly helpless, that Jomar gave an agonized moan.

"Ailia! We can't just stand here! We've got to help her! One of you, fly up and catch her!"

"She's not just Ailia," said Damion, a touch of pride in his voice. "She's a power, Jomar—and now she can command other powers."

Lorelyn's voice caught on a sob. "She looks so alone."

As they watched, something stirred in the shadows of the window above. They saw the form of a night-black dragon emerge, like the darkness come to life. It too leaped forth, wings drawn in close to its sides, diving straight at Ailia.

Ailia flung out her arms as she fell, the wide sleeves blowing back so that her arms showed thin and white. Her hands moved upon the air. Light flowed from them toward the monster, but the rays were deflected as if by some unseen shield.

Lorelyn turned in distress to Damion, and saw that he and Ana and Andarion wore expressions of concentration. *They are helping her,* she thought, comforted. *Giving her their own power.*

The dragon seized Ailia in his claws. But again a white blinding light flared forth, so that it seemed as though he held lightning in his grasp, or a star. They plunged through the air together. Then at last he roared and released her, and she dropped—a mere dozen feet above the ground. She landed on her feet, stumbled and fell to her knees. Then she struggled back to her feet again. The dragon pulled out of his dive and soared upward.

"Now they will fight," said Ana.

King Andarion spoke in tones of sorrow. "My doing. This is all my doing: Morlyn is my own flesh and blood. Without me he would never have been."

"You have nothing with which to reproach yourself, Majesty," Ana replied. "You are not the first whom Valdur has used and deceived. But look now, they are coming together."

"Just the two of them? No armies, nothing?" Jomar asked.

"Each of them *is* an army, Jo," Damion said.

AILIA WHIRLED AROUND, SEARCHING THE desolation for her foe. Then she saw the dragon that had been Mandrake perched upon the curtain wall, black under the blue star. He roared a command, and firedrakes flew up in a mass of clamoring wings from the brimstone deeps of the great pit, and there were a million shadows within the ward: shapes springing up everywhere as he summoned them, demons of this world and others that materialized at his whim. Elombar was there at their head, clad in armor, leading them as their captain into battle. An army marched toward her, made up of grotesque figures neither human nor animal, summoned out of the Ether to war with her.

She called on her own powers, and felt them course through her as through a channel. And there were radiant forms, figures with shining faces and trailing wings, encircling and protecting her. But still the dark host marched upon her.

DAMION AND THE OTHERS GAZED on the field of battle.

"I see—things out there," said Lorelyn. "The shadows—and lights—like armies fighting—"

"Yes, I see them too," Jomar said.

"The hosts of Heaven and Hell," said Damion.

They saw a bright light glowing out on the plain—the Stone in Ailia's hand.

"It's all happening just as the old stories said it would," Lorelyn whispered. "The Princess and the Prince, the Stone, the dragon. But our enemies have their own prophecies, haven't they?"

Damion nodded, but said nothing.

They watched as the Stone's radiance wove to and fro in the midst of the battle. Above the fortress the firedrakes soared upon the night wind, the black dragon wheeling in their midst.

"They must come together," said Damion, as if to himself. "This only delays it." He watched as vapor flowed from the dragon's form.

Light and shadow rippled and surged across the ward. There seemed to be to the anxious onlookers more darkness than light.

"This is the place of his power," said Ana. "The Dark One made sure that the duel happened near the seat of his strength, to upset the balance."

"Fight him, Ailia!" cried Lorelyn. There were tears in her eyes. "I always believed our side was sure to win—that it was all or-dained . . ." Her voice died away as the full horror of uncertainty seized her. Jomar laid a hand on her arm.

"It's not over yet," he said, his voice rough.

Ailia stood still as the spirit-forms swirled around her. A vast blue-edged cloud boiled above, filled with flickering lights and bel-lowing with thunder, looming in menace over them, as if it were alive. Long tongues of lightning streamed between it and the tow-ers of the Citadel. Then, amid the fitful flashes, she saw a dark shape emerge from the cloud's depths. A Loänan, its once red scales and streaming mane now turned cinder-black, its eyes blazing with infernal light. She readied herself as the dragon came swooping down, trailing filaments of vapor from the edges of its wings and settled upon a pinnacle on the outer battlement.

The celestial armies drew back, making a circle about the two pivotal figures in their strife. Damion and the others watched at the edge of the battlefield.

Ailia faced the dragon, her breast heaving, and hands clenched at her sides. The doom—Mandrake had feared nothing could defeat the doom, and he was right. She felt despair like a leaden weight, drawing her down into black depths. Slowly, she advanced.

He leaped down and advanced toward her on foot. The dragon's eyes—Mandrake's eyes—stared at her, black ringed with burning gold: like the horrific hole in the sky above, framed in fire. Mandrake's eyes, but not his spirit. Something else stared at her out of those black swollen pupils. She saw herself, white and minute, reflected in them—small and lost in the darkness that did not end with his eyes. She backed up and he stalked her, until she stood at the very brink of the pit.

But she was not abandoned. She felt her mother's sheltering presence, and knew it had always been there at the edges of her mind. Other spirit-presences hovered and enfolded her. She lifted her gaze again, hating the thing that had taken Mandrake from those eyes. There was strength in her—not a match for the power before her, but power of a different kind. To take a dragon's form herself, to try and fight, would only delay what she must do. She reached out with her thoughts, touching the black malice of the mind within the dragon, seeking Mandrake in a last desperate appeal.

And then the dragon was upon her, charging, reaching out with talon and fang. The Star Stone was knocked from her hand, and rolled away upon the ground.

THE PALE, SHINING FORMS OF the Archons of the light vanished, like candle flames that had been extinguished: only the shapes of shadow remained. Ana and King Andarion were no longer there. The radiance faded from the Star Stone, where it lay on the edge of the chasm. Damion and the others drew nearer to the place where the Princess lay, no longer caring about their own danger, drawn to the motionless form that lay before the dragon. Was Ailia dead? Her face was nearly as white as her robe.

And then they saw her stir. She moved her head from side to side, moaning, but did not revive. As they watched in horror, the dragon raised his talons to strike. A wall of shadowy shapes surrounded him: they could not enter that dark circle and give aid to Ailia. Auron and the cherub circled above, but they could not penetrate the barrier either. The dragon lunged forward, and his claws closed on Ailia.

"No!" screamed Lorelyn. But there was nothing she could do: her sword and her courage were useless now.

AILIA WOKE IN A DARK place.

She seemed to see a sky above her, filled with a dull light. It was featureless, without any sun, moon, stars, or clouds to be seen. Its color was indefinable: too pale to be called red, too hot to be gray, it yet had some of the qualities of each. It was like the color seen against one's eyelids when daylight shines through them. Ailia sat up and looked about her. She was in a wasteland, bleak and barren, empty as far as the eye could see. And yet she felt that she was not alone. A presence was there, watching, hovering . . .

"Who are you?" she whispered, rising to her feet. "Who is there?"

The Presence that she sensed answered, "Dost thou not know? I have been with thee all this time. Do not be afraid. Nothing can harm thee now. Behold me: I am Athariel, lord of the Heavens."

A shining shape coalesced out of the murky air a few paces away from where she stood: a radiant figure, with golden hair and crown, snowy robes and wings. Never had she beheld a beauty so pure, so unsullied by pain or sorrow. Ailia bowed to the ground, overwhelmed. This was the very highest of the high Elyra. "My lord—"

"Daughter," the Archon said, "thou hast come unto join us in the High Heaven. Here I must leave thee, for even I may not remain."

Ailia straightened and stared. "High Heaven—what have I done, lord, to deserve so great an honor?"

"My daughter," said the seraph, "thou hast died."

"Died," she whispered.

"This is Death, Ailia Elmiria. These are the celestial lands that the souls of the dead inhabit. And thou art now one of them. Thy mortal form was destroyed before thy spirit could reclaim its Archon nature. Thou hast lost the fight, but do not despair. Thou shalt have thy reward all the same." He pointed, and she saw now faint flickering forms, like the shades of men and women and other beings. They were standing still as statues, or wandering aimlessly about.

She lowered her gaze, unable to look at the milling souls. She had pictured High Heaven as a place of beauty, not this dull colorless waste. Was this what awaited those who died—no glorious afterlife, only a shadow-land of phantoms? And she had failed in her task. What reward could she possibly merit?

The Archon seemed to hear her thoughts. "Thou must put aside all thou thought thou knewest," he said, "and accept this fate."

Ailia made herself walk through the crowds of phantoms. There were figures of people long dead, servants of the enemy whom she had seen fall in battle. She saw Naugra there, and Syndra, and Erron Komora, but they looked at her without recognition, their eyes vacant. It was terrible: within these ghostly forms the Light still lived, and was with them imprisoned in the darkness—like bubbles of air trapped in a mire. She could *not* accept it. Her soul rebelled.

Ailia turned and looked at the Archons' bland beautiful face, the face that had never known suffering. "You are well named the Deceiver," she said, "Valdur Elvatara."

The angelic figure changed, expanded, metamorphosed into a towering shape of scales and fangs, curling claws, wings vast and dark as night, jaws that drank in the light. The black dragon towered over her, growing ever larger and darker, sprouting more heads from its neck like a hydra: monstrous heads with fangs or tusks, scales or bristles, no two alike, all hideous. A command roared forth from the multiple mouths, and in answer a figure that had been lying in a heap upon the ground leaped up, as suddenly as a puppet on strings. Ailia gasped. It was Khalazar.

"I am the God-king!" the apparition cried. "Worship me, and you will be spared!" His eyes were wide open, mad and blind; he spoke not to her but to some imaginary audience. "I am Khalazar! Worship me!"

Ailia shuddered. This was heinous, cruel beyond bearing. Valdur was mocking his own deluded thrall. And those other phantoms, they were all the same, each locked in a separate hell, moaning and gibbering. She could endure it no longer.

"Stop!" she cried. "This place is not real, it exists only within Valdur's mind! You can leave if you want to!" But they only babbled on, incoherent, drowning out one another so that she could catch only stray words here and there: "It was none of my doing! Will no one listen? You know I meant for the best, always . . ."

"Free yourselves!" she cried. "He has no power to hold you against your will!" But the maddened spirits would not hear. The many-headed beast bellowed again, and they all turned on her in a mass. Horror was all around her, wraiths and demons with leering mouths crowded upon her. Wherever she looked there were more of them, legions without number. Ghostly hands groped for her. She called on Damion, on Ana, on her mother, on all of her friends in turn. None answered: they were far from her in this unending nightmare, this pit of despair. Then she glimpsed, at the edge of her sight, the one figure in all the wasteland who had not moved at Valdur's command, but still stood motionless and alone.

As the others closed on her she called his name.

"NO!" SCREAMED LORELYN.

Not an instant of time had passed for the Tryna Lia's companions. Lorelyn had nearly completed her cry of denial; the others still stood grief-stricken and helpless, unable to tear their eyes from the spectacle.

The dragon reared, releasing its grip on Ailia's body, wings beating the air. The reflected star glared from the blackness of his eyes, and his jaws were flecked with foam. From the depths of his throat a rattling cry came. The long dark head swung to and fro, the tail coiled and uncoiled as though possessed with a life of its own. Again he raised his claw as if to tear at the girl's lifeless form; and again the claw halted in midair, clenching and opening convulsively. Then the head ceased its jerking, lunged down and closed its jaws on its own forelimb, tearing and rending its own scaly flesh with its fangs.

"What is he doing?" exclaimed Lorelyn.

The black dragon's head swung around and down, biting at its own armored breast savagely. Blood flowed from the wounds. The jaws that nothing could withstand met the impervious scales—and were stronger, for never had Valdur imagined that he might do harm to himself.

"He's mad," said Jomar in slow wonder. He pointed with his sword to the shapes of shadow. "Look! They're fading!"

They watched the shapes wisp away. Nothing stood now between them and the figures of Ailia and the dragon.

"Now!" shouted Jomar. He and Lorelyn ran at the dragon, their blades swinging.

"Stop," cried a voice.

Damion turned at the cry, and going to Ailia he knelt beside her.

She was alive, propping herself on one elbow, the other arm outstretched. "Don't," she gasped, "there's no need—he is gone . . ."

The dragon began to shrink, to change. Its color turned from black to fire-red. And then in its place a strange figure lay there, a man with a scaly face, horned and taloned. Blood from wounds to the throat, neck, and chest flowed freely over the tattered rents in his dark robe. The face, its eyes unfocused, turned toward Ailia. The panting mouth strove as if to speak. Ailia rose to her feet and rushed to the monster's side. She held the hideous head in her lap, stroking the shaggy dishevelled mane, and wiped away the blood from the face, weeping quietly all the while.

"Ailia," said Jomar.

"Let her be," said Damion.

"But—the monster—"

"It's Mandrake. Valdur is gone," said Damion. "He fled from the pain. He never could endure suffering, as mortals do."

For a time in that vast ruinous place there was no sound but for Ailia's quiet sobs. Leaning forward, she spoke into the dragon-man's scaly, pointed ears words that none of the others could catch. But as he heard them, Mandrake opened his filming eyes and fixed them on her face. And as the others watched, once more he was transformed. The wings, and tail and horns, were gone, absorbed in the shadows, and the scales sloughed away while a human face began to emerge slowly out of the monstrous countenance. He extended to her a claw, and it became more human in shape as it reached for her. She put out her own hand, and the claw touched it and became a hand also. Her other hand went to his face. She kissed him, passionately, first on the brow and then on his mouth. At last it was Mandrake the man who lay there, a monster no more but beautiful as he had been before his possession. "I called on him," said Ailia. "And he came to me." She had known the very moment when the Dark One departed in defeat. "He took command of his form again, and wounded himself to drive Valdur out."

Mandrake spoke, his voice a rasping whisper. "I have known you. I have seen the stars, the worlds with all their wonders. I feel no regret now that I lived." And then his eyes closed, and he was still. Her head bent low over his, hiding both their faces with her falling hair.

Suddenly there were ethereal forms all around her again: Eliana, and Andarion, and the golden-haired figure of her mother. Elarainia spoke to her daughter: "Ailia, my dear, do not weep. It is over. He has saved you, and you him. He is at peace now. The enemy is gone from him, and from Talmirennia. Valdur truly is a prisoner now, for his spirit has no house on this plane and must join his material form in the black star forever."

Brannar Andarion's face was haggard with grief. "We will take my son's body back into the Ether with us. That is how the greatest of the Nemerei choose to pass from the world, and that is how we shall honor him."

And Ana said to the Tryna Lia's companions, "Ailia's powers were always her weakness, never her strength. The temptations they offered were nearly fatal to her more than once. In the end it was her courage and compassion that saved her and all of you, not the sorcery that was a stumbling block to her from the very first."

The figures began to fade away from sight again. The body of Mandrake was gone. The Princess knelt alone on the ground, her arms empty. "Ailia," said Damion softly, "Ailia, come home."

She looked up at him, tears still streaking her face. Her lips moved soundlessly.

"I can take you to where there is no pain," said Damion, kneeling beside her.

Her head drooped, came to rest against his shoulder. Then, slowly, they stood together. And it seemed to Jomar and the rest that in the next moment it was no longer the two familiar figures that stood there, but two radiant forms, winged with white fire, and their eyes burned like stars. Only for an instant did the mortals see the vision, as they held their hands up against the unbearable intensity of the light. And then the two figures were no longer there.

Those that were left stood still for a moment. Even Taleera could find no words to say. A cold wind crept across the silent ward, from the ice-clad mountains high above.

"Let's go," said Lorelyn. "Now! I hate this horrible place!"

It was dark, but Jomar could tell that she was crying. He stooped, picked up the Star Stone where it lay upon the ground, and together they climbed onto Auron's back. Then together they flew away while silence once more settled on the court of night.

21

The Celestial Empire

THERE WAS GREAT REJOICING IN Arainia when the friends of the Tryna
Lia brought the Star Stone to Halmirion. In the city of Mirimar it
was as though all the year's festivals were being held at once: the
streets were hung with banners and silver stars, bells clanged from
every tower, lamps and candles glimmered from eaves and tree
branches, and fireworks were set off in the streets. People ran about
embracing strangers, dancing around bonfires, splashing in the fountains, shouting and singing from rooftops and balconies. The stellar
war was over! The Tryna Lia had conquered her adversary! Exactly
how it had happened no one was sure: there were many conflicting
reports. Ailia had fought Mandrake in a duel and slain him—Ailia
had fought his whole army single-handed and won—the host of
Heaven itself had come to her aid. Only when the days passed and
it became apparent that the Princess was not going to return, did the
mood grow more somber. News of her withdrawal into the Ether
traveled swifter than light through the worlds of the Celestial Empire. The crystal palace in the field outside Mirimar sat empty, the
Dragon Throne unfilled. Yet Ailia was still the ruler of Talmirennia:
since she had not died, there could be no other claimant. There was
some talk of placing an image of her upon the throne, like the statue
of her mother in the chapel of Halmirion, though this idea was soon
discarded. Talmirennia, it seemed, would have no mortal ruler.

The sibyls conferred with the father of the Tryna Lia, and at last
a decision was made: the Moon Throne was left empty, while the
crown and scepter of argent were placed on the Dragon Throne.
There anyone could come, to look on the Stone that was once more
set in the crown, a token of the Old Ones who still watched over
the Empire from afar but would never again rule Talmirennia or its
creatures. From now on they would rule themselves.

*   *   *

ONE EVENING NEARLY TWO YEARS after the last battle, the friends and
family of the Tryna Lia gathered in the gardens of Halmirion. King
Tiron had since departed to live in the forest by Hyelanthia, where
he could be near the lingering presence of Elarainia, and the palace
had become a guesthouse for visitors to Mirimar and its shrines.
Among the guests staying there at that time were Jomar and Lorelyn, Ailia's foster family from Mera, and the woman Mag from
Nemorah with Twidjik, as well as Auron and Taleera—who took
their human shapes, so as to be able to converse with the members
of the group who were not Nemerei. They talked together in low
voices of all that happened in the great war, and what they themselves had seen and done, while Dani and Lem played with the amphisbaena upon the lawn.

Auron said, "Without Mandrake to hold it together the Valei empire has crumbled. The goblins have all gone back to fighting one
another, since they are no longer afraid of their ruler. King Roglug
has been proclaimed the new Avatar, against his will and much to
his alarm. The last I heard of him, he had fled to some far-off world.
The cherubim will not pursue him, saying he is too unworthy a
quarry for them. The Darklings have no desire to war with us now
that they are without a true leader."

"And so are we," said Lorelyn sadly. "I know Ailia would say that
we don't really need her anymore. But it just won't be the same
without Ailia and Damion. I miss them."

"So do we," Jaimon said, and his relatives nodded and murmured.
Jemma put her hand on her brother's shoulder.

"We miss her also," the amphisbaena chittered, raising his front
head. "She made us feel safe, always."

Lorelyn leaned down and scratched Twidjik's ears. "How is it
with you in Nemorah?" she asked.

It was Mag who answered, for the benefit of Jomar and the other
Merans, "The Overseer has lost much respect in the eyes of his
people. He did not slay the dragon-god, as he boasted he would do.
He brought the destruction of their city on them instead, and many
blame him for that. They see now that Ailia's ways were wisest. We
are ruled by a council, appointed by the citizenry, and we are building a new city by the shore of the sea. Mai and Teren will raise their
children there."

As Mag was speaking, Lorelyn noticed a pair of figures approaching from across the lawn: a fair-haired Elei woman and a man. The latter was tall and regal, with a grizzled beard, and he carried in his arms a small boy perhaps two years of age. Jomar and the others noticed Lorelyn staring, and they too turned and saw the new arrivals. Then, as the Meran family and Mag and Twidjik gazed on in wonderment, the other four made obeisance to the man.

"Andarion," said Auron, "you honor us."

The king set down the child, and stood smiling at them. "I am but a man now, as other men. I have chosen to remain mortal, and not linger in the Ether when I depart this plane. I begin a new life now, in which I hope to redress past errors."

"Majesty," said Taleera, "Ana spoke the truth: you have nothing with which to reproach yourself."

"Have I not?" he asked. "It was my treatment of my son that brought about his end, and nearly destroyed Talmirennia. Only the Tryna Lia prevented it. I do not return to claim my kingship, but to live the peaceful life I should have pursued from the first. I dwell now in a world of the Elei, and I have wed"—here he turned with a smile to the lady by his side, who returned it—"and am a father once more. This is my son. I intend to love and care for him, and so make amends for my neglect of Morlyn, which caused such sorrow for so many." He took from around his neck an amulet with a dragon on it. "This was found in Morlyn's undersea castle, in the world of Nemorah. It is all I have of his."

"Mine," said the boy, reaching up for the gleaming thing with his small soft hand. His father gave it to him.

"Yes, it is yours. You see?" Brannar Andarion said to the others. "Can a soul come again into the world? Strange things may befall those who bear Archon blood. But I believe it has come to pass: he has a new life, and a new body that does not owe its existence to the intrigues of Valdur and the Loänei."

"Mandrake?" said Lorelyn. The boy turned and fixed his large blue eyes on her.

"It is not the name we gave him at birth," his mother said. "But he will answer to no other. I knew when I first looked into his eyes that this was an old soul."

"Extraordinary!" said Auron. "I have never heard of such a thing."

"If only Ailia could know this!" sighed Lorelyn. "It would have made her happy." She watched as the child went to join the two other boys in their games.

"There, I am sure she will, if she does not know it now," soothed Taleera. "We must not speak of her as though she had died." But at her words a little silence fell, and they spoke no more of Ailia.

Sometime later, when all the others had gone into the palace for their night's rest, Lorelyn and Jomar continued to sit alone, watching the stars emerge from the deepening sky. "What will you do when your life ends?" Jomar asked presently. "You're half-Archon too. Will you just die like Andarion, or stay in the Ether the way Damion and Ailia have?"

"Stay in the Ether?" said Lorelyn. "No. I want to know what lies beyond it. This Empyrean, or whatever the Nemerei call it. Why should I hang about the Ether when you die, and your spirit passes on? No! You'll go nowhere, Master Jomar, that I can't go too."

Jomar looked at Lorelyn, her blond head shining silver-gilt in the light of the stars and the Arch of Heaven. It had grown long, flowing down to her shoulders. She seemed to him in that moment more beautiful than ever before—this woman who could be like an angel if she desired, dwell in the eternal paradise of the Ether; but would instead give this up, choose rather to be as other mortals. He put his arm around her shoulders—and then, hesitantly, almost shyly, he reached out and twined a lock of her hair around his forefinger, where it gleamed like a ring of bright metal. "Lori—I've been thinking," he said. "Of going back to Mera, to my people. They still want me to govern Zimboura, and Kiran says he's tired of being king. I wondered if you'd like to come with me." He kissed her. "To rule by my side." And he added, with his look and touch, *To be with me always.*

She moved into his embrace, with her answer already in her eyes.

"ALWAYS YOU RETURN TO THE mortal plane," said Damion.

He and Ailia stood together atop a high hill, in the world where Damion had first encountered Andarion. The desertscape surrounded them: craggy buttes and rippling dunes, under a sky thick with stars and scattered with moons showing various phases. The land was desolate for the most part, without so much as a thornbush to break its monotony of sand and stone. The water that had carved out its dry gullies must have vanished many eons ago. In the far distance they saw, rising high into the sky and glowing in the moon's light, towers and pinnacles and pyramids so huge that Ailia had taken them at first for more mesas and buttes. They looked old beyond reckoning, like those she had seen in Ombar, pitted and scarred and crumbling. About them was the only remaining vegetation and a gleam of water: a last oasis of lingering life. Ailia thought she could see, carved on the side of one ruin, the half-effaced forms of winged colossi.

She and Damion were never apart now. Sometimes they wore ethereal likenesses of the fleshly forms they had worn when in the worlds, but for the most part they went formless and free, as pure essences within the great surging seas of quintessence that made up the Ether. No mortal language could describe their existence then, though Ailia often wondered how she might try to explain it. The old senses of the flesh were gone: sight and hearing and the rest. Yet there was something of all of them in the ecstasy she now knew: as if she listened to soaring strains of music; gazed on pure light; tasted bliss; and touched other El, in a way that did not merely connect her to them as a handclasp or a shared thought might, but made her utterly at one with them.

Damion was her tutor now, for during her time on the lower plane she had begun to forget her true nature, and needed to be taught again what it was to be an El. It was good, she felt, to return to the Ether's light and harmony, leaving behind the darker, lower realm where suffering and sorrow reigned. But she began to wonder if perhaps she had changed too much while she was in the lesser Heaven. Somehow, she felt drawn to the lower plane still, despite all that it had done to hurt her. Damion did not feel the same. To him the Ether was home, and a welcome release from the troubles of his earthly life. She could not make plain to him how she felt, for she did not quite understand it herself. But it was true, what he had said: she kept leaving the Ether to visit the material worlds, disguised as a sylph, or a cherub, or a dragon. Often he joined her. Once she and Damion had been swans, flying above their own white reflections in a world of clear turquoise waters that had never yet known any life of its own. And they had walked in their own forms on a planet that had no sun, but wandered freely through the heavens. On its lightless plains there were living crystals—*terebolem* the ancients called them—that glowed with their own radiance like venudor, and released emanations of bright quintessence like tongues of fire. Talmirennia was full of wonders.

Now Ailia sighed as she gazed on the sky of Meldrian. "What is wrong?" Damion asked.

"I keep thinking of those poor souls I saw in Perdition."

"Souls are only held in thrall to Valdur by their own consent. He persuaded them that they could not leave: but it is not true, and now they have seen that for themselves. Mandrake was able to break free by helping you; others may follow his example. The idea of *escape* has been planted in their minds now. If they seek it, then Perdition will be emptied, and all the enemy's spoils taken from him."

This thought comforted her. "The light there in the sky—is that the dawn?" she asked presently.

"Yes—but a dawn like no other you've ever seen. Here you'll see not one sun or two or three, but all the suns of Talmirennia in their glory."

They watched as a radiant spiral of unnumbered stars rose up slowly through the sky, leading their eyes to its incandescent center as if they were drawn into a whirling dance. Ailia gazed again at it in wonder. In a soft voice she quoted the Vision of Welessan: "'And I was raised up even to the sphere of the outer stars, and beheld beneath me all the Lesser Heaven, as it were a turning wheel.' How beautiful it is, Damion!"

"Very beautiful. You look on the Celestial Empire as Athariel himself once did, from his Cherubim Throne. And now," said Damion, "look behind you!"

Ailia turned. "What is it? I see only a few stars, scattered about in the void."

"Not stars, Ailia. Talmirennias. They are so remote that they appear as mere flecks of light, but each is as big as the Great Dance itself." She stared, enraptured, realizing that she looked at galaxy upon galaxy, a universe vaster than all her imaginings.

For a long time they were silent. Then Ailia spoke again. "How long has it been since the battle of Ombar?" she asked. "I have lost track of time in the Ether."

"Twenty years have now passed since the war ended."

"Twenty years!" cried Ailia. "So much will have changed in the mortal worlds. They will all be older—my father, and my Meran family, and Jomar and Lori. I so long to see them again."

"You can visit with them if you please."

"I wonder if Jo and Lori wed, and had children," Ailia said. "If so, the children will be grown by now." An ache of longing came into her voice. "I have missed so much. They chose to stay in time, in the stream of things. One day I will remember them, and go to see them, and they will be gone."

Suddenly she sprang up and returned through the portal from which they had come. He followed her, and they passed through the Ether, through the choiring realms of light. At last Ailia paused before one ethereal portal, leading into the world of Arainia.

"I must return," she said. "Not to visit, Damion. But to remain. It is where I belong now."

"I cannot go with you," said Damion. "The Ether is more home to me that any of the mortal lands I knew. Of course, you are still half-human and your mortal life never ended." He looked on her in sorrow. "Must you leave?"

"I am too much changed. I yearn for the mortal worlds. I cannot go back to what I was before."

"Ailia," said Damion, "you need not return to the material plane. Your task there is done. You said yourself that it is better for the mortals to have no ruler, and govern themselves."

"I did not go merely to perform a task. And I do not go now to rule, or undertake any other duty. I asked to be chosen for the errand long ago because I desired to be as mortals are, knowing all they know. And there is so much of their life I have not yet seen and tasted and felt. I have not known age or death. And if I remain an Archon, I shall not ever enter the Empyrean."

"If you do enter it we will be sundered from each other. The place of the Archons is the Ether: we do not go where mortals go."

She could not bear the sorrow in his voice: it recalled to her the anguish she had felt when she had believed him dead and lost to her. "Damion, my love, all created things have an end," she said, placing her hands upon his shoulders and gazing deep into his eyes. They shone with the reflected glory of quintessence. "The Ether has not always been, and perhaps when both it and the mortal plane are no more, all divisions will cease. I cannot believe we will always be apart." And she turned toward the ethereal rift. "Yes—I am sure that we will meet again."

"Then I can be reconciled to it," said Damion, clinging to her, "if I have that hope."

"There is always hope," said Ailia. For a moment her hands held fast to his; then gently she slipped hers free. Leaving him, she stepped through the portal into Arainia.

She stood within the Gate of Earth and Heaven, and before her the bridge of stone spanned the gulf between the portal's lone pinnacle and the mountaintop where the towers of Melnemeron rose. The wide lands lay below, and on the eastern horizon was a glimpse of the far-off sea. She felt cool of wind, warmth of sun, and the gentle pull of the earth beneath her binding her to itself.

After a moment she knew, by the fading of the light, that the portal had closed behind her. She did not linger any longer in that place, but with a swift stride and never a backward glance, she set forth across the bridge.

APPENDIX

TRANSLATOR'S NOTE

It will be apparent to any reader of the *Kanta Meldralöanan ad Try-namiria* ("The Book of the Dragon Throne and the Moon Princess") that the codex is as much a literary work as it is a historical account, and I fear that much of the original flavor imparted by its unknown author has been lost in this translation. It is also impossible to know exactly when and where the events of the *Trynamiria* (as I understand it was commonly known in its place of origin) took place, though hints in the text suggest they occurred at least a thousand years ago. One thing is clear, however, and that is that the humanoid beings the text describes are too like us not to be close relatives of ours. There is little doubt that our own Earth is their "original world," and while some of these beings have been strangely altered in appearance, there are others who would likely not cause a second glance were they to walk down one of our city streets. It is interesting to speculate what changes have since occurred in the worlds they inhabit, seeing how greatly our own civilization has progressed in the same amount of time.

As to the provenance of this copy of the *Trynamiria* and the accompanying documents, many of them fragmentary, it is a mystery and will likely remain so. The same applies to the manuscript that serves as a sort of Rosetta Stone, making this translation possible, though that at least appears to have originated here on our Earth. (But that merely deepens the mystery.) The three excerpts given below are taken from parchments that seemingly date from different eras. I would surmise that the first comes from either Mera or

Arainia, and was written after the true nature of the "Archons" was revealed at last to the people there. As to the other two, they are certainly Meran writings, and come from much earlier eras. The first of these is an account by an official emissary of the Maurainian court, describing to his monarch what he has learned in Trynisia of other peoples and worlds. This would place the time of its composition sometime within the early days of the first Commonwealth. The second, a brief overview of Meran history, seems to come from an educational text (no doubt used at the Royal Academy in Raimar), and must date to a period after the Dark Age when most scholars believed the island of the Elei was a fable.

Of the Beginning of Days and the Ordering of the Celestial Empire
(From the Imperial Archives of Eldimia)

The *El*, that we call the Archons, were before any other thing that was made. Their place was the Mid-Heaven, or Ether, that lies above our plane of Lesser Heaven but below the glory that is High Heaven; it was given to them to be their home. Though its true substance was the divine element of quintessence, yet images appeared in it at times of things that were yet to be: living dreams of the Maker, of worlds and beings still to be created.

When the lower Heaven was formed in a burst of light, the Archons delighted in it and went down into it to play. Still greater was their joy when suns and worlds appeared out of the primordial fires. Many were drawn to these spheres, claiming them for their abodes: but the higher ones among them cautioned that this starry heaven, unlike the Mid-Heaven, was not created for them alone. They would have to yield the worlds one day to whatever beings arose within them. For this was to be the plane of mortal creatures, which would be animated by sparks of the divine spirit from above, yet formed out of the same stuff of which the stars and worlds themselves were made. And so the Lesser Heaven would belong to them, and they to it.

But at first the Archons were free to possess it. Some went to dwell on planets and made their homes in air and water, earth and fire. Many learned to take material forms in the likeness of mortal creatures that did not yet exist, save only as images on the timeless Ethereal Plane; or else they took fanciful forms that combined the anatomies of many different creatures. Others of the El disdained to take any form, and dwelled only within the stars, as bodiless spirits. Thus the first division of the Archons was made, between the *Elyra* or High Ones, and the *Elaia* or Lower Ones. The latter learned to alter the substance of matter, and they reshaped the planets as they pleased, changing winds and tides and climes, raising up valleys and casting down mountains. They delved deep into the earth and toyed with the gems and ores that they found there; and they created for themselves new metals and crystals like orichalc and adamant, from which they fashioned for themselves objects of beauty. The first of these treasures was a pure crystal without flaw, the only gem of its kind, which they presented to the star-dwellers as proof that perfection could indeed exist within earthly things. Many of the high spirits were swayed by the argument, and some went to dwell within the wondrous Stone, and filled it with their radiant presence. Afterward, some of the Elyra consented to visit the planets, and even to walk upon their soil in material forms. But they never made their homes there.

When the first living creatures emerged within the worlds, some Archons were ill pleased, not wishing to renounce the plane in which they took such pleasure. Yet most welcomed the advent of the mortal beasts and beings, and watched over them and guided them as they claimed their mortal realms. Those Archons who had chosen to inhabit planets rather than stars were closest to the living things, and helped many of them grow to wisdom, and showed them how to enter the Mid-Heaven and so pass freely from world to world. The first beings that rose to wisdom under the reign of the Archons were the Loänan. The Archons appeared to them in dragon-form, and tutored them and persuaded them to abandon their more barbaric ways. They learned to draw power from gold and silver and gemstones, and flew through the Ether to other worlds. Next to arise were the unicorns or *Tarnawyn*, and after them the firebirds. These three peoples formed an alliance under the aegis of the Archons. Then many more and younger races appeared, and the old Empire of Talmirennia was formed: a great realm connected by ethereal portals, watched over by the dragons that were oldest and wisest.

The Archons also made a study of the seeds of life, and learned to alter living creatures as they had altered the worlds: they made strange and unnatural beasts and beings, sphinxes and chimaeras and cherubim. These last are said to have mated with high Archons shape-shifted into like forms, and so they declare themselves to be the true heirs of the Empire. The Elyra desired that they should guard Talmirennia, and watch over those things of power that could not be unmade and might fall into the possession of mortals, causing them harm.

There was one planet in particular that brought forth a numberless multitude of creatures, and some of these the Archons took and bore with them to other worlds. Among them were the forebears of the human race. Like all mortal things they were brutish and coarse at first, and the Archon Elarainia, who was then nurturing the living things that had risen in the world she claimed for her own, was troubled when many of the alien creatures were placed in a neighboring world. But Elmera her sister Archon, whose world it was, loved her adopted children. Mera was barren save for some sparse forest and a few fierce beasts, and she wished to see the new beings thrive there. She counseled Elarainia to withhold her judgment yet awhile, and see what came to pass. And in Elmera's sphere humanity grew in wisdom, and learned the use of tools, and to make objects of beauty. Then the Archon caused one northern isle to grow warm and fruitful, and she set in it humans from various lands whom she thought wiser and gentler than the rest. For, she said, by placing these apart from the rest of their kind she could cause them to become truly enlightened beings, that might later serve as an example for the others and teach them in turn. The people of that island (in later days named Trynisia) she called the *Elei*, the children of the gods: for she allowed the lesser spirits to mingle with them for a time in human form and instruct them, and even take some of them for mates, to bring forth offspring that were half-divine. And the Elei grew in grace and knowledge, until the Archon of Arainia herself became fascinated, and left her own sphere and dwelt among them for a time, taking the likeness of one of their kind. Her own world had as yet produced no thinking beings like these, and although she still could not abide the Merei (those humans in other lands of Mera that remained crude and barbarous), she made a path through the Mid-Heaven between the land of the Elei and Arainia, so that the latter might visit her world if they wished. And the Elei who crossed the Ethereal Plane and found themselves in Arainia marveled at it, and desired to remain there. For fair as their island was, it could not come near to the beauty and bounty of this world that lay closer to the sun; and the spirits had since departed from Trynisia, as Elmera desired them to: but the sphere of Arainia was full of Archons still.

Elarainia pondered their plea, and said at last that she would suffer a small population of the mortal beings to remain within her sphere, so long as they did no harm. But no Merei must ever set foot in it, nor look on it save in a vision, for she would not have that race do violence to its beasts and birds and forests as they did to those in their own world. And so it was that many of the Elei went joyfully to dwell in that blessed sphere with those they called their gods. And as the Merei grew wiser with the passage of time and the gentle influence of the Fairfolk, Elarainia relented yet again and permitted some of them to journey to Arainia also; but still they were not permitted to dwell there.

The Archons had also taken the ancestors of humanity to many other worlds, and they too found wisdom, though their bodies often took different forms: they became the Maliji or amazons, the woodwoses, and the hobs. Some of the Archons deliberately altered the human form, turning them into sylphs and undines, centaurs and satyrs. And of the beasts that were also taken from their original world, some also grew to wisdom: these became the nagas, pucas, kitsune, and others.

At that time the emperor of the Archons was Modrian, lord of a black star: he reigned in a winged man-form on the world of Ombar, with the Star Stone set in his crown. The human beings taken to that world had grown into strange and hideous creatures, owing to its unwholesome climes, and to the Archons called incubi and succubi that took them for mates by force. But despite the protests of the other Archons, Modrian would not free them, preferring to watch for his amusement the savage history that unfolded. Then the Archons became divided a second time, between the followers of Modrian and those who rejected his ways, and they went to war.

The mortal creatures were drawn into the struggle against Modrian's domination of their worlds and lives. The dragons learned that Modrian had been breeding creatures called firedrakes from members of their race: these were less wise than true dragons, and they could spit fire and fumes from their mouths. The Loänan grew divided over whether to disdain these creatures as abominations, or accept them as their blood kin. Soon the dragons were at war as well.

Modrian then summoned the spirit of the star Azarah, who was one of those that served him, and commanded him to cause his celestial sphere to pass through the cloud of comets that surrounded the star Auria—the star that was the sun of Mera and Arainia. And it was done, and the other Archons fought with him and his minions and pursued them into the upper airs of Mera, where their captain Athariel struck the Star Stone from Modrian's diadem with his sword. It fell to the earth, onto the island of Trynisia that he had intended to destroy.

Once Modrian was driven back to his own star and confined within it, the other Archons, surveying the ruin of the worlds, knew that the time had come for them to withdraw from the lower plane. Only at a mortal's behest would they enter that realm again. They went to dwell in the Mid-Heaven, leaving the Lesser Heaven to mortals. But they remained vigilant, for Modrian had vowed to return and revenge himself upon them and the mortal creatures they loved.

As for the Elei, they thrived both on the Isle of Trynisia and in Arainia under the guardianship of the dragons and the cherubim. They learned to construct flying ships and chariots to carry them safely through the Ether, so that they might seek out their kindred who dwelt in other worlds. They encountered first the children of the Elementals, whose planet-homes circled their own sun. Then traveling farther, they discovered the peoples who dwelt among the stars, and the wise animals also. The latter had learned to take human shapes, though in their own worlds they kept their original forms. At long last the Elei met with the firebirds, the Tarnawyn, and others of the Elder Races, and were joined to the Celestial Empire.

As for the Archons, they observed all this from the Mid-Heaven, but obeyed the Pact that they had made and intervened in the doings of the mortals only when summoned by them.

But Azarah's passage had unleashed many comets that still swept toward the planets of Auria, and could be diverted only by powerful sorcery. The starfaring Elei were able to undertake this task, with the aid of the Loänan and cherubim; but the firedrakes and the goblin-folk of Azar fought with them in the void, and many comets passed through their net. The goblins also captured flying ships from the Elei, and learned to captain them. Amid the battles and great devastation that followed many worlds were laid waste; the greatest sorcerers of the Elei were diminished in number and Arainia lost much of its knowledge; and in Mera the people came to fear and hate all sorcery, whether black or white, blaming it for the Great Disaster. With the ethereal portals closed and none left who knew how to open them, those Merei who were visiting Elarainia's world were unable to return, while the few Elei who remained in Mera were forever exiled from their kindred in Arainia, and their race diminished and died.

It was agreed then among the Elder Races that they should not interfere at that time, but rather await the fulfillment of an old prophecy: they would not resume their commerce with humanity until one arose who was both human and Archon. This heir foretold of the old Empire would guard it against Modrian's return, wielding for its protection the Stone that was the Archons' greatest treasure and the home of their high kin.

Of Our Kindred in Other Worlds

. . . I am pleased to inform Your Majesty that our embassy was well received in the land of Trynisia, and that in addition to giving us welcome the Elei were willing to instruct us concerning their own race and also their brethren that dwell among the stars. The reports are now verified that came to our attention concerning the superlunary realm known as the Celestial Empire, and the paths that lead through it. The Fairfolk have mastered the art of traveling through the heavens by these ethereal routes, and have established colonies in celestial bodies much like those our own kingdom has established on remote islands. There are indeed Elei living in the sphere of Arainia, as Your Majesty has heard; for that star is not composed of fire, like the fixed stars of the celestial sphere, but is a world like ours containing earth and air and water.

Its bright glow, like the moon's, is caused merely by the reflection of sunlight. And as I am on the topic of the moon, I should add that it too is a world, and has also been settled by the Elei. Everything is lighter there, so that a bar of iron weighs like a straw, and the lunar Fairfolk have made for themselves feathery cloaks which they use to fly through the air. I have procured a powerful spyglass so that Your Majesty may observe for yourself the meres and woodlands of Numia.

The Elei have also a thriving commerce with races of men and manlike beings that dwell in distant worlds. Concerning the latter, Your Majesty will be interested to learn that not all are unknown to us here on earth: some indeed have appeared in our mythology and in the wonder-tales of other peoples in Mera, perhaps because the memory of true encounters with these beings lingers on, or it may be that the poets who wrote of them were the recipients of divine visions. A brief description of each of these alien races follows.

The Hobgoblins

There are several varieties of hobgoblin or hob, not to be confused in any way with the more dangerous goblins, to which they are not closely related. The *boggarts* are small, dark, and hairy with vestigial tails, and are playful and mischievous. The smaller, more delicate *pixies* are also playful and capricious by nature. The *fenodyrees* are larger (though not as large as we), heavyset, and have enormous noses: they are, despite their grotesque appearance, hardworking and good-tempered beings. All hobgoblins live in subterranean dwellings, called by them "hob-holes."

The Undines, or Mermen and Mermaids

These beings are the offspring of human forebears and the Archon inhabitants, also called undines, of the watery planet Talandria that is visible from our world as a star. Like their divine forebears the mer-folk possess fishlike tails in place of legs, and dwell in the deeps of oceans.

The Dwarfs, or Gnomes

The children of the planet Valdys (and of the earth-Archons who were likewise known as gnomes) have an unusually short stature owing to the more powerful force of gravitation in that world. They are strong and sturdy however, and long-lived. Owing to inhospitable conditions on the surface of their world, they spend much of their time underground, in natural caverns and subterranean dwellings they have delved for themselves out of the living rock. They love precious stones, gold and silver, and all riches of the earth, which they fashion into elegant adornments for their lords.

The Sylphs

This is a graceful aerial race from the moon-worlds of Iantha, descended from unions between Archons of the same name and human beings. They resemble their Archon ancestors in form, with slight and delicate bodies and long diaphanous wings. They are gifted sorcerers, and can pass from one celestial body to the next through the Mid-Heaven, even entering the upper air of Iantha to ride its winds.

The Dryads

An arboreal race from a far-off forested world, dryads are descended from Archons known as *hamadryads*, who are said to have an affinity with trees. They have a peculiar empathy for all green and growing things. They dwell in houses shaped from living trees, for they will cut no wood, taking it only from trees that wind or old age has felled.

The Satyrs and Wood-nymphs

This strange race also claims Archonic descent. The women are very beautiful, but the men are all born with the hind legs and horns of goats. They call their ancestors "the gods" and themselves "demigods." They are most probably descended from the Archons known as *oreads*, that dwell in hills and forests. Both the men and women are renowned for their love of dancing and music.

The Centaurs

Another of the curious races created by the Archons' intervention with the stuff of life itself, the bodies of the centaurs are a strange meld of horse and human. They claim no divine descent, but are proud nevertheless of their connection to the Archons. They rarely mingle with our kind, not because they disdain our company, but because their unique form makes it difficult for them to enter men's dwellings and other structures.

The Harpies

The only human portion of a harpy's anatomy is its head. The feathered bodies of these creatures give them far more in common with birds. Their young hatch from eggs, and they live a century or more. Little else is known about them, for their fearsome nature discourages closer study.

The Sphinxes

The most peculiar race of all, the sphinxes are a combination of not two but three different kinds of creatures. As with the harpy, only the head is human. The body is leonine, and is further adorned with the feathered wings of a bird. The sphinxes are extremely ancient, having been created—it is reckoned—by the Archons more than a hundred thousand years ago. They prefer warm climates, and are a cultured race with a great fondness for riddle games.

The Cyclopes, or Arimaspi

It is not known whether this race was purposely altered or if it developed on its own. Either way, it is difficult to see the advantage of exchanging two eyes for one, though the single eye of the Cyclops is undoubtedly keen and far-seeing. Theirs is a simple pastoral society, but they are exceedingly fond of gold and gems—a predilection that has landed them in trouble with the race of the cherubim more than once, as many of the Archons' enchanted treasures are made of these things.

The Androgyni

This is a most singular race, whose members are neither male nor female but possess some attributes of each. How their genders came to be blended one into another, instead of being separate as in our kind, is not known: their history does not tell of it, and they say that they have always been as they are.

The Pygmies

I have written of the dwarf race, whose members are only half our height, but the pygmy people are smaller still. They barely surpass two feet in height, and consider our kind to be giants. (Only the pixie-folk are smaller, and not by much.) They dwell in caves or in little mud huts that they decorate with feathers and shells, and they ride on goats and sheep instead of horses. They are hard put to defend their crops from the wild cranes that share their world, and that seem to them like great winged monsters, owing to the pygmies' insignificant stature.

The Amazons

The amazon-race is one of the few that received no Archonic intervention whatsoever, but developed entirely on its own. Placed on a warm jungle world in ancient times, they exhibited a warlike temperament from the first, engaging in millennia of internecine warfare. One tribe finally rebelled against the rest, its women uniting to defend their children from harm by learning and mastering the arts of war. The female armies defeated all the others, and assumed a dominant role in their world. They have grown taller than their men and stronger, and are deeply distrustful of any new races they encounter.

The Woodwoses

The woodwoses or wild men arose from early ancestors placed by the Archons on a cold and densely forested world. In order to remain alive they grew thick pelts of hair, while remaining human in every other way. They can be wild in their behavior, prefer their food raw, and usually sleep out of doors, but will adjust their manners according to the company they are in, even to the point of donning some token clothing for modesty's sake.

The Demonspawn

The creatures called Demonspawn or *Morugei* consist of four separate groups, all of them brutal in nature and uncouth in appearance. The *Anthropophagi*, named for their cannibalistic habits, are in turn composed of several races: many-eyed, one-legged, bird-footed (the *Struthopodes*). The *Cynocephali* have the heads of dogs and are dull-witted, having been bred for docility and loyalty.

Then there are the *goblins*, each individual uniquely hideous and barely recognizable as human, with grossly distorted features; the large, brutish and slow-thinking *trolls*; and the equally large but far more cunning *ogres*. There are rumors of even more terrible creatures in the benighted world from which the Demonspawn come: the ghouls and vampires that feast, respectively, on dead flesh and living blood. But it is not known whether these truly exist, or are merely myths in which the Demonspawn believe.

Of the Seven Kingdoms of Mera

Trynisia

The peoples of Maurainia had long been aware of the existence of a race that dwelt in the far north, variously referred to as the *Elei*, the Fairfolk, or the Hyperboreans. They appear first in the myths and legends of the northern tribes, where it was said that they led an idyllic life in an island paradise untouched by the surrounding cold, and lived for more than a hundred and fifty years. Theirs was an easeful, pastoral existence, it was said: they had but one city, built on the summit of the mountain Elendor. The myths told that they learned their language and many other skills from their gods—who were also their progenitors. They believed in an enchanted sky-realm, which differed from the Heaven of other faiths in that they believed they could enter it while still alive, and that they even had kindred dwelling among the stars.

The first Merei (that is to say, non-Elei) people they contacted were the tribes of Rialain. Shards of Elei pottery and some of their jewelry have been unearthed in the frozen north of that country. They were driven away at first by the native people, however, and made no permanent settlements. Some were captured by warriors, and became thralls or concubines: many Rialainish people claim descent from the Elei today, and declare that the gift of prescience or Second Sight that is widely reported among them is their Elei heritage. In later times the Elei returned, moving farther down the coast to Maurainia, and created settlements along the then uninhabited Coastal Range. They befriended the natives over time, and set up trade with them. They did the same in the northernmost country of the Shurkanese in the Antipodes.

In the latter days of the Third Millennium they went to war with the Zimbouran people, supposedly over the theft of a sacred gem from their chief temple. It was the first war they had ever waged: minor skirmishes with an unknown, possibly mythical race called the Morugei (described as hideous, misshapen offspring of demons) were the only other conflicts in their recorded history. They required the help of the warrior king of Maurainia and his armies in order to overthrow the Zimbouran king, whom they also described as a demon's spawn. The war lasted for more than three years, but the enemy surrendered at last and sued for peace. But Elei civilization did not long outlast Zimboura; for mere decades after their triumph the great cataclysm of 2497 N.E. brought a swift end to their domination of the Commonwealth. The race has since interbred with others and died out, leaving only ruins, relics, and the dead language of Elensi as its legacy. The Elei homeland of Trynisia has never been found, leading some scholars to question whether it truly existed.

The Western Continent

Our great continent is made up of a triad of nations, home to three distinct peoples: Rialain to the north; our own kingdom of Maurainia; and Marakor in the south. All these countries were once a patchwork of smaller, warring kingdoms until about three thousand years ago. Menyath the Great, first king of Maurainia, conquered the tribes of hill and plain and united them over the course of a thirty-year campaign, bringing them at last under his rule, and reigning from his kingdom in the east. The southern kingdom of the Marakites was formed as an alliance to face this threat of a unified Maurainia. The Rialainish also remained proudly unconquered, and declared that their reputation for ferocity kept them safe, although it is said that in truth Menyath had no desire to annex their cold and inhospitable lands. Nor did he take the Elei settlement on the eastern coast beyond the Range, which remained independent. It is said the mountains proved too great a barrier for his armies, and also that his men had a superstitious fear of the "children of the gods" who dwelt among those distant peaks towering over the eastern plain. Embassies were sent instead, and over the next century peaceful relations with the Elei were established. At about this time the Maurainian prophet, Orendyl, established his One Faith, and Menyath adopted the new religion and insisted that his subjects also convert. His motive in this may well have been more political than spiritual: for no doubt he saw one dominating faith in a single deity as yet another means to unify the disparate tribes. The Elei retained their old traditions, but they and the Maurainians continued to live in harmony, with the faithful interpreting the Elei gods as "angels" while the Fairfolk added Orendyl's god, Aan, to their own pantheon.

Six centuries later a new threat came from Valivar IX of Zimboura, who sent his fleets in many forays against the Continent. The three kingdoms formed an alliance, and the Elei settlements of the coast and Range were incorporated into Maurainia. Emissaries were also sent, it is said, to the Elei of Trynisia, who proposed that a new Commonwealth of nations be established. The Kaanish people of the Archipelagoes, also fearing the Zimbourans, asked to be included, as did the Antipodean kingdoms of Shurkana and Mohar. Valivar was succeeded by the still more rapacious King Gurusha. In Maurainia, the new-crowned King Brannar Andarion resolved to meet this foe on his own ground. A fabulous tale had already arisen that declared Andarion to be the offspring of a mortal woman and a faerie, and as this put him on something of an equal footing with the "semidivine" Elei he no doubt encouraged its propagation. He led his army and that of the Elei across the sea to Zimboura, where he killed Gurusha in single combat, ending the threat for that time. His choice of an Antipodean woman to be his queen was perhaps designed to help relations with the peoples of the Eastern Continent, though the union proved disastrous in the end, and his one son later rebelled against him and was slain in a siege of Andarion's own castle. Regarding Brannar Andarion's own end little is known: he has no tomb in Maurainia, and therefore it must be presumed that he died in a foreign land. (The mythmakers declared that there was no tomb because he did not die at all, but was permitted to enter the Faerie Realm of his supernatural sire, where he lives on to this very day. Some also declare that he will return at some future date, as yet unrevealed.)

After the Disaster it is said that Maurainia fell into chaos because it was left without the spiritual center of Trynisia. However that may be, the king left no heirs and in the early days of the Dark Age the Patriarchs of the Faith were obliged to set up a theocracy until a true heir of the realm could be found. Forgetting all treaties, Marakor and Rialain took advantage of their neighbor's disarray to make forays into unguarded territories of Maurainia, and it seemed a relapse into the barbarism of the previous ages would result. But the theocrats anointed King Harron I, thus bringing the Interregnum to a close. Modeling himself after his idol Menyath the Great, he reunited Maurainia and drove the Marakites back behind their former borders. His successor, Harron II, signed new treaties with both Rialain and Marakor, and announced the creation of a second Commonwealth embracing all the Western Continent, as well as several outlying colonies on islands that Maurainia had seized. The Dark Age was ended.

The Archipelagoes and Antipodes

The history of the Eastern Continent is sadly marred by an almost continuous strife that goes back to epochs before recorded history. It has at various times been the home of no fewer than four empires, each of which has struggled for dominance over the centuries.

The oldest is that of the Mohara in the south, who raised the first cities along the river deltas of the western coast. Their later history was plagued with tribal warfare, which ultimately caused the people to abandon the city-states and return to living off the land as their forefathers had done.

Next to arise was the empire of Kaana. It lasted for a thousand years, dominating all the Continent not only by the great strength of its armies, but with its art, music, poetry, and philosophy. The Kaans were first to explore the sea, and they claimed as their territory the many archipelagoes there. But Kaana too declined in the end, perhaps by overextension, even as the kingdom of the Shurkana arose in the north. (*Shurkana* comes from the Kaanish words *shur Kaana*, or "beyond Kaana.") The Shurkanese too were a wise and ancient people, and their growing realm might also have come to rule the Antipodes in time. But another rival nation arose to challenge their might.

The Zimbourans came out of the harsh steppes of the southern peninsula, a land into which the Moharas seldom ventured. Hardy and warlike, with pale skin and the strength of spirit that enables a people to endure bitter weather and scant food, the southern tribe drove the Dogoda people with whom they shared the plains to the extreme tip of the peninsula, and to the very edge of annihilation. They then began to push northward, seeking for fertile lands with gentler climates, but were ill-received by the Moharas due to their religion, which required human sacrifice. This practice was abhorrent to all the other Antipodeans, and because they would not alter their ways the Zimbourans were shunned, and they were excluded from the Commonwealth. In retaliation, or so it is alleged, their King Gurusha later arranged to have a sacred gemstone stolen from the High Temple of Trynisia. But even without this excuse, war between the Zimbourans and the Commonwealth lands was most likely inevitable. Their defeat at the hands of Andarion, and the Disaster with its ensuing chaos, left their kingdom in ruins for some time. Helped by their fierce resilience, however, they were first to recover from the cataclysm, and went on to conquer and despoil the Moharan lands before overrunning the Kaans' decrepit empire. The last remaining Kaanish people fled across the sea and resettled in the colonies of the Archipelagoes, which had become an island empire and flourished under the old Commonwealth.

PRONUNCIATION OF ELENSI WORDS

Elensi words are pronounced as follows:

Vowels

A—always has the short sound, as in *flat*

AA—has a long, drawn-out "ah" sound; before R, pronounced as in *car* (In some instances I have rendered it as A for easier reading, as in Aanaa—Ana, Loänaan—Loänan)

AI—as in *rain*

AU—another "ah" sound; before R, pronounced as in *oar*

E—always has the short sound, as in *bed*

EI—like the German *ei*, an "eye" sound

I—like the French I, an "ee" sound

O—always the long sound, as on *bow*, except when it is the penultimate letter in a word (e.g., *Damion, Halmirion*), in which case it has the short sound as in *iron, lion*

OA—not a diphthong as in *road* but two distinct sounds, as in *coagulate.*

U—always the long sound, as in *tune*

Y—always a vowel, never a consonant: has the short I sound as in *win*, except before E, when it takes the long sound, as in *wine*

Consonants

G—always pronounced like the G in *goose*, never as in *gin*

S—pronounced as in *so*, not the Z sound in *phase*

TH—always pronounced as in *thin*, never as in *then*

Note: these rules do not necessarily apply to words in languages other than Elensi, i.e., Zimbouran, in which the letter Y *is* a consonant.

GLOSSARY OF
EXTRATERRESTRIAL WORDS

Ailia: (AY-lee-a) Elensi *ai + lia*, "lode star." Island girl who joined the quest in Mera to find the Star Stone; later revealed to be the Tryna Lia.

Akkar: (AH-kar) Moharan. God of the earth, consort of Nayah the sky-goddess.

Ana (AH-na) Elensi. Wise woman and guide to the Tryna Lia. See *Eliana*.

Andarion: (an-DAR-ee-on) Elensi *aan + darion*, "Lord Knight." Title given to King Brannar of Maurainia in the Golden Age.

Arainia: (a-RAY-nee-a) Elensi *ar + ain-ia*, "bright homeland/sphere." Second planet in the Auria system.

Ardana: (ar-DAN-a) Elensi *ard + aana*, "the Lady-wood." Forest in southern Eldimia, held by the Elei to be sacred to the goddess Elarainia.

Arkurion: (ar-KYOOR-ee-on) Elensi *ar-kuri + on*, "bright torch bearer." First planet in the Auria system.

Auria: (OR-ee-a) Elensi *aur + ia*, "place/sphere (of) life." Elei name for the sun.

Auron: (OR-on) Elensi *aur* + *on*, "vessel of life." An Imperial Loänan, friend and protector of the Tryna Lia.

Azar: (AZ-ar) Elensi *azar*, "calamity." Name for the planet of the dwarf star Azarah. See *Azarah*.

Azarah: (AZ-a-ra) Elensi *Azar'ah*, from *azar* + *rah*, "bringer of calamity." Name of a small dim star that became trapped in the Auria system's gravitational field. See Terrestrial Terms: *Disaster, the.*

Damion: (DAY-mee-on) Elensi *dai* + *mion*, "welcome messenger." (I have simplified the spelling of this name from the phonetic *Daimion*, as there is an English name, Damien, pronounced similarly.) Priest of the Faith and companion of the Tryna Lia.

Elaia: (el-LAY-a) Elensi *El'aia*, from *el* + *laia*, "lower gods."

Elarainia: (el-a-RAY-nee-a) Elensi *el* + *Arainia*. Name of the goddess of the planet Arainia; also, the mother of the Tryna Lia.

Eldimia: (el-DEEM-ee-a) Elensi *Eldim'ia*, from *el* + *dimi* + *ia*, "(the) gods' beauteous country." Land in the world of Arainia to which the Elei fled after the Great Disaster.

Elei: (EL-eye) Elensi *el* + *ei*, "children of the gods." Ancient race now vanished from Mera. They had special powers of the mind, believed by them to be the result of a divine ancestry.

Elendor: (el-EN-dor) Elensi *el* + *endor*, "holy mountain." Sacred mountain in Trynisia, on whose summit the holy city of Liamar was built.

Elensi: (el-EN-see) The language of the Elei. From Elensi *el* + *ensi*, "holy tongue" or "gods' tongue."

Eliana: (el-ee-AH-na) Elensi *el-i* + *aana*, "lady (of the) spirit host," or "queen of the faeries." Former queen of Trynisia; see *Ana*.

Elmir: (EL-meer) Elensi *el* + *mir*, "spirit power." The concept of Spirit, represented in Elei art as a bird.

Elmiria: (el-MEER-ee-a) Elensi *el* + *Miria*. Birth name of the Tryna Lia.

Elyra: (el-LIE-ra) Elensi *El'yra*, from *el* + *lyra*, "higher gods."

Entar: (EN-tar) Elensi *en* + *tar*, "great worm." The old stellar empire of Modrian-Valdur, known to humankind as the Constellation of the Worm, represented in astronomical illustrations as a dragon devouring its own tail. The red star Utara corresponds with the dragon's eye, the blue star Lotara is its tail, and Vartara, the black hole that is Lotara's binary companion, is identified with its mouth. See *Lotara, Utara, Vartara*.

Falaar: (fuh-LAR) A cherub guardian of the Tryna Lia. This is an approximate phonetic rendition of his name, which means "Sun-hunter."

Halmirion: (hal-MEER-ee-on) Elensi *Halmiri'on*, from *hal* + *Miria* + *on*, "Castle Moonbearer." The palace of the Tryna Lia in Eldimia.

Hyelanthia: (hye-el-AN-thee-a) Elensi *Hyelanth'ia*, from *hy-el* + *antha* + *ia*, "cloud-country belonging to the gods." Land in Arainia where the Elaia were said to have dwelt.

Ingard: (EENG-gard) Elensi. Famed knight and friend of King Andarion.

Jomar: (JOE-mar) Moharan. One of the Tryna Lia's companions, a warrior of mixed Moharan and Zimbouran heritage.

Kaans: (KAHNS) Kaanish. The inhabitants of the Archipelagoes of Kaan in Mera.

Khalazar: (KHAL-a-zar) Zimbouran *khal* + Elensi *Azar*, "born under Azar." Name of the king of Zimboura in Ailia's day. The "kh" sound is pronounced like the "ch" in the Scottish *loch*. (The western peoples, who had no such sound in their language, pronounced the name "Kalazar.")

Kiran Jariss: (KEER-an JAH-riss) Zimbouran. A Zimbouran ally of the Zayim.

Liamar: (LEE-a-mar) Elensi *lia + mar,* "star city." Holy city atop Mount Elendor in Trynisia.

Loänan: (LOW-a-nahn) Elensi *Loänaan,* from *lo + an + aan,* "lord (of) wind (and) water." See Terrestrial terms: *Dragon.*

Loänanmar: (low-a-NAHN-mar) Elensi *loanan + mar,* "city of dragons." Largest city in the world of Nemorah.

Loänei: (LOW-un-eye) Elensi *lo + an + ei,* "children of wind and water." Race of beings descended from unions between humans and Loänan transformed into human shape.

Lorelyn: (LORE-el-in) Elensi *Lor'el'yn,* from *lora + el-lyn,* "daughter of sacred sky (heaven)." A gifted Nemerei and friend of the Tryna Lia.

Lotara: (low-TAR-a) Elensi *Lot'ara,* from *lot + tar-a,* "tail of the worm." A star in Entar, the constellation of Modrian-Valdur. It is companion star to Vartara, the black star. See *Entar.*

Marakor: (MA-ra-kor) Marakite. Country to the south of Maurainia in Mera.

Maurainia: (mor-AIN-ee-a) Elensi *Maur + ain + ia,* "homeland (of) the) Maur (tribe)." Principal kingdom of Mera's Western Continent.

Meldramiria: (mel-druh-MEER-ee-a) Elensi *meldra + Miria,* "throne (of the) moon." The Tryna Lia's throne in Eldimia.

Meldrian: (MEL-dree-un) Elensi *meldri + aan,* "lord of thrones." An ancient world, the capital of the Celestial Empire from the days of the Archons.

Melnemeron: (mel-NEM-er-on) Elensi *Melnemer'on*, from *mel* + *ne-Mera* + *on*, "repository of the lore of the Not-world (Ether)." Place in Arainia where the Nemerei gather to learn and share their knowledge.

Mera: (MARE-a) Elensi word for "earth" or "soil," also used by the inhabitants of the third planet of the Auria system as the name for their world.

Meraalia: (mare-AWL-ee-a) Elensi *Meraal'ia*, from *mera-al* + *lia*, "star stone."

Miria: (MEER-ee-a) Elensi *miri* + *a*, literally "of radiance." Elei name for Arainia's moon.

Mirimar: (MEER-eem-ar) Elensi *miri* + *mar*, "radiant city." Capital city of Eldimia.

Modrian: (MO-dree-un) Elensi name for a deity, chief of the sky-gods (but subordinate to the supreme deity of High Heaven). Said to have rebelled and been defeated by the other gods of earth and sky, who confined him in the Pit of Perdition. See *Valdur*.

Modriani: (mo-dree-AN-ee) Elensi. Term for a small sect of Maurainians who worshipped Modrian-Valdur and looked for his return. The members of the Modrianist cult believed that the world was an evil illusion cast by the other gods, and that Valdur must destroy it in order to set humanity free.

Mohar: Moharan. Country south of Zimboura, now an occupied territory.

Mohara: Moharan. A people of the southern Antipodes.

Moriana: Elensi *mori* + *aana*, "lady/mistress of the nights." A title given to Mera's moon deity; also the name of Brannar Andarion's queen.

Morlyn: (MORE-lin) Elensi *mor* + *lyn*, "night sky." Son of King Brannar Andarion and Queen Moriana.

Morugei: (MOR-oo-guy) Elensi *Morug'ei*, from *moruga* + *ei*, "children (of) the night-haunts." Also Demonspawn. The mutant humanoid races that worship Valdur. These creatures are reputed to be the misshapen offspring of true humans and evil incubi. They include numerous races, whom I call here Anthropophagi, trolls, ogres, and goblins. The first three subspecies breed "true," passing on their characteristics to subsequent generations, but among goblins no two individuals are alike, and even their offspring do not resemble their parents. However, the goblins have a higher intelligence than the other races, and are more skilled in the arts of sorcery.

Nayah: (NYE-uh) Moharan. Goddess of the sky in Moharan myth.

Nemerei: (NEM-er-eye) Elensi *ne-Mera* + *ei*, "child/children (of the) not-world." ("*Ne-Mera*," "Not-world," is a literal translation of the immaterial dimension here called the Ether.) Beings able to communicate with their minds alone, in addition to other psychic powers.

Nemorah: (nuh-MOR-uh) Loänei-Elensi. A world once inhabited by the Loänei, now home to human beings.

Numia: (NYOO-mee-a) Elensi. Elei name for Mera's moon.

Ombar: (OM-bar) Elensi. Principal world of the star-state known as the Constellation of the Worm (Entar) ruled in ancient times by the Archon Modrian-Valdur. Ombar orbits so close to its sun, Utara, that it suffers from "tidal lock": one side of the planet is always turned toward the sun and the other turned away. As a result there are two realms in Ombar: the eternally hot and barren Daylands, and the Nightlands of perpetual cold and darkness. A thin strip of twilight lies between the two realms, and here most of the planet's creatures live.

Orbion: (OR-bee-on) Elensi. Name of the Celestial Emperor.

Rialain: (REE-a-lain) Elensi *Riala + ain*, "home (of the) Riala (tribe)." Country north of Maurainia in Mera.

Syndra: (SIN-druh) Elensi. A Nemerei woman of mixed Elei and Merei parentage who betrayed the Tryna Lia.

Taleera: (t'yuh-LEER-a) T'kiri. A friend and guardian of the Tryna Lia. (The name is pronounced with a little roll to the R that makes it sound almost like an L.)

Talmirennia: (tal-meer-EN-ee-a) Elensi *tal + mir + en + ia*, literally "all-power-great-place." Elensi name for the Celestial Empire.

Tanathon: (TAN-uh-thon) Elensi *tana + thon*, "tree eater." Species of large saurians inhabiting the world of Nemorah. There is reason to believe these giant reptiles are not indigenous to that planet, but are descended from sauropods of our own Jurassic period, brought to Nemorah from our world by the Archons.

Tarnawyn: (TAR-nuh-win) Elensi *tar-na + wyn*, "white serpent-foe." Unicorn.

Temendri Alfaran: (tem-END-ree AL-fa-ran) A world colonized by the Loänan, where many races dwell and meet.

Tiron: (TEER-on) Elensi *tir + on*, "blessing-bearer" or "blessed one." Name of the father of the Tryna Lia.

T'kiri: (t'-KEER-ee) T'kiri. An avian race, called "firebirds" by humans because of their brightly colored, bioluminescent plumage.

Tryna Lia: (TRY-na LEE-a) Elensi *Tryna Li'a*, from *tryna + lia-a*, "Princess of the Stars." Prophesied ruler awaited by the Elei, said to be the daughter of the planetary deity Elarainia.

Trynel: (TRY-nel) Elensi *tryne + el*, "royal and divine." A title of the Tryna Lia.

Trynisia: (try-NEE-see-a; try-NEEZH-ee-a) Elensi *Tryn'isia*, from *tryne* + *is* + *ia*, "royal beloved country." Land of the Elei in Mera, abandoned after the Great Disaster.

Trynoloänan: (try-no-LOW-a-nahn) Elensi *tryno* + *loanaan*, "dragon prince/ruler." A male leader of the Loänan.

Twidjik: an amphisbaena of Nemorah.

Utara: (yoo-TAR-a) Elensi *Ut'ara*, from *ut* + *tar-a*, "eye of the worm." Red star in Entar, the constellation of Modrian-Valdur. See *Entar*.

Valdur: (VAL-dur) Elensi *val* + *dur*, "dark one." Name given to the god Modrian after his fall from grace. Later appropriated by Zimbouran clergy as the name for their chief deity.

Valdys: (VAL-diss) Elensi *val* + *dys*, "dark dwelling." The fifth planet of Auria's system.

Valei: (VAL-eye) Elensi *val* + *ei*, "children (of the) dark." The followers of Modrian-Valdur.

Vartara: (var-TAR-a) Elensi *var* + *tar-a*, "mouth of the worm." Black star in Entar, the constellation of Modrian-Valdur. Also called the Mouth of Hell. See *Entar*.

Wakunga: (wuh-KUNG-guh) Moharan. Shaman of the last free tribe of Moharas.

Yehosi: (yuh-HO-see) Zimbouran. Chief eunuch in Khalazar's palace.

Zayim: (z'eye-EEM) Moharan. According to Mohara legend, a divinely appointed savior who would one day free them from enslavement.

Zimboura: (zim-BOOR-a) Zimbouran. A country in Mera's Antipodes.

GLOSSARY OF TERRESTRIAL TERMS

The words below are taken from our own terrestrial myths, languages, and cultures. I have utilized them for parallel concepts found in the worlds and cultures described in this book.

alerion: a feathered flying creature of Temendri Alfaran, similar to an eagle but without legs, and with a wide gaping mouth in place of a beak.

alicorn: the horn of a unicorn. It was said to have a precious gem at its base, and to possess miraculous curative powers.

ambrosia: the Elmerei possessed an elixir, given them by the gods according to tradition, which was taken from a fruit called the "food-of-the-gods." It was said to augment the latent powers of Nemerei.

amphisbaena: name of a two-headed snake in medieval myth, here used for a creature of Nemorah.

Anthropophagi: deformed humans, one of the races of the Morugei. This name (meaning literally "eaters of men") belonged to a similar race featured in medieval European mythology.

Archons: a term used for an ancient race of beings that once dominated the galaxy and were worshipped as gods. Believed by some to be the origin of the Elaia, "lower gods," in Elei mythology.

aspidochelone: a whalelike creature from our own mythology, that was sometimes mistaken for an island by sailors. If they lit a campfire on its back, the creature would submerge and drown them. It would seem that the inspiration for this myth is an actual beast in the world of Nemorah, though how our own storytellers learned of it remains a mystery.

Avatar: a term taken from Hindu tradition, here meaning either the physical manifestation of a god or else its representation by a mortal being in such a way that the divine being can be said to be literally present.

basilisk: a small, multilegged, reptilian creature of Nemorah with poisonous breath. Sometimes confused with a small flying creature of the same world, known as a cockatrice, because both have beak-shaped jaws and jagged crests resembling a cock's comb.

Celestial Empire: the realm of the Archons. The constellations in Mera's night sky were seen as hegemonies of these divine beings, the star-states in which they dwelt. Later mythologies during the Dark Age came to describe this stellar empire as a mystical country in the sky.

cherubim: gryphons; winged creatures who serve the heavenly powers as steeds and guardians. The word *cherub* comes from ancient Hebrew mythology, and was used for a divine gryphonlike creature (not to be confused with the Renaissance version, a cupidlike winged figure).

demon: an Elaia; spirit closely linked to the plane of matter. The word is here used at times in its classical sense, the "daimon" of Greek myth being a supernatural, but not necessarily malevolent, being; very different from our modern understanding of demons.

Disaster, the: I have translated the great cataclysm of 2497 N.E. as the "Disaster," since it literally involved an "evil star." Approxi-

mately ten millennia ago, a small "rogue star," probably a brown dwarf, entered Mera's solar system and became caught in the sun's gravitational field. In passing through the cometary cloud, it sent dozens of comets plunging toward the inner planets. This bombardment continued sporadically over thousands of years. From descriptions of the Disaster in Mera—"stars falling from the sky," earthquakes, volcanic eruptions, dust-clouds obscuring the sun (hence the appellation "Dark Age"), it would appear that one or more fragmented cometary nuclei impacted with the planet. The damage to the moon and other planets is also consistent with a cometary bombardment.

This accords well with the mythical account, in which the god Modrian-Valdur sent his lieutenant Azarah to destroy the world, all such higher spirits being associated with stars. Azarah also brought with it a single planet, the ill-omened Azar of Elei lore.

dracontias: according to folklore, a "magic stone" or jewel that lies inside the head of a dragon. There is in fact a crystalline substance located in, and extruding from, the Loänan braincase, which is said to amplify the creature's extrasensory powers.

dragon: the oldest intelligent race in the known universe, the dragons or Loänan are giant saurians that do not in the least resemble the monsters of Western myth but are closer to the *lung* dragons of China: supremely wise, almost godlike beings, benevolent in nature (with a few exceptions). They are able to shape-shift, can exercise power over the elements, and may live for a thousand years or more. They come from the area of the galaxy known to Merans as the Constellation of the Dragon, and travel between the stars by entering a hyperspatial dimension known as the Ethereal Plane.

eidolon: on the Ethereal Plane, the illusory "body" of a spiritual being that enables it to interact with other such bodies; also anything on the Ethereal Plane that resembles something on the material plane.

Elementals: Elaia-spirits that are attracted to the material elements of water, earth, air, and fire, and to worlds that abound in these elements. In the Auria system the Elaia took on humanoid forms, and

passed on those forms to their half-human offspring, who were named for their divine ancestors: the undines (or mer-folk) of Talandira, gnomes (or dwarfs) of Valdys, and sylphs of Iantha. On the planet Arkurion no human could live, and the Elementals there interbred with indigenous creatures known as salamanders.

Ether: a dimension of pure energy beyond or "above" the material plane.

glaumerie: an illusion cast by faerie beings on mortals. Some human sorcerers are also able to create illusions.

gnomes: see *Elementals*.

Mandrake: (*man + drake*) English equivalent for the Maurish name Jargath, "dragon-man."

orc: a marine reptile of the world of Nemorah, with a streamlined, almost whalelike body, fins for swimming, and long jaws filled with serrated teeth.

ornithopter: literally "bird wing," a term for any craft that flies through the air by mimicking the wing beats of a bird. In our world such craft are not practical on a large scale, but the flying ships of the Elei stay aloft in part through sorcery.

quintessence: the "fifth element" in old Meran cosmology, a substance superior to the four material elements of earth, fire, water, and air. Celestial objects and divine beings were believed to be composed of quintessence. It most likely derives from the old Elei concept of *elothan*, what we might call "pure energy."

salamanders: creatures that dwell in Arkurion, the fire-world (not to be confused with our small and fragile amphibians of the same name). Their scales, and the silk and wool they produce, can resist the fiercest flame. See *Elementals*.

shamir: a small wormlike creature that secretes a powerful acid in its mouth, enabling it to bore through solid rock.

sibyls: prophetesses; holy women of the Elei faith who are believed to commune with the gods and received from them visions of the future.

sylphs: see *Elementals*.

Tree of Life: the ambrosia tree; also, the symbolic representation of the universe as a tree.

undines: see *Elementals*.

venudor: a gemstone that shines with its own inner radiance.

wyvern: a two-legged flying reptile of Nemorah. Though wyverns somewhat resemble dragons, they are smaller and are not intelligent. Wyverns are large enough for a human being to ride on, though they are difficult to tame.

About the Author

Alison Baird is the author of *The Hidden World, The Wolves of Woden, The Dragon's Egg,* and *White as the Waves.* She was honored by the Canadian Children's Book Centre Choice Award, a Silver Birch Award regional winner, and she was a finalist for the IODE Violet Downey Book Award. She lives in Ontario. Her Web site is: http://webhome.idirect.com/~dbaird.